I0607175

SHE REFUSES TO LEAVE

Ken Anderson has a film, television, and sound recording background. He produced the successful and widely acclaimed movie, 'Naturally Free', this feature film was distributed throughout Australasia and the USA. Ken has now turned his skills to authoring; 'She Refuses To Leave' is a fictional novel which is an outstanding contribution to the genres of Mystery and Romance. Utilizing his interest in cinematography, his characters maintain a screen-like effervescence. They become energised with subtle close-ups and believable dialogue, the reader quickly synchronises with these characters and relishes their direction.

Ken's style of writing is unparalleled in today's world of literary offerings. 'She Refuses To Leave' is superbly written and employs a spiritualized approach. The book could be likened to the classic movie, 'Ghost' which starred Demi Moore and Patrick Swayze, although 'She Refuses To Leave' has its own individuality, with an equally important message.

Ken has lived in California, USA but now resides in Sydney, Australia.

SHE
REFUSES
TO
LEAVE

KEN ANDERSON

National Library of Australia Cataloguing-in-Publication entry:
Anderson, Ken, 1945-author
Dewey Decimal Classification: A823.4
Fiction: 1 Mystery 2 Romance 3 Spiritual Themes

First published 2013 by Eaton House Publishing, Sydney Australia
www.eatonhousepublishing.com
eatonhousepublishing@bigpond.com

ISBN: 978-0-992-36641-4

Available in e-Book
ISBN: 978-0-992-36640-7

Photo: Dreamstime
Photographer: Bowie15
Cover Design: Vila Design
Typeset by: Eaton
Formatted by: Maureen Cutajar

SPECIAL THANKS

This book would not be possible without the investigative work of Beverley Malone whose attention to detail became a pivotal tool in capturing the essence of this story.

To Lyn's family, I realise how intrusive my questions became – thanks for indulging me.

To Patricia Stone, whose obsession for editorial accuracy surpassed my expectations together with her unique ability to encourage.

To the many who assisted with this novel: thanks again, especially to Robin, Lisa, Bob, Sara, Mary, Nicole and the team at Eaton.

To Amber, whose name almost made the book – my apologies grand-daughter.

SHE
REFUSES
TO
LEAVE

PART ONE

THE EARLY YEARS

PROLOGUE

I sensed her eyes following, I glanced briefly and sure enough it was Lyn Monday, through hundreds of screaming adolescents who twisted and turned in a carnival of blurs and school-yard colours. Lyn Monday's smile tunnelling that vibrant maze, then she fluttered her eyelashes – coyly, embarrassed, I had caught her out. She giggled to her girlfriend. I can't remember the friend's name or what she looked like for Lyn held my attention.

Those eyes, the colour of emeralds, cool, tantalising with a phosphoresce spark. I smiled back but now she wasn't looking, however that first exchange was enough to last a lifetime.

A lifetime, it seemed an eternity, much had happened since 1955, I was young, ten at most and smitten, although age has nothing to do with love, you are either in it or out of it. All I know is, those memories remained strong, compelling and what followed was no accident…but why Lyn Monday?

CHAPTER 1

——◀○▶——

THE TRAP

When confronted with truth, some shy away, others embrace it. They are the realists, the ones who manage time, create order and procure an opportunistic placement in the universe. My name is Shaun Reece, I wasn't a realist then, but I am now, I would give anything to have my time over and those seventeen good seconds.

It began in 1945.

The Pez dispenser, sherbet powder, twopence watermelon and a brown mantle radio form some of my recollections but these are interruptions I can live without, I'm having enough trouble retaining the thinking process without those short-circuit jabs of intruding trivia – the important memories are barely existing.

What I do remember is my mother; she was a beautiful woman with a charismatic face, tall, slender and devoted. She was the youngest of five children. Her eldest brother was a habitual gambler whilst the youngest played games with property. Both became rich but only one kept his fortune. Her sisters were close and just as interesting; one a moralist who lobbied politicians for honesty, while the other insisted on individual perfection – both became frustrated with the world. How my mother fitted in often bemused me, however she did bond the family and this regardless of the arguments and deep divisions.

At the age of twelve, she chose her middle name Lorraine, rather than Ann. This suited her better and was a popular choice. The use of her second name was an espousal of the German/French province called Alsace Lorraine which suffered during the First World War.

In contrast to war, Lorraine attracted many friends, loved musicals and was a passionate ballroom dancer. In 1933, a motorbike ran her down – an accident that nearly killed her and ended her dream of becoming a dancer. Years later she described the motorbike's scorching motor searing her skin until rescuers pulled the twisted machine from her crumpled body. She was hospitalised and rehabilitation became a slow drawn process. She recovered physically if not mentally and by some serendipitous creativity she met a handsome charmer named Paton. His parents were at the same dance hall and cunningly organised the introduction. Lorraine fell heavily, her first true love, while Paton slowly succumbed to this relationship.

In 1937, they married and joked how they had gone overseas for their honeymoon, a harbour ferry trip from Sydney Cove to Manly, a total of forty-five minutes. Life was good – Lorraine was in love. A year later at the start of the Second World War they had their first child, he was born with birth defects and passed two weeks later. He was buried at Rookwood, the largest cemetery in the Southern Hemisphere. Years later I remember visiting his community grave and making a white wooden cross to identify his minute resting place. The cross is gone now and no one knows his exact location.

The aftermath of the Great Depression, the motorbike accident, losing a child and the uncertainty of her husband at war produced cracks. Her own mother passed and with each event my mother's self-esteem eroded. Her confidence floated like the tide, one day high, and the next the lowest of ebbs. She wondered if she would see her husband again, the Japanese bombings increased, along with her apprehensions.

Like so many through the Second World War she struggled to keep her emotions intact. She devised a plan, a surprise, which at least gave her direction. She saved every penny, simply going without. She scrimped and wrestled with a meagre budget, there were candles for lighting, a kerosene stove for cooking, a jumper and two blankets for heat, everything was recycled even the tea leaves. Toilet paper was a luxury and replaced with newspaper. Coupons allowed access to food and a distribution system that appeared fair on the surface.

The closing chapter of the war saw the allies winning but at an enormous cost. There had been years of death, destruction and miserable doubt. My mother was again pregnant, a fruitful result of my father's leave application and when the war finally closed she presented him with what was now two surprises.

I was the first surprise and born in 1945, perfectly normal. Although that sounds patronisingly aloof, I'm not. I'm of average intelligence, tall, with reasonable looks and glad I survived the turmoil and genetic trap. Through the early years, an occasional boil had ruptured the skin and was treated by Watkins Black Ointment which I recommend, similarly a bottle of Vemol scalp conditioner kept wayward hair in place. I often wonder what my father thought of me.

The second surprise was more a secret; my mother had saved enough to pay out the mortgage. After years of deprivation she had accomplished the impossible. For these times, the eradication of a home loan was a contradiction in terms whichever way you looked at it. However, the deeds were in my father's name and he refused to thank her. Over the coming days, months and years she remained bitter, couldn't he say, 'Thanks', not once did he mention her incredible accomplishment – not once.

My mother constantly refreshed my memory, "Why couldn't he say thanks?" of course I had no answer. For her to hear the word would have meant everything but he never approached the subject. I found this strange; initially I put it down to him being embarrassed a woman could accomplished something that was his responsibility, or was there something else? Something I had overlooked.

By now, my parent's relationship was faltering and my mother's confidence had all but eroded. God knows what went on in those far away ports – these were crazy times. I suspect my father may have wandered. I never knew but I am sure my mother did.

Lorraine was a perfect mother except for her insecurities which festered as two gnarling forces each determined to undermine and attack her. She became anxious and prepared me for the day my father would abandon us. She was convinced it was going to happen. She prepped me continually. She even covered the subject of herself passing and advised my father would "take up with another woman instantly". She told me what to expect from my new mother. I had no reason to doubt her for my father was not a family man and he stayed well clear of anything I would participate in. My father's father was the exception and he would ride his push-bike thirty miles to see me compete in sporting events. He died of lung cancer – his special mix of roll-your-own had taken its toll. When he passed, I was training for athletics at an oval next to the hospital. I immediately did a lap of honour and regardless of the pain ran faster than I thought possible. I hoped this was a fitting tribute for I had nothing else to give. My mother's protection of me worsened. She erected a force field of defence, albeit one where I doubted everything, a solid barrier of uncertainty. She stated, "Every girl is a potential trap." And this was just the start of her prompting; disturbingly, I accepted everything with blind faith.

Somehow, my parent's marriage hung together by the slimmest of threads, then as if trying to speed up my father's departure or at least trying to bring her prediction true, my mother tried to kill him. I had no idea what her frenzied attack was about, except there was a lot of yelling as he held her wrist, the one with the twelve-inch blade and then he laughed contemptuously into her contorted face. My father comforted me later and said, "Parents fight sometimes, it is nothing to cry over," which I had done all Sunday afternoon. It must have been something huge, for no one tries to embed a blade that big unless you have pissed them off. The police never came and we gingerly got on with life. My mother was subdued for weeks.

It was my first year of high school. The school was new and built from prefabricated concrete, a radical departure from bricks and mortar. It consisted of 150 students who quickly discovered it was their job to initiate the teachers, for some it was their first year of teaching. This initiation was a test of wills where some passed, some floundered. As for the students, they were a creative bunch, one even testing the headmaster's patience when he rolled a humongous wooden container down a steep hill at the exact moment the headmaster turned his car from the parking lot onto the street. With some creative driving he survived this attempt on his life and the next day we witnessed a brutal public retribution, clearly a headmaster running out of patience.

My class was the lowest grade possible, a class made up of delinquent misfits. My allocation to this class was a mystery, I expected a higher grade. The teachers struggled to maintain discipline and mainly supervised the child minding. I remember three morons at the back of my class swigged from a flagon of fortified wine. By the end of the period, one was so inebriated he spewed all the way to the toilet block. One classmate raped a girl in the train. Then a group of five from my class formed a social club and invited a girl from the local girl's school to attend. It was just an excuse for sex, strangely she didn't mind and they took photos of this orgy, more explicit than I had seen and she returned time after time wanting more. Each week the smile on her face widened as she controlled more of the boys, there would be something like twelve now, all lining up and buzzing like bees to honey. When I saw her last photo, she had a glazed transcendental look, peaceful, out of it, her trip worth the exposure. Strange, there was a lesson here, for she controlled everything. She may have trapped the boys into thinking she was theirs but the truth was the photos showed another side. She received far more from this experience; the boys were ostracised and their fornicating ways stopped. The girl walked away posing as the victim, no girl could be that deranged! Maybe my mother's warning was right, 'every girl is a potential trap', regardless, her comment had me wondering. But now I was determined to escape this idiotic group and to find a class without disruption and mayhem.

I worked my butt off for the first six months, and it worked by receiving a promotion of three grades. Here I needed to work even harder to catch up. Having missed six months of education was an enormous setback, however at the end of the first year I became the school's first head prefect where I remained in that position until I graduated. I was grateful to have received a street education from this class of misfits for I knew all the troublemakers and what their capabilities were. As prefects, we ran a tight ship and soon there was pride in belonging. The school excelled in all things, academic and sporting. We had debating groups, cadets who trained with real ammunition and the first canteen in Australia to sell salad sandwiches.

My mother continued to guide me, warning that, 'Girls are trouble, big trouble'. It was a new repertoire but with a similar theme. She didn't include, "Beware the Ides of March" but given the opportunity she may have, she did however organise my social calendar, which meant church fetes and Sunday school classes followed by church; however, even in that sin-free environment, she could not have foreseen the danger.

I was not far off my fifteenth birthday. I arrived home confronted by my mother. She looked different, her eyes wide, forehead furrowed and her neck flushed with concern. Her hand held an envelope and I noticed it quivering incessantly. She warned, "Don't become serious with any girl. Play the field and ignore this love letter from Witherspoon." She flapped the envelope in the air as if it was a marriage contract.

I queried, "Chantal from church?" My mother already knew what was in the letter. I wondered how she could reseal the envelope.

My mother had contrived an answer and this before I had slit the envelope. I remember her advice implicitly, "Tell the girl you never received her letter." It was simple, problem gone. Honestly, I was more shocked that a girl found me interesting I didn't ponder my mother's advice. Poor Chantal had poured her heart out, devoting her body and soul, shit; we were of the same religion, a match made in heaven, except I felt nothing, absolutely nothing for this girl, except a high level of embarrassment and all this while I had listened to the minister's Sunday sermon. There were obvious temptations sitting right next to me. My mother emphasised, "You see what I mean, this is what I've been talking about, be careful."

Days later at the dusty stairs of the nearby train station, Chantal was waiting. She asked, "Did you receive my letter?"

My mother's planned response was on the tip of my tongue, "What letter? I never received a letter."

It was only then I realised the implications, I was bald-faced lying, I flushed, my eyes darted precariously, everywhere except Chantal's face. She went quiet, knowing I was full of it. Any dignity callously stripped, Chantal's face grimaced, her dream all but a nightmare. Her shoulders slumped and then she faded away. I felt bad but that was the advice my mother gave and she had to have known the ways of women. But I had lied! What were all those church sermons and Sunday school lessons about if we couldn't tell the truth? Chantal scurried across the road with a few friends and later stopped coming to church. In hindsight, I should have ignored my mother and spoken to Chantal. It would have been kinder to say, "Sorry, I don't feel the same."

Some weeks later, I caught my mother steaming my father's letters; she read them and resealed them. She never saw me looking. What was going on? Was she spying on both of us?

Some days later…

"Shaun," it was my mother calling from the back door, "Shaun… dinner," and she banged on a huge pot made from aluminium as if she was in charge of a mess hall. I was a mere thirty yards from our house and hiding in a tree. It was a huge eucalypt with a broad fork towering some twenty-five feet above the ground. Every day after school, I went through the same ritual, a prerequisite for someone without brothers or sisters. I made my own fun and nestled into its comforting divide, here, in private moments I surveyed the neighbour's backyards, the Stephen's and the Byrd's and on the adjoining property to my rear was a tennis court being no further then thirty feet and seldom used except when I ventured in. From here, I could view the distant ridge that formed the midpoint of the town called Berala. At its highest peak was my old primary school, built in 1924, a large two-story building of brown brick and rendered cream concrete. It was difficult to forget this school as each day proved an enriching moment. It had everything, an active sports program, many energetic teachers, opportunity classes, bullies and most importantly, Lyn Monday, who was the most beautiful girl I had ever seen, she enjoyed life and compounded friends at a tremendous rate. Beautiful Lyn Monday, her lithe figure and long auburn hair had caught my interest since the age of ten. Her entrancing green eyes tantalised my very soul, we never spoke, we only looked at each other, strange but that was the way it happened. Words became redundant, looks did the damage and I didn't object one bit. It felt superior to talking and it stirred every emotion. Words could only drift, only to be hushed by the seasons; besides, what could be said that the eyes couldn't? Don't ask me how this worked, it just did.

My mother returned to the back door and there was one last exasperated bang at the pot; I knew this was the final call. I scrambled down the rough bark using the embedded nails for footholds, then without showing any eagerness I casually meandered towards the back door, picking up a bicycle, my hand crafted boomerang and several basketballs all strewn haphazardly over our large but narrow backyard.

As I entered the house, my mother ordered, "Wash up. Have you been up that tree again?"

I nodded and caught her smiling. "Is dad working late?"

Her smile changed to a snarl, "Yes, I'll ask him to check you before he goes to bed."

I washed quickly.

My mother sat opposite as I forked a lamb cutlet and became her captive audience, "Before your father gets home I need you to understand."

"Does this have anything to do with you arguing?"

"It might, remember I will always love you no matter what." She patted my hand for reassurance. "I think your father is seeing someone."

"Who?"

"I don't know but we need to be prepared, we may not be able to stay here much longer."

Panicking I questioned, "We have to leave the house?"

"Possibly, just be ready to move."

She hugged me and a tear slipped her cheek. Was my father really cheating? I felt sick to the stomach.

Then, as if I didn't have enough to worry about, my mother's warnings increased, as if she sensed that love letter was just the tip of the iceberg, 'Have nothing to do with girls, they're trouble, a trap,' all said as if girls were the vilest of creatures. I couldn't believe she said those words, wasn't she a traitor to her side? My frustration grew.

Lyn Monday still gave me those enticing looks but with milling girlfriends and my mother controlling every blink, romance seemed impossible, I was close, but miles from reality.

CHAPTER 2

ANY DAY OF THE WEEK, EXCEPT MONDAY

Nothing happened with my father, not the slightest hint of impropriety or any suggestion we would move out. At every opportunity my mother continued to guide me. Every day became an anti-climax although I was glad this real life drama never eventuated. Eventually, I began to doubt my father's infidelities.

For me, girls were another matter and it appeared my mother's warning might have been right. What happened next had me searching for answers. I had received an invitation to a party on the far side of town. I barely knew the birthday girl, a Janet Carson. She had placed a tiny brown envelope into my hand and said, "Make sure you come!" I didn't know any of the boys. Why was I here? Why was I suddenly set free? Where was my insulating force field of defence? I was questioning everything. Why after all this time had my mother allowed me to go to this party? She didn't even know the girl.

The house was a modestly built weatherboard cottage and after knocking on the front door, the disinterested, already intoxicated parent casually directed me to the side garage where the action would take place. I could hear the music playing, Dion's – 'Run Around Sue', the treble needed adjusting but as the turntable was a basic set-up, they could only adjust the volume. Six girls were on one side of the garage, the same number of boys on the other. The boys had been hand picked, preselected candidates but I suspected it was more than a budding romance these girls were after. They buzzed excitedly on their half of the garage. They giggled, perused, and flirted. They applied make-up and complimented each other on how gorgeous they looked. I was feeling like a piece of meat. I had no idea who had hand picked me. It was obvious we were the sheep...err rams, all being herded together where the girls would select one and guide us through the turns, hoops and hurdles. Every manipulative part of the night including our first game of spin the bottle had been sneakily orchestrated. The neck of the bottle rotated through at least a dozen turns and stopped a second later at Claire Fields, the most outgoing and provocatively dressed of these predators. She had huge breasts and caked on foundation applied with a shaky hand. Her lipstick was a bright pink that had a wet glistening look and her nuggetty build gave her the distant appearance of a road worker. She smelt like rose water, sugary sweet. Every available crevasse liberally doused for maximum effect. She stood in the middle of the circle and spun the bottle to see who would be her victim. What are the odds of being the first boy up? I had never seen the game played only heard of it. I took the lead and planted a peck on her spatulated cheek, my first kiss. She was as surprised as I was and blurted out, "What...? That's it?"

Ok, she wanted lip, it was obvious from her reaction, and when I tried to correct my mistake, she gushed out, "Don't bother." I was left – bent over with lips pouting as she sat down leaving me exposed like an idiot. I returned to my seat thinking, 'What a bitch'. When I think back to that time, I was fortunate to be naive and inexperienced for it saved me becoming a victim to these little tarts. Not all the boys were so lucky and sacrificed more than they should have. I escaped early, embarrassed, but also relieved.

Maybe my mother was right, maybe girls were out to trap you. I didn't tell her about the raunchiness portrayed that night but I sensed she suspected something for the next time I asked to go to a birthday party, she flatly refused. I worked on her for weeks but she wouldn't budge, an ornery position considering these were good friends. She gave no explanation, she simply said, "No," I still regret missing that party.

Lyn Monday still occupied my mind but I hadn't seen her for ages. Then a few weeks later I entered a dimly lit milk bar in town, simply called… Pauls. Lyn was already there. As she turned from the counter, she smiled and walked up to me. She was so beautiful. She flicked her auburn hair behind her shoulders and spoke for the first time. Her green eyes sparkled even in this twilight environment and then fiercely locked onto mine. Her energy buzzed all around me. I felt hot and cold all at the same time. Her eyes danced wildly. What she said next and how she said it had my heart pounding, she moved closer to my ear, now only inches away, I could even smell her subtle fragrance, "Do you like me?" as if this was the next stage to our relationship.

Shit! I needed to speak… I swallowed, stammered, and spat out, "… of… course."

That was all I said, my face went blood red, my mouth dried, in essence I seized up in panic, I turned embarrassed and walked out of the shop without buying a thing. I closed my eyes and dreaded my cowardice. There was something happening, however at a level I didn't understand. Was she trying to trap me? Good… great… but still, what should I do next? I had been brainwashed to reject the enemy and had no idea what to say or do. How could someone come up to you and say that? It was so open, some might say trashy but not from my perspective, for it was a genuine and honest question and I blew it.

After that, we often exchanged glances and coming from Lyn Monday that was enough, but now I was convinced she would never talk to me again. I felt guilty for not continuing the conversation. Was it the beginning and the end, all wrapped up in one short conversation? I continued to keep Lyn Monday a secret from my mother.

Then some months later my mother surprised me, "You know Felicity Moss, Taren Moss's daughter?"

"Yes," I said with caution.

"You know your school dance is next Saturday?"

"Oh right, the dance." I had dismissed the idea of going.

"I was talking to Taren at work and we decided you should take Felicity."

"Like, a date?"

My mother casually replied, "It's no big deal, all you have to do is ask."

I must have appeared reluctant for my mother asked, "What's wrong?"

"Nothing," I couldn't tell her about Lyn and when it came to girls, I was an abysmal mess. Maybe a date might be a good. I glossed over what sinister motives lay ahead and considered Felicity's assets. She was cute with tight drawn pigtails and rapidly developing breasts. Her legs were finely toned and that caught my attention. She lived within three hundred yards of my house and nothing was happening with Lyn Monday or Tuesday Weld, an unreachable actress pinned to my bedroom wall – I needed experience before trying again.

At the dance we held hands and talked aimlessly, then returned on the last train. It was then I discovered Felicity Moss's secret, she was primed and ready to go, she whispered, "They don't need to know what we do."

"You mean our mothers?" We both knew our mothers would want details.

She nodded.

The red rattling train approached the station and shuddered to a stop. We descended the station's steps, the very steps where I had lied to Chantal Witherspoon.

We walked slowly. I was unsure what to do but never expected Felicity to pull me into a deserted shop's alcove. All I could see was her outline, impressive figure and then her breasts against my chest, teasing and incredibly soft.

"… go on."

My hesitation was obvious and to move the pace along she held my hand to her breast. I swallowed. She rested her forehead against mine and said, "I have always loved you."

Shit.

I brushed her fair hair behind her ears and leaned close to kiss her. Again, I learnt that girls think a lot more about kissing for no sooner had we made contact when she opened her mouth and gushed at me with a lip movement that had zero suction. Her wet mouth felt like an eel. I ended up kissing gums and teeth but thankfully – no tongue. Where had the lips gone? It was unexpected compared to the intensity of her body. After that kiss I knew I could never be serious with Felicity. She seemed embarrassed. It was over in an instant. I didn't know what to say. We adjusted our clothes and walked on silently. I left disillusioned.

I had a million questions but most importantly, why had my mother organised this date? Was Felicity the type of girl my mother accepted? Without that kiss I may have gone further. Was kissing the Richter scale of emotions? I didn't contact Felicity after that, much to the disappointment of the mothers. My mother wanted to know how the date had gone, "I had a great time," it wasn't a lie exactly, for this date had been rewarding. If nothing else, I had rounded first base. Maybe we both gained something. And what was it with my mother's choice of girls – if she chose the girl, did it become the lesser trap?

Would I ever have that second chance with Lyn? How would she have kissed? If I had controlled the milk bar conversation I would have known by now, however with Lyn, kissing seemed secondary. It was her eyes that held my attention. I couldn't explain it but something was stirring me to react. She was the most vibrant, effervescent creature to occupy my dreams.

I formed a friendship with a Josh Freemont, a high school classmate. He lived a few blocks from Lyn Monday's house, a sheer coincidence… Chantal Witherspoon, the love letter girl also lived close by, only ten houses separated Lyn and Chantal.

Josh was good looking with fair hair. He was an inch shorter than me – so six-foot one. We trained for athletics although I never officially raced against him as he was a year younger. He was quicker, not by much but enough to edge me out over a hundred yards. We became super competitive with everything.

We shared many moments, we spoke of girls, I discussed Lyn Monday and my deepest feelings and he discussed girls that held his interest. We were young but old enough to work at Christmas for the Post Office, called the GPO then. Here we sorted the mail and later I became a telegram boy, a plum job where I'd cycle untold miles to dodgy addresses.

Many times, I returned to Paul's Milk Bar hoping to correct that meeting with Lyn. If only I had the chance to have that time over. However, she never came back. I flushed each time I thought of that day and my brief embarrassing conversation. You ask someone if they like you and he answers, "…of… course," This clumsily delivered response gave her no hint of my true feelings and then to add insult to injury, I turned and walked away, leaving her like Claire Fields had left me, hanging, eyes closed and puckering for that ridiculous kiss. Lyn must really despise me, she obviously expected more.

Robert Freemont was Josh's brother and was celebrating his 21st birthday. He was four years older than Josh. Josh had the looks, Robert being the older brother had more common sense. We celebrated his party by building a bonfire and allowing huge explosive devices like bungers, rockets and other paraphernalia to be ignited. The fire roared in the middle of their backyard and 'Fever' played seductively through the portable sound system. Seats for the girls and the boys stood near a portable table covered with a plastic tablecloth. The alcohol was for the aged drinkers and the juice and carbonated lolly water for the under age, surprisingly, few knew how old they were that night. The air was still, then, invaded by fireworks which thundered the night sky. During this deafening outburst Lyn

Monday arrived. I had no idea she was invited. I had a lump in my throat, instantly the crescendo stopped, at least for a few seconds while everyone gazed in awe. Her hair was shorter but she still looked gorgeous, I studied her sleek fluid movements. She had it all, the looks, the stature, the voice, the openness, and the absolute presence of someone special. Just for a moment I thought I detected the fragrance of soap, clean and fresh. She wore dark blue sneakers, jeans and a trendy t-shirt which had high cut sleeves, enough to expose her slender arms.

The lump in my throat tightened. She smiled at me coyly, similar to that first time at school. The thunderous claps started again and Chantal Witherspoon appeared through the gun-smoked mist like a girl on a mission. The girl I had lied to. The girl I had scorned and rejected although her love letter was incredibly brave...

'My body burns when I think of you'.

I felt embarrassed for lying, I needed to apologise, later tonight perhaps. She cast daggers at me and turned her back but before she could settle she had to jump sideways to avoid a string of jumping-jacks.

A game was organised after the bungers had scared the girls shitless. A game called Captain Blood's Eye. A lame game, that was to take the most fragile female present and produce a terrifying scenario where she caused the Captain permanent eye damage. All that was needed was a chair for the victim to sit on, a blindfold, an over ripe tomato and an eye patch for the person playing the Captain. Of course, Chantal was the most highly-strung girl present. It appeared her reputation preceded her and when twenty guys and nineteen girls are volunteering your services, it becomes difficult to say no, although I think the majority of the girls didn't mind, none wanted to go first and when Chantal edged forward, they seized her election with gusto.

Positioned in the middle of the yard, Chantal was close to the bonfire but not that close to be a sacrificial lamb. It just made it easier to see. She was blindfolded, her shoulder length hair carefully removed from her face. I remember her white t-shirt clung tightly to her ample breasts and her small waist had a belt, a large leather device that could have doubled as a barber's strap. This device held up her crisp white jeans, which had black embroidery around the pockets to counter the starkness.

The person having the most experience with this game played the Captain, he portrayed the 'Aye', and 'Shiver-me-timbers' exactly like Long John Silvers from Treasure Island. Chantal's hand was taken from its clenched position and hesitantly placed on the Captain's face, she felt his mouth, nose, left eye, ears, and then she felt the patch on his right eye. The guys were trying not to snigger. An explanation was given that the eye was lost in a battle against the King's men, where a sharp spear had plucked it out. Here it remained on the tip for everyone to see. However, the Captain didn't take this lying down; he killed his attacker, and recovered the eye. However, even though he tried, the eye never went back quite the same way. Chantal's finger touched the eye patch again. She felt the patch move. Suddenly there was a realisation she was going to touch the Captain's bad eye and she squirmed in her seat and screamed hysterically. Many hands held her to the seat and she was requested to extend a finger. "Nooo," she screamed but the finger, with some help became straighter, reminiscent of a rigour mortis victim. Without warning, her finger skewered the overripe tomato with a slurping sound that drew, "Oh," from the crowd. She became an emotional casualty, her breathing increased and she ripped off the blindfold unable to contain her composure. Everyone was laughing except me. I felt sorry for her.

She looked at me with daggers. Christ, I was the only one not laughing, however she singled me out for a broadside. "It's not funny being used, you fucking liar." The over ripe juice ran down her shirt and a large clump of pulp hung precariously to her finger and then dropped to her lap. She began crying and her aides in waiting, two loser girlfriends rushed to her and pulled her aside trying to quieten her. Everyone was laughing, and she continued her abuse at me as if I was the only person of interest, "I've seen how you've been ogling her," and she pointed to Lyn Monday as if she was a prized heifer. For once Lyn Monday looked embarrassed, I was dumb founded.

Robert's parents ushered Chantal into the house and proceeded to clean her up. They may well have considered calling a
doctor. I looked at Lyn and all we could do was shrug. As the
night wore on, Lyn Monday was 'hit' on several times but each
advance repelled. I made up my mind to make a move when
some idiot placed a bunger into a glass bottle and lit it. It blew
glass shrapnel at all the revellers. Several people, including myself were hit. A glass shard passed right through my hand and
the cut began oozing similar to an abattoir's beheading. As I
left for emergency, Lyn Monday whispered to me, "Sorry, I
wish it could be you." That comment had me wondering, what
did she mean? "Sorry, I wish it could be you."

There was no time to talk and I was ushered away.

I saw Josh Freemont some weeks later, "What happened after I left the party?" He was lay-back about the events only
mentioning, "Chantal left early, the bonfire was extinguished,
and to prevent further injury my father confiscated the fireworks," he then casually divulged, as if an after thought, "Oh
yeah, a few days later Lyn Monday committed suicide."

"… what?" I stammered. The blood rush from my face and a
roaring tremor quaked my body.

"She died," he said with a blasé detachment as if it was an
everyday occurrence.

My face was clammy, "What happened? She's only seventeen!"

Still clinically removed from the emotion he replied, "Was
seventeen… I don't know anything else."

I was too shocked to probe. I had missed the funeral, and I
instantly missed Lyn. I stopped seeing Josh Freemont after that
comment, it was the way he replied – 'Was seventeen…' I
couldn't understand this lack of feeling. It wasn't his fault, for
he had no attachment to the most beautiful girl that ever lived.
I ached for another chance but knew I had blown the opportunity. I couldn't bring myself to grieve – I wanted opening not
closing. Was this a cruel hoax? I clung desperately to that
premise – my only hope.

CHAPTER 3

WHEN YOU LOSE A MONDAY,
THE WEEKS GO SO QUICKLY

Six months later

I adopted Roy Orbison's, 'Only the Lonely' as my theme song. The days were difficult, I'd wake up with Lyn Monday and I'd go to sleep with her. I would dream of being together, holding hands, even kissing. Her breath was sweet, her touch soft and caressing. Her caring voice filled my head with whispers, "I love you." However, she never said that, we had never even touched and my mind was being creative. I enjoyed what little memories I had of her – those energetic eyes, her coy smile and the tiny freckles that dotted a perfect face – all good memories except for my stupid response to her question, "Do you like me?" and now this disastrous, intrusive finality being an impossibility for me to accept.

Why had she taken her life? I considered I might be responsible, perhaps I had upset her that day at the milk bar; maybe she had lost confidence and it had unlocked a pocket of insecurity and once started, it took control. Maybe she was no different from my mother with loads of uncertainty and precarious fragility. What was different? Physically, she had cut her beautiful hair. It was barely longer than my own. Her hair had to be one of her most auspicious features but it made no difference to me, it was still Lyn.

There was no point talking to her family or friends who would have been reeling from her action, "Sorry, I wish it could be you," what was that about? It seemed important, I remember her eyes locking onto mine, almost pleading; something was up, again a passionate delivery. I regretted being rushed to hospital, if only I had let my hand bleed, maybe a few seconds longer and I would have had an answer. "Sorry," what was that about? Had she done something wrong and felt the need to apologise?

"... I wish it could be you," then suicide, her death didn't make sense, there had to be a reason. I couldn't let her go; I needed a start not an ending. I felt so empty; there was no way to say goodbye and only seventeen good seconds to remember her by.

Another month passed a total of seven months.

It was yet another party and Del Shannon was hitting high notes with his hit 'Runaway', not that I had been to many parties that rocked, however I did kiss a girl named Brenda, she was a part of a small group of friends who worked for a large department store. Somehow, we gathered weekly, utilising the weekends to have fun. We knew each other and it seemed the right amount of girls and guys, just enough to go around. We had car trips, beach parties, and backyard soirees. It was a good scene and something I needed desperately after Lyn's death. Anyway that kiss of Brenda's; the kiss was superb and every boy commented that out of all the girls playing the spin the bottle game she was the only one who raised the bar of expectation. Her lips were warm, encouraging, affectionate, and had a little movement that thrilled. All the boys felt it, discussed it and unanimously voted her number one. Nothing ever happened with Brenda who quickly found a boyfriend and couldn't make any more of our get togethers.

A year later

My mother wasn't well; the first sign that things were amiss was her preparation of food. She stopped cooking weekly favourites and struggled with her work, having arguments and disputes over the smallest of matters. I was cut loose, a strange feeling when I had had years of nurturing and direction. Her control slackened, initially I thought it was a trap to catch me out but she didn't seem to care any more. It was as if she had been a tightly wound spring all her life, one full of energy but now the spring had slackened and she was suddenly inert. She still cared but never to the same extent, the weeks held no hope of a recovery and her brothers and sisters pestered my father for medical intervention.

I now had my driver's licence and it was a lot easier taking a girl out. My closest friend through high school was Rob McNee, Rob knew Samantha-Jane Creighton and set us up on our first date, a double at a drive-in. Samantha was an attractive girl with a bubbling personality. As soon as she bobbed her head into the car, she grinned, it was an enticing look, a face of innocence, mystery and fun, all rolled into one. Her cobalt eyes complimented her sandy coloured-hair which reached midpoint down her back. Samantha's figure was incredible. I helped fasten her seat belt and she giggled at the attention, embarrassed, I smiled back.

Rob was with what's-her-name and I insisted he take the front bench seat while Samantha and I commandeered the rear. I remember catching Rob looking at the movie and then back at him kissing what's-her-name. Don't ask me what was playing on the screen, all I know was it was a double bill and we lasted to the last frame. The moment Samantha and I kissed was like years of pent up energy releasing. To her credit, she did prevent me going into her bra to check out her equipment. Maybe it was because we had others in the car or maybe she had high morals. Not on a first date was commendable.

With Samantha, she hissed sexuality, I felt comfortably horny and we explored every facet of kissing imaginable. There were no wet eel or abalone lips. There were no teeth or gums and her make-up had been prepared with care and not a spatula. She had a lingering scent that drove me wild and she later told me she had borrowed a puff from her mother's perfume armoury. With the mechanics of kissing, she rated a close second to Brenda; there was hardly anything between them. Brenda had that little thing going on that played a game with you. However, Samantha was ultimately more passionate with her body, and that surpassed Brenda by a mile.

I was in touch with Samantha the next day and we made plans to meet again. We duplicated the previous night's marathon and our lips became chaffed. Again, she prevented me from going all the way. We talked a lot and I found out so many things about girls. We were getting serious. Each day without fail we would catch up with one another. Then we moved to another level, she wanted me to say, "I love you."

I just couldn't. To start with, there was my mother's warning, "Every girl is a potential trap," and then there was Lyn Monday who was still alive in me. I'm sure I did love Samantha but my mother's influence and Monday's memory were always the most predominate of forces.

I broke away, although it was hard, I thought it was best. We were becoming far too serious for kids so young. The weeks passed and I honestly missed her. However, I had burnt my bridges and had to live with the consequences. Weeks later, unbeknown to me, Samantha had set up an accidental meeting on a North Coast Beach. She knew I would be there with Rob and his family over the Christmas break and she had the perfect excuse, her work mates were Rob's twin sisters. Samantha asked me in a moment of solitude, away from Rob's crazy family, "Why don't you want to see me?"

I responded, "We are different religions, it won't work," it was such a lame excuse but not necessarily a lie for Samantha wore a crucifix and was clearly Catholic, the arch rival of us Protestants. I even remember my Minister advising against mixed marriages. Although he was referring to black and white, red, and yellow, but he let slip once that Catholics were a force to be reckoned with.

However, Samantha had all the answers, "I'm not Catholic, I go to the same church as you but a different diocese, I even belong to their fellowship group."

"But you wear a crucifix."

"My mother gave it to me as a Christmas present, everyone's wearing them."

Well, that should teach me to be simplistic – brainwashed and a sitting duck. I was unsure how to handle romance other than on the most basic of terms.

Samantha surprised me further when she asked, "Did your father put you up to this?"

"No, I've never discussed it with him."

"I don't believe you, your father told you to break up with me."

"No."

"Your father hates Catholics!"

"I'm not sure he hates Catholics, he calls them names but I'm sure he doesn't hate them. I swear he never said a thing."

"I still don't believe you but now that you found out what religion I am are we going to get back together?"

"Ok," I had nothing to argue with and straight away, we made plans to see one another. She was prepared to fight for me and that was good. There was no trap here, I think!

It was confirmed, my mother had developed Alzheimer's, a debilitating degeneration, her protection of me was completely neutralised and I enjoyed this relationship with Samantha which was both physical and mind boggling open, except for one thing, Lyn Monday! I regretted keeping this secret, but nothing could be gained – only doubt and repercussions. I had to move on. We made plans through the week and by the weekend we acted out those arrangements. We were into each other and that was unique, refreshing and steamy. Like moss needed rock, as Bogart craved Bacall and Ed 'Cookie' Burns authenticated 77 Sunset Strip. We became a team, united by affection and I assumed love for one another. Here we would weave those spare moments into our unique fantasies. We made plans and stuck to them and often returned to the drive-in and raced my Holden at over 100 miles per hour into the outside dippers, a mile long course of hills and dales. It was hair-raising stuff for once you were in the hollows there was no way to turn the wheel. Sadly, some people perished and the council graded the road to prevent further fatalities. In the end, the road resembled a bowling green where life became mundane and boring.

CHAPTER 4

THE SECRET REMAINS

I continued to think of 1962 – what a year for heartbreak, Lyn passed and soon after: Marilyn Monroe. I remember exactly where I was when Marilyn Monroe died; strangely, I was at a friend's house, fifty yards from where Lyn Monday died. Altogether, a disastrous time and on reflection, a decade to end all decades – Joe DiMaggio cried for Norma Jean. The Berlin Wall divided more than a nation. Neil Armstrong walked on the moon and Marianne Faithful sang, 'Those were the Days My Friend'. Did J.F.K. die at the hands of the Soviets? The tide remained high then slowly ebbed, nothing changed for me, except change itself, a numb feeling, and Samantha – if only she knew.

I valued the past, thinking retro and savouring those late fifties and early sixties. Why hadn't I seen much of Lyn Monday in those final years? I was probably in the 'black-hole', the nickname for a tiny room no bigger than 10 x 6 feet, a laundry converted to a photographic darkroom. It had one boarded up window, completely inoperable and with no vents, although it had a rattling old green fan that pushed hot stale air around with waves of uncertainty. This 'black-hole' was a unique place where I could think, a mature alternative to climbing a tree and far more creative for a teenager on the cusp of ageing. For my efforts, the rewards justified the hours. I was processing colour photographs, a first for Australia and the applications proved endless for there were commercial customers, weddings, portraitures and amateurs keen to replicate the professionals. Black and White became passé as everyone wanted to see rich vivid colours. I set up agencies to increase the business. All told, there were only three people in Australia who could do this work and I was one of them and at the ripe old age of fifteen. So much happened around this time that school work took second place. I was incredibly busy. Initially, I controlled the chemical's temperature by buying ice from the ice works some two miles away and then walking the ice block home on my bicycle's handlebars. It was always a race to get back before the ice melted, especially in the middle of summer where temperatures soared in excess of 110 Fahrenheit. I survived these darkroom sweat baths by using breathing techniques that controlled my metabolism, similar to Shaolin Monks who I heard can drastically reduce heart rates, even stopping them. I never tried that.

There were no books or courses to refer to, only trial and error. I was ahead of everyone, with the exception of one company based in America. This successful large consortium decided to open in Australia and spent millions setting up laboratories. Before I knew it, my unique schoolboy enterprise had competition. When you're at school there is no way you can compete with these multi-nationals. I thought I could and developed a faster turnaround, instead of having a one and a half hour processing time I converted the chemicals to operate at higher temperatures. More heat, more ice, it was a vicious cycle. I had to safeguard the sensitive emulsion by adding inhibitors and I managed to split the processing time by half. I was going great guns speeding up production but this multi-national just put on an extra shift and doubled their capacity. They had more and more outlets opening while I struggled with assignments, in the end I conceded their victory.

It was way too late for Lyn Monday, but then again maybe

not. For some strange reason it felt like she was still with me. The unexplainable, she was here but wasn't. I missed her enticing smile but knew I had recall of every second spent together. I rationalised: not hard when seconds were all there had been. Again tormented by the lack of a true relationship, so why was I obsessing about her? Then, as if to exacerbate my situation, the Mommas and the Pappas recorded 'Monday, Monday'. They had no idea why they wrote that song but I did! Would I ever get over Lyn?

Not long after I fell into a plum job making feature movies and commercials, 'Anyhow, have a Winfield and Ajax the foaming cleanser', were some of the television catch cries audiences adopted with enthusiasm. The commercial world was alive but the movie world was struggling. I escaped the Vietnam draft, again a loser, but somehow I felt grateful. Feelings surfaced, was I a coward? I was once.

I spent a long weekend camped on a beach on the Mid-North Coast filming the Australian Surfing Championships, the first event of its kind. The waves were poor, barely three feet and when I returned with the film footage, it was processed, edited and showcased on television. That couple of minute's segment ran every Saturday for eight weeks and the interest it generated staggered me. Letters of congratulations flooded the television station. Encouraged, I produced a surfing movie, which did scattered business across Australia except for Sydney where it played to packed houses. There was so much happening I acquired 'occupational tunnel-vision', a fixation to achieve at work; maybe I did this to escape the truth.

I had met Samantha two years after Lyn had died. It was three years later we ventured north, our first time away and to the same location as the surf meet. We were playing Jan and Dean's, "Surfin' Safari'. I stopped the car abruptly and turned the music off. Samantha was surprised when I asked her to walk a steep headland, quite a hike from the car. She refused point-blank, and it was only through intense pressure that she relented. I remember saying, "You'll be sorry."

"Why?"

"It's different but I guess you will never have the chance to see it again."

"Why?"

"Because if you don't get off your fat lazy arse, I'll never bring you back here."

"Am I getting fat?"

"Mm, I think you could do with some exercise."

She opened the door and replied, "Alright, I'll go, but this better be good," expecting the view to be the piece d' resistance.

As she walked ahead of me, I checked her rear – it was perfect!

"Are you looking at my fat arse?"

"Me? No. Why would I do that?"

It was a perfect day and from this naturally high outcrop the panorama proved majestic. Below we could see bronze whalers feasting ravenously on schools of silver floundering Snapper. Samantha asked, "How many sharks are there?"

"I've seen six, maybe seven."

It was nature at its finest, brutal thrashing savagery but nothing we could do other than remove our gaze to the horizon. I held Samantha tight, her head rested against my chest. She tried to make light of the carnage by teasing, "I'm glad I insisted you join me."

I replied mockingly, "I'm sorry that I was hesitant." She smiled knowingly. I whispered close to her ear, "And that comment about you needing exercise, forget it, I think you are just perfect."

"Thanks and you're not too bad either."

In a moment of peace we held each other close, a warm sun, a light breeze and a briny ocean air was enough to pacify the most verbally minded. We hadn't spoken for five minutes and when I thought Samantha had her fill of picturesque imagery I asked softly, "Will you marry me?"

Samantha turned, stunned. Her eyes were moist, then she wept, we kissed, her wet cold cheeks a stark contrast to her warm curvaceous body. She continued hugging me.

I asked, "Is that a yes?"

"Of course I will, I love you."

We kissed again. I hugged her tight but didn't say a word. Did she notice I couldn't say, 'I love you'? I hated myself for the deception, how could I continue loving someone who was dead? Was I insane? Samantha deserved better.

After returning from that trip we would drive untold miles to have privacy, somewhere so isolated no one could find us. Thankfully, our car never broke down on those desolate National Park trails for they were rough going, especially at night. We always brought supplies – food, drinks, and became experts at devouring long bread rolls jam packed with an assortment of short cuts, salads, cheeses and relish. We gulped drinks and consumed runny cream doughnuts still warm from the fryer. Surprisingly, Samantha remained as trim as a girl on a skimmed milk diet.

One night we left the car and made our way cautiously down a craggy cliff face where a deserted beach welcomed us. We swam naked until midnight with the waves crashing resoundingly against our freezing bodies. When we reached the shoreline, we briskly rubbed each other down. The stars were powerfully inspiring and we felt insignificant under God's creation. I lit a fire. The smoke drifted north, finally spiralling into the heavens. We linked hands to reinforce our commitment... again I remained silent. I could have said, 'I love you' but was scared to slip up. One mistake, one faltering tone and I'd be saying, 'Oh yeah and by the way, I'm also in love with another girl – unfortunately she died!'

No one could imagine the pain. I must admit I was feeling empty, no answers just questions. We lay on our backs trying to catch our breaths, here I tried to dismiss the past but instead I shivered. The misty glow of the moon shimmered with a blue cooling tinge and a breeze sprang from the south whipping zestfully across white-capped waves. We had had enough. The fresh air bit at our skin and our goose bumps had goose bumps.

The day of our marriage was a nervous event and my parents buzzed from our house to Samantha's. My mother was

excited, almost understanding the fuss. We exchanged silly im-
mature notes and Samantha kept them. Years later I couldn't
believe what I had written, 'If I'm late, start without me', and
then 'What time is it again'? What a jerk, regardless of my vain
search for humour we did marry and in a beautiful church on
one of Sydney's northern beaches. The day was a blur. I cannot
blame the alcohol for I only had a sip of champagne and if it
had not been for the photographs I would have sworn the
ceremony never took place.

After the wedding, I had moments of doubt. Flashes of 'Lyn'
short-circuited my brain, static recalls, and those words, "Do
you like me?" these continued to be replayed with absolute clarity. Had I led Samantha on? Little pangs of guilt surfaced – this
was absolute stupidity. I felt happy and miserable at the same
time. The months merged and I purposefully found things to
distract my attention.

CHAPTER 5

◄❴O❵►

THE FREEDOMS THERE, JUST COME AND TASTE IT

Samantha asked for kids, so I obliged, we became passionate about children and within five years we had two girls, the eldest Tamara, the spitting image of my mother, a competitive girl with everything and the youngest Kem, a spitter, a regurgitating victim of reflux. I loved these girls. I was mellowing and passionately accepting the role of fatherhood.

I changed jobs and began a career as a sound engineer. I remember the special master edit that was required for Neil Diamond's hit, 'A Hot August Night' and how the duplicators ran hotter than hot trying to keep up with orders. However, I couldn't free myself from the bug of movie making and used every available moment to produce a feature film, it was about the skills of professional motorbike riders and the freedom enjoyed when hitting dusty off-road trails in their attempt to escape the city. This was creative rewarding work however funding a feature film project required a lot of money, so Samantha and I did everything. Samantha became an accomplished sound recordist who with her shotgun-microphone could intimately hear the conversations of people hundreds of yards away. Swearing at the race pits was common and I'd often lowered the camera to see her blushing. To produce the movie cost $10,000 and years of intense labour, the money was a pittance for feature film budgets. I thought people wouldn't take us seriously so I informed the distributors we produced the movie for $100,000. Even then, they laughed at us. No one could produce a movie for $100,000. That was what I was afraid of, however that $10,000 personal investment was a lot of money, we had just bought a house and the repayments were crippling. Things were tough and we had our G rated movie premiere during the September school holidays and at the most unlikeliest of venues – raunchy Kings Cross. Metro Goldwyn Mayer; our distributor advised it was the only theatre available and this would be our premiere location.

Very few people ventured to the risqué Cross – and the movie drifted into a void all of its own. After all the publicity, nothing happened. Blood sweat and tears had produced the movie and we had high expectations. For two months, we drifted along hoping for a miracle. Samantha became frustrated, we knew we had made a good product but everything was out of our hands. We could do nothing other than resign ourselves to failure, a bitter-sweet time for us. We had mounting debts, little money and it was nearing Christmas. Samantha was nervous and the cracks began to show, she spat out, "Look at the mess you've got us into, we'll probably lose the house over this."

I couldn't understand this reasoning, we were partners in everything but before I could explain the phone rang, it was Alistair McDowell the head of Metro Goldwyn Mayer. He announced, "Congratulations Shaun, your movie has broken box office records and the kids are lined up around the block. We're out grossing Walt Disney big time; every theatre is going to want it. I just thought you would like to know."

I wasn't even aware, "What venue?" I asked shocked.

"Goodwood, in Adelaide, it has just gone crazy, congratulations again!"

You can imagine my disbelief, and then I remembered Samantha's comment, "Look at the mess you've got us into..."

The timing of that phone call was odd being the exact moment following Samantha's outburst, Samantha looked at me perplexed, I stroked my chin, determined to savour the moment, "Guess who that was?"

Samantha's face changed from morbidity to exaltation however her timing could not have been worse. I understood her frustration but it was at the expense of us? Her stinging rebuttal was the start and the beginning and now there were two problems confronting our marriage. Regardless, our movie went around the country breaking records. During a cyclone in North Queensland, we lost a drive-in screen and could only run for two of the seven nights. We still managed to gross $8,000 from that location. The movie's production to box office ratio was a resounding bonanza!

We made plans to move, not to a new house but to another country and this being our opportunity to distribute the movie internationally. My youngest daughter was now three, her reflux condition had settled but she remained with an ornery disposition, especially with people who were clearly in the wrong. She reminded me of my aunt who lobbied politicians for justice. Kem was a nightmare to take anywhere for she corrected many, admittedly a lot deserved a good swipe but not from someone so young. God only knew when she was going to open her mouth for when she did the earth shook. On our flight to America she advised smokers to extinguish their cigarettes as they were clearly in a non-smoking section and they did for fear of being reported – I loved her guts!

We settled into a small Californian community in the San Bernardino Mountains called Blue Jay. It was a picturesque pine forest sitting a 100 miles east of Los Angeles. It was frequented by sightseers, rattlesnakes, coyotes, squirrels, scorpions, bears and of course Blue Jays a native bird. Close by were ski resorts and notably Liberace's house which nestled close to a lake. His grand piano sat in the front room and only yards from the water. We enrolled Tamara in school and she had an American accent within three days. Kem tried to copy her and rolled the American accented rrr's like a dog defending a bone. She started preschool shortly after.

Samantha loved the wilderness, searching for Indian arrowheads and insisting on exploring trails, but suddenly her zest for nature took a slide. We had a two-story condominium, bedrooms downstairs, the living up. Samantha was making the girl's beds when from behind she was pounced on by what she thought was a bear. She screamed so loud I spilt my coffee and I scrambled downstairs to find her face down with her shoulders pinned to the bed. The scene was hilarious as a giant Irish Setter tried to lick her. After pulling the dog away from her trembling body, Samantha calmed and ventured closer, not that close, but enough to say... 'Hi'.

Blossom, the red haired setter adopted us and although she belonged to a neighbour spent most of her time with us. She smothered the girls with affection and became their protector. No stranger could approach. Blossom rescued Kem when she fell into a snowdrift and continued to go beyond what Lassie or Rin Tin Tin could conjure up in their half hour episodes. She protected the girls with a passion.

We must have appeared uncharacteristically foreign to these mountain people, we had strange accents and a life style that was all hustle and bustle, then, as if pitying us, one local advised, "Always keep the pantry stocked and ensure you have snow chains but most importantly remember to keep a large plastic bag in the car."

We followed his instructions to the letter but couldn't figure out why a large plastic bag. The weeks unfolded and there was still no clue, we understood the need for food when snowed-in, the snow chains made sense but a large plastic bag didn't. Weeks later the first fall of the season dumped many feet of white powdery snow. The ploughs worked overtime keeping the roads clear; however, the bitumen remained slippery and dangerous. It was time for the snow chains. Then I realised the significance of having a large plastic bag. When fitting the snow chains you knelt in slush or on the clean plastic bag. It was good advice!

We explored and fell in love with the country. The scenery was magnificent with expansive deserts and dry-river washes waiting patiently for rain. We played the odds in Vegas and the slots machines nearly wiped us out. With nothing to lose, Samantha placed her last quarter in a machine and pulled the handle. With fingers crossed, the tumblers aligned and the machine went crazy. Samantha won three thousand dollars, less State and Federal taxes, however if she had bet a dollar, she would have won a Ford Cobra. We were ecstatic with the win but wondered what the return trip would have been like in a high performance V8. Later we traversed Death Valley on one of the hottest days imaginable and survived. We ventured into Arizona, Utah and New Mexico. Once off the road, flash floods became a concern and we constantly surveyed the cactus-strewn horizon searching for billowing threats of grey. Luckily, the dust swirled to our backs and the trails ahead remained dry. With only five percent humidity, it was a guarantee of clear skies and pristine Sierra Mountains – here snow-capped peaks reached for the heavens as if God somehow lived there.

The locals were genuine people and I have fond memories of Mrs K short for Kuzmick. She cared for our two daughters while we organised distribution of the movie in Hollywood. We met an interesting array of people and I remember the actor, Cornell Wilde, then briefly we met the President of the Adult Movie industry, Mike Freiberg; minutes later I saw him arrested for trafficking blue movies across state lines. This was the time of Linda Lovelace's Deep Throat and the movie house on Sunset Boulevard ran for eight years showing that one movie. A Japanese airline would touch down in Los Angeles and a bus would deliver the next session's audience and afterwards would escort them to the airport for their return flight to Japan. I sat next to Francis Ford Coppola in a restaurant and our host tipped one hundred dollar bills – the attention he received was mind blowing. We had never seen such excesses.

Our feature film opened with Dino De Laurentiis's, 'King Kong' and broke theatre records, however we could never have imagined that theatres would take six months to pay and that was after putting pressure on them. The movie industry is a percentage game where a predetermined split determines your return. However, we had trouble with theatre staff manipulating the figures. Eventually, we would turn up to a theatre to count the 'heads' to ensure honesty prevailed.

My parents visited us for Christmas. My mother's disorientation was obvious for she wanted to get back in the car and go home, she couldn't even remember the long-haul flight. Her face lacked make-up and her beautiful oval face had become puffy and grotesque. Dad was having all sorts of problems getting her to co-operate. After a few weeks my parents returned to Australia and we followed soon after to assist my father.

The movie industry was struggling. I looked for work while our agent in America went to work collecting overdue cheques. Rather he went to work on us and commandeered all the cheques boosting his own bank account handsomely. He refused to give us the money or hand back our car. It was only when we employed the services of a private investigator that we saw some action. The report stated he wet himself when bailed-up in a dark alleyway one night and gladly handed over the car. We had co-written a screenplay together but the treacherous son-of-a-bitch took my name off the credits and sprouted it as his own – I learnt a lot from that agent.

The seventies were memorable and of course, I will never forget my ex-agent and President Richard Nixon who were similar in many ways. Amorous hippies expounded love not war, which was an excuse to fornicate and achieved nothing except media attention. There was the invincible Evel Knievel, Grease, ABBA and of course, Elvis, who was still King!

CHAPTER 6

―――◄○►―――

UNEXPECTED EVENTS

As my mother's condition degenerated, my father devoted himself to caring and refused to place her in a nursing home. It was only through desperation he let go and this being kinder to have her admitted to hospital as she had developed ulcers that began eating her heels. She could no longer walk and died soon after at the age of sixty-five. When it counted, my father attended with compassion, she couldn't have hoped for more. Maybe he did it out of guilt, I will never know.

I had the chance to tell my mother I loved her before she passed. I doubted if she could hear me in her comatose condition. My father viewed my mother in state, something I preferred not to do. I can't remember her funeral, strange, important events blocked from my memory; I was numb, although I remember getting a parking ticket while arranging the funeral details. I fought the parking ticket and won, so something positive came out of this sad affair. All I knew was, my mother's advice gave me no opportunity to know Lyn Monday. Why had she done this to me? Her advice had gutted my confidence, my very soul was scared, and I doubted I would ever get over that girl and the secret I had kept all these years.

Weeks had passed since my mother's funeral. I still couldn't remember a thing. I had barricaded my mind into tiny compartments where memories were stored but not categorised, here a time capsule inside and a vague recall on the outside. My secret appeared safe from Samantha, maybe in time I might forget – I doubted it. I felt sad, nothing could correct the past, and nothing could bring back my mother or Lyn Monday.

I kept my distance from my father, seeing him occasionally. Each time he appeared unchanged, I didn't know if he was the cause of my mother's demise. He seemed upset with her passing, maybe it was my mother's interpretation that was skewed.

My two daughters occupied my thoughts constantly. They were growing into beautiful girls, my eldest a sporty adventurous type while the youngest was still intent to correct imperfections in others... she did this charmingly, always with a smile and a "sorry". She had developed incredible people skills, which ensured she 'stung' with the kindest of intentions.

Months later, after a dental appointment, Samantha returned home, she saw me sitting on the sofa and disappeared into the bedroom. Minutes later she called, "Shaun?"

I discarded the magazine and stood in the doorway to see what she wanted.

"What happened...?"

With the exception of a tightly wrapped sheet, she was naked, "Forget what happened at the dentist, come here," she smiled the wickedest of grins.

She held out her hand but instead I took hold of the sheet and gently peeled away the layers, kissing her body as I went. She arched her back and sighed. I lay beside her. I noticed her breathing increase to short sharp pants and then sweat began to spot her forehead. I whispered softly into her ear, "You're very sexy."

She replied, "Stop talking."

I wrestled her into the middle of the bed, puppy play really and then we rolled into ecstasy. Her hands gripped the sheets. Suddenly it was the law of the jungle passion I never knew existed. I caught her reflection in the mirror, she was beyond satisfaction. I should have realised she had a vulnerable egg just hoping to be nourished. From our coupling grew a tiny pod, a caring and understanding son, born exactly three months short of a year. The moment he breathed, he attracted attention for he urinated on the obstetrician. We named him Joel Reece. As he grew older, he broke regional records and ran in State Championships. He was the teacher's pet and a perfect son, not the slightest hiccup of angst. School was a fun time but I knew learning wasn't his forte. His passion was basketball and for his height, he was talented. He was over-looked for representation when it mattered but his skill levels were superior to many tall gawky guys who stood under the hoop, touched, and dropped. In his Nike elevators, he would proudly take the court standing a whopping six foot-two, enormous! Well only in spirit, if not in basketball height. I remember eight three pointers per game being his point guard average.

He had a tender side, show him a dumped kitten and he would have a home for it in no time. 'Missy' owed her life to him and all her dumped brothers and sisters survived because he cared. They had excellent homes to see out their years. He loved that cat and that cat loved him. He also loved life and a good laugh. Being accepted was important and on reflection, this was his weakness.

So these were the eighties, Madonna failed her audition for Fame, while Boy George looked nothing like one and Conan the Barbarian was grooming himself to become the Governor of California. Great Britain and Argentina rattled sabres for control of the Falklands and again that year there was the Iran versus Iraq war. The doomed space ship Challenger blew apart and spread despair like the AIDS virus. Tom Selleck torched the hearts of young ladies while the Ku Klux Clan torched anything that would burn – they left American skies glowing with sinister overtones.

The years were racing, we were into the nineties; I kept working, trying to blur the past. Events merged, each competing against the other, there was always something happening. Michael Jordan was just as popular as the Spice Girls, INXS's Michael Hutchence died. Britney Spears stole every guy's heart. There was always someone doing something to someone, OJ Simpson cruised the freeway with a procession of police in tow and later was set free. There was Kosovo and later Desert Storm. Bill Clinton never had sex with Monica although he tried his hardest. Samantha and I had our own problem, a jarring reality show before reality shows became famous.

Joel was eighteen. He had scraped through high school and was following his passion into the hospitality industry where he quickly found a job at a suburban hotel, part of a large international chain. He was working the front desk of the hotel with another staff member when two gunmen forced their way through the front doors, assaulted both and robbed the establishment. Bruised and battered they called the police who arrived quickly but the culprits were long gone. To be bound – kicked and robbed at a front desk by two desperadoes intent on killing produced cracks, similar to my mother's fragility. The police had no chance of apprehending these low lives.

Gradually, Joel's personal relationships faltered. He began drinking to dull the memory, maybe not the biggest challenge anyone has faced but certainly a challenge for someone so young and whose faith rested in others.

For safety concerns, Joel changed employers and moved to a high-rise international hotel owned by a Korean consortium. He was at this city hotel for only six weeks when the clouds of change grew dark and ominous.

What were the chances of being held-up again and so soon, or at all? This time, the robbers had planned their attack from within the hotel using a room that was undergoing refurbishment. To stage this robbery they used room 306, I'll always remember that number and I will always remember how my son spoke of the terror produced there. Really, he didn't have to speak; I could see the drama etched into his face. Joel and another employee were subjected to four hours of brutality and their lives were constantly threatened. Joel was again beaten and the robbers escaped with a small fortune in cash, credit cards, traveller's cheques and jewellery. Surprisingly Joel looked the same on the outside but deep within, he was hurting, a virtual sandbar waiting to be under-mined.

The nightmare continued, Joel thought he was being followed. Was he becoming paranoid? But what appeared as delusional ravings of a post-traumatic stress victim turned out to be a disturbing and accurate observation. It was the unthinkable, Joel became the suspect to this robbery and a huge police task force began gathering evidence. They deduced it was an inside job. The police proceeded to bug our house then instigated a surveillance operation equal to a Keystone Cop episode. Our phones were tapped – they broke into Joel's car by smashing a side window. Nothing was stolen – not even his money, however, every conceivable item was searched. When I complained to the police they refused to deny or admit to the break-in. They looked guilty, strange behaviour for law enforcers. Now I was concerned these cowboys may plant some form of evidence, anything to achieve a result. However, all they proved was their incompetence and their ability to drive my son crazy. The cowboys lingered and their round-up continued for months. In the end, there was no evidence, not one question was asked of Joel, and no charges were laid. The real perpetrators went free and at an enormous cost to the community. By this stage, Joel was looking terrible and his doctor prescribed medication to help him sleep. Because the police had such a high profile, many friends deserted him for fear they may be drawn into this nightmare. Our lives were in total disarray. I couldn't imagine how Joel was fairing. Joel Reece, my son – the one who cared for others was a mess. Mix in several girlfriends with precarious situations and we had a melting pot of volatility, in the end he couldn't think straight and although never diagnosed as such, he broke. He came home one night looking drawn, his expression beyond tired, he said goodnight, and asked us to wake him in the morning adding, "I've booked the wrestling on cable."

The next morning, we let him sleep as late as possible but when Samantha went to wake him, he wouldn't answer the door. Finally, I broke the lock trying to gain access. There was no response after shaking him, only a deep death rattle emanating from his chest.

The wailing of sirens became intense and my life became

surreal, having the central image sharp but the edges soft and blurry; it was as if an artist had taken to a canvas with sweeping strokes and was deliberately shaping my existence. He must be a bastard, can't he paint sharp edges? Why does everything look blurred? I'm sitting in the lead ambulance on the way to hospital clearing a pathway for the second, the one carrying my dying son. Get the image sharp, paint with clarity for Christ sake. Get these dumb cars out of the way. I can hear everything but feel nothing. I am beyond numb.

I wait in emergency with my painful memories and by the time Samantha and the girls arrive I have nothing to add, there are no updates. We pace the waiting room nervously. The first doctor cautioned, "Your son may not live, be prepared. His blood analysis is indicative of those who have taken a critical overdose. The ambulance officers gave us these sleeping pills. Do these belong to your son?"

We nodded. We were convinced he didn't attempt suicide for he was adamant to watch wrestling on cable. He was passionate for each broadcast. Did he take the wrong dosage or being groggy, did he take repeated dosages? The toxicology report had no way of determining amounts. Maybe we would never discover the truth.

At the end of 48 hours, there was no change. Joel was still unconscious, his breathing assisted by a respirator, he looked terrible. There were tubes and wires going everywhere. Another doctor moved our concerns to a new level, "If he develops pneumonia, do you want us to save him?" How could you ask that question? Utterly exhausted we returned home. I had a shower and cried more tears than water spurting for freedom. I had never cried like that, a lot for my mother but this seemed different, more intense. We continued to harass the hospital for updates. When we returned we found a chaplain praying for him. She was a nice lady who used the power of silence to extract the raw emotion. She just looked sad. Samantha cracked, Joel was going to die we both sensed it. The longer he stayed in a coma the worst his condition would become. Then, after five days in intensive care, we were informed he was going to be moved."

"Where to," I asked.

The doctor replied, "High dependency," as if this was a common occurrence.

"Why?"

"There are other patients requiring intensive care. We have to make room."

Joel was trolleyed into a small ward with little equipment which also had three female patients crammed in like sardines.

In our fragile state, we monitored him carefully. The nurses were busy, stretched to capacity. We observed his heart rate, blood pressure, oxygen levels, reflexes and we also provided stimuli but nothing happened. Each day was a blur with no change. It was clear that Joel had brain damage.

During a shift change, a nurse asked if she could pray for him. We naturally agreed. She said a kind prayer but nothing out of the ordinary, however... at the end... she simply stated, "The angel's are looking after him." I instantly felt energised and re-markably, Joel showed signs of improving. It was a force so powerful I couldn't dispute its origin. Angels were never my strong point when studying religion, in fact, I had dismissed them as fanciful imagery but now the strength of that prayer be-came overwhelming. Why couldn't this have happened with the chaplain or any of the others with good intentions? But angels?

Because he had showed signs of responding, he attracted at-tention. He had visits from the Neurological Department and the Brain Injury Unit who seemed intent on staging a turf war. They both wanted him and openly argued their case. The doc-tor fighting hardest for my son offered us the chance to see their brain injury unit, a separate care facility near the helicop-ter base. It was a large modern building positioned deep within the hospital's grounds. We were shocked. The patients were such a contrast to the main hospital. Some had no control of their bladders, some screamed without warning, vicious cutting words. Some beyond frustration, some compulsively lapping the corridors but regardless the doctors and staff were compassionate and caring. My son was set up in a ward with six others, a long room but well equipped. The unit was highly organised and they were fighting hard for my son, what a story this would make if only the outside world could stomach the truth.

The following weeks proved just as difficult. There was not one patient who didn't have a story, all different but all with the same outcome – they were brain injured. Nothing is perfect, visitors rape patients, there are arrests, patients come in varying degrees of anger, some from failed suicide attempts to crashed skulls from car accidents, none receive a social elevation above the next, all have a problem that needs fixing, some get close, others relapse, many stroke out and die. Some escape, a sad world hidden away from the mainstream of society, the rejected, the unlucky and those broken.

Joel was little more than a vegetable and for three months he remained unconscious. Samantha and I stayed with him everyday, throughout all the operations, the soiled bedclothes, physiotherapy and the cleaning of his tracheotomy whenever it gunked up with phlegm. I loved my son. I couldn't bear the thought of him gone and I fought by his side. He recovered, enough for Samantha and me to wheel him out of the Brain Injury Unit exactly ten months to the day, different people with different lives.

My daughter, Tamara stayed in touch with my father, I had stopped seeing him. Maybe it was my son's condition that was more important or maybe I felt singed by his treatment of my mother. Maybe my life would have been different if he had communicated with me. What went wrong?

Then I received a phone call from my father's retirement home. The Director said, "I'm sorry to advise but your father has passed away. A nurse found him lying on his bed, the phone was off the hook as if he had been talking to someone. He went peacefully. I'm very sorry, would you like to see him before we make arrangements."

On the way to the retirement home, Samantha and I collected Tamara who advised, "You're not going to believe this, but I was speaking to grandpa only thirty minutes ago when suddenly the connection was cut; you know what I said to him...?" Tears stained her tired face, "I told him I was having a baby. He was excited for me but then the line went dead or so I thought, he must have passed when he heard the news. This is so sad, one life is terminated another starts, the cycle continues though."

This was devastating and fantastic news all at the same time, which made just another bizarre moment.

When I saw my father prostrate on his bed he looked at peace, his mouth was open and I tried to shut it – it would be more dignified closed. Then I did the unthinkable. I kissed him, my father who had caused my mother's problems, I forgave him, I don't know if I had the right to do that but it helped me, I hoped it helped my father but now it was too late for answers. I knew I should have cleared the air before he passed but the pain was so intense I couldn't bear the moment.

After the funeral, I had plenty of time to think. I felt at peace with my father and that kiss was important, I hoped he realised I cared, although I still had reservations for no amount of debriefing would erase my concerns and what had happened to my mother.

I regretted those missed opportunities. If only I had grabbed those moments and ran with my instincts. Maybe I should have helped my mother, maybe I should have revealed my feelings to Lyn and maybe I should have spoken to my father. I was just too scared to hear the truth and now it was too late.

PART TWO

THE PRESENT

*Like drifting on a rising current, her spirit sought me
out until I had no alternative but to ask…
what happened to Lyn Monday?*

CHAPTER 7

◄○►

SPORT ON MONDAY

Where had the years gone? Financially, Samantha and I were secure, we owned our house but had an investment property geared to the max.

My daughter had a son named Drew now aged six, tall for his age and keen on sport. He was full of questions and often reminded me of myself at that age. These were the years for grandchildren as the cycle started afresh. Now I looked forward to visitation rights which were frequently unscheduled.

On this particular day, Drew had a sporting meet. This was a courageous school program which offered children the chance to compete, something frowned on years earlier. Although well intentioned, the school system tried to shield them from the sun's rays, pollution and over-exertion. Suddenly there was a turn around, similar to when we ran, jumped and let our minds be creative.

Little Drew's athletic carnival had been set down for a Thursday but the rain bucketed down. The school had no alternative but to cancel the day. By the following Tuesday the grounds were still soaked and the white chalking machine refused to mark the soggy field. They postponed the day and rescheduled the event for the following Monday. Sure enough, the ground was perfect.

Drew returned at the end of the day and announced he came second in the two hundred-metre sprint, he bubbled with excitement and I congratulated him. He ventured, "I came second last in another race." He was so proud!

I said encouragingly, "That is very good Drew."

You can say all this stuff when you are a grandfather. What I have not mentioned is my daughter, Tamara, thrives on competition and had spent some years competing at world championship level. I saw her being within the top ten for her chosen sport and fiercely competitive. Years later she was still a highly competitive individual being a solicitor, a sports scientist, and recently beginning her Masters at Law. The troubling part came next when my daughter returned to receive Drew's news, she appeared excited but I knew her too well, she was disappointed with a second spot, so we didn't even mention second last. In her mind, there was no second, third or fourth, you either won or lost.

I sensed her disappointment, it was in the eyes, the delivery, and I can tell what my daughter is going to do even before she does. Anyway, Drew was brimming with excitement and Tamara braved on, pretending second was great. Suddenly Drew needed to justify his position and said, almost apologetically, "Some kids wore spikes!"

That was enough, Tamara spurted out, "Little Athletic Kids... really? They let kids that young wear spikes?" The air mixed with tension, it floated high, held with expectation. Tamara would use anything to justify a 'loss'. Of course, no one likes running against spiked kids, especially if your sneakers are a notch above a Dunlop Volley. Drew looked flustered.

I felt for the poor kid and overnight I decided to explain what had happened to me. I drive Drew to school each day so I had a captive audience, I began by saying, "Do you want me to tell you about Lionel Lynch?

"Who, Granddad?"

"Lionel Lynch," I reiterated. "He always beat me at Primary School. I always came second, no matter what the event. It could be running, high jumping, long jump, he always beat me.

Then we moved to different high schools. The next thing I knew I was winning every race and event. Every year I would be the school champion for my age group. Lionel was never at district carnivals and I expected to see him at the regional run-offs, but he wasn't there either. I was sure he would be at the State Championships all warmed up and ready to beat me. He wasn't there either. I never did see him again. Maybe, I just got stronger and he became slower. Don't be concerned with coming second. Second is great. Think of my experience with Lionel Lynch and eventually you will win."

Later that day I reflected on my conversation with Drew; where had Lionel Lynch disappeared to? His times in primary school were good enough for a State berth. He too, was super-competitive. Something had to have happened to him. Maybe he moved interstate. That might explain it.

Then I thought of Josh Freemont, my mate from high school, he was a year younger but an exceptional runner. Then the strangest thing happened, all those memories from the past flooded at me like an avalanche of smothering rock and silted debris. I thought of my parents, my friends, my relatives, where I had lived, what I had done, where I used to go and who I'd seen... the images flashed brilliantly before me, swirling my body like a pulsating aura. Not surprisingly, Lyn Monday spun herself through this maze of imagery, coyly enticing with tantalizing eyes so captivating it was all I could do not to melt.

After all these years, she was still making eye contact. Hot and cold shivers ran my spine. After forty-five years of repression my memories were in tact, Lyn Monday was exactly the way I had left her, the milk bar, the awkwardness, the lack of words in our conversation, they were all there, embarrassing, but still crystal clear. I remembered her soft skin and those fluttering long eyelashes. Eyes so deep you felt like diving in, immersing yourself into that emerald sea of intrigue. The bonfire's reflection shimmied against her fresh cut hair and she shrugged her shoulders as she had done before. Her face so beautiful, the most beautiful girl I had ever seen. Suddenly those eyes looked down, sad. Oh so sad, and then a single tear slipped her cheek dropping timely into space. I blinked to erase this interruption. This wasn't my memory of her. But she was here. I reached out but something was wrong, no matter how far I stretched, she was unreachable… only a metre away. But how? Was it my imagination or some form of apparition? A real live encounter and a moment to make me a believer, it was over-whelming. Her hand moved to her face and wiped the trail of that lonesome tear. She looked up, just staring at me and waiting for a response…. this was Lyn, my Lyn Monday! Before I could react, I recognised her voice, a pleading… "Help me," no different from when she spoke in the milk bar, a haunt-ingly familiar tone, clear as a bell.

Emotion took hold. I shook my head hoping to clear the panic. I ran outside the house and sucked a huge breath of wintry air, my hands were on my hips, I bent over to catch my breath, similar to a sprinter after a race and tried to settle my distress. The more I inhaled the worst I became. My heart was racing, my forehead spotted. I couldn't breathe. My body swam in sweat. Vomit rose, burning the back of my throat. Stifling, suffocating, and the nau-sea wouldn't settle. I fought the urge to be sick.

"Samantha," I screamed and collapsed onto the nearest gar-den seat where I remained for a split second, then, slid onto my knees holding my chest in panic. The blackness rushed at me and engulfed everything except a pinprick of intensity, a light so determined to survive this darkening magnitude and this was all to do with my Lyn, my… nothing! I felt devastated and my tears flowed like a summer storm. Why was everything dif-ferent? Why was this happening? Every ounce of energy drained from me and the last thing I remember was the light quickly extinguishing.

A male voice was next to my ear, I remember him counting slowly, "One… two… three." Then without ceremony, I was in the air and dumped like a side of mutton onto an ambulance gurney. Its directional influence resembled a shopping cart, a rattling old runaway on a steep car park. The shock reverberated through my body and I pulled back hitting my head on something.

I was alive and in hospital. There was no vice gripping my chest but my head-ached. I felt depressed. The doctors questioned me but I refused to participate – what could I say, "A girl... a friend... just paid me a visit." They could all go to hell! What would they know about Lyn Monday? What would they know about spirits? What did I know, except this was real and I wasn't about to let her go!

As the medication wore off, I felt like shit. I didn't want to face anyone and my eyes felt more comfortable shut. I could hear the doctor reporting to Samantha, "Nothing is showing up in the tests. His blood pressure was high on admission but now normal. We tested his blood chemistry and there was nothing to suggest drugs or other complications. His cholesterol count is perfect, in fact, for someone his age, he appears incredibly fit, his heart looks normal. Has he had a history of similar attacks?"

Samantha considered, "No... I can't even imagine what could have caused this."

"Think carefully, has he had anything happen that may have led to this panic attack? Is there any reason for him acting morose and uninterested?"

"No, absolutely not. Everything has been fine."

"Then I'll leave you with a referral, Doctor Roberts is a smart cookie who specialises in neurological and episodic events. Something has happened and the doctor needs to establish what? Your husband needs a management plan should another attack occur."

Surprised, Samantha asked, "A shrink? You think this was a mental problem?"

The doctor's voice dropped several decibels but loud enough for me to hear, "Absolutely, don't worry, a mental condition is most times manageable, Doctor Roberts will sort him out."

I felt like calling out, "You idiot, get me a second opinion," but my body refused to co-operate.

Samantha thanked the doctor who gave me twenty-four hours before discharge. Samantha pulled back the curtain and came bedside to hold my hand, "You heard all that, right?" My throat was croaky and dry, "Yep." I still preferred not to open my eyes, but scoffed angrily at the doctor's evaluation, "He's a clown."

"Shaun, I need to know what happened."

"I wasn't doing anything special, I just needed to get outside and into the fresh air. There was no physical activity, nothing out of the ordinary. Then the pain started, shooting barbs right across my chest. I even had pain down my arm."

"Well... thankfully it was not a heart attack but something happened. You scared me Shaun and what is this with your eyes, why won't you open them?"

"The lights are too bright."

"I can turn them off."

"No, I'll just keep them shut for the time being."

"Ok... so there is nothing that you can add to this mystery."

"No, nothing," I lied, how could I tell Samantha about Lyn Monday after all these years? I felt guilty, as if I had betrayed her.

"Shaun, get some sleep and I'll come by after dinner."

I did sleep and way past dinner. When I awoke, Samantha was preparing to leave, "Oh, you're awake?"

"I'm sorry, it must have been boring for you?"

"No, not really."

"Why do you say that?"

"You've been talking in your sleep and I've heard enough to know something is troubling you."

"What?" I asked defensively.

"Something big is happening on Monday."

"Monday? Did I say anything else?"

"Just that, over and over, you kept repeating it was Monday. I don't know what Monday has to do with anything. Try to think. What is going to happen on Monday?"

Feeling powerless I stumbled, "Nothing... absolutely nothing... nothing I know of."

Samantha paused, cautiously, she knew me better than anyone but decided to leave my fragility intact, at least for now. "Can you open your eyes when I'm talking to you?"

"Later maybe."

"Okay then, rest up and I'll see you in the morning. Whatever is the problem, you know you can tell me."

"I know."

I didn't know, for this was different, Lyn Monday was the only secret I had kept from Samantha and that was as bad as having an affair – torrid, steamy and illicit. I tried to reason this out. I had only spoken to Lyn Monday twice in all the time I had known her, so why was I feeling guilty? We had never touched or kissed and when I did talk, the words were stupid and meaningless. There was eye contact – that's all. The only contact that made sense was how she looked at me, each gaze binding me closer and closer until I ached for the next – a special intense bond where nothing else mattered. Now after all these years, her presence tormented and teased again. I felt miserable, the lowest point of my life and to think she was right there in front of me. Again, I left her standing, again I walked away without answers. Why was she doing this? Why now after all these years? Was it true, did she cry? That single pouring of emotion, so intense I felt devastated. I was again reliving the past. The only thing resurrecting me from this agonising pit was a glimmer of hope – Lyn had been in touch and how could I ignore that, but as a consequence my life was going to get worse – I could just tell!

CHAPTER 8

———◄○►———

MONDAYITIS

While Samantha watched me sleep, she overheard me mention 'Monday'. From my aimless ramblings, I spoke 'Lyn Monday's' name and this to the point of obsessing. Samantha thought I was referring to a day of the week. What did Samantha say? "… over and over you kept repeating it was Monday. I don't know what Monday has to do with anything. Try to think."

Samantha would be relentless until she knew the truth, always ferreting out the details, it wouldn't be long before I broke and exposed my secret.

Broke – that was a laugh, I was already broken! Still, I didn't have the heart to destroy Samantha's faith in me or was it because I could foresee the enormous complications that would accompany the truth. Whichever way I looked at it, this secret was entrenched and there was no way to explain or justify it.

Throughout the night, I drifted in and out of sleep. A twilight zone – never too deep nor completely awake, disturbed sleep fuelled by churning emotions. Two young nurses came into my room making whispered chitchat. It must have been the boredom of the job for they jibbed one another constantly. Then they left me alone for several hours. About three o'clock they came back. I still pretended to be asleep. They seemed so young, nineteen, maybe twenty. How things had changed, they seemed experienced on every subject, although what came next surprised me...

Within a whisper of all whispers one asked, "What's his problem again?"

Were they referring to me?

"Ssshh, don't wake him. The doctors think some form of trauma, but he's not opening up. He's good looking, don't you think. For an older guy, not bad."

"Yeah, the spitting image of Harrison Ford."

They both giggled at the movie star reference.

"You're not interested are you?"

"I'd consider an older man, just think of the experience he would have. I'm sick of guys our age who have no idea how to romance you."

"Would you do it with him?"

She paused, "Yeah, maybe. You?"

"Maybe, he has a certain charisma happening, it would be interesting."

"He's married. I saw his wife leave as I came on shift."

"Oh. What's she like?"

"Attractive, but... she was upset... the way she was behaving was the most peculiar thing."

"Why?"

"She looked like she had seen a ghost. She was pale, her face drawn and I bet she couldn't wait to get home for a good cry. I thought she would burst into tears any second."

"She's probably upset by him being in hospital."

"Maybe."

Samantha was near tears? I hadn't noticed but the nurse had. As they exited the door, I opened my eyes. That's when the youngest spotted me. She almost died from embarrassment and nudged the other. The door closed, and I could hear their voices from the corridor, they were arguing, I couldn't hear exactly what they were saying but after a minute, the youngest bounded back in. She looked worried as she came close, "Sorry, you won't tell anyone, will you?"

"No, it's cool," I put my hand out for an introduction, "I'm Shaun, pleased to meet you."

She replied, "Leah," she looked embarrassed. "I'm sorry, I thought you were asleep."

"No big deal."

"Okay? So we're good about everything?"

I nodded.

She walked towards the door, turned and smiled. The door came to an abrupt close and the room felt empty. What was happening with Samantha? I had no idea she was hurting that badly. Maybe while I was sleeping I had muttered something else.

At home, Samantha hovered around me like a hallway monitor. The nurses were right; she did appear strained, although to address this problem was far more than I could manage for the moment. I watched television, played music, a song for all occasions, 'Blue Bayou'. Then I began writing a new book on inspiration. I spoke on the phone with my grandchildren. My son kept checking on me, which was unnerving. It felt like suicide watch. Dr. Roberts's card was on the fireplace just to remind me to make an appointment. I ignored it, instead I kept thinking of Lyn Monday. Something was wrong, what did she need help with? A bad feeling gripped my gut and wouldn't let go. I knew I had to ask questions, research and stealthily investigate but after forty-five years the chances of finding answers would be difficult, people would have moved, records erased and Lyn Monday's parents were likely to have passed. Maybe her friends might help. The trouble was, I couldn't remember their names. Was Lyn all I paid attention to? Pretty much!

I needed a plan. The more I thought the worst my predicament became. It was bizarre, the whole thing was crazy, why probe into her death after forty-five years? Then suddenly, I decided it was too left field and dismissed the idea completely, a moment of clarity. The whole experience had come to me during a period of trauma. Not an ideal analytical environment and I was already a sceptical individual. Besides, it looked a waste of time – so that was it... over – kaput – finitio!

What did she need help with anyway? Hang-on, I thought I decided not to pursue this. There was no chance of forgetting Monday, my head churned for answers and the notion wouldn't leave. What could I do anyway? If I gave myself forty-eight hours rest, I could watch some movies, go for walks and call friends. Maybe dinner, only then might I be able to rid myself of this crazy compulsion to investigate.

I dialled some friends we hadn't seen for ages. They could only go out tonight which suited me perfectly. Siobhan was an attractive talkative woman, easy to communicate with while her husband, Tom, usually sat there, moody, and nodded, only getting involved when asked a direct question. Samantha was keen to go and it would be good to catch up with people we hadn't seen for ages.

We arrived at a villa styled eatery with a narrow lane way entrance. This led to the main restaurant which was always a buzz with media personalities and high-flyers. I spotted Siobhan and Tom from a distance, Siobhan was wearing a low cut black number revealing her ample cleavage, it amazed me how her dress remained attached as there were no straps and her shoulders were exposed for all to see. Nice breasts. Samantha nudged me politely to stop gawking. Siobhan's red hair reached the middle of her back and she looked more striking than the last time I had seen her, which was when exactly? I couldn't remember; all I could remember was she controlled the conversation then, and I expected no less tonight. She was considerably younger and hadn't aged a bit, there was still time to have a family, pity she hadn't for it may have given her something to think about other than herself. Tom was casually dressed, also good looking although his shoulders had rounded as if he was carrying the weight of the world. His black hair, I suspect was retouched to reveal tiny snippets of grey, a look that wasn't altogether unappealing. At least he cared for his appearance. When I kissed Siobhan's cheek, it felt flushed but surprisingly her hands were cold. Siobhan and Tom had already ordered drinks. On closer appraisal and after shaking Tom's hand he looked the worst for wear, his hand continued trembling and his demeanour decidedly frazzled. Siobhan explained that on the way to the restaurant, they had hit another car; Tom's fault and the other driver had threatened him, a road rage incident that needed reporting. He planned to do that later but in the meantime, the accident played heavily on his mind. He was concerned with the time it would take to file the report and this meant missing our dinner date. That for Tom seemed far more important than addressing potential violence. He was always one to be in denial.

We started with bread, then giant sized entrees and when the main course arrived we were still discussing which lawyer should represent Tom. This car accident had heavy overtones and the potential for ethnic thugs to enforce demands. The other driver had sighted Tom's driver's licence and knew exactly where to find him. Tom was drinking heavily. In reality, Tom was scared to go home and now Siobhan tried to curtail Tom's excessive drinking but it was a losing battle. By dessert, they had worn us out and had drained themselves of every last tit-bit of accident information. Samantha invited them to stay at our house for the night. They considered, almost in a collective moment, "And how are you two going?"

I looked at my watch. It was exactly three hours since we had arrived and this was their first question about us. I answered, "Just great."

Samantha looked surprised, examined me closely and divulged, "Shaun's just got out of hospital. We thought he had a heart attack but as you can see he has made a full recovery." Tom, in a moment of infinite wisdom, spouted, "You look like shit. What happened?"

"The doctors don't know for sure, it's a worry these days, they all look like they have come from the university crèche, they're so young, what experience could they possibly have?"

Samantha was determined to put my case out there and said, "He's lying, he had a panic attack and he won't tell me what caused it or what he's feeling."

Siobhan was a marriage counsellor and a public relations consultant and that disclosure had her attention. Mention feelings and the professional thinks, 'Hey, a short-cut to resolution,' she patted me on the hand as if she understood. She had no idea!

Regardless, Siobhan sensed she could help and gazed longingly into my face. I recognised the attempt to question by silence. I'd seen this approach while my son was in hospital. Make out you care, use a Jack Benny pregnant pause and let the victim feel obligated to spill their guts. It's an old trick. The server arrived just in time to save me. She placed four plates of rich creamy tiramisu's in front of us. It tasted heavenly and I decided it would be aberrant to divulge repressed feelings by adding curdling memories. I escaped by saying, "Tom, you probably thought you would get your head kicked in after that accident, how about another for the road?"

Tom's capacity to sponge up alcohol was becoming legendary and he nodded and tried to figure what dessert accompaniment was the most powerful. Siobhan to her credit didn't let go, something like a fox terrier coming back to a bone, "Shaun, I'm aware that you're sidestepping this issue, let me help you. Pleaseeee… go on be a honey."

I nodded, but not a commitment. 'Honey', like was she serious, like I'd trust my precious feelings of Lyn Monday with this control freak, maybe in another life where we were both amoeboid cells floating in a slimy pond.

Samantha gave me one of her looks. Sometimes I was a highly trained recruit that snapped to attention, sometimes, but not this time. "There's nothing happening, there's nothing to talk over."

"Bullocks," Tom declared.

"What?" I said surprised.

"'Bullocks Run' sounds an interesting dessert wine, let's get a bottle."

"Good idea, where's it made?"

"The Clare, great wine country."

"What type of wine are we talking about, Sauternes."

"No, Gewurztraminer."

"Ah, perfect."

Siobhan was relentless, "Tom? What are you doing? Can't

you see this time is for Shaun, forget your wine and help out here will you?"

"What can I do?" Tom returned to me and asked, "Another woman, hey! Have you been fooling around, getting a bit on the side old chap," he leaned forward and shook my hand as a form of congratulations, "If so, make sure she's a 'looker'. It's not much point going through recrimination and stress for an ugly bitch."

Siobhan snapped, "Tom!"

"It's true, what's the point of fooling around with an ugly bitch. It's a different thing if you're talking marriage."

Siobhan was casting daggers, but Tom seemed oblivious to her warning, "Tom… I don't think you should drink any more." She edged his glass away but it was too late for prohibition.

"Hey… remember the song…" as if what he was about to say explained everything, "If you need to be happy in your life, never get a pretty woman to be your wife."

I said, "Mm… I'm not sure those were the exact words."

Tom slurred, "Whatever," then, as if driven by a serendipitous moment he began to melodise the chorus. He used a dialect similar to the singer, the one who made the song famous, however and annoyingly each word massacred the original, "If you want my personal view, get an ugly bitch to marry you."

I stammered, "What?"

"That's right."

I queried again, trying to make sense of his gibberish, "If I fool around, make sure it's with a good looking woman? Then you're giving advice about marrying an ugly…"

"Bitch," Tom quickly assisted.

I corrected, "… woman… you're saying it's best for a happy marriage. Christ, do you have a death wish?" I looked at Siobhan who was steaming.

Tom continued on the road to hell, "Affairs are one thing, life commitments another. You're not going to marry this bitch you're having this affair with because you are already married. So go for it!"

Samantha's eyes rolled back and Siobhan's mouth dropped.

Tom's inebriation was worse than I realised, even his speech was becoming slurred.

I had a need to confess, I said softly, "I'm not having an affair," although I refused to look at Samantha and now that I had made this public announcement I felt guiltier than ever.

I thought I had problems. However, compared to me; Tom certainly had issues and enough to divert Siobhan's attention. There was a deathly silence as Siobhan figured what to do, then within two breaths Siobhan laid it on the line, "Into what category do I fall – Tom? What is it again… ugly bitch? Maybe you realise the mistake you have made. What is it?"

From the tables surrounding us I could see other diners move uncomfortably in their seats. Some looked embarrassed. I know I was. Siobhan was good looking, certainly not ugly, she scrubbed up well, smelt over perfumed sometimes leaving a stale after five stench resembling expired facial cream but when the calculations were done she wasn't deserving of Tom's disloyalty. I could see Tom struggling and I could imagine plans for a divorce. The dessert wine arrived and Tom took this opportunity to skull the first pouring, "Delicious, everyone has to try this."

Siobhan ordered, "Tom. If you drink any more, you can go home by yourself."

"But we're not going home honey, remember we're going to Shaun's place tonight and you're going to help him with his problems. Right Shaun?"

He whispered something under his breath which none of us heard, I had the advantage of sitting opposite and could read his lips. It looked like, "Good luck Shaun, you're going to get screwed over."

"What did you say darling," an icy tone accompanied Siobhan's delivery.

"Why nothing darling."

"I thought you said something about how life's a bitch now that you're living by yourself."

"What? No. Why would I say that?"

"Because that's pretty much your only option."

CHAPTER 9

NOT THE BERBER

There was a buffer of empty tables surrounding us, Siobhan and Tom's tirade had cleared the restaurant. The Maitre'd looked stunned while Samantha's shocked face said it all, we were witnessing the end of a marriage and there was nothing we could do; it was like watching a train wreck in painfully slow motion.

We left Tom and Siobhan's car in the car park and bundled them into ours. Tom sat in the front and Siobhan and Samantha the rear. There was an icy divide. I couldn't just start up a conversation with Tom as that would have looked like I was taking sides. I didn't want to talk to Samantha and certainly did not want to get into a discussion with Siobhan. I tuned to a radio station that was playing a half hour segment on the Door's greatest hits, anything to create atmosphere. To my relief Tom asked me to pull over but no sooner had he opened the door and placed his feet on the ground when he vomited over his shoes in his attempt to hit the gutter. He groaned painfully, as we sat, me thinking, better here than on the Berber carpet.

Siobhan didn't budge only huffed and Samantha looked at the passing traffic. This wasn't such a great idea catching friends up but we were committed. I reached into the glove compartment and secured several tissues foreseeing an end to Tom's predicament, a moment when he could wipe his face and shoes and we'd be closer to finishing this nightmare. While we waited, I wound down the windows and inhaled some of the finest carbon monoxide fumes just hoping for a passive host.

I ventured, "All done are we Tom?"

"Almost," came his feeble response. "I think the chicken was off."

Shit, I had chicken as well. My stomach rose to meet the expectation. I dismissed his suggestive tone and considered the volume of alcohol the main offender, but still, poultry?

The remainder of the trip would take 30 minutes, the sky looked ominous and I could hear distant claps of thunder. I turned up the radio to hear 'Riders on the Storm', it seemed fitting. It began to rain and the wipers squelched annoyingly against the glass. The storm rolled towards us and with such intensity I drove into a drive thru restaurant. Here we ordered coffee. I shouted through a one-inch gap in the window, even then the rain was so intense it pelted sideways and I received a drenching. Luckily, the pick up point was undercover. The sky exploded with lightning bolts which raced against each other in large horizontal lines, twisting and turning into the other until their long tendrils rose up and spat out a crescendo of thunderous claps.

The ground shook and hail pelted down.

Tom looked petrified.

Then out of the blue Samantha stated the obvious, "These strikes are close."

I was going to reply but was distracted by blasting car horns to our rear. The next in line wanted us to move and then the next. I refused to budge; we were the only ones undercover. No one had a death wish to confront us and eventually their honking subsided. When the violence subsided we drove off quickly and as expected the horns started up again – a final act of retaliation.

Tom, belligerently spoke, "A... holes, the whole worlds gone fucking mad!"

I had to agree, putting his wife and himself into that equation.

We settled Tom into his own room with a pull out sofa bed. There were extra towels for its protection and we gave him two buckets in case his body felt like repeating its vile purging. He was quickly asleep. Siobhan showered in the main guest room and donned Samantha's satin dressing gown. The one I love. I wondered why she didn't put on pyjamas although she appeared comfortable, maybe she slept in the nude, now there was an image I could ponder for a while.

She sat on the opposite lounge and asked, "Ready?"

"Ok, let's do it," Samantha said excitedly but Siobhan stifled her eagerness by replying, "Samantha, I would prefer to do this one-on-one with Shaun."

Samantha was expecting to be a part of the debriefing process. She rose looking disappointed but touched Siobhan's hand as if it was a girly thing and something 'hip'. She then kissed me on the top of the head like a lost soul who would benefit from this counselling. Samantha went directly to bed and Siobhan settled onto the lounge drawing her legs under her. She raked her hair with her fingers, smiled and sat back exposing toes, heels, calves and inner thighs. A lot of flesh remained uncovered and that three quarter length dressing gown wasn't cutting it. I noted again how beautiful she was and that her body smelt fresher than before.

"Comfortable?" she asked. I nodded and my mind began working overtime trying to come up with some way to sidestep the pending questions. "Tom and you are a little fragile at the moment?" I asked.

She didn't answer; she shook her head to show a look of frustration.

"How long have you two been married."

She answered this time but the reply was curt, "Too long."

"Shame, damn shame, what happened?"

'What do you mean, what happened?'

"Tom and you?" if I could get the subject onto her it might sidetrack raising my issues.

"It's over, I've had enough, I don't want to talk about it, I'd rather be helping you."

"Oh... no chance of a reconciliation?"

"As if – I don't want to talk about it."

"No kids, no chance for a family then."

"Shaun, I appreciate your concern but there is nothing to tell you. Honestly I don't want to discuss Tom," then Siobhan asked, "Did you have a good night?"

I paused, if I said yes, I'd be lying, if I said no, she'd want to know the reason. It had everything to do with how callously insensitive these two had become. It was a no win situation, "No, it was pretty much a non-event for me."

"Why Shaun, what's the matter?" She did appear to care but she might have been hoping that question would lead to my precarious state and fruitful answers.

"You need to consider others, you're so wrapped up in yourself there's no room for friends." It was true and I couldn't think of anything else to divert her attention. Siobhan sat stunned. She hadn't expected to have herself examined.

"Give me an example Shaun?"

"Good try, Siobhan. This interrogation isn't going to happen. I have no respect for you as a counsellor and as for you as our friends; Tom and you have stretched the limits. Why don't you go to bed and get some rest." Blunt, brutal, hitting over the head type of psychology and it seemed to be working; of course this approach was contrived.

Her bottom lip quivered. Siobhan began to cry. I hate it when women do that, now I felt guilty, you just can't get up and leave, their emotions come in waves and they need nurturing, anything to prevent a total meltdown – regardless, this was a better option than her analysing me.

"I'll get some tissues, maybe three scoops of ice cream to start with." She nodded. She knew the routine but her teary condition was worsening. "I'm sorry Siobhan, I should have kept quiet, I'm not the same person since my hospital stay."

"No, it's nothing to do with you, what you're saying is true, we've become insensitive to others. Sit closer, I appreciate you being so blunt," she tapped the seat for me to join her. "It's so true, we have been totally selfish and uncaring," there were more tears to reinforce her plight. Her porcelain skin glowed a deeper shade of rouge, all the way from her neck to her flamed hair. Her dressing gown had opened revealing her left breast. What a figure! She held my hand. Twenty seconds later I prised free and announced, "I'll get the tissues and the ice cream tub. Two spoons, hey!"

While in the kitchen, I used the phone to make a call.

When I returned the lights had been dimmed and Siobhan was still teary, she had done nothing to cover her exposed nipple. Again, she insisted I sit next to her.

"I'm so sorry Shaun, I should never have tried to help you. Can you forgive me?"

"Sure, I have forgotten what we're trying to achieve anyway."

"Good," she bent forward and kissed me on the cheek. She stayed close for way too long, her mouth brushed against my cheek and lingered, her breath came in short sharp spurts as if out of breath. She held both hands tight and nuzzled my neck. "You're making me steamy Shaun. You know I have this thing for you." She pulled back to check my reaction, "It's alright, I won't tell anyone, Samantha will not suspect a thing. It will be our secret, you know I love you!"

Samantha turned up the light to full intensity and announced, "Ice cream… you little devils, fancy keeping that secret from me."

Siobhan wrapped her dressing gown up tight. "We're all finished here. I was just saying to Shaun we should get you to join us. Shaun needs intensive professional help and nothing I can accomplish in one session. I'm tired, I think I'll go to bed, thanks for a great night and thanks for putting us up." She left the room in a rush.

"Thanks for rescuing me Samantha."

"I couldn't believe she'd do that and with me in the next room. Did you contemplate going further?"

"Of course not, I was just wondering how far she might go. It's flattering if nothing else."

"Yes; highly flattering but what would I know?" I noticed an edge to the compliment.

"Err, thanks."

"So you got no where with Siobhan?"

"Well... no." I think Samantha was discussing my therapy session, either way it was a NO.

"Best to lock our bedroom door."

Well she might warn, another time, another place – Tom was an idiot!

I lay awake thinking how close I had come. If I hadn't had the foresight to phone Samantha, I may well have been another notch on Siobhan's belt. She was an attractive woman and had a figure to die for, there was also the fact she said, "You know I have this thing for you..."

I was hot just thinking about her. Samantha cuddled in close and I let her soft whispered snores comfort my apprehensions. Gradually I drifted into that same darkness and subtle tranquillity.

At three fifteen, an enormous bang came at our bedroom door. It startled the life out of me and Samantha literally rolled out of bed. The banging persisted. I hit the bedside lamp and shouted, "What's happening? Who is it?"

"Quick, help me," Tom shouted, his voice near panic.

I unlocked the door to find Siobhan lying face up on the kitchen's cold ceramics. She was twitching violently.

Tom was beside himself and said, "I heard this crash and went to investigate. That's when I discovered her like this."

A carton of milk had been dropped and it contents had pooled on the floor. A glass tumbler had shattered on impact and blood seeped from cuts near Siobhan's shoulders. I kicked the largest shards away to prevent further injury but these cuts didn't appear anywhere near as serious as the uncontrollable spasms her body was experiencing. Her head was at a strange angle, her eyes gone, rolled back, whitewashed, a once beautiful woman now reduced to helplessness as rippling waves of convulsion seized her body. She wriggled violently and her face, distorted, maligned with pain and emphasising her wretched predicament.

"Get her into the recovery position," Samantha shouted.

Maintaining his level of panic, Tom said, "Christ, what is happening to her?"

"Has she had an epileptic fit before?" I shouted.

"No, never." He was unable to turn his stunned gaze from his wife's distress.

"Call for an ambulance, quickly… Tom go, go now!" I pushed him towards the phone, which did unravel his fixation.

We couldn't even approach her as she was thrashing violently.

Samantha yelled, "Get a pillow to protect her head. Hurry Shaun. Christ, she's starting to foam at the mouth. Siobhan can you hear me, try to relax, help is on the way."

The ambulance guys arrived. They gave each other a cursory look that signified drug use and a wild party that had gone horribly wrong.

"What has she taken?" was their first comment.

"Tell us, what did she take?"

"We don't know; we were asleep."

"Tom, does she do drugs?"

"No never."

The paramedic asked his assistant, "Check the signs." He looked at Tom and directed, "Sir, check her room, maybe there's something…"

His assistant interrupted, "Her breathing is laboured… she's going into shock." Siobhan stopped breathing. The paramedic began cardiac resuscitation. He double palmed her chest and asked, "Is she allergic to anything?"

Tom answered, "Not that I know of and there's nothing in the room."

"We need to get her stable before we can move her… she's back. Blood pressure is low, very low, a heart rate of… 35.

Siobhan finally stabilised and they transported her. She was admitted to the same hospital I had left days earlier. We waited for two hours before the doctor presented himself.

"She's fine, strangely quiet. Is that what she is usually like?"

Tom responded, "No, most times she's an annoying bitch who won't shut up."

The doctor looked surprised but accepted his bitterness. He had seen it all, even if he was only in his late twenties.

"You can see her if you like. We will run some tests and pinpoint what caused her seizure."

"So it was a fit."

"It appears so. The important thing is she is going to be fine. She has had a shock so one visitor at a time. Try to limit your time to five minutes. She is very tired; her body has gone through a lot."

Tom went first and spent less than a minute. Samantha went next and lasted the entire five minutes. When she returned she was ghostly white. I had no opportunity to speak and when I entered the room I found Siobhan supported by three pillows. She looked tired, her hair roughly combed and frizzy. She was dressed in an ice blue hospital gown; the top two straps were undone due to the cuts on her shoulders. It fell, exposing the top half of her breasts. Even in her worst of moments, Siobhan was strikingly attractive.

Before I could say a thing she offered, "Shaun, I'm sorry, really sorry, can you forgive me."

"Of course, no big deal, the main thing is you are alright."

"Shaun that was a terrible trip, I felt defenceless, it was overpowering, even the lightning and thunder wasn't that bad."

"What happened?"

"The brilliance was beyond description." She closed her eyes. She continued but with tears streaming her face, she didn't even bother to wipe them. "I was scared, really scared. Don't hate me, I couldn't stand it if you do."

"Why would I hate you?"

"I'm disgusted with myself. It's too distressing to talk about it, just forgive me. She began weeping. I gave her a hug and kissed her on the forehead. She was having trouble letting go. Then suddenly she pushed me away, "She won't hurt me again, will she?"

"Who?"

"You know."

I asked, "Who… you mean Samantha?"

"No… for Christ sake, the other one. I'm so sorry Shaun, I didn't know."

"What other one, what happened?"

"A warning Shaun, I'll never do it again."

"A warning? Who from?"

"I didn't realise there was someone in your life besides Samantha. You better go!" She rolled over and wept uncontrollably. I was stunned. Did Siobhan know about Lyn? If so, how? I was in a panic. Did Siobhan say something to Samantha?

When I returned to the waiting room, Tom had gone for a coffee. Samantha looked upset. She cast daggers in my direction. There was a deathly silence. If Samantha could have swung a punch she would have, the only thing saving me was her inept biomechanical ability, regardless she shoved me with both hands which had me adjusting my balance.

I stammered, "What was that for?"

CHAPTER 10

———◄○►———

RELUCTANT AND NERVOUS – THEN CAME THE BLOODHOUNDS

Tom remained at the hospital, it was a decision brought about by frugality rather than anything. He had something to say to Siobhan and it would be a pointless exercise returning with us. The air was icy anyway, I decided I didn't like him and he probably didn't care for me. Tom never thanked us or apologised for their strange behaviour, he just rolled along as if the last twelve hours were an everyday occurrence and as for Samantha… well, her frozen silence continued. I was jumping ahead of the action realising the game was up. Siobhan must have mentioned what happened, or enough to steam Samantha into action. And as for that push, I was grateful I wasn't at the top of the stairs. A few times in the past I had seen Samantha lose it but always recovering minutes later – just enough fury to get you thinking.

On our way home, Samantha staunchly faced the passenger window, she never spoke and it was a nervous drive. I didn't know if she would attack or quiz me until I became – 'dry-cleaned' of the truth. Knowing Samantha, she would probably use both tortures to ensure the right amount of discomfort. How would I handle that moment? How much did Siobhan know?

I glanced briefly at Samantha. She still looked upset. At home, the kitchen floor was a mess. I picked up scraps of medical tape and discarded vials. I turned the tap and waited for the bucket to fill. One hand held the mop the other hand drummed the bench top. Samantha passed by without a word and went to the cupboard, she returned with a bottle of heavy-duty bleach. She liberally poured a cupful into the bucket. For a moment, our eyes locked but neither was ready to argue over what had happened. The repugnant stench of bleach helped divide us.

I cleaned the floor, tipped the water out and repeated the whole process three more times. It was overkill but I felt I had to do something before going to bed, anything to clean the house and to bleach my memory. By the time I slid between the sheets, Samantha had settled and smiled weakly. We held hands with a tight grip. Before I let my body relax, I said, "Some night."

She was quick with her response, "And?"

"Tiring."

"Do you want to talk about it?"

"I'm really tired, I'm not even sure I could do the subject justice right now. I'm not even sure I know what the subject is."

Samantha rolled over. There appeared no animosity or was it my imagination.

When we awoke I realised it was my imagination.

"Feel better?"

"Yes."

"Good. I've got a question for you."

My heart sank.

"Am I going to lose you?"

"What? Of course not."

"Are you sure?"

"Of course."

"Siobhan mentioned there is another woman in your life. I asked her if she meant herself but she just shivered and said no. She didn't want to discuss it any more, so I think it's only fair to ask you the question. Is there someone else?"

"Samantha, I don't know what's happening. You do trust me?"

"I did until I spoke to Siobhan, as each minute passes you are testing my patience."

"Samantha it's not that simple."

"Does it have anything to do with your stay in hospital?"

"I think so."

"Does it have anything to do with Siobhan?"

"Maybe, there seems some type of connection."

"What happened? This other woman... is who exactly?"

I reinforced, "Christ Samantha, we have been through so much."

"So there is another woman?"

I was silent

"What's happening, I need to know." I knew she was drawing teeth, suddenly there would be a yank and within seconds I would be clutching an empty hole of feelings, "There is someone... another..."

"Woman?" she added.

"No, a young girl."

"Girl?" her eyebrows raised up questioningly, "How young?" she snapped.

"Seventeen."

"Christ Shaun, you're not involved with someone that young?"

"No... listen; it's not what you think."

"Is she attractive?"

"Somewhat... listen..."

"Have you known her for long?"

"Yes. Look Samantha..."

"How old was she when you first met?"

I felt flat and she refused to break the line of questioning, "Nine or ten."

"Shit, that is disgusting, that would make you..." she paused doing the figures, "In your early fifties."

"Samantha, you don't understand. Stop jumping to conclusions."

"Do you love her?"

Exasperated I spat out, "Look Samantha, she's dead... alright... she died at the age of seventeen, long before I met you... she's dead, she's no threat to you, no threat whatsoever. Just leave me alone with this, I'm trying to work out what's happening and I need to be left alone."

Samantha climbed out of bed and paced the room. It must have been thirty seconds before she spoke with a vile intensity, "No threat you say... no threat, what happened to Siobhan then? I just happen to believe there is life after death. What happens when you die Shaun? Is your spirit going with her or with me?"

That question shook me and her demanding attitude produced a shock wave of intensity, "Don't be ridiculous. That is such an outrageous hypotheses, who knows where we go? I might be in hell, you in heaven, we might be somewhere else." I hadn't worked through the repercussions of dying but it was an interesting scenario. Would I ever see Lyn Monday again? Shit, maybe there was a chance.

Samantha commented, "I accept this all happened before I met you but it's obvious you never got over her. And the worst thing is, you never told me."

"Samantha..."

"Did you love her?" she wasn't finished with me, this was the icing on the cake, the piece-de-résistance, if she could secure this information I was finished.

I refused to answer, anyway it was too late for words, Samantha began crying, I tried to console her but each attempt made the situation worse. "I admit I have feelings for her but she has been dead for forty-five years." I whispered as if embarrassed, "But now she wants my help." I realised how ridiculous it sounded when the words passed my lips.

She seized the moment, "See... you're talking in the present tense, she's alive in your mind. Hell, how did I get to this point in life, only to find my husband's infatuated with some girl who's been dead for forty-five years, let me guess her name... Monday, right... that's it!"

I nodded... exposed!

Samantha was bright, sometimes too bright, she looked startled as the pieces fell together, "Wow! You discussed her in your sleep to the point of obsessing. How can you help someone who is dead? I'm having a problem understanding this. Why... why now after all this time? I'm going to lose you, I can tell."

"That is ridiculous."

Samantha stood with her hands on her hips and demanded, "You can start by telling me everything."

I insisted Samantha sit close as I confessed. Her body was stiff as if tensile steel supported her shoulders and back. She wasn't looking at me but I could tell every word was being archived for later. It felt better to relieve myself from the burden of secrecy but I sensed it did nothing for Samantha. I gave her the simplified version. I went light on my feelings for Lyn and I certainly didn't mention her eyes for fear of upsetting her further.

If I had grieved for Lyn, maybe none of this would be happening. Maybe I'd be a normal person but still my mother had screwed with my mind until it was a fine maze of contradictions. Was there any hope? Anyway, I didn't come calling, Lyn Monday did! With the right justification, anything was possible. When I looked at Samantha's vacant stare, I knew things weren't sitting right.

Later that day

I needed someone to talk to, someone not affected by emotion, anyone but Samantha.

Unknown to her, I phoned a counselling service. They didn't ask for my name which was a relief, it was a no commitment service provided by a local church.

The person at the other end of the phone was caring and thorough asking a dozen questions. I explained I was having trouble letting go of this girl who died, someone special who had been in my life. I was feeling empty about this relationship and had upset my wife.

The counsellor questioned, "So, if I asked what you are feeling now, what would your answer be? Give me one word."

"Guilt more than anything… I have let others down by refusing to accept this girl's death."

"Guilt? I don't understand why would you feel guilty?"

"It was a girlfriend I hid her from my wife."

"So you were having an affair behind your wife's back, then your girlfriend died and now your feeling guilty about the affair."

"No, I didn't have an affair, I never cheated."

"I'm sorry; I'm not following, if you didn't have an affair, why are you feeling guilty?"

"I really have no idea, when you put it like that, I can't imagine how I got into this mess in the first place."

"Why don't you have a talk to your doctor, he may prescribe something to relax you. The way I see it, your problem is forgetting."

"Most times I have problems remembering."

"Oh, was it a traumatic death and you're trying to block the pain."

"No, no, nothing like that, I just feel numb, as if this person is still with me."

"That can happen sometimes, give your self another month and things will settle. We can organise for you to see a counsellor, I have to admit that was my best option when my mother died. That one on one is better than talking to a voice at the end of the phone. Sometimes it is difficult to grasp what is happening, each case has its own individuality."

We were drifting; I asked if I could call back.

"Of course, take care."

Now I pondered the guilt trip, I had done nothing to compromise our marriage. Christ, I hardly knew Lyn! She had died before I met Samantha so I didn't need to feel guilty or explain myself. My mind was short-circuiting and others were in this drama with me, poor Siobhan; what did she experience? What happened proved this was real and she had to be the raw unabashed example. Why warn her off? Was that even possible?

Then my mind changed direction for the umpteenth time, Lyn Monday was dead and how could I rationalise it any other way. I resolved to feel more for Samantha, she was the one I had committed to, I needed to try harder. I needed to get beyond Lyn Monday and all this hocus-pocus of afterlife's recall. Its drawing consequences were getting me nowhere. I had to get a life, there was no way to correct the past, why had Lyn Monday waited so long? Why had she suddenly appeared? It was too late now, I needed to concentrate on Samantha, she was my life, my direction, there was nothing happening except... except... Lyn Monday was back!

CHAPTER 11

───◄○►───

THE FAX

The question continued to haunt me. Why did Lyn Monday visit? Why seek me out, why not her family? Was I the only person receptive? Maybe it was difficult to circumnavigate the afterlife, could there be barriers, insurmountable problems with communication. Was I the only person she could see in this foggy world of reality? Lyn must have known I would help, but help her with what? It was beyond frustration, maybe I was crazy, yeah crazy, if not, I soon would be.

Samantha was still cool, any conversation curt and to the point. We wandered the house and did our utmost to avoid each other. The rooms, all nineteen of them were not big enough – even opposite sides of the Super-dome would have been too close. Where possible, I tried to act normal. Why was this happening? I continued to feel guilty. My biggest hurdle was this gut-wrenching nervousness. I hated gut-premonitions for most times they came true. One day I would have to research this phenomenon – I was convinced it held the key to unlocking mysteries. It would probably make a good book.

Then it started, the more I thought of Lyn Monday the more I thought of Lyn Monday. Obsession possessed me; I had to find out what she wanted. I had no idea why I was thinking like this. Who would be the first person to contact? Who would know about Lyn? I couldn't even remember what high school she attended. Why didn't I remember that? This was ridiculous, my mind was being selective, a few memories were crystallising but with other's they were the vaguest of recalls likened to a spider web, patiently waiting for a collection, but now a gentle breeze swayed the gossamer structure where hope drifted by, some snared, most lost. Still, that gut retching nervousness gnarled my core, it refused to let go, something was up; something big was about to happen. The hairs bristled my neck, an uncomfortable sensation, I turned quickly but there was nothing other than a cool breeze wafting through the window, it blew defiantly in my face. It lifted papers off my desk and scattered them across the room. It was no sooner here, than gone. I collated the papers and returned them to the desk. This time I felt the wind rising but instead of letting the papers scatter, I placed my hand on top until the wind subsided. Was this a signal? I lifted my hand and faced the window. The breeze rose with my expectation. The papers lifted, fluttered and stayed aloft longer than they should have. They finally settled onto the desk rather than the floor. I smiled and the breeze caressed my body, a slight pressure similar to waves caressing a shoreline. Unbelievable, was this Lyn Monday again? Then there was nothing, the breeze was gone in an instant.

I had to act. I figured I would start a search for Lyn's grave. I knew the cemetery from my childhood, a vast collection of plots, tens of thousands, however the only thing I didn't know was how the office co-ordinated the burial details or provided information. In desperation, I called the cemetery and found an interesting fact. Any deaths before 1976 were in books and after that date they were on a computer database. I spoke to a helpful person by the name of James who said he would begin a manual search. Keeping in mind privacy laws, I told him Lyn Monday was my cousin and I was hoping to collate the family's whereabouts, a means of preserving our history. I had lied but it wasn't a strong enough reason to stop me; I was prepared to do anything for answers. James went to a lot of trouble and after several days, he reported he couldn't find a match.

Puzzled by this, I called back several days later and asked the most basic of questions, "When you search the records, is it for the whole cemetery?"

"No, this is the crematorium. Try Anglican, Catholic, Independent which will include Methodist, Baptist, Presbyterian and there are community graves and of course further additions like Chinese, Islamic, Greek, War Memorials etc. Each has their own office you will need to contact them individually."

I couldn't help but ask, "Why don't you guys get together and make up one central register?"

James's response was, "That would cause too many problems." Even in death, religion continued to divide us.

I had wasted days; I was a complete amateur when it came to researching deaths.

Maybe Lyn didn't die after all, or if she did, maybe she was in a different cemetery. Maybe her cremated ashes were elsewhere. There were so many options.

I decided to take a different tack. I went to the phone book and looked for my old mate, Josh Freemont from high school, the one who informed me of Lyn's suicide. I found one J. Freemont living in Sydney and it was just by sheer accident I spotted an R. Freemont further down the page living at the same address. It must be his brother Robert; the one who had the bonfire party.

I hesitated, after all these years to suddenly ring up unexpectedly, what would he think. What do I say? I decided not to think and punched in Josh's number but there was no answer. It rang out for several days. In desperation, I called the R. Freemont's number and a woman answered on the third ring.

"My name is Shaun, I'm not sure if I have the right number, is Robert there?"

There was a few seconds silence, "No sorry, Robert died last year. What do you want exactly?"

"I'm very sorry, I had no idea. You're Robert's wife?"

"Yes, I'm Jean. Did you know Robert?"

"Yes, I knew him years ago. I'm very sorry," I paused, "I'm trying to contact his brother Josh, I went to school with him and would like to catch up."

"Is this about a school reunion?"

"No, I just want to catch up."

"You know Shaun; it's weird that I got this call."

"Why?"

"This number is a dedicated fax line. I never answer it, but today I was sitting by the machine when it rang and for some unknown reason I picked it up. I'll get Josh's phone number for you, he's living up the coast."

There was a twenty-second delay and she returned with the number. I thanked Jean and apologised for disturbing her.

After days of dead ends, my first clue was an intercepted fax call – bizarre.

I phoned Josh straight away. Initially he had trouble remembering my name but after some gentle prodding the penny dropped. We discussed his work. He was a university lecturer for those disadvantaged by distance, if a student wished to complete their curriculum by the internet, he was the man, he told me his students achieved a higher state average than students having an up front lecturer, which I assumed meant in your face rather than anything else.

We skipped through the years thinking fondly of several teachers from high school and whose encouragement forged our career paths. The topic rested with wives and how he was happily married with three children. He had two girls and a son, the rebel of the family and surprisingly they were the corresponding ages to Tamara, Kem and Joel. Life had been good for Josh, he told me he was going to Morocco for a holiday and would be staying in a villa by the sea. We ambled for an hour then I said, completely 'out of the blue'… "Lyn Monday!"

That was all I said, "Lyn Monday!"

He jumped right in and said excitedly, "She was my girlfriend."

Just like that, he said, "She was my girlfriend."

What shocked me was the excitement in his voice, he literally bubbled like champagne and flowed down the line with such enthusiasm I had trouble composing myself. Shit, he never told me she was his girlfriend. Not one word, in all the time we were mates and all those times I had confided my deepest feelings for Lyn. I felt betrayed.

He continued, "She lived in the Avenues." His voice was still on a high.

Unfazed, I asked, "Didn't she die?"

That's when he went quiet. Strangely quiet and the delay was embarrassing. I could tell he was trying to recall our last conversation, which was...

"Oh yeah, Lyn Monday committed suicide."

"...what?"

"She died."

"What happened? She's only seventeen!"

"Was seventeen... I don't know anything else."

I again asked, "She died didn't she?"

He finally spoke – a strange and lengthy deliberation that must have lasted fifteen seconds, "... mm, might have?"

"... mm, might have?" Shit, if she were my girlfriend I sure as hell would remember her committing suicide. There was no way anyone could forget Lyn Monday. She was not the sort of person you forgot, not for a moment.

It was obvious I couldn't trust him and five minutes later, I finished the call with the intention of getting together after he returned from Morocco. My body was shaking and the vilest of thoughts raced through my head. I was so worked up I felt like vomiting. Did he have dementia? Unlikely, he recalled everything else so accurately and he had kept his relationship with Lyn secret for all these years – why?

If Josh wanted Lyn, I would have reluctantly accepted it. However, a secret, a lie, a cover up and it had taken forty-five years to be exposed. Back then, why didn't he just tell me he was her boyfriend and why now did he go strange when I mentioned her death? He had to be hiding something. There was no other possibility. I tried to think of a reason, but the lie was the most significant piece of evidence. Lyn was such a vibrant person I never accepted she extinguished her own life.

Was Josh the reason Lyn asked for help, was there something sinister brewing, something that needed exposing? Josh Freemont, who would have thought? No wonder he dismissed my query so rapidly back in 1962 and now this second time as our conversation degenerated into a gnarling state of polite acceptance. The chances of getting together after his Morocco trip seemed as unlikely as raising the Titanic.

Why did he lie?

I remembered Lyn's final words to me, this just after the glass shrapnel ripped through my hand, those precious last words when I was being rush to emergency,

"Sorry, I wish it could be you."

Now that comment made more sense. However, what happened soon after for Lyn to have taken her life. Hold on, if Josh was lying, there was a chance Lyn was alive. I had not been able to find her burial location. I must admit this was a strange revelation, one where I stacked hope upon hope. I searched the white pages directory and listed every Monday in the hope of finding a lead. There were none.

I closed my eyes and recalled my experiences. I had sighted Monday's presence, I even tried to touch her, she was close but unreachable, I heard her voice asking for help and I had experienced Siobhan's seizure and this according to Siobhan was a warning to stay clear of me. Because of these signals, I sadly dismissed the possibility Lyn was alive. Again, I was numb.

My daughter Tamara's heightened spiritualism was a by-product of her recent divorce, she needed something to fill the void and her constructive advice was, "If you need help, acquire the services of someone professional."

Whom did I know who was an expert with deaths? Who would sniff out the past and knew their way around cemeteries?

Who knew more of our convict history and discovered Samantha was related to a bushranger, the more I thought the easier it became – Beaulieu Parkes… of course. She was Samantha's niece. A vibrant attractive woman, mid forties and from a family of five children, although a little wacky sometimes, she had literally run away with the circus when she was young, toured all over and was street-savvy and her obsession with the dead was strange and renown. She had settled into her second marriage and had heaps of time on her hands. The only hesitation I had was that she was a stirrer who relished any opportunity to unsettle me. Regardless, I could do with her help but I would have to be careful, she was close to Samantha.

I spoke cautiously, "Beaulieu, Shaun here."

She queried, "Shaun who?"

"Shaun Reece, Samantha's husband."

"Oh, Shaun. Yes of course. How are you?"

"I'm fine and Samantha sends her love," I lied.

"What's up?"

"I'm trying to track down some information and wonder if you could help. A girl died some time ago, her name was Lyn Monday. I need to find her grave."

"Some time ago, you say. What age was she and what was the year of passing?"

"Seventeen, I think the year was 1962."

"You knew her well?"

"Not that well. I went to school with her, that's all." I was thinking, 'keep it low key, and don't raise her suspicions, if she suspects anything she will pounce quicker than a mountain lion'.

"Why this sudden interest?"

I expanded, "This all started when Drew came second in his sporting carnival and prompted me to think about my sporting achievements at school, then I thought of this girl and something about her suicide didn't sit right. I called a high school friend and suddenly he went strange, really peculiar when I mentioned her death."

"Mm, a mystery, ha, ha."

I didn't tell Beaulieu about Lyn Monday's spirit, or my obsessed feelings for this girl nor anything to do with Samantha's vexation; I kept the whole matter as simple as possible. With Beaulieu, every detail was sacrosanct so you had to watch what you said. I gave her what little information I had.

Beaulieu's voice lifted, "How enticing, in simple terms you want me to find the grave and what happened to this girl?"

"Is that something you can help with?"

"A dead girl's grave, suspicious circumstances, ha, ha." She did that little laugh sometimes. It wasn't really a laugh, more a sleuth inspired exclamation. "Yes, I can help you. Does Samantha know about this girl?"

"Of course. Thanks Beaulieu, you're fantastic." I cut the call knowing it was question time – on my life, my predicaments, if I kept talking, Beaulieu would have me exposed within minutes. It was one thing Samantha knowing and another that I was researching Lyn's death, anyway, Samantha may never find out.

Samantha appeared in the doorway, she said in a frosted tone, "Why would you drag Beaulieu into this? Why?"

CHAPTER 12

―◄○►―

CERTIFIED BY THE CERTIFICATE

Why couldn't I use Beaulieu to help? I was desperate for answers however it did nothing for Samantha who diced carrots with a keen determination and with a knife as equally as sharp. Her neck was rigid as if turning would break the fixation. The poor carrots were the bunt of her aggression, she asked again, although she knew the answer, "What is the reason you called Beaulieu?" she lifted her head to hear my response, she was testing me, for a second her hand stopped the decapitation. She poignantly waited.

"Err... I know Beaulieu researched your family's history so she might be able to find this girl's grave site."

She let the knife fall, slicing green foliage from thick orange sticks, "The week girl, huh?"

"What?"

"The Monday, Tuesday, Wednesday... you know, the everyday of the week girl, the one you're obsessed with each day."

"Yeah, that's the one, excuse me for caring."

Samantha smiled curtly. Was she indifferent to the subject but possessively aggressive of the attention I gave Lyn Monday?

Something was different, strange… was I pushing Samantha too hard? If I discussed using Beaulieu's investigative skills, I'm sure she would have vetoed my request. This was a no win situation and I was a fool to think I could slip by the net of family unity; anyway, Beaulieu was working on the case and the end justified the means, that was all that mattered. At this moment, I didn't care what Samantha thought; there were just some things too important in life, or for that matter death.

Beaulieu began an information overload. Interestingly, a group of genealogists had circumvented the cemetery and photographed every headstone. My head ached at the enormity of the task. Consequently, they had produced a DVD and Beaulieu just happened to have one and rang me back with her findings. Sure enough, Lyn Monday had died, buried in 1962. My heart sank. Beaulieu supplied her headstone inscription then added Lyn's father died some years later. His grave was close by. Well here was my proof, but there was no mother. Was she still alive?

I began a physical search of my hometown to find Lyn's mother, while Beaulieu conducted a mysterious search of details she kept to herself, although we agreed to give each other feedback when something cropped up.

In the hope of getting Samantha involved, I asked her to join me. Our first destination was the 'Avenues' in Berala. The streets were wider than I remembered and the demographics had changed, I knew Lyn lived near a private golf course but I couldn't remember which avenue – they all looked alike. Forty-five years on, my mind had a glazed opaqueness which gave translucent information, annoying, for I desperately needed precise facts. I stopped the car just as the postman was doing his rounds. I remember working for the post office and if someone knew where a person lived it had to be the postman. What were my chances of picking the right time he scampered pass? I did a mental calculation, a thirty-second window of opportunity over a 7 hour-period, being… an 840:1 chance. Wow, you wouldn't want to bet against those odds. Although I was excited, my question about a Mrs. Monday living in the Avenues proved disappointing. The postman covered all seven avenues but had no recollection of that name. I refused to be deterred and started knocking on doors asking if anyone knew. The first person I came across was a young guy, nineteen or twenty years of age, I commented, "She would be in her eighties," He was suspicious, a by-product of a turbulent area. Regardless, he called his mother who advised she had lived here for thirty-one years but had never heard of a Monday living in this street or nearby. She suggested I ask the lady who lived on the corner, a mere thirty metres away. She had resided there for fifty years. She didn't know her name, which was a sad indictment on the area. There was no answer. I drove down the street and came across a greying senior dressed in starched whites – her bowling attire. She didn't know her either and had lived there all her life.

I felt frustrated. I hadn't achieved a thing. The next destination was the cemetery, several kilometres away. This was a strange experience for I knew the religious denomination where Lyn rested but it was a huge rolling necropolis and literally thousands of headstones dotted the landscape. I thought we would have to transverse hills and dales, however I had pulled up exactly at the grave site, a mere five metres from the road, I couldn't have planned it better. Was she guiding me?

"Samantha commented, "That was luck. Something is going right for a change."

"Yeah," but I knew this wasn't luck, it wasn't even chance, this was a drawing. I dismissed doing the figures. The chances were too remote, the odds too odd.

It was just those few steps and here she was, the absolute proof, her name, her special place with white marble and greying concrete, her plaque was stark polished stone with black engraving. This was all that was left, but still, I knew she wasn't resting here, not her spirit, she was anywhere but here, anywhere but in this grave. She was never going to be happy here. The way she pulled her hair from her face, that smile, you understood how special you were in her presence, she rocked, at least she rocked me. I sat on the grave's edge and reflected… why take her life? What possible reason had driven her to that finality? My grand plan was to wait until I had matured before I attempted a relationship. How imbecilic, I cringed at my stupidity. What an idiot. What was I thinking? How long was I going to wait? Fool… with my mother's reasoning it would never happen.

Samantha began clearing the years of debris, "This is very sad," she said, "What happened to her, Shaun?"

I noticed a change in her resolve, maybe a mellowing "I have no idea what happened other than she committed suicide… it is sad. Such a waste!"

"Did you go to her funeral?"

"No, I found out she died a couple of weeks after, it was too late to say goodbye."

Her voice had an excitement, "Well, this is it then, this is your chance to say goodbye."

"What do you mean… say goodbye… I can't say goodbye."

"Of course you can. I'll go back to the car if you need privacy."

I could tell Samantha cared but didn't understand the enormity of my situation. How could I say goodbye, how could I accept something so final after all these years? How could she understand my desperation? Then I found Lyn's father's grave in the next row. My throat was dry and my head ached, what a disaster. I returned to Lyn's grave and sat close to her headstone.

Samantha commented, "You look sad Shaun, cry if you want, it will make you feel better."

I looked at her startled, 'Make me feel better'; nothing could make me feel better.

I tried to stand but my legs refused to co-operate. Samantha looked up, "Shaun, give me a hand with this rubbish."

"Give me a second," I fought back the emotion. I tried to focus on something else, a crow, for some reason this bird stood proud and defiant, jet-black and challenging, it flapped its wings and flew overhead, landing four rows over. I tried to focus on this King of Graves but it was a strange sensation, as if I was the intruder, the one who had to leave. I tried to match its rebelliousness but nothing happened, my legs were still pins and needles, redundant paralytic stumps. The bird flew away with a squawk, proclaiming he was the winner.

"Shaun, the rubbish?"

"Ok."

"Reflecting…. the good times I guess. Take your time then."

"Reflecting… good times?"

"Yes, you're thinking of those special moments with her. You're thinking, 'what if I buckle, become emotional, Samantha will hold it against me,' however you're wrong Shaun, men cry, I'm a compassionate person – just let her go. Just let her go."

She looked into my face begging me to crumble. I fought the urge. Nothing would strip me of my determination, Lyn Monday lived, and to burst forth with grief would end her and me, this was the only thread linking us, I had to salvage something from this disaster.

After an awkward moment Samantha said, "I'll leave you, take your time," she returned to the car.

What was she really thinking?

I tried to move my legs but again they refused to co-operate. My arms worked but my legs felt numb, I rubbed them hoping the circulation would return. I tried once more. They refused to act. Was Lyn controlling me or was I a victim of my own mind game, an ingrained flaw that had taken years to surface. To prevent the appearance of being an idiot I leaned across the grave and removed several handfuls of composted silt. I tossed them onto a vacant lot. If Lyn was holding me, how long before she would let go? I looked at Samantha, those short five metres away, and we exchanged looks, we smiled, it appeared the longer I stayed the more understanding she was becoming. She finally wound down the window and asked, "Just to remind you, the gates close in five minutes."

I had been sitting on Lyn's grave for ages. I whispered, "Alright Lyn, you can let me go, I'm going to help."

I stood instantly.

Samantha asked, "Did you say something?"

"Yes, I said sorry."

As I entered the car, Samantha examined my face, she said, "I hope I receive that much attention when I die. What was it, one hour and fifteen minutes?" Her hand reached across and patted me on the knee, a compassionate touch but it made me feel uncomfortable.

When would I find out what Lyn wanted? Why me? Was it because I held an eternal flame; was I the only one who cared? What a strange situation. I had no one to talk to then and now I had no one who could possibly understand. Samantha was trying but you can't ask for a time-out for a lost friend, a girl, one you're keen on – no wife is that understanding.

We drove home, everything a blur. Samantha opened the front door and we entered the house. I sat stunned, unable to move, little flashes leading up to this moment were bizarre, the event of Lyn's presence requesting my help, then my admission to hospital and the warning for Siobhan to back away. Josh Freemont's lie, admitting he was Lyn Monday's boyfriend. Did Lyn need me to correct the past? Was there something amiss? Lyn certainly knew how to grab your attention and all this because my grandson came second in his race.

The next day Beaulieu phoned, "Shaun darling, I have Lyn Monday's Death Certificate, would you like me to email a copy."

"Already? How did you get it so fast?"

"Efficiency. You seem very anxious, or is it my imagination?"

"Your imagination. Thanks." I hung up quickly.

I waited for the email. Knowing Beaulieu I escaped lightly, she was onto my every emotion. Any deviation from the normal would be picked-up. She was as if a little girl trapped in a woman's body, bored silly and teasing anyone that crossed her path.

The email arrived and I clenched my teeth. The type fitted a rigid template, clinically determined. There were tiny rows and columns and I could imagine the typist clanging at a mechanical typewriter with a steely determination. I envisaged bifocals and a discerning eye to aid this Coroner's report.

It coldly read...

Lynette Martine Monday: I never knew her middle name. Was that French?

Dental Nurse: Where did she work? I couldn't remember.

Female: I nodded approval. Then next line read, Age: 17 years, a misty cloud prevented me continuing. I wiped my eyes, a private moment – a rare lapse of concentration perhaps, then on the next line the tragedy continued, the date of her death and at her parent's home in Berala. This was not long after Robert Freemont's birthday party, that disastrous bonfire celebration, what an understatement; there was Chantal's meltdown and too much drink. Some idiot dropped a firework's bunger into a glass bottle and several of us ended up in hospital. It may have been worse with someone killed. I remember Lyn's precious last words before I was rushed away, "Sorry, I wish it could be you." Why did Lyn say that? Did she prefer me to Josh Freemont?

Confused, I continued reading... Her poor father reported her death. No parent should bear that responsibility. I skipped to the cause of death...

'Chloral Hydrate and bromide poisoning self-administered but whether wilful or otherwise the evidence presented does not enable me to say'.

What was Chloral Hydrate? I knew what bromide was from my photographic days. It was used as an inhibitor but Chloral Hydrate was a mystery.

There had to have been the police inquiry, the medical examination, an autopsy, the release of the body and then the funeral arrangements. Her parents would have been beside themselves. What was strange; there was no way to distinguish if Lyn committed suicide, there may have been another reason. So why did Josh Freemont say suicide? It was Saturday morning when Lyn's body was discovered and by Tuesday morning, she was buried. I couldn't believe the finding, and where was I when this was happening? Probably locked up in that miserable darkroom, I couldn't believe Lyn Monday was dead... I gritted my resolve and refused to let her go. Couldn't anyone else see this? She was alive and this regardless of some stinking Death Certificate. Christ this was hard, I had seen her grave and Death Certificate but still... she had been in touch... she had been close, she wanted help, but why the mystery? If she could communicate once, why couldn't she again? This was my biggest hurdle. What were the ways of spirits? I had no idea. Had she taken forty-five years to reach me, and then it was over, a bizarre fleeting visit. Now there were signals, little reminders she was near, but still, she was too far away to make a difference; I ached to hear her voice, see her smile. This was frustrating and to make matters worse, this report mirrored my son's tragedy, he survived – she didn't. Then another connection, the presiding minister at Lyn's funeral was Reverend Lester Bouvarde, the same minister whose son helped me develop and enlarge photographs of several bikini-clad hostesses after the official opening of the Berala Shopping Centre.

When Samantha saw me, she literally reeled, "Look at you, you're a mess. You have to give this up. Do I have to call Beaulieu and tell her to stop?"

"Whatever for?"

"You know Siobhan is still in hospital."

"Why is she still there?"

"She isn't coping and honestly, neither are you."

"I just need some time."

"Maybe a holiday then?"

"Absolutely not," even surprising myself with the intensity.

She huffed. I turned unable to communicate further. The tears were welling and I felt like shit. Samantha was right, I did need to get a grip.

Then as if I wasn't in control of my actions, I blurted out, "I'm going to the hospital to see Siobhan."

"I'm coming too."

"No, I've got to do this myself."

"I'll keep you company in the car and wait in the car park."

"Alright."

We drove in silence. I was surprised by my dogged determination, I couldn't even imagine what Samantha thought, for I was visiting a woman who had hit on me, almost compromising our marriage but she had also experienced Lyn Monday and I was desperate for that information.

The first thing Siobhan said was, "Shaun, what a surprise. It is so good to see you. You know Tom and I separated, I haven't seen anyone since."

"Oh Siobhan, I'm sorry, you must feel..."

She interrupted, "I'm sorry I came onto you, that was a mistake, can you forgive me?"

"Of course, forget it. Siobhan... I had to see you for... confirmation. You know that... girl."

She nodded.

I nodded. We both understood.

Siobhan asked, "Was she close?"

How could I answer that question? I must have looked perplexed for Siobhan continued, "Anyway, it is good to see you," she smiled.

"You must be upset separating from Tom."

"No, not in the least, our problems had been building, maybe as long as eighteen months."

"I feel responsible, if only I hadn't asked you and Tom out to dinner."

"Don't say that. You had no control over what happened."

"How do you know?"

"Shaun, it's no secret I have liked you for a long time, during an argument with Tom I told him of my feelings, that's why we kept away but when you called and invited us to dinner, I didn't have the strength to say no. A few drinks later I felt uninhibited. You were close and I had to tell you how I felt, what I didn't count on was that girl. Can you believe we are talking about a spirit here, unbelievable! I'm sorry Shaun; I shouldn't have told Samantha about her, I was a mess at the time and not thinking straight."

"I know; your comments unleashed more than Samantha's wrath."

"Oh Shaun, I'm so sorry, I was worried about Samantha being hurt, you have to look after her."

"I think Samantha will be fine. We need time, it will pass." It

was strange how Siobhan was concerned for Samantha all of a
sudden. She was quite prepared to have an adulterous relationship with me.

Siobhan asked, "What type of relationship did you have
with this girl?"

"It's difficult to explain. I went to school with her, something happened. I have no idea what but for some reason she
took her life." I surprised myself when I added, "She has asked
for my help."

"She said those words?"

I nodded, "I can't believe I told you."

"Why?"

"I feel uncomfortable discussing it, as if its all fantasy, I'm having trouble getting my head around this. When you were trying to
psychoanalyse me after dinner you would never have believed me.
It's only because you experienced this that you believe."

"I believe, absolutely."

"Thanks, you doubt yourself sometimes, what has happened
makes you question everything."

"Shaun… I've had time to think and what I said about loving you, I mean it. It probably won't change a thing, but at least
I tried. You don't mind me being so open?"

"No, of course not. Honestly, it's refreshing but why tell me?
Why now?"

"It just feels right, I've been bottling up my emotions for too
long and I've resolved to be more forthcoming, regardless of the
backlash. I was put on notice to back away, I'm figuring if this
girl doesn't make her move now, she will later, she may respect
what you have with Samantha and wait until you pass. Shaun,
I've never been so scared but I'm not going to be bullied. At
this point, I don't care. I want you and that's all that matters."

I ignored her last comment, "How do you know she'll make
a move?"

"I know women and what they want, you definitely have
two, well three. With me around I can see why she became protective of you."

"Siobhan really, things may have been different for us in another time, I think you're a stunning woman but I just can't fit anyone else into my life right now."

Siobhan shook her head at my emotionless delivery and said, "Remember, I'm the only one who has experienced this first hand, without me you'd still be wondering. I'm your justification; your little ..."

"Siobhan?" I cautioned.

She shivered a little but still managed to flutter her eyelashes, "Sorry, just remember you're not going mad. We have both been drawn and survived. Your journey was subtler than mine, be careful. Look out for Samantha. She is the innocent victim in all this. Call me if you need to talk."

"Thanks."

I kissed her on the forehead, knowing this was just the beginning of a strange journey and somehow Siobhan's involvement was just starting. As I closed the door, I thought of Samantha. What a guilt-trip and over absolutely nothing but with Samantha I had this unwritten rule to tell each other everything. I did, except for Lyn Monday and here lay the problem, I knew Samantha would never forgive me.

As I returned to the car park, I passed hundreds of cars all neatly racking up parking fees, each minute was a bonanza. It was a sheer co-incidence I ran into Leah, the nurse who had looked after me in hospital, she had told her work mate that sleeping with me was an option – a light hearted discussion, theoretical at best, but one I had inadvertently overheard.

"Leah... you're on your way to work?"

"Mr. Reece."

"Shaun."

"Sorry, Shaun, yes, I'm late as usual."

"I never had the opportunity to say thanks."

"For looking after you?"

"Yes, and for the encouragement... you know."

"It was nothing," she giggled with embarrassment.

"It was what I needed at the time, a little boost. What I'm saying is, thanks and don't feel guilty."

"I should never have discussed sex at work. It's totally embarrassing, you know we get caught up with institutional mayhem, hospitals are renown for strict guidelines and procedures, sometimes we become... flippant... careless... it was late," she smiled sheepishly, "I have to rush," she bent forward and innocently kissed me on the cheek. She added a hug and patted me on the back, "Bye Shaun, thanks for understanding, take care."

"Bye Leah, and don't work too hard," I waved goodbye as she disappeared down the fire stairs. I thought... nice girl.

CHAPTER 13

LEAH

Samantha was a mere six car parking-bays from where Leah and I were talking, as I opened the car door Samantha asked, "She didn't hit on you?"

"No, not really."

"Are you sure?"

"Of course she didn't."

She lifted an eyebrow and gave a questioning look. "You don't sound convincing."

"Err... we kissed and she gave me a hug, that's all."

"What did you say to her?"

"Err... just small talk, really nothing important."

"Like?"

"I told her not to feel guilty about what she said."

"And that was?"

"Why do you need to know?"

"I'm sitting in this car park thinking, what else could go wrong. Then I think maybe it's nothing to worry about and the strangest feeling comes over me. As if I can't trust you any more. Why would I feel like that?"

"Gee Samantha, she's only a kid, and kids get bored, alright? Give her a break."

"Everyone is a kid to you Shaun, can't you see she has enough maturity to want to sleep with you."

"Yeah, and her work mate as well, but they are innocent... really."

"Her work mate as well? What in the hell are you talking about?"

"Leah, you saw me talking to her..."

"Who in the hell is Leah?"

"A nurse who looked after me, I saw her in the car park. She just gave me a kiss and hug... what?"

"Oh nothing. That explains everything. Sleeping with this nurse and her friend would be acceptable to me, no worries with that, that is completely innocent; I can't even imagine how I could question your loyalty under those circumstances."

"Samantha, stop picking at everything, these girls were just having fun, nothing happened, Christ they're young enough to be my daughters."

"I wouldn't go there if I were you. You're in enough trouble with that seventeen year – old Day-Tripper."

We drove in silence, I assumed she meant 'Lyn Monday'. I didn't dare ask what 'Tripper' meant, although it had to be a reference to Lyn's visit.

Minutes later, as if she was anxious for an answer, "You know I meant Siobhan... did she hit on you?"

"Oh her, Siobhan... of course not, no, she won't do that again," I fibbed. "And by the way, Siobhan and Tom have separated."

Samantha commented as if her voice was winding down for a slow motion replay and it came out as... "Thattt... isss.... sooo... sadddd."

It was unconvincing, as if Siobhan deserved what she got. My head was spinning. I needed to do something to refresh the spirit and rejuvenate my values, so I asked, "Would you like to go for a drive?"

"Where?"

"A surprise."

This was something I needed to do, somewhere to reconnect

to ensure my roots were strong. I may have grown but I wasn't sure the journey taken was the right one.

I asked, "Samantha, what is happening to us?"

She smiled but it was forced, more like a chameleon changing colours, "Well where do I start, let me see, oh yes, that secret you hid and then all the little secrets attached to the big secret. I thought we told each other everything, how many secrets do you have Shaun?"

"I'm sorry Samantha, I never realised the implication. I never wanted to hurt you."

"You never forgot her, why?"

"You could never forget a girl like her, I don't know why I never told you, she had died before I met you, it's just... I thought..."

"Yes?" she questioned, "You loved her?"

"I hardly knew her. I don't understand any of this."

"Why all this mystery and subterfuge?"

"I honestly don't know. I'm sorry, will you accept my apology?"

She sat back in the seat and sighed. There was no answer and we remained silent.

The moon looked enormous and rested on the horizon, a golden husk mellowed by mist and salt air. By the time Samantha realised our destination we were committed. Her attitude was different, as if eager for the adventure; "You're not walking me down that craggy headland again are you?"

"Yes, and I'm insisting you peel off every last ounce of clothing and skinny dip with me, like the last time we were here."

"Shaun, you are the romantic aren't you?"

"We need to do this Samantha, even though we may get pneumonia."

She gazed at me as I pulled the car to a stop and went to her side to open the door.

"Alright, I guess you know what you're doing," that was all she said. I took her hand and led her down the steep incline where the rocks were loose and crumbling. I forgot how rough the terrain was and cursed when I slipped taking Samantha with me. We came to a resounding stop, inches from the precipice and all Samantha could do was giggle – like we were still in our teens, "Are you alright?"

"I'm bleeding from cuts and scrapes but who's complaining. This is exciting,"

When we reached the bottom, we were able to walk in ankle deep sand and without hesitation we stripped off and bounded around like puppies in a pet shop.

When we hit the water the shock was startling. The water was freezing, however we both persisted and then she began splashing huge sheets of water with discerning accuracy. I dived below the surface and came up between Samantha's legs where I lifted her onto my shoulders and held her above the rolling surf. "Put me down you big lug, put me down and fight fair." When I refused, she bent forward and kissed my lips. Similar to when we first kissed. I lifted her off my shoulders and spun her body around. I looked into her face and saw her young girl's smile return.

"You're very sexy," I said.

"Shaun, let's make love here, please not on the gritty sand."

I bent to kiss her and was surprised by her strength, her arms wrapped around me with such intensity that the air dislodged from my lungs. Stretching on her toes, she reached up and bit my bottom lip. It was a hard bite and I tasted blood. "Alive enough for you? Can you handle a woman this passionate?"

"Yeah, I always have."

"Show me!"

I did, I lifted her off her feet and settled her into our most intimate of positions. She shrieked at first but seconds later she began sobbing uncontrollably. Her face was close against mine, our steamy breaths panting heavily against each other. The briny air invaded our nostrils. As I waded through the water, she clung tightly around my neck, her nails pressuring my skin, more from passion than her fear of tumbling. The water swirled in foaming suds that determinedly followed us. As a larger wave rolled towards us, I eased Samantha against its force and she relaxed, letting its strength settle her onto me. She shuddered at the intensity – we were alive! The backwash withdrew her body slightly then another wave forced her at me until we were in rhythm with nature. Wave after wave gave us slow penetrable sex and finally after ten minutes we climaxed simultaneously. Samantha screamed aloud. I thought it would destroy our moment but it only seemed to intensify the passion.

"I love you," she declared.

I smiled back.

Again, the cold defeated us and we ran as fast as our tired legs would allow. Our clothes were discarded somewhere… I was sure we had left them close. However, my doubt had been raised when I couldn't find them. There was no wind so they couldn't have blown away. Coming off the steep face of the headland limited our search and I deduced the clothes had been stolen. When I mentioned this to Samantha, she froze and looked around. Could someone have been here, watching? Had they seen us? Had they heard Samantha's rapturous outburst?

The moon was higher and the beach shone brightly, more brilliant then I ever remembered. I checked the sand for extra footprints. There were none, only our tracks.

Weird.

Resigned to the fact that the clothes were gone we gingerly climbed the cliff edge and found the car intact and thankfully the advantage of having a concealed key. Samantha searched the car for anything to hide our nakedness. There was nothing other than the tissues kept in the glove compartment. We were at a reorder status, there were only four tissues remaining, Tom had used the balance. Samantha laid one across my genitals as that should take care of any prying eyes and she did the same, clasping the remainder in case she needed to cover her breasts. As I drove down the dusty dirt road I glanced at her, Samantha's face was drawn and she looked straight ahead. Her figure was magnificent. She had really looked after herself. I softly spoke, "That was great." However, she wasn't listening.

"Who was there Shaun, did they see us?"

"I think someone is messing with us."

"Who?"

"Probably young kids out for a lark." I didn't believe that for a minute but it was more convincing than me saying 'maybe Lyn Monday turned up'. "You did enjoy yourself didn't you?"

"Shaun, tell me what you really think happened."

"No."

"No? Why not?"

"Because this conversation and its direction will take longer than the trip home and it will have lasting repercussions."

"That serious."

"Yeah."

"Well, you better tell me what you think."

"You have competition."

"Who? Not that spirit girl again," she said in a bitter tone, "You're telling me this dead girl is messing with us."

"I don't think of her as dead, just the opposite. Maybe that's the problem; I just refuse to admit she's gone."

"Christ Shaun, she's dead, alright, over forty-five years ago. You've seen the Death Certificate. You have visited her grave! What further proof do you need?"

"I know she's dead, but she isn't, and that's the trouble. I was hurtled into hospital for no apparent reason and remember Siobhan saw her too – she wanted me to warn you. I think this girl has become jealous of what we have and is trying to scare you, consequently we are driving around buck-naked and God knows what looks we will attract when we hit the city limits. Samantha, I've had these bizarre experiences and honestly, I'm worried."

"Shaun these experiences are explainable, I refuse to be a party to your paranoia."

We drove in silence for a while. In a moment of absolute insanity I laughed to myself, I could see a funny side to this, the stolen clothes was a childish prank but a signal to let me know she was around. All these years nothing and now suddenly things were happening; why? I would swear Lyn was sitting in the back of the car watching us act out a play. She neither encouraged nor discouraged, she was taking me somewhere and each step was slow, deliberate, as if planning each move, until – checkmate!

Samantha broke the silence, "Shaun, please answer me, why are you still in love with her?"

"I…"

"It's alright, I won't bite your head off, I need an answer; silence is not helping your cause."

I felt my swollen bottom lip, the one Samantha drew blood from, it wasn't her best example, "I don't know. It's so long ago; I can barely remember her face."

"Shaun, I need to know what happened between you and her."

"Absolutely nothing, and that's the worrying thing, I never touched, kissed or even held her hand. We only spoke a few words over all those years."

"Something happened. What did she say?"

I pulled the car to a stop.

I looked at Samantha and said, "The only words she ever said were, 'Do you like me'? and years later just before her death she said, 'Sorry, I wish it could be you'."

"And how did you reply to both?"

"I'd rather not discuss this any more. I wiped my eyes and went to start the car but Samantha touched my arm and insisted, "You stopped to talk, finish it – now!"

"When Lyn said, "I wish it could be you," I didn't say anything because I was being rushed to hospital with a bleeding hand. However, the first time was a disaster, I was in a milk bar and she walked up to me, smiled, moved closer, I was so caught out, we were inches away, then she said, "Do you like me?"

"And she said it exactly like that?"

"Yeah, I just froze and panicked, all I could muster was a few words…"

"And they were?"

"Of … course…"

"And that's it? That's all that was spoken between the two of you?"

"Yes. She was genuine," as if that needed to be said. I know I spoke only two words but the moment was intense."

"Well that should cement a life time bond," She shook her head feeling exasperated.

Samantha thought seriously, "This is all to do with what? How many words are we talking here, eleven at most?"

"I know, it's stupid, I feel such an ass."

"Something else must have happened; think back."

"No nothing, I didn't see her much, the only thing I'm having problems with is her ... Err."

"What?"

"It is ridiculous."

"No what?"

"Her eyes were green, hypnotic; it was all to do with her eyes. They locked onto me and have never let go."

"Shit," Samantha spat out. "Of course. That's the most powerful thing that can happen."

"Are you playing me? You think I'm being stupid."

"No, that explains everything."

I wasn't convinced, "How?"

"I read a book once on entrapment. The eyes are the most powerful of forces. Whole countries have gone to war over how some man became smitten with the look of a woman. You're not the first and I dare say, not the last."

"I agree, but she's been dead for forty-five years. There is something else happening, I'm not sure I can handle it."

Then Samantha response shook me, "Shaun, I want you back, you're somewhere but it's not here, you need to get over this, it happened, it's happening but that's it, no more!"

CHAPTER 14

GREEN LIGHT, LITTLE GREEN MONSTER

We were parked by the side of the road. I was glad the car's windows were frosting, not a negative when naked, even so Samantha was determined to continue our conversation and more importantly determined that I should forget Lyn. She demanded the whole matter be resolved, "No more, absolutely no more," but from my perspective it was far from a fait accompli. Through frustration she spat out, "I'm glad that's over."

It was typical Samantha, take the lead and be the boss, anything to prevent the meltdown? For Samantha to adopt this attitude she had to feel threatened but I sensed my obsession was only a part of the problem. Admittedly, my secret was probably the most threatening thing that could happen to our marriage. Most partners wouldn't give a rat's arse but with Samantha it was important, a matter of honour where I had deceived her, loved another and this while we had been intimate. During our time, not a single word from me. We had gone through countless trials together, we had always been truthful and forthright, we survived because of our frankness but this was different and she knew it. From our marriage, I had kept something back; it was something rotten, something browning at the core. Samantha now knew I had loved another and a strange vulnerability settled upon us. My betrayal was similar to treason and regardless of Lyn Monday being dead there was now this wedge; sharp, dividing and splintery, driven hard, which would take a Herculean effort to extract, I couldn't tell Samantha I loved her, I just couldn't and she knew that.

Love – what was it anyway? I knew how I felt for Lyn; I knew how I felt for Samantha and our children. I remembered how I loved my mother, all different types of love. So why couldn't I tell Samantha I loved her? I did love her but it was different. She expected 'uno, el supremo, top deck', all encompassing love. Only one love, a selfish possessive love, no room for anyone else, it was good in a way my mother died, she may have been a threat to Samantha. Samantha would surely have been a threat to her.

I was bitter at Samantha's dogged determination. To forget Lyn Monday was impossible. I was unable to contain my bitterness and seconds later I lashed out for justice, "Samantha, I'm not buying your assessment of the situation. You're just too ready to dismiss what is happening."

Samantha was cool, with a stare to match, "Like?"

"Maybe this girl wants help, maybe she needs the past corrected, maybe she needs to say sorry and wants me to do that, you see that happening on television all the time. Something profound is happening here."

Samantha raised her left eyebrow questioningly, "Fantasy time isn't my forte, but what if it is true, why after all these years? Shaun, from her circle of friends was there anyone as caring and as giving as you? Is there anyone who has kept her memory intact and refuses to let go. Obviously, she was attracted to you back then but you weren't ready, however now, that's a different story. As annoying as this is to me, there is no way I'm getting you back unless you walk away. Otherwise, you'll have to make a decision between us."

Shocked by her ultimatum I responded, "No... I can't."

"You must, there can't be two, only one. Your spirit girl or me!"

Samantha refused to accept Lyn Monday, point-blank. She owned me and we had a marriage contract as proof. There was no way she could accept anyone else and refused to entertain Lyn Monday existed – of course she didn't.

The upside to this downside was that Samantha had capitulated when saying, "Wrap this up, you have three days to do it." I gauged this to be a reluctant decision but one where she thought I should be weaned, rather than go cold turkey.

I turned the key and started the car's demisters. A minute later the windows were clear although my mind was numbed by fog. Christ, we had been discussing our future in the nude. Half an hour later I was pulled over for speeding; I was such a mess. The officer tried not to laugh and when I told him we had had our clothes stolen he became sympathetic enough to ignore the fifteen-kilometre excess and let us off with a warning. Samantha clung tightly to her tissues, which did little to cover her curvaceous figure or intense embarrassment.

Once home I instantly researched the Coroner's findings, every hour was precious. The drug Lyn had overdosed on was a sleeping potion with a street name of 'Mickey Finn'. A residual memory had me thinking of spy and detective stories where groggily headed heroes became waylaid on their way to solving the mystery. I knew about 'Mickey's' as a kid, everyone who watched television or listened to radio dramas knew of this sinister doping drug, a date-rape drug similar to Rolhypnol, but why was it responsible for Lyn's death?

The overdosing effects would take place in thirty seconds. Lyn would have been confused, vomiting. Her speech slurred, followed by general respiratory depression. Then she would have experienced low blood pressure and convulsions. I felt nauseated. Christ... I could not believe my son's overdose paralleled Lyn's death.

The first question that came to mind, how did she induce this Mickey Finn? She may have had access as a dental nurse. Did she have any idea she was taking something so powerful?

Was it slipped into a drink without her knowledge? I thought of Josh Freemont and the vilest of emotions surfaced. That liar, what role did he have in all this? Was he instrumental in her death? Was he taking advantage of her? Why did he conceal her as his girlfriend?

The clock was ticking. I emailed Beaulieu requesting she continue the research.

I dreaded the early hours of the morning, for that was the worst time for recurring memories, I was always a light sleeper but now I was lucky to catch a few hours at best. My study was subduedly lit from an eerie green banker's lamp, I could hear the low rumble of the refrigerator going through its automatic defrost cycle and then the dishwasher timer engaged, it banged and shuffled plates until there was nowhere else for them to settle. I slumped into my office chair and caressed the soft leather. I loved that chair, I constantly utilised the rocker. It helped me think of better times. It went anyway, up, down, tilted with lumbar adjustments, having eight controls in all. The only thing it didn't have was a vibrating massager.

With Samantha's deadline looming I shelved plans to write a new book

Inspiration in the Modern Work Place

I just didn't have the motivation to be inspiring others, and besides, there were eighty-five similar books in the market place. The golden rule I had found was always to do something no one else had, to be the first. That led me to question myself, if I was so pedantic about the golden rule, why did I start writing about 'inspiration'? Growing turnips would have been easier.

What was I thinking? The question was, what was I passionate about? Think... with other books I had written, the subject adopts you, it's strange for you have no control, absolutely none. With a self-imposed bet, I scribbled the first words that came to mind...

Lyn Monday in large flowing letters and then I reinforced it by going over each five times. Lyn Monday was several-fingers tall and dropped shadowed with lines so fine her name had its own depth of field. Maybe I could write a book about Lyn, and I added…

The Novel

Maybe hide the drafts from Samantha and adopt a pen name. I thought about that some more.

If I had the courage to pursue this relationship, it may have saved her life, we could have married and had a lifetime of memories. Lyn Reece would have been her married name. I wrote that down as well… again large, bold…

Lyn Reece

I was truly rambling and coming up with any ridiculous idea, again those fine lines to reinforce her name, but could I do justice to this novel? There was enough passion; definitely, I decided to attempt a draft, a private tribute to Lyn however no one should know…

Samantha shouted in my ear, "Lyn Monday the Novel!"

I jumped with fright. I never sensed her leaning over my shoulder. She said belligerently, "Did I scare the hell out of you?"

Red faced I tried to recover, "Shit Samantha, I thought you were asleep. When I left, you were snoring."

She ignored me and snatched the page from my grasp, "I don't see an Samantha Reece written down here, so I guess Lyn's winning, right? Hey, what's this… Lyn Reece? My replacement?"

"Samantha don't."

She turned to go, but I grabbed her wrist and held it tight.

She struggled to free herself but I held on, she angrily quipped, "You're a shit."

I felt the need to apologise, "I don't know how to let go, I'm sorry Samantha, you know I…"

"Love me, is that what you want to say?"

"I'm trying."

"Years of waiting for the words. Shaun, it's not going to happen, is it? You can't say love, can you? Not to me! And this is a different kind of love you have with this girl, honestly, I'm mad as hell. There, I said it, mad, angry, and pissed-off, anyway you interpret it. I can't compete with someone who knows how to play you like this, I'm a mere mortal Shaun, no tricks up my sleeve, and I can't zap you and put you into hospital to get your attention. All I can do is be me, and I guess you're tired of that, especially when a seventeen year old is flirting with you. I've decided this must end, now! You don't think, breathe, or talk about her any more, understand! That's the end of it."

I closed my eyes and let her wrist go, knowing she grasped the situation perfectly.

Determinedly she said, "Come back to bed, it's cold."

When I returned five minutes later Samantha was on my side of the bed, "Hold me Shaun, I need you," she sounded desperate almost pleading as if this might be our last chance. I held her close and with such intensity I thought she would break. I smelt her hair, which was like the scent of Lavender. It was uplifting and invigorating however in the background my mind drifted back to Lyn. I was definitely crazy.

"I'm sorry Samantha for putting you through this but I can't control myself."

We drifted together breathing contentedly like Siamese twins. I knew her possessiveness was rising and we were more like brother and sister rather than lovers. Every word strained and ripping us apart, I drifted to sleep but couldn't settle. Each time I awoke my body swam in sweat; it would have been an hour later when I felt an Arctic freeze invade my body. I tried to pull the covers up for protection but for some reason I couldn't find the blanket's edge, before I could do anything else my body went through a strange warming process, beginning at my feet and ending at my shoulders. I drifted again comfortably lulled by this tight cocoon of peaceful serenity. I stirred again, I turned to check the time, it was 5am, and I rolled over and tried to settle but felt the need to rise. My eyes sprang open similar to a trapdoor. I rolled onto my back completely refreshed. A strange invigoration possessed me and what came next I could not have imagined. The heaviest of weight settled across my body, evenly pressured, all the way from my toes to my head, every inch weighted to the shape of my body. It was oppressive and with each moment its intensity increased. It was hard to move. I refused to call Samantha, who appeared peaceful, but then my breathing became laboured and there was a difficulty to inhale, as if a boa constrictor was squeezing the very essence out of me. The weight was overwhelming but somehow I managed to slide out of bed and land with a thump on the floor. I was completely out of breath and shaking. The weight had lifted, a few more seconds and the pressure would surely have crushed me. I was breathing rapidly; my heart had to be pumping 200+. There was a need for me to work. I staggered to my feet and crept quietly to the office. I didn't delay and began writing immediately…

Lyn Monday the Novel
© *Shaun Reece*

I felt more at ease but it was still hard to concentrate after that second signal. The first had been the panic attack, which appeared life threatening and now this immense weight, a bone-crushing wake up call. When Lyn Monday wanted your attention, you jumped!

I coded the computer to prevent Samantha's access. I also decided not to discuss anything with her, now another secret. As soon as possible I spoke to Beaulieu and made plans. I would see her in one hour. I told her I was writing a novel about this girl, I just hoped she wouldn't talk to Samantha.

I was out of the house before lunch and driving east. Last night's incident was playing on my mind. I felt better Lyn was back. I knew Lyn would never harm me although the force she used was concerning. Why grab my attention this way? Why create such mystery?

Beaulieu's house was a turn of the century Federation, built from large sandstone blocks and held defiantly by thick mortar. The roof had grey slate shingles with federation red guttering and this skirted a huge wrap around veranda. When I rang the brass doorbell I couldn't hear a ring so I decided to knock as well. The security door opened slowly and stopped a quarter way – frozen. Then as if Beaulieu recognised me, she opened the door fully without a word and turned, leaving me no option other than to follow.

Her high-heeled stilettos clicked-clacked on the tiles and I tried to oppose the drumbeat, ensuring my individuality, with Beaulieu it was something I needed to keep in mind. Her long jet-black hair swayed from side to side, it had a sheen, similar to shampoo models on television. She turned to ensure I was following. Her face was pear shaped with a rich peachy complexion. She was tall with a stunning figure, a trimness that seemed unkind to women her age and especially those carrying thickened thighs and rolling hips. She turned without acknowledgement and continued down the long corridor, she called out, some five paces ahead, "And Samantha, how is she?"

"Just fine."

"You'll say hi for me."

"Sure. I think she's planning a few days away." Create doubt and stall for time, it was my only hope.

She turned, smiled and pointed to the sofa, "We'll do tea… high tea, I don't have many chances to do cucumber sandwiches, I hope you like sandwiches, cakes and tempting morsels. I didn't have much time to prepare. Your announcement was sudden. Let's eat."

"Looks delicious."

We sat and she poured from her finest china. I felt I was at a child's tea party except the standard was considerably higher than the last time I had partaken of… 'tea'. On that occasion, my young cousin had use the toilet water to fill her teapot and this created all types of coughing and spluttering when my grandmother discovered what she had been served.

Still pouring from a height, Beaulieu peered above her bifocals and asked, "So you need a researcher, let's talk money first, let's get the dread out of the way, then we can relax, I charge $5.00 per hour plus expenses. Would that be suitable?"

"We're not in China, Beaulieu."

"I like to think I am, if I prepare for their standard of living now, I'll be the only one who is able to adjust quickly when they take over."

"I never thought about that, would you like me to pay you in; what's their currency?"

"U.S. dollars."

"Of course."

"Should I transfer the money into your bank or should I send it via FedEx."

"You have a wonderful sense of humour Shaun, I'm sure we will bounce off each other like magnets from opposing poles. Now, I must warn you, my sense of humour is weird."

"Really?"

"Oh, yes, you will be absolutely enthralled by my wit, intrigued by my research and most importantly, my thoroughness to detail."

"I'm sure," her thoroughness to detail was a given, although I had doubts about her wit and her comment concerning intrigue, worried me. She had lived in England for some time playing netball and working through a bitter divorce. Regardless, she retained a sense of humour that was outside the square. Her voice was her most striking feature. She said with an authoritarian air, "Now, is there anything else you can tell me about this girl?"

"Not really, I can't remember much." The last thing I needed was for her to be conversing with Samantha. Swapping notes on my feelings and my morbid attachment would be a disaster. Reinforcing my story, "All I know is, this school friend of mine, Josh Freemont went weird at the mention of Lyn's death, an over the top type of freaky weird, strange behaviour and he was lying to me about their relationship. I caught him out on that lie and he knows it. I doubt he will call me after he returns from Morocco."

"He wasn't distressed that you were mentioning Lyn Monday?"

"No. Initially I'd call his attitude elated but when I mentioned her death, he seemed detached. Really Beaulieu, I don't have much more to give you."

"So you are writing a novel on this girl?"

"Yes."

"Shaun, this will be a challenge for you."

"Why do you say that?"

Beaulieu looked up, caught my eye and answered, "Well you don't seem to know too much about this girl, so it will be a short story then!" I smiled sheepishly, she was onto me, she had dangled the bait and I had grabbed the hook. She added, "So we are finished, I'll keep you posted." I knew Beaulieu would interrogate me later.

I rose. She directed me to the front door, "And so the mystery begins, ha-ha!" her voice trailed the corridor. There was that little laugh again, sleuthing, intriguing, never a nervous inflection, being more an authoritarian one with sophistication and class... add a little flair with her English adopted plum and you listened. A woman who researched the dead, it was a hobby, one where she devoted herself to unravelling the past and deep dark secrets. Who would have thought?

After saying goodbye the security door closed with a bang.

Would Beaulieu be on the phone to Samantha already? I was close to answers but also close to trouble.

CHAPTER 15

◄○►

BEAULIEU

The journey home was one of reflection; I was obsessed with Lyn. Why go against Samantha's wishes and use her niece Beaulieu for research, was I mad? If caught, I stood the chance of undermining our very foundation, regardless Beaulieu was researching Lyn's death and I felt confidently euphoric. Nothing would stop me, however at the back of my mind I knew there would be a reckoning, one where the crap would hit the fan.

Once home I thought of Beaulieu and within seconds, the phone rang. I could have picked it up on the first ring but decided to let it ring to four.

"Hi Beaulieu, so soon."

She dismissed my small talk with, "Are you ready Shaun?"

"For what?"

"Are you sitting down?"

"Yes."

"I don't want you distracted; this needs your full attention."

"Yes, yes, go on, you're sounding more like Samantha."

"Good. I'm not sure you want this."

"Beaulieu, get on with it, what do you have?"

"The Coronal Inquest's transcript."

"The what?"

"The inquest into Lyn Monday's death. Are you sure you want to proceed?"

"Of course."

"This information is brutal, if you had any attachment to this girl, maybe you shouldn't hear this."

'Had any attachment', was the key words, "I had no attachment to Lyn," speaking in past tense. It was a different story if talking in the present tense, "Tell me Beaulieu, was she pregnant?"

"Yes. How did you know?"

My throat went dry and it hurt to swallow, "I just knew," I said sadly.

Beaulieu continued without hesitation, "Lyn didn't commit suicide per se. The coroner's finding left that open, he couldn't determine if it was wilful or not. Of course, that was on the death certificate and you saw that. Here is the interesting part, she had booked a driving lesson for the following morning and asked her mother to wake her. So suicide seems unlikely."

My mind drifted back to my son, Joel, who had booked a wrestling program on cable and asked us to wake him in the morning – no different!

"Shaun, there was another guy involved, his name was Malcolm Shallier, they were seeing each other on and off for a year, Lyn claims it was his baby but he denied it. This is the interesting thing; Malcolm Shailler was the local pharmacist."

"You're kidding! It's just too long ago, I can't remember him."

Beaulieu determinedly continued, "And he supplied the mixture that killed her although it was prepared some months earlier."

I queried, "What, that Mickey Finn?"

"I think it was referred to as a sleeping potion."

"But still referred to as a Mickey Finn, so why did she need a sleeping potion?"

"Her doctor's report claimed she had a bad back. Shaun, you are sitting down, right?"

"Yes. There is more?"

Beaulieu was wound up tighter than a cuckoo clock, "Besides denying the baby was his, this pharmacist, Malcolm Shailler gave her unauthorised tablets called Amenorone Forte which required a doctor's prescription; Shaun, do you understand what that means? He just handed her these tablets to abort the foetus. Highly illegal, however nothing happened to him. No black mark against his name, he just walked away without a reprimand. No wrap over the knuckles or concerns about his unethical behaviour. Because the tablets were not the cause of death, it wasn't such a big deal. However, I've looked up the side effects and if Lyn had survived, the baby may have been deformed; it was a drug similar to thalidomide. Leading up to her death, Malcolm Shailler and she argued, there was no support from him. Lyn must have been in a terrible mess and scared to tell her parents. Shaun, this is the crucial point, in his statement and taken by the police immediately after her death, Malcolm states he couldn't remember Lyn's last words, he only remembered Lyn mentioning the red mixture, that Mickey Finn sleeping potion and should she take it? What a contradiction hey! What a strange thing to say, one minute he can't remember but the next he can. What I find peculiar is the dates included in his statement, for example the conception date is way out, his police statements claim Lyn began her periods during the holiday weekend June 6 and then she phoned him on June 29, twenty-three days later to say she was one week overdue. That's complete nonsense. My estimate of when she fell pregnant is May 20 – 22 giving her approximately 5 – 6 weeks before she confirmed the pregnancy."

"But why would he lie about the dates?"

"He hoped to disprove he was the father, he claims they broke up for a short time, so manipulating the dates worked in his favour. Neither the police nor court was alerted to this, they let Lyn down terribly. The autopsy report showed she was pregnant, nothing to show how developed the foetus was. How could they overlook something so important? Besides the dates being manipulated, Malcolm also had a lapse of memory on some important issues, however when the subject was not that critical his memory returned. Why did Lyn ask him about the red medicine, that Mickey Finn other than for his guidance as a pharmacist? The tablets didn't abort the pregnancy so what was next, a dose so large it would make her sick, enough to lose the baby? He probably advised her to take the red mixture hoping that would fix the problem one way or the other. He pleaded ignorance when asked if he knew the potency of the red mixture. Why wouldn't he know? He was into his third year of study as a pharmacist. He was desperate, what with a fledging career and mounting debts, he didn't want excess baggage and this was emphasised in his statement. At that point, the police should have been investigating his motives but they didn't. Another interesting fact, he was six years her senior."

I stammered, "Six years... older, that's a big age difference."

Beaulieu added, "She was only sixteen when he started seeing her which made him twenty-two. I hope he learnt something from all this, terribly sad, it's a shame."

I responded bitterly, "Shame, yeah, a shame." There was that word again – shame. It was a shame she died and it would be a shame if nothing was gained. It's a fucking shame if there is no shame. What a useless word? How inert can a word become? I felt numb.

Beaulieu asked, "Shaun, are you alright?"

"What... err, of course? I'm just thinking."

She added, "I have something else."

As if on autopilot I managed, "You're a miracle worker." I imagined her smiling because there was a little pause.

She started again, "I have his address and phone number."

"Really?"

Beaulieu asked, "Do you remember where Josh Freemont lives?"

I went quiet.

Beaulieu answered for me, "I did a search and you won't believe this."

"What?"

"They live next door to each other, both have lake front properties."

"Christ, this is unbelievable." I had information overload.

"I'm scanning the documents to you as we speak. You should get them soon."

Besides the churning within, I managed a weak, "Thanks," and hung up.

My mind was spinning, a boyfriend, I had no problem with that, that was Lyn's choice, but I wasn't happy that Malcolm Shailler was using her and where did Josh Freemont fit into this? If he claimed Lyn was his girlfriend, it had to be prior to the relationship with Malcolm Shailler or at the same time, whatever, it was a well-kept secret regardless of the timing. But why and whose baby was it? Now there was another death, one I hadn't considered – the baby.

Suddenly I realised Samantha had been standing in the doorway, she moved into the study a mere metre away and asked, "What are you doing?"

Knowing I was busted I blurted out, "I'm researching that girl again. Honestly I don't care what you think."

"You didn't talk to Beaulieu again, did you? Tell me you didn't."

"Yep, sure did, I'm up to my neck in research. So there it is – the truth!"

Samantha was speechless and it was several seconds before she could say, "You've gone against my very wishes. Are you an idiot?"

I shrugged knowing it was better to keep quiet.

She asked, "I've lost you haven't I?"

"Don't be ridiculous."

"Each second is becoming a nightmare Shaun. Can't you see what is happening here? This girl is making you deceitful, gone is the person who discussed everything, every subject was approachable, however now you've changed and your life is one big secret. This is unhealthy, your fixation with the past and this

dead girl is sick. You need to get a grip. You need to stop dragging Beaulieu into your morbid fascination. God knows she is
so bored she'll jump at any opportunity to assist and once that
starts you'll be feeding off each other."

"Samantha, sorry, I can't."

The phone rang again. The timing was perfect and it cut
Samantha off.

I answered, "Yes?"

It was Beaulieu again, "Are you busy?"

"No, go ahead."

Samantha sat and drummed her fingers on the desktop im-
patiently. It was hard to concentrate with Samantha's cool close
intensity, "Right," I kept repeating.

Beaulieu asked, "So, what's your opinion?"

"On what?"

"On what I've just told you, how can you not have an opinion?"

"What's the question again?"

"Where are you today Shaun?"

"Sorry, I was distracted."

Beaulieu asked, "Should I call back?"

Samantha could hear every word and nodded her head for
me to do that. I doggedly resisted her intrusion. This was a battle for control.

"No, continue, it's just, I'm coming to grips with everything."

"You sound... distant..."

"It's nothing."

Then Samantha spoke loud enough for Beaulieu to hear,
"Shaun, get off the phone and grow up." Samantha rose and at
the same time pushed her office chair into the bookcase. It
tilted precariously then crashed to the floor. Samantha stormed
out of the study.

There was several seconds delay, "Was that Samantha?"
Beaulieu questioned.

"Yes, sorry about that, I forgot she wanted to go shopping
and I kept her waiting."

"You should go."

"No, it doesn't matter any more, she left without me. I apologise."

"Are you sure?"

Samantha was right, I was becoming deceitful; one lie was leading to another. I had a flash of this repulsive person I was becoming but I overcame that desire to self-evaluate, "Beaulieu, please continue."

Beaulieu checked, "I did mention Malcolm Shailler has a business on the Central Coast."

"I think so."

"He also has some problem with his legs and needs an operation for an old football injury."

"They should give him a spine while they are at it."

"Nasty. I liked you better when you weren't paying attention."

"He is married?"

"Yes, to a Sheila."

"You don't know her name?"

"Yes Sheila; what is wrong with you? Her full name is Sheila Sarah Shallier and they have been married for forty-one years. I think she prefers the name Sarah. Their old house is still on the market, it's worth 1.8 million."

I commented, "A substantial asset. He must have enough cash reserves to purchase his new home. You never found out why he moved so close to Josh Freemont?"

"My research can't fathom brain waves, documentation only. Opinions, desires and the comings and goings of our mere mortals are out of my realm."

"Do you know what he looks like?"

"Better, I will send you a photo."

"You have a photo?"

"Yes, that's a part of my research."

"I'll email you a copy... I'm sending it now. Any second you should be able to access it, he's good-looking."

I loaded the attachment... seconds later, "The photos loaded." I was surprised, "So you call this good looking."

"Of course. Who wouldn't?"

"I guess you're right and obviously Lyn thought so. Beaulieu, his posture resembles someone standing over a bench for many years, his shoulders are very rounded. Where was this photo taken?"

"Near his home, I think."

"His legs are in white stockings, why?"

"Maybe the aftermath of his knee surgery, those types of stockings stop blood clotting."

"This photo isn't the clearest but I wouldn't put him in the good-looking category, average I'd say."

"Well there you have the difference between the sexes."

"I refuse to be drawn into a 15-minute debate on what constitutes a good looking male. Maybe you are right. In fact you are."

"You're a disappointment today Shaun; sometimes we could have discussed a topic like this until your face glowed beetroot red, the funniest of sights." She chuckled to herself.

"Hilarious, but you're not drawing me on that subject. Is that all?"

"No, I would like to apologise to Samantha; could you ask her to call me?"

"I wouldn't worry; she's probably over her hissy-fit by now and has forgotten it even happened."

"Still, I feel terrible, I've taken so much of your time; life is precious and each second valuable. You need time together to nurture a relationship. A marriage needs constant maintenance, give and take is what it's about."

"I'll remember that."

"Goodbye Shaun."

Within a blink, Samantha was framed by the doorway, "Finished this time? You know I can hear everything you say... I had a hissy-fit did I?"

"Look Samantha, you want me to be this other person, I just can't, I can't forget, Lyn died a long time ago but it's real; alright? Her death appears suspicious; I have to investigate what happened."

"Really? Investigate? No, this is more. You have changed. Look at you, you will do anything to get close to her, your imagination is rampant, you crave the next intervention more than life itself, you're a spirit junkie and nothing will stop you. There is nothing to support your belief. Shaun, grow up!"

"Samantha, you're being ridiculous, it's this unreasonable attitude of yours that has forced me to act irrationally. Without your jealous interfering I wouldn't have to go underground."

"You should be so lucky to have someone as caring."

"Caring is one thing, a dictatorship is another. Lyn is out there somewhere, I'll find her. I love her." I couldn't believe I said… 'I love her'… for once the words had left my lips there was no way to retract them.

Samantha was stunned then silent; she managed, "… I'm leaving… I can't take this any more, you're in love with a memory and everything that has happened is a product of your warped imagination. You are seriously messed up, the visit, the request for help, all fantasy; this is the real world, not a misty dream where a girl waits patiently for you."

"You are wrong."

"Good luck, you're going to need it."

Samantha slammed the back door and her favourite figurine, a ballerina, fell from the cabinet, smashing into a thousand pieces. I heard Samantha's car burn rubber down the drive and with a roar she accelerated away. She had had enough. I regretted that critical error but I didn't regret the years of emotion finally surfacing, it was time to stand up for myself. When I told Samantha I lived in a dictatorship that was true. Through the years I had been manipulated into accepting every whim, every, 'I want', it was like Samantha had become the spoilt child of the family getting her way with absolutely everything and I just accepted it. However now, Lyn had 'stirred the pot' and I wasn't bending. No one was going to mess with 'Lyn Monday'.

I realised the loneliness of my situation. The hours drifted into days. My son was staying with friends and there had been no word from Samantha. Where had she gone? I called but her phone but it was switched off.

On numerous occasions I heard Samantha's car rumble into the street and each time I checked the window but it was my imagination playing tricks. Now I was hearing things! As the night settled the house made the strangest of noises. I waited patiently however with each passing minute my concerns were escalating.

CHAPTER 16

TAUNTING WITCHERY

What I needed most was time to think. Lyn needed help and I was determined to assist – but with what? My marriage was in jeopardy, balanced between fragile and precarious, a strange feeling with little direction. My attachment to Lyn was my only motivation to keep going. Was I the victim of a fanciful imagination stuck steadfastly between the afterlife and a pathetic existence? I realised I was at the crossroads. Samantha was heading east and I was drifting north. This had been happening for years. And those hurtful words…

"Lyn is out there somewhere, I'll find her. I love her."

Had I become that insensitive? Definitely, but there was something else happening, more than justice and emotions to correct; but what? It was a gut feeling – I had never felt so strong about anything. I still couldn't dismiss the thought that Lyn had played her role in my unravelling and then Samantha's exasperated meltdown. Samantha was right, I was eager for the next intervention. In one way it felt good to be away from Samantha's stymied stubbornness. She had made it clear, Lyn or her, not both; but Lyn was dead, or was she? Samantha was alive, or was she? Whichever way I looked at it, both were jealous, possessive and determined to control me. Lyn's motivation was by far the strongest; I could never resist a damsel in distress and those mystic eyes so captivating, she was still snatching my emotions. If she returned, I would be ready. But why had it taken so long to contact me, forty-five years later was a long time and she was running out of time.

Then I thought of Beaulieu, why was Samantha concerned for her niece? I hadn't detected anything unusual with Beaulieu; however my fascination with Lyn may have clouded my judgement. Samantha maybe right, Beaulieu was always compulsive and the subject of Lyn addictive. Beaulieu's motivation was different from mine, hooked in another way, the research energised her and once started she craved the accolades. Snippets sucked from the vaults of archives, databases and fellow time travellers whose minds refused erasure. This was her buzz and with each discovery it fragmented into a thousand pieces, she could never be satisfied. Samantha may be right, Beaulieu and I might be feeding off each other but I certainly wouldn't accept Lyn as a misty dream of fantasy. Samantha was definitely wrong on that point. I would have to watch Beaulieu and keep her grounded. I couldn't allow her to be trapped. I knew of no one as dedicated and reliable, she was my priority to protect. Then I heard a ping, she had sent me an email, cheerful and innocent but its contents were deceptive and a trap. This electronic message changed everything. Beaulieu may have had my sympathy seconds ago but after reading the text, I was concerned. The subject line simply stated:

Shaun Darlin', an innocent enough introduction for the gullible, I wasn't!

I couldn't help but feel most of the questions were irrelevant and the others skewed for bias; she was pushing my buttons hoping for a reaction. I took a deep breath, I never expected her to move this quickly.

There were a total of five questions…

Question 1:

Do you remember the lady that owned the shop near your primary school? (She may have been a relative of Lyn Monday).

I remembered the shop but not the lady who owned it. I typed 'no', however I changed my answer to 'yes' when a snippet of recall gave me the answer, 'Madeline, I think'. I encountered this lady every school day, sometimes twice a day. Strange, I was unable to recall her face. Why would Beaulieu need this information?

Question 2:

Do you remember the grand opening of the Berala Shopping Centre?

The question was bizarre, what possible connection did it have? I typed 'yes'. I remembered taking photographs of bikini clad girls who were handing out something unimportant and then rushing to the darkroom to develop the film. Helping me was Jeff, the Presbyterian minister's son; we enlarged the girl's shapely figures onto a 20 x 16 inch print and keenly perused the resolution, then, a day later, the local newspaper ran the story. Jeff considered a career path in glamour photography but his father spoke to him of temptation, lust and how much money there was to be made from having a medical degree. Interestingly, his father had conducted the funeral service for Lyn.

Question 3:

If I find anyone from Lyn Monday's family, what do you want me to say?

Easily answered, 'nothing, leave it to me'.

Question 4:

What happened at the Berala train station?

Well, besides lying to Chantal Witherspoon about her love letter, there was one other catastrophe. It was early morning when a heavy fog shrouded the platform; here a stalled train waited for assistance. Out of the misty depths charged another train back-ending the first and killing scores of people. Chaos ensued and the word spread quicker than a telegram boy on a downhill run.

Then years later, while waiting on the railway platform, I remember talking to a crotchety grey-haired guy who explained how he had represented Australia in the Olympics. He described how to prepare for a running race and drew a line in the crushed gravel. He knelt down to show me a new racing technique called 'the bullet start'. This guy was a legend, I never did ask his name but that start enabled me to have a blistering getaway in every race. I virtually hung over the starting line a foot in front of everyone. This annoyed many competitors but it was a legal start.

I answered Beaulieu's question with, 'train crash' – another question without purpose the only thing achieved was the reinforcement of drifting memories. The most poignant of all questions and I assumed the reason for the email.

Question 5:

Did you love Lyn Monday?

Beaulieu was heading for the juggler – crafty! And with the truth she would have me.

I typed, 'no'. Again, it was all a matter of tense – if she had written, do you love Lyn Monday? I would have typed, 'yes', or would I have given her that satisfaction?

Semantic or pedantic – what right to mess with my feelings? I hit the send button. I had told Beaulieu, "I can't remember much about her", meaning Lyn. Instantly she doubted me and became determined to prove otherwise. Beaulieu was definitely feeding off me, caught up in the research and seeking my truth. I suspected I was her highest priority, while Lyn was mine.

I had to stay ahead of the game, remain cool, she was a crafty witch! I really didn't think of her as a witch until this very second, and then I imagined her stirring the pot and adding bat wings and frog gizzards and a print out copy of my email. All the answers stewing to spelling time; was I serious? My mind was spinning. Minutes earlier I was concerned for her but now I thought she was devious. What was happening to me? Samantha was right when she said, 'good luck, you're going to need it'.

Regardless of my reasoning, my patience lasted fifteen minutes, I couldn't stand it and I called Beaulieu.

"Beaulieu, Shaun."

"Yes Shaun, fine day."

"Indeed," it was as if we had crossed paths in an English country garden and next we would be discussing roses and petunias.

"I've just returned from the garden where I've been..."

I interrupted, "Smelling the roses?" I said it with a venomous twist.

She hesitated, "No... spraying for bugs, messy business as you can imagine."

"Talking of messy. Your email, what's the story? Bored silly are you?"

"What... what do you mean?"

"Well, I've answered all your questions but you probably haven't had time to open this pot-pourri fanciful list, you really are a piece of work!"

"Shaun... what in the hell are you talking about?"

"You're not happy just to research this story you have to go that inch further and see if you can get a reaction."

"Well, if that was my intention it seems to have worked. What question stirred you the most Shaun?"

If I told her, I'd be playing her game, in fact I was playing, she had me exactly where she wanted me, "No, you tell me what question."

"This is so childish, really Shaun, are you so caught up with this girl you can't reason a little argument for old times sake. Anyway, I'll play; let me see... of course. This girl's family. Would they be alive? If so, would they talk to you? And who would do the talking... maybe her mother? A relative? Should I hand over those details when you are such a basket case? I suggest you see a doctor."

"Don't cloud the issue. You know something."

"Of course."

"Really?" She seemed so confident.

"Are you taking bets?"

"Of course not, I have complete faith in your ability to research and more so in your ability to pry."

"And you ring me to do... what? Rip shreds off the only person with answers, the only person who can help."

I took a deep breath trying to contain the wrath, "I'm curious, that's all."

Beaulieu asked, "How do you want me to handle Lyn's family?"

"I'd rather do that, you know it's personal."

Beaulieu replied somewhat quizzically, "Really... really? I had no idea. Personal you say? Why? What happened for you to be this secretive?"

I cut her off, "Beaulieu, if you know about the family, tell me."

Smugly she declared, "Yes, I've spoken to Lyn's mother, I had no idea this was such a personal issue. I am sorry."

I was flabbergasted. Then I realised the significance, "She is alive?"

"Of course she is, if I spoke to her."

My throat seized and I thought of the milk bar, Lyn, those eyes.

"Is that all you can say. How about, good job with the research. Look Shaun, I'll send you an email on how to contact her. Sorry about jumping the gun. Oh, by the way are you looking after my aunt?"

"Who?" I was still reeling from the information.

"Samantha, your wife. Say hi for me."

"Oh, Samantha, of course," Did Beaulieu know Samantha had left? "Oh sorry, the neighbour's dog just got loose, I have to go, I'll ring you back," it was better to get off the phone than be drawn.

Lyn's mother was alive – now I had a predicament. If I couldn't talk to Lyn Monday, how in the hell could I talk to her mother and after all these years?

Fifteen minutes later, the phone rang.

I answered cautiously, "Yes."

"Canine clear?"

"Yes Beaulieu."

"I forgot to tell you."

"Is this important?"

"Of course... I explained to Lyn's mother you are writing a novel on growing up in Berala."

"What else did you say?"

"Now this bit was creativity on my part, I said you were a nice person, imagine!"

"That was the best you could come up with."

"It's difficult when you're adlibbing."

"Anything else?"

"Let me think. Yes, I asked if you could speak to her and ask a few questions but she said she hadn't lived in Berala for many years and didn't know if she could help. She mentioned she never had children."

"She said that! You must have the wrong person."

"No, I don't make mistakes. Go easy on her, this is a sensitive area."

"Ok."

I didn't know how to handle Lyn's mother's comment, 'She never had children'. Was she in denial or staying clear of the subject? I understood her pain, what had this poor woman experienced? I was sad but then angry. Why wasn't she proud of her daughter? I remained with this vile unadulterated ire and by morning, I tried to look from all perspectives, why would anyone want to recall bad times, it was natural for her to shut out a third party.

Using a crystal ball could prove handy for Bess Monday's response, especially when I divulged, 'I know everything about Lyn's death'. Would she hang up on me? If I had trouble speaking to her daughter, how in the hell was I going to talk to this higher authority, her mother! My mother's warnings were streaming at me like ribbons attached to a fan, fluttery but still determinedly directional. 'Every girl is a potential trap,' true so true and a trap from the moment Lyn had looked at me. Should I pick up the phone? No, this was too important. My whole life's issues centred on this one call, this was the chance to address mistakes. I deliberated. I couldn't make the call, my throat tightened. Why make this poor woman recall sad times, although she had dismissed Lyn as a part of her life. Hell, I could procrastinate all day. Frustrated, I picked up the phone.

"Hello… Bess Monday?"

"Yes."

My heart thumped and my hands began shaking. "My name is Shaun Reece. A friend of mine called you recently and said you may be able to help. I'm writing a novel about…"

"Yes go on."

"Your daughter… you see… I went to school with Lyn… I had a crush on her… a long time ago," like now, "Anyway, I was wondering if you could help me."

There was a long pause and beads of sweat spotted my forehead.

"You knew Lyn?"

"Yes, I don't want to upset you but I was hoping you might help."

"What with?"

"I know what happened to Lyn and I need to check some details with you."

"You know what happened?"

"Yes. I suspected there maybe more to Lyn's death, something suspicious. This is very upsetting for me as I can imagine it is for you. I don't expect you to understand but I want the best for Lyn's memory."

"You know about Malcolm Shailler?"

"Yes," I was close to tears and I'm sure she could detect the warbling cracks in my voice.

"So you know everything."

"Everything."

"Mr. Reece, I'm about to leave, I'm sorry. I need time to think."

I asked, "Can I call you back?"

"Yes, maybe in a couple of days."

At least she didn't hang up on me, I felt terrible putting her through this ordeal and I was amazed I had made it to the end of the conversation. That had to be the hardest thing to achieve. I felt elated I had surpassed my mother's drama and had stood on my own. I had actually spoken to the closest relative to Lyn Monday – her mother. How sad for her, Lyn's death would have created such a void. I knew how I felt and could imagine it being ten times worst for her.

There was still no direction from Lyn. What did she want me to do?

Several days later, I lifted the phone and replaced the handset; what if Bess wouldn't talk? I tried again. On the third ring, "Hello."

"Bess, this is Shaun Reece. Is it alright to talk?"

"I'm not sure I can help, it was a long time ago. How did you find out about Lyn?"

I had no alternative but to push my book. I couldn't say I had a visit from her daughter, I couldn't say Lyn was responsible for putting Siobhan in hospital, I couldn't say my wife left because of my obsession for... enough! Explaining a novel was far easier, "This all started with my grandson coming second in a race, after that I thought of other athletes from school and then the strangest thing happened, I started to think of Lyn. I will not hide the fact I liked Lyn, although that relationship never went anywhere," I swallowed hard, "But what did happen was a strange feeling, something wasn't right, that feeling continues to plague me. I told you I'm writing a novel, it's called... Lyn Monday. I'm hoping to tell Lyn's side of the story."

That started the waterworks, Bess was crying, I was equally emotional.

I gathered enough words to say, "I don't know why I'm writing this, it just feels the right thing to do."

Almost undecipherable, she sobbed, "I'll... have to hand you to my sister... before I become an uncontrollable mess... I'm sorry."

There was a gap of thirty seconds as the crying continued.

A younger voice more controlled and polished announced, "I'm sorry, Bess is too upset to continue, may I help you. My name is Robin."

"I'm sorry for upsetting Bess, it was not my intention, if you want me to hang up I will, we are a bad combination, too many memories."

"I maybe able to help, I was close to Lyn. I lived two doors from her. I was five years older than Lyn but went to most of the parties and events she did. Bess tells me you're writing a book."

Robin was easier to talk to and I re-established my composure, tentatively I asked Robin, "I need assistance with some questions, can you help?"

"I'll try."

"Do you remember a person in Lyn's life by the name of Josh Freemont?"

"No, that name isn't familiar."

"He claims Lyn was his girlfriend."

"I can't remember him, it was a long time ago. How exactly did you find out about Lyn's death?"

I explained my grandson race and my school days, "Honestly, I had the strangest of feelings, something was terribly wrong. I know you will have a problem believing this."

Robin asked, "But how did you know about Malcolm Shailler?"

"I accessed the court transcripts which gives me a fair insight into what happened – it's a matter of public record. Could I ask if you think the Coroner's Inquest was handled correctly, in other words, were you satisfied with the finding?"

She paused and cautiously replied, "One is never satisfied, especially in these types of matters."

"Of course," she was on guard and to probe further would be non-productive, "Once you have digested everything, could we talk later?"

"Yes, that is probably a good idea."

We exchanged phone numbers. I thanked her and apologised for upsetting Bess.

I still had no idea what Lyn wanted, however I had achieved a lot, I had faced my demons and had survived, for me it was my Everest. I was glad Bess had broken down for it showed she loved her daughter. She should have been proud of seventeen good years; I probably had seventeen good seconds. Regardless of our time, we both loved Lyn with intensity. I'm glad I was a witness to that raw emotion!

CHAPTER 17

THE MIND DOCTOR

Bess's emotion had renewed old feelings. My hands had a slight tremor as I moped around the house ignoring all but the essentials. There were two things important, to establish if I wanted Samantha back and of course what to do with Lyn. I paced for hours and stopped in front of the mantelpiece. I removed the psychiatrist business card and made an appointment. Doctor Roberts was an episodic events expert and was waiting exclusively for me, or so her secretary said.

I arrived at Doctor Roberts' office. Her rooms had expansive views overlooking the harbour and I feared her account would reflect this Double Bay address. I wasn't disappointed; her secretary addressed the payment immediately. I folded the credit card receipt with two sharp creases and secured it into my back pocket. I waited patiently for ten minutes and gathered this opportunity to sort the events into an order of credibility. Several minutes later it became apparent my integrity was going to suffer, there was no way to explain the past.

Soon a red-eyed woman with platinum hair and pencil thin lips retreated from the therapy room – accompanying her was a strange looking woman who seemed too old to be a doctor. Her eyes looked weary, nevertheless, actively scanning the room.

This had to be Dr. Roberts. The only thing resisting my departure was the calmness surrounding her for she had an inner peace that was attractive. She patted the platinum blonde on the shoulder and whispered, "See you tomorrow my dear."

"Come in," she looked down to read the file's name, "Shaun," she said surprised for some reason. She walked ahead of me with small steps that were half the capacity of mine. She queried, "Celtic back-ground are we?"

"Some connection to the Emerald Isle."

She stopped, turned to face me and said, "Well Shaun, I start by telling each patient the same thing, then I finely tune the session to accommodate their needs, this is how it works… have a seat." We settled into opposite chairs. The bi-fold doors were open allowing fresh salt air to tingle our senses. I looked past her across the bay, she coughed to grab my attention, "You pay, and I listen. If I have to painfully extract the information, you will eventually go broke and we will both be unhappy. I will lose a patient and you will have lost time and money. I suggest you divulge your problem and quickly. Do not imagine for a minute that you will arouse, shock, or offend me. I have heard it all before, trust me, I'm a doctor." She smiled as if that was a joke and this humour was from a brimming repertoire. I smiled in case it was expected.

She glanced at her watch and opened my file. She clicked her pen ready and expected me to barrel roll over Niagara. I was hesitant, "When you are ready," she prompted.

I was nowhere near ready. The best I could come up with was, "It's simple really, I'm married, have three kids, all grown up of course. Incidentally, been happily married for ages, sorry, I left that part out. Recently I was in hospital suffering a stress attack. I thought it was a heart attack, the doctor from the hospital referred me to you." That wasn't too bad for an opening salve.

She frowned disapproval and quipped, "Yes, I can see how simple this is, if only every case had this simplistic nature to it." She slowly scribbled something onto her pad. I figured she wrote 'dumb ass' or something similar to remind her of my cantankerous stupidity.

I mustered a pathetic, "Sorry."

Doctor Roberts stopped writing and looked up, "Shaun, nothing is ever simple and nothing works as planned. That's why they invented Murphy's Law."

"Murphy's Law?"

"Yes."

"I don't think they invented Murphy's Law; they just named a conclusion after it. If something can go wrong, it will go wrong. There was no invention per se."

"Oh really? That's interesting. Shaun, you see the trap you're falling into here, I will listen all day. So far I worked out you are having marital problems and you are here by default. I guess you are doing this to save your marriage. Right or wrong?"

"Right and that Murphy's Law question was a trick, right?

She smiled, a little turn at the corners of her lips. She demanded, "Shaun get on with it, I know when someone is humouring me."

I had never experienced a woman with such face slapping audacity. It took a few seconds to compose myself but when I did, the flow came unabated, "I have repressed feelings about a girl who died years ago. Recently these feelings surfaced as a panic attack. I never did get over this girl's death, I refuse to let go, for me she isn't dead, not her spirit, she is still here. I've seen her. Does that make sense?"

"Your proof?" she asked.

"The most convincing proof has to be a friend who was hospitalised for getting too close. She was flirting with me and I think my spirit friend warned her off – a jealousy issue. You can see why I was hesitant in telling you this – it's bizarre! Of course none of this has gone down well with my wife. I've spent so much time dwelling over this 'spirit' it has become an obsession. I feel such an idiot. Her eyes have to be my strongest memory and incredibly drawing, they were green, tantalising and seductive, I can't get them out of my head. When she appeared recently she asked for help, I have no idea why or what she wants. There have been a number of unexplained events and co-incidences. Understandably, my wife isn't handling this obsession and has left me."

Dr. Roberts asked the strangest question, "Who is paying me? You or your wife?"

"Me I guess." As strange as her question was, it seemed relevant.

She then asked, "So, whose interests do I have – yours or your wife's?"

"Mine, I hope."

She announced, "I know where this is heading."

"Where?"

"One of two places. Regret or happiness, which would you prefer?"

"Happiness."

"So how do you get happy?"

"I have no idea."

"Exactly. That is why you are here. The question is if you shut out your memories of this girl would that make you happy?"

"No."

"If you churn over these memories until you're a basket case, is that better?"

"Not a great option but better than shutting out her memory."

"So there you are, you have direction. Trust me; the answer is coming, so be patient. There will be more pain and then that will subside, eventually you will settle."

"Am I going to get over this girl?"

"No never and why should you? What makes you happy Shaun?"

"Nothing now, but I can't stop thinking about her."

"Then that is the way it is. Engross yourself in her, if that is what you want. If you are being obsessive, then that will pass and this will enable you to get on with your life. If you stay in this guilt trap you'll never progress."

"But what if I'm going mad, my wife thinks I am."

"Shaun, you are not mad, in love maybe, but certainly not mad. Who said you cannot love a spirit? Relax, enjoy her, and if you want your wife back, great, if you do not, well you had a number of great years and it is over. Remember not to delve into something others want. You have probably done that all your life. Shaun, it's… me time. Say it… me time."

I whispered, "Me time," I continued to feel such an idiot.

"Feel better?"

"No, just guilty and stupid."

"Of course. That will change, the guilt part at least." She smiled. "Great news Shaun, this is your last session, so you don't have to worry about going bankrupt."

I smiled, at least there was some good news.

As I stood to leave she asked, "Do you feel anything different?" She looked into my eyes with clarity and understanding, "Do you sense something?"

I stopped and for some strange reason shut my eyes. A breath of light warm air wafted into the room and caressed my neck, arms, and gently pressured against my body.

"Yes," I said shocked.

She smiled. "I am also a believer Shaun, and this is a good omen and a great presence. Something good is going to come out of all this. I can just tell. When it does, phone me and tell me what happened."

"Of course, thank you."

She bowed gracefully and swept her arm before her, directing me to exit.

When I drove home, I was full of optimism but upon entering the front door I realised years of marriage sat precariously balanced. There was no message from Samantha. The house felt desolate and I drifted into that void of depression which I had left only hours earlier.

CHAPTER 18

KNOCK THREE TIMES

After Doctor Roberts's evaluation, there was a direction for happiness, however that path resembled a minefield, consequently the 'black-dog' followed me everywhere. There would be casualties. I felt low just thinking about it and poured myself another drink.

I don't know how long I had stewed over the issues but I had convinced myself I wasn't budging, Samantha would just have to accept that. When would I see her again?

I lay on the sofa. I must have drifted to sleep but jumped when three loud knocks overpowered the doorbell. Cursing at the interruption, I staggered to my feet and opened the door. An invigorated voice from the darkness bellowed, "Shaunee, you look absolutely terrible, have you been drinking?" It was Siobhan.

"Yes, do you want to join me?"

She moved gracefully through the doorway and glided past. Her untethered red hair swayed tantalisingly from side to side, "What smells?" she questioned.

I didn't answer.

"Incidentally, I'm just out of hospital feeling perked up and ready to go."

"Great, what do you want to drink?"

"Is Samantha here?"

"No, she left me." I thought I detected a smile. "Bourbon on the rocks? I only have JD."

"Is there any other kind?"

"Well, actually yes, but… what are you doing here Siobhan?"

"I called by to thank you. Incidentally, I'm making plans to go to London."

"Why?"

"A break. Talking of breaks, what happened with you and Samantha?"

"She had enough of my afterlife obsession. It was one of those shit days, you know how it is," I slugged back the glass and poured another.

"Can I sit down?"

"Do whatever you want, it doesn't matter any more."

She did, pulling back her flowing red hair and kicking off blue stilettos. She sat close.

"Shaun, when did you eat last?"

"I don't remember. I'm not hungry."

"I do a mean Spanish Omelette. I'll prepare a feast, especially for you."

"Probably not."

"I'll try anyway; I'm a good cook, you'll have to try me."

I thought the emphasis on 'try me' had more to do with something else, rather than cooking.

"What's this mess? Did Samantha throw this at you?"

"I think so, something came hurtling through space." She was referring to Samantha's figurine that had exploded into a thousand pieces; I had left it as a reminder of how fragile life could be.

Siobhan whipped eggs as if she had installed new energiser batteries, "Tomatoes?"

"Samantha probably didn't buy any," but I was wrong. Samantha had stocked the refrigerator, "Yep, there are six."

"Why haven't you shaved Shaun, that growth must be days old?"

I felt my face. It felt like a six-day growth. What had Dr. Roberts thought of my appearance? Had Samantha been gone that long?

"What's happening to you Shaun? It's that girl, isn't it?"

"Yeah, she was so young, no one cares, no one except me, and now it's too late."

"I care Shaun; what happened to her?"

"She died after receiving bad advice, sinister or manipulative, who knows, it doesn't matter any more, she's gone."

"Shaun, she's around I'm sure. I can vouch for that; remember what happened to me." She hesitated, "I can't stand this any more. Shaun, can I tell you something personal? Promise not to get upset."

"Go on, even if I said no, I have a feeling you'll still tell me."

"You need a shower."

I replied defensively, "You're an expert on hygiene now?"

She nodded and I could tell from her look I must be alarming to the senses, "Go and shower and I'll turn the hotplate down but pleaseee hurry."

I loved that, those extended words which added zest to her sentences. Siobhan probably got her own way all the time. As I left the room, she smiled innocently and said, "Hurrieee."

"Alright, alright, I'm trying, alright," even startling myself with the abrupt attitude. Why was I being short with her, she was only trying to help, maybe one drink too many – "Sorry!"

"Accepted, but you are being brutal. Regardless, I like you as a dark morose individual who's angry with the world but I'm afraid your bite will be wasted on me. Have your shower and eat, then we can grow morbid together, let me into those dark nooks and crannies."

"Your poison and I thought you were recovering. Fancy wanting to delve there."

"I'd go anywhere with you Shaun, now go." She smiled as if she meant it. Imagine Siobhan addressing real problems with me; I mellowed instantly.

I gave my body the once over with oozing hot water and a

body wash that smelt like sheep dip. I later read it was a treatment for head lice, probably left over from the grandchildren. Regardless it foamed up well, I even put on a conditioner, a sign a man is caring for himself.

There was a knock at the door just as I turned off the tap.

"Can I come in?"

"If you must subject yourself to every vile piece of imagery."

The bathroom was misty but not that much to hide my credentials. The door crept open somewhat tentatively. She peeked a look then smiled. Somehow, she managed to keep eye contact although I was expecting her gaze to drop any second.

"A towel?" she asked.

Without waiting for a response, she pulled Samantha's towel, the largest fluffiest wrap off the rail and proceeded to pat me down.

"What are you doing?"

"Drying you down. You've kept in shape Shaun, just like I imagined." Her eyes were now drifting.

"Thanks for the company."

She knelt at my feet and lifted her head, she said with sincerity, "Let me pamper you; any objections?"

"None that readily come to mind."

It was one of those moments guys dream about, an attractive woman at their feet and their caressing hands rubbing miracles.

I felt obligated to say something, especially to remove my mind from erotic-embarrassment, "You know, I've got this whole retro existence going on at the moment."

"Really," she replied, still briskly invigorating my skin.

"Yeah, a dual life addiction where you can immerse yourself into total darkness and then within a flash you can be uplifted to moderate depression – two for the price of one."

She lingered, my body was badly in need of melody, "The food is on the table and getting cold, hurry along." She smiled again, rose from her compassionate position and left the misty surrounds of this steam room and me, a man with unfulfilled desire, I blow-dried my own hair.

When I tasted the omelette, it was divine, Samantha never cooked Spanish, always plain old Ozzie tucker with an Orleans's flair, "This is good," I declared, she touched my hand, "What does Samantha cook?"

"Her speciality is blackened steak, she claims it's a Cajun influence but I don't know, I suspect over cooking and the accompanying vegetables are also crunchy. Even her sausages are burnt all round and slit up the middle then she dams the gravy in a pile of mash. Just once I'd like a sausage intact. Of course, her speciality is Vegemite on toast layered with a fried egg and a snip of parsley. Then for an extra special treat she sometimes warms Apple Danish."

"Her own creation?"

"Once removed from the box."

It appeared I was famished and anything put on the table quickly disappeared.

However during this time Siobhan appeared to be holding back, a cautious, hesitant approach, then and without warning she asked, "Do you want to come to London with me?" she moved closer jumping her chair and holding my arm intensely. I was stunned, however the idea was enticing. To get away and visit castles, tombs, heritage buildings and years of crumbling tradition seemed extremely pampering. "Would we visit the Tower of London and see torturing devices and implements to maim and kill."

"If you wish, I'm at your disposal. We could see a show; I hear they are planning a return of the Phantom."

"The comic book hero?"

"No, the musical silly. I'm at your disposal." There, she said it again.

"Err..." I quickly changed the subject I wasn't sure I could handle the next step, "Talking of disposal, your cooking was excellent, let me do the dishes."

She smiled, "Forget the dishes, lets adjourn to the sofa," Siobhan sat close, "I want to know where you're up to with this girl. You liked her a lot?"

"Yes."

"What sort of relationship did you have?"

I replied, "A distant one."

"What does that mean?"

"We only said a dozen words in all the years we knew each other."

"Well how come you have this intense connection with her?"

"Beats me."

"What was her name?"

"Lyn... Lyn Monday, I think we both wanted something special to happen but I was too young for a commitment."

"What makes you think that?

"Siobhan, it was just a childhood romance, an infatuation, where everything goes wrong, alright, no big deal," it was, "I must be going through a mid life crisis or something."

"Shaun, you know I'm the only one beside yourself to be exposed to this phenomenon and I know there is more to this than a childhood infatuation. You love her?"

I was shocked she used love in the present tense, "Yeah, strangely I do, do you find that bizarre? Do you think I'm weird?"

"Of course not, you are extremely fortunate to be in love, and I understand your predicament more than you could imagine. I admire you for having the courage to stand up for what you believe. Shaun, do you know about layered love?"

"No?"

"This is a term describing one's affection for others, like your mother is one form of love, while with a brother or sister, you could love them equally but differently, again with a friend, a girlfriend and a wife, all different loves and being layered upon each other, all important and fulfilling but certainly not monogamous. There is no such thing as being devoted to a single entity, only in an insecure world. With layered love it builds until you're 'brimming' and the more you have, the more you can give to others. I'm the first to admit people should develop their love and not inhibit their emotions. Of course, not every form of love demands sexuality. However many loves start out with lust, sometimes this is the basis for love, however love is more complex that just a one-nighter. You should never mix the signals, many people do. Take your reflexive action in the bathroom, I touch you, you being a normal male have a response, it wasn't love, it was what men do, they think sex, again you shouldn't mix up these signals nor should you feel guilty, it happens, it is completely natural. Remember, love comes later, again a difficult subject to define because of the varying degrees of intensity. So why do women expect one person's loyalty. Some go beyond comprehension, even resorting to brain-washing to maintain the hold, and once that starts, it limits the layering, then the male feels guilty and soon the marriage is stifled. The layering process, the one that creates the return of love is in shut-down, the marriage is self-defeating and under stress."

"Wow," that was all I could muster, I understood her theory completely, and I even endorsed it.

Then she shocked me further, "Shaun, I decided to try again. I don't care about Samantha or this Lyn, I'm back! Regardless of the outcome, I'm prepared to fight for you. I love you."

Still reeling from her confession I said off the top of my head, more to fill a lull in the conversation, "You're like Jack Nicholson."

Siobhan questioned, "What, like in the movie 'About Schmidt', someone caring and dedicated?"

"No, just Jack using a similar line as in the 'Shining'... 'Heeere's Johnny so Heeere's Siobhan'."

She said, "Very funny, I'm talking love and pouring my heart out while you're trying to be a comedian. You know your problem. You need a reality check. She snuggled closer and wrapped her leg across mine until her toes parted my legs. Let me look after you Shaun. Let me be your reality check, let me show you how to love."

I nodded. Could I really be agreeing to this?

"Now, what did this Lyn do to you that put you into such a mess?"

I explained each brief encounter but she wasn't convinced. Then I explained how Lyn's entrancing eyes held me captive and that's when then I hit the jackpot. Samantha had come to the same conclusion, which just reinforced my belief that I was under Lyn Monday's spell!

I was surprised when Siobhan said, "For a test only Shaun, I want you to kiss me."

"What are you talking about Siobhan?"

"Trust me, and to start with, you don't ask a woman why she wants to kiss you, you just do it."

She rose, pulled up her dress and straddled my lap. She moved her flaming locks off her face, wriggled her body to get comfortable and held my head tightly with both hands. Her head moved closer and her lips touched mine, gently. She lingered for a few seconds. I was hot and flustered. She was warm and close.

"Why did…?"

"Shh, we're not finished."

She touched my lips again and with more passion this time, her head rotated for a better angle. Mm… not a bad kisser.

When we broke apart, I was gasping for breath, "Wow!"

"We are not done here."

She returned, only this time with that little game, the one I had encountered years earlier. A Brenda kiss, the one where all the guys voted her number one.

Panting, I blurted out, "I see."

"No wait, there is one more."

She smiled seductively and moved against me again. Her mouth opened and we were engaging tongue and swapping angles until it seemed only fair to let her have her way. It was ten minutes later when we stopped.

I gulped at her body's intensity. "Ok, so what was that test about?"

"That test was for me, this next one is for you, it's about the eyes."

"Eyes?"

"Yes, look at me."

"Ok."

She looked normal, attractive and sexy, nothing out of the

ordinary for a beautiful looking woman many years my junior. She was incredibly hot and I felt every impulse awaken.

"Look this time."

There was a twinkle of mischief happening. I managed, "I see."

Somehow, her pupils looked huge and drawing then they danced wildly as if I was the only one on her mind. Another pool to dive into and immerse yourself – the attraction was identical to Lyn Monday's and I swear for a moment I saw a greenish tinge.

"The reason I'm doing this is because ..."

"You don't have to explain a thing."

"Are you sure."

"Oh yeah, you want sex."

She laughed. "Later on. I am trying to explain that women can be manipulative. Some have the gift, some don't. If you have it, you most times use it. Did Lyn Monday ever use her eyes like that with you?"

"Oh yeah. All the time, it was how we communicated I guess."

"If she used them on you, she would have used them on others. It would be rare for a person that gifted to remain a monogamous gazer. She had other boy-friends?"

"Yes."

"Honestly Shaun, a girl with that sort of gift is not going to sit around wasting her talent. These other guys would have been zapped as well. Shaun, I don't think you were an exclusive person to see those eyes operate. She may have realised her mistake by not fighting enough for you and now she's trying again."

"Siobhan, you just helped me through a major crisis. You can't believe how helpful you've been."

"I am good, aren't I?"

"You are actually, although this isn't just about love, there is something else going on. Siobhan, Lyn selected me to help her in someway. I can't lose sight of that but what could she possibly want?"

"I have no idea. I figure you'll find out when she is ready."

I lamented, "You're right, I shouldn't push so hard for answers, maybe by doing that I'm blocking her returning."

"Maybe, I have no experience with that, maybe it is best to relax and see what happens. After a moment's deliberation, "Are you comfortable with me?"

"I never thought I'd say this but surprisingly yes."

"How did I rate as a kisser?"

"Five."

"Out of five?"

"No ten," I lied.

CHAPTER 19

THE KISS TO END A RELATIONSHIP

Siobhan could capture and duplicate every kiss I considered important, she could also replicate Lyn's seductive heart stopping gaze, that look which had held me spellbound for years. Why had it taken so long to realise? Where had this woman been all my life? And now she presented her argument with such clarity it was difficult not to believe... Lyn may have used her eyes with others. She certainly had other boyfriends. Maybe I had overplayed Lyn's affection for me.

Siobhan then announced, "Not good enough, five out of ten is pathetic, we need more practice," and she straddled my lap again, looked into my eyes with a little grin, hoisted up her dress revealing taut inner thighs and repeated the whole torrid process. Our lips were locked and she leaned above me, slightly, just enough to ensure I was pinned. I wasn't going anywhere; I didn't want to, strange how my emotions could be changed so quickly.

Surprisingly, I didn't feel the slightest pang of guilt as she wrestled a willing victim. Samantha was now a distant memory... until I heard a cough... just one, an accentuated bark crudely delivered. I wanted to ignore it... I reluctantly opened my eyes, "Shit… Samantha…" I stammered for control, holding Siobhan at arms length. Samantha was leaning in the doorway arms folded and had been there… "Samantha… how long have you been standing there?"

"Long enough to know how unfaithful my husband is and how our 'friend' has no qualms stepping into my place."

Siobhan casually replied, "Samantha, things have changed." She climbed off my lap, pulled down her dress and sat at the end of the sofa. "It's no secret, I want Shaun, you walked away and it was as if fate brought us together. We've made plans to go to London."

I was flabbergasted.

Samantha stood shaking. She went to speak but her throat seized, resulting in a high-pitched squeak, she refused to continue for fear of appearing ridiculous. Her eyes pleaded for answers.

I requested, "Siobhan, can you give us a few minutes."

"I'll be in the kitchen."

When Siobhan left, Samantha questioned, "How long has this been going on?"

"It started a few minutes ago," I could tell Samantha didn't believe me.

"Is this what you want Shaun?"

"No, I want you Samantha but you were suffocating me. Can't we start again but have more understanding for each another?"

"This is me, take me the way I am, no adjustment, no twitching my dials to get the perfect woman. What is it then?"

"Well, I want to continue with Lyn's…"

"No, absolutely not."

I couldn't speak. Years of fond memories surfaced and then disappeared as quickly as they came.

"Well?"

I felt rushed, "Samantha, I don't want to say this but you really have become obstinate, there is no space left for discussion, no room for negotiation."

Samantha demanded, "I want a divorce!"

"It doesn't have to be like this, maybe you are in shock, you're angry, I apologise, I never wanted you to see me kissing another woman... I'm sorry."

"The kettles been simmering for too long, it's enough, I can't handle your infidelity with spirits or mortals, you've done your darnedest to push me away and it worked. I'm leaving."

Resigned to her direction I asked, "Where are you going to stay?"

"Why here Shaun, this is my home."

"Of course, where have you been staying?"

"In a hotel room, I cried continuously however now I'm over it. I need a new life away from this nonsense, and where will you be staying?"

Strangely bitter, I twisted the knife to extract the right amount of damage, "Apparently, I'm off to London and after that, who knows. You have the house Samantha, I don't want anything else, just enough to live on and maybe that money pit on the coast, agree?"

She snarled, which I took as a yes, "I have to say something Shaun, and you know me, I tell it as it is. This isn't going to last with Siobhan, this will be a fling, a once off affair; I assume you haven't gone all the way yet. Think of the age difference, shit, she's young enough to be..."

I interrupted, "Not really," although Samantha wasn't that far off the mark.

"Anyway, I'm bitterly disappointed in you Shaun. After all these years you've changed and for the worst. You've made me feel redundant, cheated and robbed of everything. You can have that stupid investment on the coast you deserve the pain."

"Samantha, you have every right to be bitter. I can't believe we are doing this although I don't think there is an option, we have grown so far apart there is no way to return, honestly I never saw this coming, I'm sorry for the heartache, I never wanted to hurt you, you do believe me."

"No, I don't, you knew before we were married that something was wrong and you refused to tell me. That's when this started. Christ, I can't believe we are discussing a dead girl being the catalyst in breaking us up; do you realise how sick that is? Then you move onto that flaming harlot." She twisted sideways to sight Siobhan but luckily she was out of view. She returned with venomous snipes at me, "Now go, before I do something stupid. I'm really about to lose it!" she sounded determined. I packed quickly taking only essentials and jagged memories. Was this really happening? Had I really left Samantha? I was suddenly elated; but why? I couldn't explain a thing, except surrealism appearing normal.

Siobhan produced a check-list for our London trip. Instead of feeling guilty about Samantha, I openly embraced the journey as a way to brush away the past, reline the cupboards and recharge the batteries. Siobhan proved that she could draw you in and hold you; there was no difference between what Lyn Monday had done and what Siobhan could produce; seemingly easy with a blink of those beautiful fluttering eyelashes. Her eyes appeared identical to Lyn's. Why hadn't I seen that power previously?

Siobhan and I went our separate ways, I insisted. I needed time to get my head around what had happened and if in doubt, pull out. I stayed at a hotel for the remainder of the night and the next day my feelings were still strong. After lunch I purchased an air ticket and then converted dollars to pounds. I was like a kid starting out; the feeling of attraction produced a heart thumping nervousness and it felt good, the chase was on and I was eager to see Siobhan again.

Later that night, we met at a restaurant, I figured with some distance between us Siobhan may have had second thoughts but she remained steadfast. I considered Lyn Monday's request for help, I couldn't ignore that but I was having problems recognising my exclusivity in her life, suddenly Siobhan had captured that entrancement and I was literally caught up with her energy, nothing else seemed important.

"Shaun, I'm so excited I could burst."

I smiled and held her hand across the table, inwardly I could have been doing back flips, the aches and pains had disappeared and I felt alive for the first time in years. I queried, "What is this place?"

"A place lovers come to find themselves, simply called... 'OS'. The 'OS' stands for Opera Singers and it boasts a lavish Carte du Jour."

It was a strange place; each table displayed a starched-white tablecloth that hung stiffly to the floor. Enormous chandeliers hung majestically from the lofty ceiling and painstaking recreations of the Masters decorated the upper walls. Green velvet lined the lower half. The restaurant hummed with excitement and that is exactly what the staff did for the first twenty minutes. Athlete's warm up and stretch; opera singers warm up and hum hoping to stretch their vocal cords. As each moment came, the chefs, the waiters, even the bus boys and the maitra'd joined in, and when it came time for us to order, a barrel-chested but handsome man presented us with menus and a full version of Oklahoma. At the conclusion, he clicked his heels as a salute and bided his time on the far side of the room awaiting our decision.

"That was different. I've never seen any...."

Before I could finish an attendant employed solely to pour water into large glasses began to sing Carmen. Other waiters joined in at the most appropriate moment, the four walls could barely contain their enthusiasm and although not a fan of opera, I was impressed. Their skill and devotions to bring this level of the art to the common diner was benevolent to say the least.

I ventured, "I hope we are able to talk."

"We have nothing to say, we know what we want."

"Siobhan, I wanted to check your still okay with this, you know I'm older than you, a lot older."

"Rubbish, age has nothing to do with it. She was just about to add something important when Franco, I now realised his name from the name-tag, came up to the table and accepted our order. He was singing Oh Sole O'Mio, which I was mellowing to, when a bottle of Dom was popped. The frosted stiletto glasses were so thin I thought the high notes would shatter the flutes. He reduced the volume and stealthily disappeared to the kitchen.

The drink waiter adopted the lead and poured the unique bubbles, the ones that remain in your mouth and danced frantically on your tongue. We toasted, tasted and continued sipping and I asked, "Why did you order for me?"

"Because I can, you'll enjoy it."

"That was Italian, wasn't it? How did you learn to speak with such fluency?"

"It's a high school thing. I ordered your favourite – Lamb's Fry."

"No, it's not, you didn't?"

"Yes, but its Italian Lamb's Fry."

"No. No, not the Italian Lamb's Fry, I hate it, tell me you didn't."

She laughed a full body tremble, completely at ease and gave me a wicked smile that was downright mischievous, "Silly, of course not. For starters, we're having oils and olive paste for dipping. Then I ordered a Carpetbag Steak stuffed with Sydney Rock Oysters and a side order of Kipher potatoes sprinkled with rosemary. Then, as an accompaniment to the side order, there are asparagus spears with Hollandaise. Don't you just love hollieee sauce?"

"Yes." I breathed as a sigh of relief. "I hate lamb. Lambed out as a kid."

She nodded as if she understood.

By the time the breads appeared, Siobhan had kicked off her shoes and had entwined her arched toes around the back of my calf. She edged it against a knotted muscle that surprisingly began to relax.

Everything in this restaurant was devoted to big and boisterous. I know of no opera singer who wants to whisper an aria, however when the food arrived our section went quiet and I noticed a lulling symphony of Mendelssohn drifting from speakers concealed in the floor.

"Do you like olives?" I asked.

"I'm acquiring the taste for them, my second time actually," I noticed it was her second bite.

"Siobhan why me? There has to be dozens of eligible guys who would fall at your feet."

"I want you."

"Why? Why me? I need to understand."

"No one else turns me on like you do and besides this isn't a new thing, I've already told you I've loved you for years. I go to bed thinking about you and I have dreams that need fulfilling. Many dreams, you'd be surprised at how inventive I can be."

"This is really flattering but I'm embarrassed, you're a stunning looking woman." She smiled coyly. "If it wasn't for what you did last night, that thing with your eyes, I don't think I would be contemplating being with you. You know I'm having problems getting over this... girl. I could never devote one hundred percent of myself to you."

"Shaun, we've discussed 'layering' that is the key to this. I realise you refuse to admit she's dead, I like that in you and why should you let go of someone you love. It doesn't worry me; it just makes you more interesting and complex. God knows, Tom was as boring as fly shit and as unfaithful as a paddock bull. The difference between you and him is that he hid his love for others and when you do that, it becomes a negative force."

"Stop Siobhan, what you are saying about Tom is exactly what I did to Samantha; I kept Lyn a secret from her. That's the reason for our break-up. My cheating on her is no different from Tom, so don't put me in a category holier than others."

"I understand but you are being honest with me and that's what matters. Of course, I feel sorry for Samantha but this will be a learning experience for the both of you. You will move on from here."

"I'm not sure about Samantha."

"That's her decision then. The way I see it, you are the sort of person who is prepared to love and not cave in to alter your opinion. You openly committed to this girl and I'm fine with that. Shaun, I want you to love me like that. Could you try? Can we try? Could you find room for me as well? I promise never, never to question your faith in me; you have my absolute resolve to support you."

"Siobhan, I doubt myself sometimes, don't count on me producing miracles."

"You still love Samantha, but differently, remember she was the one who walked away. Your love for Lyn Monday is different from Samantha's and your love for me will be different. All I need is one hundred percent of that different type of love. Don't stop loving Lyn, don't stop loving Samantha; promise?" I nodded, "Shaun, I'm excited, I can hardly wait for London, just you, me," she smiled, unable to retain her beaming grin, "It's been so long, now finally."

I wasn't sure I was doing the right thing but Siobhan was as excited as a three year old on Christmas morning and her gushing enthusiasm was dragging me along. Why hadn't I seen this side to her previously, she was brimming with great ideas, plans and… she wanted me with my baggage. The wine wasn't helping but there again it was, without its bubbly effervescence I may have vetoed her plans, but what of Samantha? Why had we ended our marriage with such haste? It was as if we both sensed the end, although Samantha would never admit it. She would play the victim for all it was worth. If anything, we knew the other intimately, we would often pre-empt each others thoughts. Over the years we had grown close, too close, and this was the problem, there was nowhere else to go but apart. Each day a repetitive unfurling of regimes and procedures, no wonder Lyn had caught my attention, and now Siobhan! Christ; what a whirlwind but somehow there was direction and an understanding that answers may perchance but I couldn't imagine how.

The night was over too soon and I looked forward to the alarm clock ringing in five hours.

CHAPTER 20

◀◦▶

LONDON OR BUST

I called a cab at four-thirty and by five, I was directing the turban – swathed driver to Siobhan's house. I still expected a complication, a headache, a tidal wave or even an outbreak of Malaria, something that might stop me leaving Australia, minutes later I found Siobhan ready and waiting kerbside. As the taxi approached, Siobhan waved excitedly. She looked gorgeous, a striking figure in green army fatigues and white sneakers, wow! I never thought anyone could look that bedazzling. Her scarlet hair hung carefree and as she entered the taxi she used those eyes to reinforce her appeal – a hint of green, a mesmerising heart stopping gaze adding justification to why I purchased the air ticket. The cab driver stowed her bag and we drove off holding hands.

At the airport, I remembered Beaulieu and called her to halt the research, the phone rang out. I couldn't leave a message. We boarded the plane in first class. I was barely able to contain Siobhan's enthusiasm and her infectious mood made light of everything, I didn't have a care in the world. The engines roared and our bodies pressured the seats on take-off, there was no retreating, no more doubt, I had broken away from Samantha and remarkably I hadn't thought of Lyn Monday for hours, not until this moment.

Siobhan asked, "Do you miss her?"

"Yes."

She said dismissively, "Samantha will be fine, don't worry."

"Sorry, I was thinking of someone else."

"Oh. That girl!"

"Yes."

"Sorry, your guardian angel and my competition."

"She's not your competitor Siobhan, you had to know her. She was… kind… considerate, she occupies my thoughts constantly; anyway, I would stake my life on her liking you." Siobhan gave me an accepting smile and sighed, it was as if that statement meant everything to her, after several minutes she said, "When we return, I will help you unravel her mystery, I will even massage your feet while you write about her."

"Sounds good, are you an expert in massage therapy?"

"Fingers that work miracles, you'll see. Shaun?"

"Yes."

"Thank you."

"Why thank me?"

"You're good for me. You think of others but at the same time consider me as someone special. I need that in a man. It feels good to be with you." It was my turn to smile. "Shaun, I can't believe you gave Samantha the house. You see what I mean? Who would break up with their wife and hand her the house without a fight? If everyone had that type of attitude there would be no need for lawyers."

"Samantha has been a good wife and mother; she doesn't need to start over. None of this was her fault and I can understand she couldn't handle what was happening but it was hard to understand her jealous and possessive nature. This whole thing is bizarre and you know that first hand. Samantha told me to make a decision, it was either her or Lyn, but strangely, it wasn't about that, not at all. It was a choice between understanding or not, it was something I couldn't let go of."

"This trip will be the best thing for you, a time to recharge the batteries."

"First, I needed to know, you have no regrets that Tom left?"

"Shaun, he was gone ages ago. I never did find out but I think he and his secretary were having an affair. What hurt most was his disappearance during the weekends, he would just up and leave without telling me and be gone for days, later citing business as his excuse."

"With you being a marriage counsellor, you never thought to correct that?"

"You realise early, especially in my profession that if something is broken, repairs are only a temporary solution. It's going to break again, each time weaker. All I was looking for was an excuse to end our marriage." She looked at me as if she had found one.

"And what about us Siobhan, how strong are we to start with?"

"Time will tell, we have the right ingredients, I have always loved you, although I realise that may not have been the case with you, for years you seemed contented with Samantha."

"Mm, contented, just drifting along, taking one day at a time and don't start me on love. I have absolutely no idea what women expect."

"I think you know exactly what love is."

I swallowed.

Siobhan continued without waiting for an answer, "This whole Lyn Monday thing has jolted you back to reality. You're a lucky man Shaun, three women to choose from, have you made the right decision with me?"

"You're a beautiful woman, and now caring, which I'm totally surprised by. You seem to have an enormous grip on where I'm at in life. I think you know me better than anyone. I don't know what the future holds but I'm game if you are."

She answered quickly, "And it will be fun finding out, a new adventure, I'm excited Shaun and if you tire of me I'll understand. No obligation, agree?"

We shook hands. Great, no pressure I thought. "Do you learn these things at marriage counselling school?"

She replied somewhat slowly, "We understand each other more than you could imagine." As I reached for the headphones, I asked Siobhan, "Guess what movie I'll be watching?"

"Let me see… it's not a movie, you're going to be listening to music, the Best of Santana then the comedy channel," she thought for a second, "Retro time with Bill Cosby."

"How did you know that?"

"It just popped into my head." She kissed me on the cheek and gave me another tantalising gaze, utilising those crazy little signals.

We were in touch and I couldn't help but feel a part of her. It was so unlike the old Siobhan who was always self-absorbed. Maybe she needed to shred Tom from the equation and have a fresh start and I noticed she wasn't wearing that perfume that went stale by 5 o'clock. She smelt fresh and I commented, "You smell nice."

"Thanks."

"I've smelt that fragrance before."

"It's just my cashmere soap," the in-flight attendant interrupted by offering drinks, to which Siobhan replied, "Bottled water for the both of us please."

"How did you know that? Normally I'd have a beer? But I thought I'd preserve the body and keep hydrated."

"I know. It's uncanny."

I looked quizzically at her and she gave me the cutest smile. I kissed her on the cheek, "You do smell good. Keep using that soap, it suits you."

"Thanks. Now close your eyes and listen to Carlos."

Black Magic Woman was playing, my favourite.

It was a long flight and by the time we arrived in Heathrow, Siobhan looked as fresh as when we started. We breezed through 'Intimidation' and our bags were already carousing the carousel, when we arrived in the Customs Hall, Siobhan lifted all the bags as if it was her responsibility to look after me. I insisted on pushing the trolley and when we came to the declaration point, we were summons through with a furious hand signal and dismissed as being desirable. Siobhan hailed a taxi, a strange occurrence for she didn't even look down the road. However, the driver was with us in seconds and shortly after we were on the motorway.

During my last trip to London, I noticed the drivers were a frazzled lot and blew their car horns incessantly. However, this time was such a stark contrast and everyone had matured with decidedly better manners. We had a speedy check in at the hotel. Siobhan insisted on looking after the account but she included my name on the registration form. Surprisingly, I was her guest and she was paying. I wondered how long this might last; at least until the credit card maxed out.

"Answer the door Shaun."

"I didn't hear a knock."

"There, you didn't hear that?"

It was the hotel in-room attendant. He wheeled in champagne, a fruit basket and a cheese platter. Siobhan tipped him handsomely and when he left, I asked, "This must be costing you a fortune."

To which she replied, "I received a windfall recently. Don't worry about the money, relax and think of me."

I kissed her neck passionately, she was driving me wild. We still hadn't consummated our relationship but any time now seemed a convenient time. We sipped the champagne. The bubbles were annoying her nose and eventually she placed the flute onto the coffee table and nibbled seductively on a cracker. She curled her legs onto the sofa and continued gazing at me. She used her fingers to rack her hair and shook her flaming locks letting the straggling ends drop below her curvaceous shoulders. Her eyes never left me. She tuned the radio to a nostalgia station that played early rock and old classics. The Chiffons, 'He's so Fine', provided a perfect backdrop.

So, with food, wine, a luxurious suite and nostalgic music playing, almost subliminally, we ventured into a state of mindless attention towards one another. This was the start of countless hours devoted to caring, without guilt, shame or remorse.

I washed her hair using the hotel's complimentary but luxurious shampoo. She closed her eyes and sighed as I massaged her scalp with more than consideration. My fingers caressed her slender neck; her shoulder muscles and the lobes of her ears, all divine to the touch. The water was warm, sensual, encouraging us to a heightened state of arousal. Sweet perfumed jasmine wafted the air. She raised her hand and I gently kneaded my knuckles against her palm until each movement became a symphony of rhythmic attention, I swear that if it was possible, our hands were already in orgasm and falling in love. Every part of my body was prepared to go through this duty of devotion, commitment and acceptance. We did. We worshipped the temple of the body. Naked, she was stunning, tight waisted, ample breasts, fine porcelain skin; there was no hint of regret. I couldn't figure out why me, there had to be thousands of younger guys out there for her.

Day after day, it rained and when it ceased, a dense fog replaced the inclemency and bringing a charcoal grey to our window. It was so thick it cut visibility to zero. The city was in gridlock, a perfect excuse to remain in our luxury suite, nick – named, the 'Kasbah'. We ate, slept and played like young lovers until the whole process repeated itself. I prayed the rain would bucket down for weeks and the mist would envelope us forever. This was the most sensual time of my life, a new steamy awakening where Siobhan kept pushing the boundaries. We craved intimacy; she kissed me everywhere, running the gauntlet of options. When we made love, there was the arousal, the caressing and a satisfying unity; those gripping cycles that drove me wild and they came in twisting turbulent sets that culminated in ferocious climaxes – a tornado of blissful rapture so powerful I craved the next. These moments could last forever.

It was early and as a form of respite, Siobhan insisted on researching Lyn Monday's death. I had left my notes behind but had a reasonable recall of events; I also remembered Beaulieu's interpretation.

"Where do we start Shaun?"

"The way Lyn died was questionable."

"There was foul play?"

"Possibly," I explained Malcolm Shailler, the pharmacist's involvement and what I knew about my lying high school friend, Josh Freemont

"What did you feel after her death?"

"Devastation, I had missed the funeral by two weeks."

"Did her other boyfriends go to the funeral?"

"I don't think so."

"That is so sad; three people close to her missing the funeral."

"Lyn died on a Saturday morning and by Tuesday morning she was laid to rest. When you think about the time frame, everything appeared rushed, especially considering there was the police investigation, an autopsy, and the funeral preparations. I don't know how her family coped. It's such a tragedy."

"Shaun, sit close to me."

"I don't dare, you know what will happen."

She smiled, those eyes shifted into gear, enticing, sensuous, it was all I could do to continue talking. I stood and moved around the room trying to focus. I changed the subject, "The weather is still zeroed-out." She patted the sofa for me to sit beside her.

I relented. She smiled contentedly as I edged between the sofa's armrest and her curves. We snuggled close, "Shaun, no regrets?"

"Absolutely not, this has got to be the best time of my life. What about yourself?"

"Do I look happy?"

I teased, "No, you look absolutely miserable; we can pack up and go if you want."

She leaned forward and whispered close to my ear with a simple questioning word that would determine my resolve, "Me?" her breath warm. Her lips brushed my lobe sending little impulses to tingle the skin. She was asking for my commitment, it was the simplest of questions, instead of asking, 'Do you love me?' all she asked was... 'Me?'

I responded, "You," she held my hand in the tightest of grips and rested her head on my shoulder, she sighed contentedly.

I needed to know, "Me?"

She didn't raise her head only breathed gently like a summer zephyr, "You."

There... our commitment to each other. Simply stated and uncomplicated: resounding and binding nonetheless.

It must have been five minutes later when Siobhan returned to the topic, "So your friend Josh Freemont was lying?"

"Yes, he slipped up on a lie, admitting to me forty-five years later that Lyn was his girlfriend. Christ, I was his mate, he never told me about this relationship even though I was always telling him how much I liked her. I feel betrayed. I have no problem with Lyn choosing another person; that was her decision, I would have liked it to be me but I was a disaster with girls."

"Shaun, that was then, now you handle everything just fine, trust me," she smiled a satisfied grin, "Tell me more about Malcolm Shailler."

"He was studying pharmacopoeia and into his third year at university. Word had it that Malcolm was handsome, a ladies man. I think Lyn was attracted to his image, many girls thought him a catch. A young girl meets a guy, six years older; she is sixteen he is twenty-two. He is charming, good looking, attentive and has a responsible job as a chemist but the problem was... he lacked fortitude."

"Did he know that red medicine could be lethal?"

"He claims he didn't until she died – a load of crap! Lecturers of pharmacopoeia had a responsibility to instruct their students in the dangers of overdosing; I find it difficult to believe Malcolm Shailler didn't know. Regardless, Shailler had a position of trust with Lyn but he let her down."

"Trust?"

"Pharmacists are revered as people to rely on. You trust them for the correct information. My thoughts are, there should have been charges laid for manslaughter and if he purposefully misled her, it maybe murder. It all comes down to the truth spoken between them. He had to have known that overdosing would be lethal. I don't buy his police statements. They were too contrived, clinical. He had a memory lapse trying to recall Lyn's last few words; which just happen to be a question about the Mickey Finn red mixture and should she take it, possibly to terminate the pregnancy; very convenient for him to forget. Why would Lyn take more than the prescribed amount unless he encouraged her or misled her?

"But for what reason?"

"He didn't want the baby and refused to admit it was his. They had many arguments; he refused to marry her. Lyn must have been petrified, alone, and having to face her parents. She would have been panicking. He may have been pressuring her to terminate the pregnancy. Remember these were difficult times and less liberating when compared to today. Malcolm must have told Lyn to take a strong dose of medicine, anything to fix the problem. Anyway, that is my theory."

"And he lied at the Inquest?"

"His evidence and statements were inconsistent.

"You sound bitter Shaun."

"I am bitter, especially when someone is used." Siobhan looked concerned, "He lied. The jury is still out with Josh Freemont but with Malcolm Shailler he had to have told Lyn to take that medicine; anything to make her sick and abort the baby. This wasn't his first attempt at a pharmaceutical abortion."

"Oh."

"I can never forgive him for this; he gave Lyn prescription tablets illegally. This was his first attempt to rid himself of the problem. He covered this up by telling Lyn the tablets would encourage her periods. Unfortunately, that is only part of the truth. These tablets were a potent drug and frequently caused birth defects. He had no right to give her tablets without a doctor's prescription. He didn't even…"

Siobhan surprised me when she stood quickly and dismayed me further when she rushed to the bathroom and locked the door. She remained there for some time. I listened at the door but all I could hear was the sound of her sobbing and then the pulling of tissues from a box. She was clearly distraught. I sat against the door, "Siobhan, are you alright?"

"I'm just upset, it will pass, I'm sorry…"

"Don't be, I should have been more sensitive."

She released the lock and the door drew open, she looked a pitiful mess similar to when she was in hospital. "I'm so sorry."

"Hold me Shaun, tightly, promise you'll never let go of me. No matter what!"

"Of course, I'll never let go, I gave you my word. Remember me: you, you just don't say those words if you don't mean them."

She cuddled closer on the couch, I had never seen this side to her previously it wasn't a bad side, this raw emotion, this vulnerable woman, once I hated her brashness but now I loved her fragility, it seemed remote our loyalty might be tested. Maybe we needed to escape the Kasbah. It was only 9 am maybe see a movie, a play, something light hearted; perhaps dinner tonight, anything to raise her spirits.

I could not have guessed what came next.

CHAPTER 21

VIKINGS OR KING ARTHUR?

Siobhan returned to the bathroom to freshen up. My mind raced for answers, what could we do? Just about anything would be a better alternative than drawing references from the past. I knew how addictive the subject was and how draining Lyn's story had become. I couldn't let Siobhan slip into that morbidity. Before I could reach a decision, the phone rang. I retrieved the handset and answered. There was no response but I could hear someone breathing, "Hello… hello," I persevered.

The call terminated.

Siobhan, oblivious to the phone call said, "I know what we can do but you'll need to be a little sneaky."

"Why?"

"Because it is closed."

"What's closed?"

"Where we are going silly."

The phone rang again.

This time Siobhan picked up the receiver, "Hello."

The call terminated again.

Siobhan looked puzzled.

"Who was it?"

"I don't know, anyway let's go."

"Are we breaking into some place?"

"Yeah, but we have every right to be there, as long as you can keep your nerve." It was a teasing look; she then grabbed her bag and held the door open.

"Do I need anything?"

"Just me," she giggled and I felt better she was over the blues.

As we exited the elevator, she held my hand and literally dragged me through the foyer heading to the front desk where the manager handed her a white sealed envelope. We exited the hotel to find a Land Rover parked out the front. It had a sticker which advertised the rental company, it said... 'NO GUYS', which I figured was a similar play on an Australian company, who used... "NO BIRDS'. She opened the envelope and withdrew a key; she tossed it into the air for me to catch and said, "Drive."

"But... I left my driver's license in the room safe."

"So?"

I disengaged the central locking and we drove away, recklessly abandoning protocol.

The day was a complete contrast to the previous, the sun was out and the road was almost dry. Siobhan didn't talk, only pointing to our direction. We were heading south, away from the city scrawl to lush green meadows and rolling hills. I suspected the beach. Siobhan sat at an angle looking at me rather than the road. It must have been forty minutes before I spoke, "I'm trying to figure out how a rent-a-car just happened to be outside the hotel waiting for us. Don't you need a contract before driving away?"

"All done when I booked the hotel."

"And our destination?"

"My place to think."

"Which is?"

"Turn left now. We don't want the main entrance, that will be shut, we want a dirt trail, keep your eyes peeled."

"A dirt trail after all this rain will be..."

"Four wheel driving, you can handle one of these beasts can't you Shaun?"

"Do I look like I've been driving Holden's all my life?"

"Mm, pretty much."

"But where are we going? Have you been here before?"

She didn't or wouldn't answer.

"There, go right and keep driving, don't slow or we'll be stuck in mud."

Five muddy minutes later; I was amazed. We were alongside one of the great mysteries of the world – Stonehenge!

The place was deserted. It looked magnificent with mossy grassed surrounds and sheer monumental extrusions, this balanced uniquely with rocky beams giving weight to the mystery.

"Siobhan, why are we here?"

"Come with me."

She was out of the Rover with a spring in her step and didn't stop until she was standing at the mid-point of this historic ruin.

"Siobhan, why are we here?"

"Shh, let me think."

She sat on a rock and closed her eyes while I walked the perimeter. I was amazed at the structure and on a sign leading to the ruins it gave theories of how man had constructed this sacred site. Although no theory could be proven the only clue lay in some of the rocks which originated from Wales some 200 kilometres away. Only fifty rocks remained. The balancing rocks weighed in at more than 40 tonnes with the uprights being considerably heavier. How could they lift that type of weight? As a final tribute the sign reported that the structure had taken 700 years to build and was over 4500 years old. Some theories considered the structure to be created by King Arthur while others had Nordic myth interwoven in its development. I guess it was no different to the Aztec and the Egyptians who had toiled for centuries to create magnificence.

I continued walking the perimeter but when I looked for Siobhan she was gone. I couldn't see her anywhere. A strange emptiness engulfed me, it was then I looked up and Siobhan was standing on top of a rocky beam. She had removed her clothes and stood with hands raised above her head – legs equally apart. I gasped. I couldn't imagine how she had climbed without me seeing her. This was not a time to call her name nor was this a time to question. I was more concerned she might fall. The sun seemed drawn to her, glowing the brightest of golden rays.

It was minutes later when she lowered her arms and lifted her shoulders several times to relax. She turned towards me and smiled.

"Siobhan," I called out, "How?"

"I practice rock climbing." She laughed, "Can you believe that?"

"Well?" I wasn't sure.

"Can you catch me Shaun? I'm coming down."

"No don't. I don't want you hurt, wait there, I'll get help."

"Nonsense," she dressed and lowered herself over the edge. I moved closer. "Wait." But she wouldn't. I looked around to see if anyone was coming. When I looked back she was several finger holds above me. She let go and with instinctive reflexes I caught her descent.

"Shit Siobhan, don't scare me."

"Kiss me Shaun, taste a woman energised."

There was no way to argue. There was no reason to. We kissed like it was our first and then I realised what she was referring to. My body lifted, she was giving me life, she was giving me years of youth, was it my imagination? What was this place? Why hadn't others realised it potential.

In the Rover I said, "You're special."

"I know, so are you."

"I don't want anything to happen to you, please don't try that again."

"I promise, it was a once off."

"Have you been here before?"

"No, first time."

That had me wondering, how did she know her way into the reserve, when it came to direction, Samantha was an abysmal nightmare. I couldn't help but ask, "If this was your first time here, how did you know it would be closed to the public?"

"After all that rain it was a natural conclusion and besides it was reported on the news last night."

"But ..."

Before I could ask she interrupted, "I studied this area as a school project. I know it backwards. You wouldn't believe I got a ninety-eight percentile on that assignment."

I told Siobhan the various theories surrounding the Stonehenge creation. She said she already knew and how they erected the stones, even how they managed to bring the stones to this location. "How?"

"Some stones were gouged from the Marlborough Downs area a mere thirty kilometres away while the rest came from Wales which is a considerable journey."

"Two hundred clicks," I advised sounding like an expert. "But to erect the stones would have been impossible. You just can't have that many hands on such a small surface, it's impossible to control."

"They built ramps and dug holes for the perpendicular supports and then used logs to slide the stones into place allowing each to drop into their predetermined hole."

"But what about those beams, the one you were standing on for example? How could they lift those so high?"

"Again a slightly higher ramp was built and the beams rolled onto the top of the supports. Later you dig away the dirt ramp, leaving 'Stonehenge'.

"Is this your theory?"

"I just know it's a magical place!"

I had no reason to question her, except for rock climbing? Maybe!

Thirty minutes later...

We stood between thatch-roofed houses on narrow twisting lanes, each snaked a compass direction and serviced the habitable down called Castle Glen. Here retailers sold everything from pork pies to pot belly ovens. We drank coffee from a tea house which seemed a ridiculous concept and they offered 'high tea' which couldn't be confused as 'high coffee'. Siobhan was glowing. The sun was warm the air brilliantly alive.

Then, as if by chance I sighted a guy looking at us, it was a fleeting glimpse. I dismissed his stare as innocent except his eyelids flittered once too often. He quickly turned. Instantly I thought of Samantha hiring a private investigator, was she checking on us? When I looked again he was gone. I remembered his shirt, a pale yellow, unobtrusive, he would have been in his late thirties with rough features as if his nose had been broken regularly. My mind was working overtime. Why would Samantha have us followed?

"Shaun? What's the matter?"

"Sorry, I thought I saw someone. It's nothing," I didn't have the heart to tell her my suspicions.

I tried to relax but should have known Samantha would never let go. It had been so simple to sever ties but now she was heading for a meltdown, something unprecedented, sweet revenge maybe, or stripping me of every emotion until I couldn't love again. I should never have mentioned Lyn Monday, talk about inflaming the enemy and telling Samantha I loved Lyn had been the biggest mistake of my life. Now, I had Siobhan creating heady imagery, what a whirlwind!

Siobhan diverted my attention, for amid these colourful shops one stood alone. It sold potions, liniments, candles, oils, tonics and spells. The signage announced, 'Future Shock'. I didn't know if this was an attraction or a deterrent however its wafting essences was as enticing as oregano from a pizzeria.

Siobhan excitedly announced, "Potions are cool," and she side-stepped into the shop. I did a fast walk to keep up. Sure enough, there were little bottles lined in numerical order, one to thirty-one. Siobhan said, "My shout," but I insisted, "Let me, you've got the room to pay for." She reconsidered quickly and nodded, adding a sheepish smile that had me worried.

"I may have left my driver's license but I always have some cash on me," I added softly, "In case we need to bribe someone."

"Whatever for?"

"Well you acted as a heathen and desecrated Stonehenge. Thank God no one caught us. Imagine the headlines... 'Aussie girl found cavorting at sacred site'."

She laughed mischievously.

We held hands and I took a deep breath. Within a minute we had decided to purchase a surprise for each other. I made her turn her back when I asked for a love potion No. 9. This was a popular choice according to the proprietor. She was a plump short woman who offered a palm reading service with every bottle, a decisive deal clincher. Before I made the transaction I asked, "Why so many potions?"

"Love is complex, I know of sixteen hundred love potions all currently available and some work better than others. I only sell the best."

"Wow, sixteen hundred, you're kidding?"

With my little bottled gift wrapped, Siobhan turned and grabbed my arm, she ventured, "Isn't he the cutest."

I smiled and the saleswoman sighed heavily, a rehearsed reaction when discussing love. I knew they were playing me, gently, as if what I was asking was venturing into a woman's domain rather than a man's.

Then eagerly, Siobhan leaned forward and whispered into the woman's ear. Her eyes widened and from below the counter she withdrew a small jar with a screw top lid. The glass was smoky and the contents undefinable. There was no label, industry standard or barcode, just the jar. Both handled it cautiously, the saleswoman refused to take any payment, however I had to pay ten pounds for my potion. I gave her twenty and as I put my hand out for the change she took my hand. She cast her eye along the lifeline more as a precursor to my reading. She looked me in the eye, bit her lip and let go. I had no idea why Siobhan was now holding my arm tighter as if expecting the worse. The proprietor revealed a change in my life and there would be a disruption with women, well that had happened already. She studied my hand again. Then she warned, "There is someone you cannot trust, take great care."

I asked what she meant but she shrugged her shoulders and looked as if only the palm had the answer. Then she announced that romance would be my guiding force. Some years of money worries then the path to riches assured. I had a gut feeling she wasn't telling me everything. She snuck a quick glance at Siobhan hoping I didn't see.

As we left the shop I couldn't contain my inquisitiveness, "What was that palm reading about?"

"Nothing, it's all silly tripe."

"Nothing? I saw the looks you were getting."

She shrugged at my attempt to pry.

"Siobhan, what's in the jar?"

"A love aid."

"A sex toy?"

"No silly," as if she needed one of those.

"But I don't understand. What is it?"

"It's a surprise. Why would I go and spoil everything by telling you."

She carried the jar in both hands as if the contents contained something unstable – like nitro-glycerine and the slightest stumble or drop in temperature could prove disastrous. We walked to the car; Siobhan seemed keen to return to London.

CHAPTER 22

———◄O►———

MY RIBS

On the motorway I checked the rear view mirror but no one was following, as a further precaution I surveyed the hotel's exterior. Next, I entered the foyer but doubled back to catch out the private investigator, but zilch!

Siobhan asked, "What are you doing?"

"Checking to see if the car was locked."

"Of course it is."

We entered the foyer and handed the keys to reception, "Drives well," I commented, "But it needs a wash."

The smartly dressed female concierge offered, "I'll look after it sir,"

Maybe Samantha wasn't paying enough for twenty-four hour surveillance. Maybe the private investigator already had the evidence.

Was my imagination playing tricks, my only concerns had been two terminated phone calls and a sly glance to raise suspicions? As I closed the hotel door a strange closeness beset me, as if the unknown would take precedence over my life. On reflection, that was how the past had unfolded so what was different? I slid the key across the table and looked at Siobhan, she was on the far side of the table facing me. Her hands still gripped that tiny jar. She carried a look that was serious, as if business needed to be completed and she needed space to accomplish this.

I asked, "Did you enjoy today?"

"Yes, of course."

"I think I'll take a shower?"

"Ok, good idea, you start." Siobhan reinforced, "You go, I need to prepare."

Something was up, "Prepare what?"

"I'll join you soon," she nodded and waved me off.

Her mind was elsewhere and I went to the bathroom and turned on the shower to remove the freezing residue always lurking dormant in long plumbed pipes. A minute later and with a splutter, hot steam began to rise; I adjusted the temperature. The water streamed and a mist enveloped the room. That exact moment the door drew open and her nakedness caught my attention, superbly figured, breasts full with firm raised nipples. She did a whole circle displaying her body, carefree as a soaring eagle. Her buttocks toned and her leg muscles firm. Her waist the tightest of circumferences, I reached out to touch her hips but she pulled away.

"Look all you want, but don't dare touch."

I looked in amazement wondering what would happen if I did. On the side of caution, I circled my finger for her to turn once more. She did and ever so slowly, as if she could read my mind. Every inch of her was of goddess proportions, an absolute Venus. The base of her back, just above her beautiful rounds were tiny dimples which I would have loved to run my fingers across, besides her eyes they had to be her most 'turn-on' asset. Her stomach muscles had gentle rolls finely sculptured and evenly spaced. They would be divine to touch; why not?

"Siobhan, can I...?"

"No... no... no touching."

I heaved with frustration.

"Your turn," she demanded.

"What."

"Your turn... go... turn around... parade."

I turned slowly, not a man thing. I felt clumsy but she insisted,

"Well, are you going all the way or are you leaving on those ridiculous boxers?"

Not enough steam to cover my assets, always the way, never enough.

I knew once they were gone I would be aroused.

She jokingly ordered, "How can I see you with that impediment?"

I tugged and dropped, leaving them at my feet.

Again, she insisted, "All the way."

I gave a double shuffle and with a kick they went flying through the air landing somewhere near the basin.

She moved close, "Shut your eyes and don't open them until I tell you."

I could feel her breath on my chest. She had to be millimetres away, her exhalations light and warm, panting and irregular, as if she was already aroused. How close could she get without touching? I imagined she was much closer, so close it was tingling my skin and bristling the finest of hairs. It was not the only thing bristling. I felt uniquely firm and without a touch to encourage me. Her breath moved lower, across the deep pit of my navel and lingered at the base of my extension, again her breath was all it took. I formed fists trying to resist the temptation to touch and look. The warmth drove me wild and extended the complete length. She must have knelt for I felt a cooling breeze from underneath. A directional wafting so minute it barely existed. My clenched fists were determined to control my physical side; my mind could look after the incidentals. I sensed her hands inside my parted legs gently airbrushing the skin then up the outside until she was at my hips. Her lips must have been next to mine, close, so close but we still didn't touch.

She circled my body and did nothing other than be close, skin almost on skin. Then she was gone and I heard the drumming of the shower spray disrupted by gentle splashes. The shower door closed with a bang. Was that it?

Her voice raised above the shower, "Joining me? You can open your eyes now."

We kept our distance in the shower. I handed her the soap and she handed me the shampoo. I craved her touch more than anything but there was something else happening here, a sense of electricity and to touch would extinguish the charge.

We left the bathroom and Siobhan commandeered the sofa watching an old movie, her legs curled beneath her.

"Siobhan, can I sit close?"

"No, later."

"Have I done something wrong?"

"Not in the least, this is just as hard for me as it is for you."

"You're teasing me."

"I know, don't you just hate having to wait but it will be better this way."

"I doubt it."

"Shaun, let's watch television."

"That's a better alternative to watching you, just sitting there, I think I'll explode. Later we can do dinner and when we come back, will we...?"

"Of course. I've got the ultimate surprise for you."

"Is this anything to do with that jar?"

"Maybe."

"But you're not going to tell me or give me a hint?"

"No, women need to keep some secrets, you know everything else about me."

"Well, I know what we can do in the meantime," I retrieved the gift wrapped No. 9.

She ripped the paper apart, "A No. 9, of course. You want me to take it, you want to ensure my allegiance, my absolute faith in you, seal my love and prevent me looking at others."

"Well no... well yes, not exactly that, more a little game we can play."

"There is no need, I'm a goner already but I'll play," but before I could say a word she twisted the top and poured the entire contents into her mouth. She swallowed and sat the empty bottle on the small table next to her, "There, I'm yours forever, satisfied."

"I think you were only meant to drink half and leave some for me."

"Oh well."

"But the poem… I'm supposed to read the poem as you drink."

"Quick," she said, "Catch," and the bottle returned to me on a straight trajectory and I turned the bottle and began reading…

LET THE ONE WHO SIPS THIS NO. 9
BLESS ME WITH LOVE SO DIVINE.
SWEET LOVE POTION NO. 9
INSURE HER LOVE FOR ALL TIME

I said concerned, "I hope we weren't too late with the poem, you're supposed to sip the potion, not gulp it down," My investment of ten pounds was at risk. Siobhan had the biggest grin imaginable as if she had been toying with me, her grin then reduced to a satisfied smile and she returned to watching the Greta Garbo black and white.

I monitored her for side effects but nothing happened. I slept for a short while and when I awoke, Siobhan smiled dreamily and said, "I told you Tom and I split."

"Yes. Are you thinking of him?"

She shuddered a little but didn't answer me.

"Siobhan, are you thinking of him?"

"Who?"

"Tom."

"Tom, why would you mention Tom?"

"I didn't, you did."

She said slightly vexed, "No I didn't."

Later we dressed for dinner, we never looked or touched in all that time; normally we couldn't keep our hands off one another, so much for a workable love potion.

Her exit from the bedroom was something to behold, not only was she dressed in a low cut slinky dress made from fabric that graced every curve, she had pony-tailed her beautiful hair to the side which would have attracted heads at Royal Ascot.

"You look stunning."

She smiled and commented, "So that's what you look like all scrubbed and willing."

We had no idea where we were going and we exited the hotel's revolving doors holding hands, a good start for a close evening. I checked the street for our private investigator but the side walks were vacant and each parked car, deserted. I was disappointed with Samantha's antics.

We walked slowly, Siobhan's high heels clicked the pavement, she asked, "What day is it?"

"Monday," I answered.

"Oh."

"Why?"

"What day did you say?"

"Monday."

"Something about today... something I had to do... can you remember?"

I stopped walking, "Are you alright?"

She ran her hand across her forehead, "Silly me. I just went blank for a second."

Strange; I placed my hand around her waist and held her tighter than I should have, I could feel her slender figure and I think no underwear.

"Siobhan, are you roaming free?"

"Yeah, can you handle a woman that wild?"

I held her as tight as possible cautious not to bruise the merchandise – we walked on.

She appeared perfectly normal, although amorous to a fault.

We lingered outside a restaurant, an old pub with a new theme called 'Cavern of Dreams', this being no further than one hundred metres from the hotel. This unique establishment oozed charm and the enticing aromas wafted through the front door making it hard to resist. Once inside, we found a booth, a flickering candle lit the table and under its intensity we perused the menu. I had second thoughts. I saw Miggly Ox-tail and White Wine Soup, it was a menu item too gross to contemplate, instead I placed my faith in Siobhan's selection. She closed her eyes, circled her finger into a wide sweep and jabbed at the menu. I could not believe how apt her selection was... 'Lover's Ribs', smoked with hickory', a serving for two – just perfect.

She worked her toes between my legs and rested her foot in the most tantalising of positions. Her eyes went to work on me; I could have melted, minutes of saying nothing, just looking at her face, such incredible beauty, her eyes flirting with me every second. It was hot and cold shudders all blending into one. I would never get over this woman, never forget the heights to which she was taking me. The meals arrived too soon and she kept her foot positioned just right, even though the waitress hovered above with only a table to block her view. The plates came with large white tie on napkins that enable us to contain the free-flowing caramelised sauce. Beef ribs, slow cooked, huge, tender, the meat was literally falling from the bone and they tasted divine. Sauce surrounded Siobhan's lips and we kissed openly saving the wet towels for later. Accompanying the platter plates was a bowl of steamed potatoes, which must have had thirty little suckers wrapped in their jackets and drowned in butter. We drank warm beer, stoutish and obscene with a thick head, higher than an inch.

"Tell me about that jar."

"No."

"Why not?" I joked, "I'm nervous," it was true, there was a certain amount of trepidation.

"You need to experience this without the hype, you need to experience this raw unique love, and you can wait a bit longer can't you? Think of me without undies."

"You had to mention that, didn't you?"

"Am I being too forward?"

"You're just great, please don't stop."

It was our night for indulgence, there was no one else in the world and then she asked the strangest question, "Where did I leave my car?"

I was already feeling apprehensive but now my concerns were multiplied – what had that love potion done to her?

CHAPTER 23

────◀○▶────

THE JAR

Why would Siobhan ask about a car? There wasn't one. Of course there was the rental car but that had been handed back. Each time she said something out of character I detected a little shiver. I hoped she wasn't getting a cold which might explain her odd behaviour... but still, that love potion might be playing its role.

I finally answered, "There is no car, you didn't bring a car. Do you mean the rent-a-car?" I reached across and felt her forehead.

She said, "Of course I didn't bring a car, we walked here. What are you doing?"

"I'm checking if you have a temperature." I took hold of her hand, "Siobhan, are you alright?"

"Of course silly, why do you ask?"

"The car... you wanted to know where you had left the car."

"Unlikely, maybe I said, 'where did I leave the jar'?"

"Maybe it's my hearing, sorry." I thought I would monitor her anyway. These strange comments started after she drank that Love Potion. What was in that vial of No. 9?

Siobhan reflected, "Today has been one of the best days for me, with the exception of this morning when we discussed Lyn,

I don't want to talk about her while on holidays, do you mind? It's not as if I don't care, it just upsets me too much. When we return to Australia, I'll be fine. Back to business then, huh?"

"I understand," in light of this morning's emotional outburst, I was going to suggest the same. I couldn't imagine the flight back, already I felt empty thinking about it. The thought of facing Samantha would be depressing, why did she need to spy on me? I resolved to ignore the problems for tonight and concentrate on Siobhan – she was my future now.

"Dessert, the final accompaniment where lovers commit their future."

"What did you just say?"

She answered, "Dessert, the final accompaniment where lovers commit their future."

"Are you reading that from the menu?"

"Yes, it says it here... see," and she leaned forward to show me the spot on the menu.

"It a selling ploy," Siobhan looked devastated at my casualness. "Siobhan, we have already committed, remember... Me: You, you do remember? You scoffed that potion and something mysterious is going to happen. Now you want me to participate with another test?"

"But this is different, it'll be fun, go on Shauneee pleaseeeeeeeeee."

When confronted by 12 vowels I always found it difficult to say no.

Hesitantly I ventured, "Alright, dessert then, a mouthful, I shouldn't have had those two sides of beef."

Again, she closed her eyes and circled the wagons before resting her finger on the first dessert heading the list, a Devil's Advocate Chocolate Cake, in the middle of each chocolate dessert contained a little card wrapped in plastic, to test your devotion, or if careless, a choking demise.

She giggled; her eyes wide with anticipation. Minutes later the dessert arrived and she read, "My test is 'FOREVER'. That is just perfect."

"What does that mean?"

"It means I'll be around forever." She smiled excitedly.

"Let me read mine. I ripped the plastic apart. It simply stated… 'TOMORROW'."

"Then we will see tomorrow. Wow, your test starts tomorrow, so soon." She suddenly looked sad.

"What does it mean… tomorrow?"

"You will be tested tomorrow silly."

"Why so glum?"

"I'm not glum, just reflective," she breathed heavily but I still thought she looked forlorn.

As we left the restaurant it started to drizzle, too light to worry about and besides we needed to walk off the meal, we were crammed to the brim with succulent protein and oily carbohydrates mostly refined from a factory. It was all we could do to walk straight. Maybe it was the stout or Grand Mariner aiding the compass's indiscretions. Whatever the reason we were satisfied and in need of nothing other than each other's company. I had never thought I could be this attached to anyone. As we walked, the alcohol possessed us. We watched the Thames flow, splattered by raindrops. The inclemency had returned and when I looked up, the Tower of London was being drenched by steam lit floodlights. We kissed passionately already soaked to the skin, I felt like humming, 'Singing in the Rain' but that wouldn't work unless I danced. I considered the Beach Boy's, 'Good Vibrations', anything to lift our spirits although harder to accomplish considering the backing tracks were mixed in post production. The air felt dense, an air of expectancy surrounded us, altogether a volatile mix for mayhem. Siobhan challenged, "So my test is forever, yours is tomorrow, are you up to it?"

"What?"

"For you, a test of your devotion, you do love me?"

"Of course I love you, but why do I have to prove it?"

"Because I ask. It is important to me, more important than you could imagine."

"What do you want me to do?"

"Put your life on the line, show me you are special."

"Siobhan, really, is this necessary?"

"I wouldn't ask unless it was."

"Then whatever you ask I will attempt."

"Swim the Thames for me." She laughed frivolously, encouraging me to be recklessness…. "Now."

"Okay."

I started to undo the buttons on my shirt. I cast my eyes across the water, the distance I estimated was two hundred metres and the tide was on the cusp. Sure, I could do it.

"Shaun, no, I'm kidding, but see, you would have. Come with me, my lover, my everything – indulge me some more." She didn't wait for an answer only dragging me along the rain drenched street until we were above steps that dropped to the river, wide enough for two, stone masoned, rough cut and lapped with water.

We removed our shoes and let the water slap our ankles. The water swirled around her dress. It was freezing, I was grateful she pulled the plug on that swimming request.

"Give me a kiss my handsome Prince."

"Siobhan this is not a scene from Enchanted."

"It is," she laughed. I kissed her. "Hold me," and with the water still at our feet I held her body close, we faced the opposite shore, her head tilted back resting against my chest.

"My Prince is prepared to swim that foul smelling river with swirling currents and dangerous rips, what am I prepared to do for him?"

"Siobhan, you don't have to do a thing, I just want you, nothing more, no proof, no test, I'm just grateful I found you."

"I must do something, it's important I give you a present, you must see for yourself that I'm committed. I'll always be there for you. Do you believe me?"

"I have no doubt but I want nothing."

A moment later, "A lift squire?" It was the strangest thing; it was the cabbie, the one from the airport. We walked up the stairs and followed him, he returned to his London cab. There were towels waiting for us. We dried our feet and sat close.

I was full of questions but asked nothing. Why did I have to prove myself? What was she thinking and did she have the cabbie on stand-by just waiting for our freezing Thames exit?

I opened the hotel's door and Siobhan embraced me, she had been crying, something I wasn't aware of. "Shaun, I promise one day you will understand how important tonight was. Can you trust me?"

"Of course?"

"Good. The jar then."

That was all she said. She went into the bedroom, undressed and wrapped her naked body in a snug sheet, tight as a cocoon, her curvaceous form still obvious.

She stood in the doorway just looking at me, no comment, no direction, as if she was somewhere else.

I asked worried, "What's the matter?"

She replied, as if this was the most important thing she had ever said, "I'm full."

"What do you mean? That you've eaten too much?" she looked at me with longing eyes. I continued the conversation as if she had answered, "Same here, those ribs were enormous."

"Mm, something like that, I'm full of everything, it's difficult to describe, full of love, happiness and life, these last few weeks have been important for me and you haven't left my side, you've indulged me, every little whim. Besides being a good friend you're a remarkable person, I just wished we could have been together earlier."

"Better late than never."

She smiled and nodded in agreement.

"To bed then? Turn off the lights."

As I did, thousands of phosphorous particles led a trail from where she had been standing all the way to the bed. The closer I came to her, the intensity increased. I swallowed. The bed literally glowed with a strange enticing energy. She opened the sheet for me to join her. My God she was beautiful, the rarest of angels any man could have witnessed. If I thought my world was spinning it was nothing to compare with the passion I now experienced. We flowed into each other's arms like droplets of quicksilver – unstable, volatile and screaming with heated fervour. She reached for the jar and threw the remainder of its contents into the air; each particle came alive and danced wildly, then gently settled over us. She quickly wrapped the sheet around us and whispered, "Shut your eyes." I kissed her neck and nibbled her skin. She sighed at each bite. I pillowed her hips and sought her strength – all encompassing, all giving and she held me longer than I knew possible. We fused as one…

ME: YOU – FOREVER.

I was devoted to pleasing her. My body tingled, every nerve ending focused, I felt every breath as she exhaled and those whispering little sighs echoed seductively, I nuzzled her softness never wanting this to end. Then I realised what was happening. A strange, exotic and somehow indescribable feeling possessed me. A phosphorescent glow produced a unique energy but with each second, as if alerted to my realisation, it petered, lacking intensity. The glow finally ebbed. I was about to say, 'I love you', but Siobhan had fallen asleep.

I cradled her head on my arm and when the pins and needles set-in I didn't have the heart to move her. Her breathing lifted her breasts with a gentle rise, she looked complete and at peace. We must have moved throughout the night for she had wrapped herself around me with interlocking legs and an arm that clung so tightly it became difficult to breathe.

When the sun beamed though the curtains, our bodies were meshed – locked tighter than a clam, "Siobhan," I whispered, "The sun is shining."

"What…?"

'What', was the operative word and remained to haunt me.

CHAPTER 24

INTERFERENCE

Streaming sunlight highlighted her curves. We lay sun-drenched, warm and comfortable but something was different. The way she said, "What?" had me worried.

"Shaun... oh, you're here."

"Of course I'm here."

"Good... have we been naughty?"

"You could say that, that has got to be the most intense moment of my life."

She stretched her body and sighed. Then she palmed both hands into a praying gesture and rotated them in a 360-degree stretch. I was amazed at her flexibility. She stopped and looked bewildered, she asked, "Have we been drinking?"

"A little, not too much... certainly a bit."

"Kiss me, show me your passion."

I raised myself onto an elbow and reached over her naked body, my lips brushed her lips. She opened her mouth slightly and let her tongue moisten our contact. Her kiss was different, not unpleasant, more experimental, as if she needed to understand the nature of our kiss, a dissecting, feeling the way, an understanding of our relationship, strange, for only hours earlier we were beyond anything so rudimentary. We were then the closest of close, we were the ultimate union.

I pulled back and asked, "What's up?"

"My head's aching. Where are we exactly? Where is Samantha, she's not likely to spring us in bed, is she?"

"Siobhan, are you alright?"

"I don't think so. Hold me Shaun." Something was up. As each second passed, I could feel her body stiffen.

"Siobhan relax. What are you thinking?"

"I don't know. I'm trying to fathom our relationship."

My heart sank.

"Why are we in bed? How did we get here and where are we?"

My throat seized. I shook my head, this couldn't be happening. Surely, she couldn't have forgotten.

Then she doubled gazumped me, "Does Samantha know about us? I take it we made love?"

"Siobhan, of course we made love. Are you kidding me?"

She closed her eyes tightly, maybe for five seconds and when she opened them they were wide with panic, "Where are we?"

"London."

Her mouth dropped, "London… England…" and she clambered out of bed alarmed, she wrapped a sheet around her body and paced the suite nervously, "How did I get here?"

"Listen Siobhan…"

She suddenly turned on me, "No, no, you listen, something bad has happened here and I'm holding you responsible. Did you spike my drink? How long have I been here?"

She had to be pulling my leg, "Yeah, you are really funny, Siobhan stop the games."

"How long have you kept me here?"

"We've been here for two weeks but…"

She held up her hand, her face pained. With a sharp tug she extended the drapes revealing a sun-drenched skyline. She took a step back, "Where are we really? Where have you taken me?" She was really losing it. The more she talked the more she convinced herself something terrible had happened.

"Siobhan, relax we are in London, I don't know what's going

on but your behaviour is worrying me."

"London… you've done something bad here," she sat on the sofa and sobbed.

Again, I tried to comfort her but she pushed me away.

"Let me call a doctor."

"Give me the phone, she dialled 000 but it was a wrong number, "Christ, you've blocked the phone."

"Who are you dialling?"

"The police."

"Whatever for?"

"To report you."

"Siobhan, I never did anything, I promise."

She challenged, "If you're so innocent, let me make my call," guilty or innocent, no winner here, and besides she was festering into a believable victim and now casting daggers in my direction. What went wrong?

Reluctantly I said, "Try 999, also ask for a doctor." I felt exasperated, I pleaded again, "Siobhan, I admit to passion but coming to London was your idea, check your air ticketing, you purchased your ticket first and then I booked mine." She didn't believe me. I added, "Remember you invited me along."

"Where are the tickets? Samantha just let you come on holidays with me, yeah right!"

I struggled to find a hard copy confirmation and then I realised it was in the room's safe, thankfully it showed Siobhan's credit card transaction but unfortunately no signature. My ticket showed a later purchase.

"You could have drugged me and stolen the card."

"Siobhan, we came here under difficult circumstances, something has happened to you, something is happening to us, I need to work through this with you."

She lowered the phone onto its cradle, "You've got five minutes, and then I'll report you."

"You need to see a doctor."

"Five minutes… start talking. Really, how long have I been here again?"

"Two weeks."

"Shit, drugged for two weeks."

"No drugs."

"It's not a hospital then?"

"What is the matter with you? That was weeks ago. You remember the flight."

"No."

"I think I should call a doctor."

"I don't know... my head feels groggy and the last thing I remember is you... walking out of my hospital room... saying, 'You're great...'"

"You honestly don't remember anything else."

"No."

I shook my head, "Listen carefully Siobhan, this is a holiday, just sex, no drugs, earthy sex, healthy intercourse, I'm sorry, but I can't explain what has happened to you. You must have amnesia, it is best I call a doctor."

She was impossible to deal with, I did call reception. They had a list of doctors eager to charge 300 pounds for a five-minute consultation. Her diagnoses' was temporary amnesia. The Pakistani specialist prescribed one Valium and rest. To his credit, he did supply the medicine and Siobhan looked at the little pill trying to decide if she wanted more clouds. Her heart was racing and I thought it better to make a cup of tea. I flushed the Valium into the Thames, more pollution.

"Look me in my eye and tell me the truth... you have been... making love to me for two weeks and I didn't know? You know what that is don't you?"

"Siobhan don't even go there. I left Samantha for you, and you remember your split with Tom."

She spat out his name in disgust, "Tom... him! Yeah... I remember him alright. But nothing else. So Samantha just rolled over and said go with me."

"No, she was as mad as a hornet, I gave her the house."

"You left her for me and gave her that magnificent house? Oh Shaun why? You two had everything. I'm not complaining you're away from her that must have taken guts."

I detected a mellowing. "Siobhan, I'm really concerned for you. As for myself, I've burnt major bridges just to be with you. Can you imagine what I'm thinking right now?"

"A little."

"Samantha doesn't forgive and when I left, it was final."

"What did we do that brought it to a head?"

"She caught us kissing; you were on top of me. Your dress was up around your thighs and it was the most passionate moment I had ever experienced, at least to that point of time. Samantha and I had moments of intensity throughout the years but nothing like that. That was the wedge. She knew, I knew and you were very convincing that our marriage was over. I had no hesitation. I think we all came to that decision at the one time, a unique moment where the universes collide."

"What about your kids?"

"They're not happy, word spread like wildfire. They hate you. The best thing we did was to come to London, it was a perfect lead up and the trip has been incredible. We breezed though every obstacle without a question and we made passionate love for two weeks. Although I think I've already covered that."

"But Samantha's a good person Shaun, maybe you should go back to her, you gave up so much for me and now I can't even remember what happened."

"Siobhan, it was time, Samantha and I just hadn't realised. She will carry the image of the two of us to the grave and that is my only regret. Try to think back to last night. Do you remember telling me you were full?"

"No, nothing, full you say?" I nodded and she shook her head.

"Siobhan, look in the mirror," she did.

"What?"

"Your neck."

"Oh, you've marked me." She seemed flattered for a brief second, maybe my imagination. Her fingers brushed her neck. I felt stupid but at least it proved our passion.

"Just like horny teenagers, you must have had a right royal time." She appeared more conciliatory and I felt relieved to be off charges.

"That girl who died, the one who warned me off, did you get over that dark infatuated obsession?"

"It's not something you get over. Siobhan, don't you remember the eye test? You were the one who helped me move on, without you I'd be like road kill, gone and squelched many times over. You saved me. I haven't even thought of Lyn until you suggested we research what happened."

"And?"

"It was an anticlimactic moment. You were too upset to continue, so we left it alone."

"Shaun, I wish I could remember."

"I wish you could remember that test, you gave me examples of how some women manipulate you... with..."

"Go on."

"Their eyes."

"I have no idea what you're on about, although the subject isn't that unfamiliar. Some guys are really taken for a ride."

It was strange, Siobhan couldn't remember anything and as each hour passed we tried to comprehend how this could have happened. She showered by herself. We both knew she was struggling. I kissed her on the cheek and complimented her appearance, which was always striking. The only thing different was her fragrance.

"Siobhan, that fresh soap scent, it's gone."

She looked questioningly at me, "What do you mean? I just showered and splashed on a little perfume."

"Something is different."

It was as if Siobhan was a different person. Was it the contents of that jar, the 'love potion', or was she experiencing a breakdown? Whatever the reason, our most intimate of times were lost forever.

CHAPTER 25

—◄o►—

A RED ROSE

Within seconds, my mind flashed back to Robert Freemont's twenty-first birthday bash. That disastrous bonfire celebration forty-five years ago and the moment Lyn Monday arrived. She looked stunning, eyes sparkling, hair short and a trendy T-shirt, it was at this point I detected the fragrance of soap wafting the air. Years of recall suddenly so clear. I could smell Lyn's fresh scent but then the smoky bonfire overpowered her delicate perfume. It was quickly diffused – then smothered. Siobhan had used that same soapy fragrance on our flight to London and each day since, however now… she smelt different, suddenly I realised.

In a panic, I ran to the bathroom and searched Siobhan's toiletry bag, the cupboards and in absolute desperation the other rooms. I returned to the bathroom and rechecked the trash but it was empty, nothing, no Cashmere soap, certainly no wrapper, only that stinking after-five perfume sitting mid-centre of the basin.

At this point, I dismissed the 'love potion' and 'dust' as being the cause of Siobhan's amnesia. In reality, Siobhan's problems stemmed from weeks of memory loss, certainly not one day and what appeared scatty questions were instead a valiant attempt to gain control. Her question, "Where did I leave the car?" being my most significant clue to her awakening. If Siobhan had previously 'encountered' Lyn's presence there was a chance she had returned and had taken control of Siobhan. My body stiffened at the possibility. My head ached and my body felt old all of a sudden. My eyes welled.

Siobhan asked from the bathroom door, "Shaun, what are you doing?"

Nervously, I advised, "… Siobhan you're not going to believe what happened."

I walked her to the sofa, "I'll give you the truth, nothing else," she nodded cautiously. How would she handle the truth? I felt gutted just thinking about it, "Siobhan, I didn't realise until a few minutes ago, but Lyn was here… and… as hard as this is to believe, I think… Lyn… Lyn Monday's spirit controlled you," I looked into her pooling eyes.

She snapped back quicker than I thought possible, "What? That's ridiculous!"

There was a delay between us. I nodded as reinforcement; Siobhan shook her head to enforce the denial. Back home, Siobhan admitted that Lyn's spirit was threatening, so now why doubt my theory? I proceeded cautiously, "This is a highly speculative notion but it makes sense," as each second ticked I began to question myself.

"Shaun, I can't handle any more surprises right now. I'm beyond fragile."

"I think it will help you understand." In hindsight I should have shut-up but I needed to talk, even if it was such an improbable hypothesis, "I think Lyn was here but I didn't realise. It's the only explanation other than you having a breakdown and I don't think that is the case."

"I think I'm having a breakdown."

"You're upset Siobhan, that's understandable. This was Lyn's way to get to me and express her feelings." Suddenly it felt a comfortable theory again, seconds before I was having doubts. Why was I drifting positions so rapidly?

Siobhan's voice came with a warning, "My mind's not into anything at the moment. Do you understand? I'm in shock. What you're saying is… I was possessed by Lyn Monday? Shaun, I don't need this, do you understand how shattered I feel?"

"Of course." I sucked a deep breath, "This was more like a borrowing, I don't like the word possessed. The word possessed seems brutal. Rest assured, Lyn did it respectably, subtly, always tender and caring, she made love a beautiful thing. She preserved your reputation. She saw a window of opportunity and grabbed it. You were available, close and had the right credentials."

"You're determined to do this… credentials? Which were?"

"Sexy, glamorous and you loved me. You do love me?"

"I did say that, but…. but… I was warned, I know I fought that but everything is so different now."

Yes the warning, such a contradiction, "Something changed Lyn's direction, instead of working against you, she decided to work within you," I could read Siobhan's face, she wasn't buying any of this. I struggled, "… the soap."

"What soap? You're determined to do this. I'll break."

"Siobhan, I've always hated that perfume you wear, sorry, it goes off about 5pm. With Lyn, I loved her soapy smell. We, us Siobhan… we discussed it over the last few weeks, even on the plane, I asked you to continue using that soap. It was a real turn on. The weird thing is, I cannot find that type of soap anywhere. It is as if she removed any trace of it. Christ, this is over-whelming and frustratingly depressing."

Siobhan snapped, "If what you're telling me is the case, your problems seem insignificant. I was used for love, right?"

"Well that and …"

"You can't answer anything else. See, it was sex, I'm right. I have no recollection of anything that happened in the last few weeks and then I find my perfume goes off by 5 pm, do you have any idea how I'm feeling?"

"I'm sorry."

"My head is spinning and you insist in overloading me with absolute nonsense. All this is unimportant, something bad happened and I'm traumatised.... enough."

As the minutes ticked by Siobhan appeared agitated with a desperate need to return to Australia. I could understand her needing a familiar environment, so with airline details in hand, she changed our booking. This gave us three hours before departure. My ticketing rode on the back of hers and I was automatically included whether I wanted to go or not.

All I could do was agree, my mind was racing but she needed to hear the truth, as improbable as it sounded, again there was no one to talk to, the emptiness was welling. It was all I could do not to rip something apart. Siobhan packed her bags in one room, I the other. What a miserable situation, so close to Lyn, so far from ever having that relationship again. There was too much pain, and what was all that crap...

ME: YOU – FOREVER

I sank into the sofa and could have cried beyond eternity.

Then I remembered that stupid test. TOMORROW! We were already here, this was tomorrow, was this the test?

It made no sense but I had promised to do something. There was no direction from Lyn. Why couldn't she tell me what was happening? Now nothing. Why merge with Siobhan and suddenly leave? It was as if the 'Cavern of Dream's chocolate dessert' held the key. From that moment, everything was wrapped up quickly as if there was a deadline, and then that London cabbie appearing on the banks of the Thames, that had reinforced her departure, only hours left, make the most of it, go... go... all weird!

I told Siobhan I had to leave, she looked devastated, there was only two hours before check-in, she stammered, her vulnerability showing "... shall I wait here?"

"No, catch a cab, I'll meet you at the airport," she looked shaken, I could read her response – 'London... airport and by myself?' She couldn't determine what to do, she looked drained. As I opened the door I reinforced, "Call the concierge, they will take our bags down and organise a cab for you."

"Will you really meet me at the airport?" I nodded and closed the door. I shouldn't have left but I needed answers.

It was a race with time. Before leaving the hotel's foyer I asked for the account, to which the front desk manager replied, "Sir, your account has been paid. Nil balance, your wife paid earlier."

"Can I have a copy please?"

She gave me a print out and I pocketed the bill to read later. As I walked through the foyer I saw that squash-nosed private investigator. He was sitting looking at me and from behind a stretched out London Times. As I approached he sought immunity by raising the paper further but I spat out, literally spraying him with saliva, "I'm onto you Dick, tell Samantha I'm coming home and will sort her out, you're such an amateur, I spotted you from the outset."

He smiled sheepishly and wiped his face. He placed the 'Times' onto his lap almost teasing me to react. Incensed, I whisked the paper from his grasp and threw it across the foyer, there was a flutter of commotion as I stormed out. There was no time to discuss his ethics. I turned left, just like last night, only this time I was at boiling point. If it wasn't for the brisk air cooling my temper I may well have returned and punched him out. This wasn't a great moment, rarely had I lost control, the only thing stopping my meltdown was the need for confirmation.

I stopped outside the restaurant, 'Cavern of Dreams'. It was shut, a sign announced...

Closed Until Further Notice

I peered through the window and could see the seats where we sat. The place was dark, dusty and uninviting, dissimilar to last night. I frustratingly banged on the chained door. Crappy feelings erupted, then I sighted the menu taped to the glass, sure enough there was 'Lover's Ribs' and the dessert, 'Devil's Advocate Chocolate Cake', great, a confirmation, I wasn't going completely mad. Then I looked for the part concerning the test information where the little plastic satchel delivered the future... I remember our conversation...

"Dessert, the final accompaniment where lovers commit their future."

There was nothing about lover's committing their future or any reference to a satchel. Disappointed, I followed last night's path to the Thames, the swirling currents looked inviting, drawing, I even thought of plunging in, doing a lap of honour like the one I had done for my grandfather when he passed. I could swim until exhausted then allow the current to slowly take me. It didn't seem to matter if I lay on the bottom of this rotting river, a fervent foul sewer for all eternity – hope gone. I was at the water's edge where lapping ripples washed my shoes… enticing!

"Squire, need a lift?"

I turned startled. It was him – the cabbie.

I suddenly felt alive, "Yes, please," he led the way.

He drove in silence. His back was straight and his neck rigid. A two-way radio had its volume low, too low, too soft to hear the broadcast. I couldn't continue this ridiculous facade and asked, "Do you know where she is?"

"Yes, waiting for you at the airport, have you had a good time this visit?"

"The weather has been a concern."

"Ahh, the weather, you make the most of things when you have the opportunity."

"So true. How do you know she is at the airport?"

"I dropped her off earlier and she sent me back for you, she's a special one that one, Squire, look after her."

"I know. How did you know where to find me?"

"Where else could you be but recapping good times, every-one wanders down to the river's edge," he turned his head and gave me a half smile, "I pick up so many fares from that spot, but don't tell my opposition," he laughed at the impossibility.

Then I asked a vital question, "Do you think she has changed in the last few weeks?"

"All for the better, and if you don't mind me adding, you look up to the challenge."

"Thanks, I think. I'm sorry what's your name?"

"Rollie."

"Shaun."

"I know."

"How?"

"Remember, she asked me to pick you up, she said it almost pleadingly, 'would you mind picking up my Shauneee', no big secret," he laughed.

My mind was racing, was it Lyn or Siobhan waiting at the airport? Was I the one having the breakdown? Everything had been real but now doubt and misgiving was stronger than common sense. I ached for answers.

"Here we are Squire," and he pulled the cab quickly into the airport kerb and rushed to open my door. I went to pay him but he said, "Prepaid; if I accepted anything further I'd have some serious questioning back at head office." He winked as if I should understand. He added, "Tomorrow."

"What?"

"Another day, tomorrow is another day, I hope to see you again," and he shook my hand firmly, "Go, catch up with her, tell her you love her, that always makes them feel special."

I was speechless, as he drove away I felt buoyed by his advice. I stopped briefly on the way to check-in and purchased the freshest red single stem rose. I held the flower to my back.

Siobhan saw me approaching and turned to ignore me, I tapped her on the shoulder, "Siobhan, thanks for sending Rollie back."

She faced me hesitantly, "What are you talking about?"

"The cabbie, you sent him to fetch me."

"No I didn't, in fact I've been thinking, its best we don't see one another again."

"Why? But I thought."

"Don't do this here, just leave me be."

"Siobhan please."

"Alright, if you insist on doing this…" She steamed, "You're messed up. I'm still reeling from being used as your little whore

– you and that girl using me was too much." That comment attracted a few stares but I was determined.

I produced the rose, "For you, see, I do care."

"We're sitting in different rows on the plane, my request. I just need to be alone, like you left me back in the hotel room. Do you know how I felt back there – crushed?" She dropped the flower to the ground. I watched the petals explode on impact and with them any hope.

My predicament was escalating, who had sent the cabbie and who was he referring to, Lyn or Siobhan? Where was Lyn now? All those years of memories and the chance to reminisce, what a waste, and when I went to say… 'I love you', who was that with… Lyn or Siobhan? Anyway, she had fallen asleep, now Siobhan was having a meltdown and Lyn was gone forever. What a miserable situation and I still had no idea what Lyn wanted help with!

CHAPTER 26

——◄○►——

SIMMER WITH MELTON

I was the last person to board and meandered to the plane's rear under protest. The very last row; what happened to first class? I didn't mind but my ticket clearly showed first class. I checked the boarding pass and it clearly stated… 'Economy Class' or should have read, 'Idiot, who didn't check the details,' and why so many kids that screamed and hooted on take off? After dinner, the hordes settled, plastic food loaded with carbohydrates, tiredness and constant droning had most with their mouths open and smelly feet invading the aisle. I listened to Frank Zappa and the Mother of Invention, I'm sure they invented swearing, an apt reinforcement at this time. After four hours, I finally acknowledged the passenger sitting next to me, we nodded, she smiled; I smiled back. I put out my hand to introduce myself, "Shaun Reece. Sorry, I've been a little pre-occupied. That was rude of me."

"No worries, I'm Chelsea Melton, nice to meet you Shaun, I needed my space as well." She was a budding university student from Australia who had just won the World Champion's Debating Final. Apparently a big deal and the media were all over the story. Why I was sitting next to her was a mystery, there was no one else seated in our row, surely they could have positioned her with fellow students, there again my allocation had been short-circuited so why should someone else escape the discomfort. Bitter, you bet! She offered me a mint. She didn't deserve my retribution and I felt sorry for being that callous. She was attractive in an old fashioned sense. She wore her hair in a ponytail, had sprinkles of freckles and I suspected contact lenses that hinted aqua over large doe eyes. Her voice was smooth and held projection, altogether a look of innocence, a girl unblemished by this harsh world. Her most prolific assets appeared her pleasant nature and the ability to reason. I asked what subjects she had debated during the competition and she replied, "One worded topics that require an argument."

"Such as?"

"Automation – Quantum – Infinity – Love."

"What side did you take for love?"

The plane hit a pocket of turbulence.

"Oh, I argued against."

The plane shook some more.

"How can you argue against love?"

"Christ, what's wrong with everyone?" her eyes filled. I figured she had something brewing and had a good reason to be upset. I reappraised my opinion instantly.

"Chelsea, I'm just asking a question. You know you're not the only person disillusioned. It has taken me forty-five years to find my true love and in a wink I lost her."

Her eyes welled and a lonely tear trickled her cheek, "Sorry, life is unfair… what happened Shaun – a car accident?"

What a predicament, I was conversing with a young girl who had no hope of understanding, "I'm sorry, it's just too painful to discuss."

"I understand, you're hurt," she wiped the tear, "I'm hurt too, if I didn't have debating to worry about I'd be an absolute mess."

"Life sucks."

"I agree."

I added, "We seem to have a lot in common."

Des Rains the team manager described by his name tag

came down the aisle checking his charges, he didn't seem that occupied with their well-being until he came to Chelsea, "Chelsea, are you alright here? Would you like to move closer?"

I looked at him in amazement. Was he suggesting I was coming onto her?

Chelsea's chilling rebuttal followed, "Don't be stupid Des."

He gave a 'huh' and returned to his seat without an argument.

Chelsea looked embarrassed, "Chelsea… was he suggesting what I think he was suggesting?"

"I'm his path to glory. Since I won the Holy Grail of debating he's been overtly protective. I hate him. When we hit Sydney there will be a media conference, every one will want a piece. This is his big chance to be recognised," she sounded empty.

"Why so glum then?"

"I've got a major problem with him…. I'm sure he told my boyfriend to get lost, though I have no way of proving it. You see, I'd been seeing this guy for eighteen months and things were… kind of serious." She looked at me as if I should under-stand the intensity of her relationship, "Anyway, when I was declared the World Champ he quickly dumped me, I think Des got to him."

"Why would Des destroy your relationship with this guy?"

"Less distraction to start with, with Des everything has a monetary value, he said I needed to focus to obtain the maxi-mum benefits."

"It sounds like your boyfriend has 'little grit'.

"You're right, oh yeah, but more like 'no grit'."

"Whatever Des said should have been discussed, and your boyfriend should have had the courtesy to talk it out. Honestly, you're better off without him."

"Who, Des or my boyfriend?"

"Both I'd say. What is Des exactly?"

"Well that's just it, I made the mistake of saying I needed an agent. Since then he has assumed the role. There was no dis-cussion, there was no agreement, he came by default."

"Well tell him, no!"

"It's not that simple, he has all the contracts in place which are ready to be signed, this world tour needs a dedicated agent to co-ordinate, without that, it's not going to happen. Honestly, I don't think I could stand him fussing around for two years, he'll drive me insane."

"Surely someone else can do the job?"

"I just don't know, there has been no time to find out."

"I understand."

"Shit, I regret winning that debating championship."

Wow, she swore and was as bitter as me. I asked, "And this was your first boyfriend?"

"Yeah and probably the last." She then asked, "You look too... mature, sorry, how could you be having women problems?"

"Age has nothing to do with it. You can be just as messed up at my age as yours."

"You're miserable, I'm miserable."

"Misery isn't our only companion. I've someone special on this flight that refuses to sit with me?"

"Why? Where? What happened?" She looked above the row of seats.

"Chelsea, it's too bizarre for someone your age."

"Shaun, you know my story, your account can't be such a revelation. Well, where is she?"

"First class, she's not herself."

"Mental problems?"

"Close."

"Is she the one, that special one?"

"It has to be, I think, it's just... this is hard to explain. Forty-five years ago my true love died, later I married, had children and then weeks ago this dead girl appears."

Her eyes widened, "She wasn't dead after all?"

"I can't do this, I'm sorry."

"You must, I need to know, please Shaun."

I swallowed, "Yes, she was dead... but not her spirit. She... merged... err... morphed my friend who I had left my wife for," there was more turbulence – the plane shook violently.

There was a huge gap in the conversation and she looked at me bewildered. I nodded as reinforcement, she asked, "Your friend, the one in first class, what connection is she to this? I don't understand."

"She is the morphed girlfriend, taken over by the spirit of the girl that died. That was until yesterday. I can tell by the look on your face your not believing this."

"Your right, I don't. How can you be taken over? That's spooky. Shaun, you're pulling my leg. You're not a weirdo, are you?"

"I think I must be."

"And I thought I had problems."

"I did warn you."

"Regardless, I love your dilemma, you seem so passionate. I wish I had someone to love me like that. Anyway, what to do? It's absolutely unbelievable, tell me, what does your friend look like, the one in first-class?"

"Scarlet hair, she has to be the best looking woman on-board, although a little self-absorbed."

"You're similar to me, falling for the lookers."

"Chelsea, you need to debate my quandary, the key to all this. It's only one word."

"What's the subject?"

"Tomorrow."

"That's easy."

"Really?"

"Tomorrow is forever." The plane kicked through another patch of turbulence.

I was astounded, "What do you mean?"

"Tomorrow never comes, so in essence it means the same as forever."

"Okay, that is one side to the debate. What's the other?"

"Tomorrow is today."

"How do you figure that?"

Chelsea explained, "Well, if we assume tomorrow never arrives then the day previous to that has to be the starting point and today must be the real tomorrow."

"Today!"

"But the day after is tomorrow. Who is right? Who is wrong? There are no winners, only how you debate the issue. It's the chicken or the egg debate, what came first."

I thought, ME: YOU – FOREVER and now TOMOR-ROW my test.

She asked, "Did that help?"

"More than you could imagine," I never imagined someone so young could be this inspiring.

"And this girl you knew all those years ago. Is she really gone?"

"Don't tell me you believe my story."

"No, no, I'm just interested how this pans out. Can you describe her?"

"Consider the most beautiful girl that ever lived with green eyes deep enough to immerse yourself, mix in a tantalising smile and bubbling personality and you have her. However, I couldn't speak to her, my throat seized every time I saw her, I panicked, she moves on but I have one thing that will never be lost – those eyes, I'm under her spell. Then she dies. A reported suicide and takes our special moments with her."

"How did she die?"

"A drug overdose. The truth, she never committed suicide only received bad advice from her pharmacist boyfriend or he tried to kill her, it was a suburban myth that she took her own life. He was a bad choice and now to add fuel to the fire there may have been another boyfriend. He was someone who slotted in during a break-up. This guy is a piece of work, he lied to me and has started acting suspiciously."

"You love her even though she had other boyfriends? That's so unique."

"My fault, I wasn't ready at the time, we both made mistakes and I'll regret mine until the day I die."

"Wow, and you still love her after all these years, and this other woman in first class is?"

"My destiny I guess, someone Lyn wanted me to be with. I have no idea why?"

"I'm really having problems believing this, sorry Shaun, can we just accept that your life is shit and you've hit rock bottom?"

I sighed and nodded, "Yep, probably best. Why hear me out if you don't believe me."

"It's the passion that I'm hooked on, I would give anything to have someone treat me like that and in light of your story, I honestly feel a lot better."

"Well that just makes me feel fantastic."

She started to laugh. I could also see the funny side. Our laughter was infectious and caught the attention of her manager who quickly rose and stood aligned with our seats. "Can I see you for a few minutes Chelsea? Some plans to nut out for the coming weeks," anything to prise her away. He looked at me suspiciously which I admit was justified when considering the topics under discussion. Chelsea reluctantly rose and after a reshuffling of students, she sat besides him, cornered at the window seat, three rows ahead. After half an hour, she returned, her face flushed and looking distraught, "What's up?"

"He wants me to move away from you."

"Why?"

"He thinks you are bad for me. You're a negative force when I should be concentrating on the press conference."

"I see."

"Yeah, I told him you're totally berserk."

"I'm sorry Chelsea, I never meant to upset anyone. I understand completely, it's best you sit with him."

"Shaun, no one has made me laugh like you and I'm captivated by this crappy life of yours, who could dream up such shit, some of it has to be true. I told Des to get lost and to forget about being my agent. What do you think of that?"

"That took grit."

"Thanks."

I encouraged, "Well things can only get better for the two of us… hey!"

CHAPTER 27

◄○►

CATACLYSMIC ADJUDICATORS

I looked at my watch, eight hours since take-off. The cabin was as messy as a teenage dormitory and the droning of the plane's engines continued to tire the senses. Of course Chelsea's confidence was being drawn from comparisons – my drama versus hers. We had laughed at the ridiculousness of my story which had made her feel good, even though she didn't believe a word. She said, "My problem is believing your story."

"Am I a liar then?"

"Oh no, you definitely believed that happened. For one thing, it's too fanciful, shit, that type of possession doesn't happen unless it's in sci-fi books or movies, you're not a writer are you?"

"Actually yes."

"You're not testing the plot of a new book on me? Shit!"

"I write non fiction." I added slightly vexed, "No, this is not a test."

"You're not tempted to merge genres, create a new reader base?"

"Chelsea, I haven't the energy for this. I'm delighted I've energised you but really it has been draining for me. This is my life, this is where I'm up to. I think it's real, I have to live with what I've experienced; I can't and won't change a thing. I have loved and lost."

"In that case you won the debate and my support."

I looked at her astonished, "That simple."

"That simple, shit simple."

Somehow, I found her use of profanities likeable, some people could get away with murder and as for her reasoning, I was gobsmacked at her maturity.

We had remained silent for half an hour when I couldn't contain myself any longer, "So, what does it mean?"

She questioned, "What?"

"When people use words… the air vibrates with energy only to have it fade, never be heard of again. What does it all mean? Where does it all end? Really, nothing changes or corrects the past. They're just empty words with hollow feelings…"

"You're not going all funny on me again? Shaun, lighten up, you had a moment, better to have love and lost… you know the rest."

She smiled and I couldn't help but feel lifted, "You're a good medicine young lady."

She said, "Probably, why are we sitting together, what's the odds, was it fate, you're supposed to be sitting in first class, I'm supposed to be sitting next to 'dick-for-brains', what's the odds? I think our lives are planned, I think you're going to be in my life for some time to come, I have no idea why this bizarre encounter has happened but I have to have faith. It might as well start with you."

An in-flight attendant rushed through a drawn curtain and proceeded towards the back of the plane. She looked distressed, then she saw Chelsea patting my arm for assurance. "Shaun Reece?" I nodded, "Siobhan is your friend, right?"

"Yes."

"We have a problem. You better come with me."

"I'm coming too," Chelsea demanded.

The attendant didn't know what to make of our relationship, "This way."

"What has happened?" I queried as Chelsea snapped closely at my heels. The attendant wasn't falling for a debriefing not with so many people looking.

We passed Des who protested, "Chelsea, where do you think you are going?" But Chelsea said, "Sit Des." He reluctantly sat.

Chelsea queried, "So your friend's name is Siobhan?"

I nodded.

"Nice name."

We dodged feet, a baby's feeding bottle and a queue waiting patiently at a rest stop. In first class, the mood was sombre, the French champagne was flowing and the Lobster Mornay was about to be served. The wide-screened televisions looked huge. Siobhan was missing, I couldn't see her anywhere.

"Where is she?" I asked.

"We have her in the staff's rest station, she can lie down there and not be afraid of others peering. She has been inconsolable."

"What happened?"

"She has been crying since take off. We checked with London and they advised you were to be sitting next to her. There appears some mix-up with allocations."

"Really?" I replied, with a level of sarcasm. "I thought I was sitting in first class, it is just fantastic back there."

She smiled, forever the airline's representative.

I returned the conversation to Siobhan, "Really, crying non stop?"

"Yes, we have a passenger who is a doctor, he saw her and wanted to prescribe something but she said no. She also said she had been drugged for two weeks and would like to remember things from this point."

I ventured, "She's very unstable and most likely referring to her hospital stay." I nodded my head hoping the in-flight attendant would accept my version. I didn't need an Air Marshall investigating the last few weeks. "Can I see her? She hasn't been herself. I'm sure I can help."

That was all she needed and pointed to a modular cabin in the forward section. I knocked on the small door but there was no answer. I turned the handle and noticed an empty tissue box, the used tissues had been thrown across the floor. Chelsea gripped my arm in case of a protest.

When Siobhan saw us her eyes widened, "Shaun!"

Chelsea and I hesitated, she looked dishevelled with red witching hair in need of a De Lorenzo treatment. Her mascara ran wildly resembling a Kiss Concert without air conditioning. Her fine porcelain skin was inflamed especially around the eyes and her puffy nose had become irritated by pulped paper fibres. "Siobhan, the flight attendant came to get me, are you alright?"

"No." I moved closer, snivelling she quipped, "Who is this? Why is she holding your arm? Are you collecting more young girls?"

"Siobhan, Chelsea."

Chelsea clung tighter, "She's just a friend Siobhan, don't worry. What has happened to you?"

She blew her nose before speaking, "The tears won't stop Shaun, like a tap. It's embarrassing and they made me a prisoner in this little holding cell."

"It's the staff's rest station, not a cell."

"It feels like a cell. Why is she here Shaun? Can't you see I'm embarrassed without inviting everyone along."

Chelsea proudly advised, "Shaun and I are soul mates."

I looked at Chelsea.

Siobhan raised a questioning brow, then Chelsea confirmed, "It's true."

Siobhan queried, "Soul mates, huh, you work fast Shaun. Did Shaun tell you what happened to me?" she used another tissue and blew harder.

"He said you were the most beautiful woman on this plane and that you've had problems lately, something about being morphed by a spirit – shit unreal! Shaun told me he left his wife for you. That must have been gut wrenching. Siobhan, you don't deserve what happened but Shaun is a good person, give him a chance and for God sake get over this self-pitying thing. I know something dramatic happened, scary even and I can understand that, however Shaun needs you now and not this distressed broken person who is letting her emotions run wild. You're a magnificent looking woman; I can see your potential but look at your swollen eyes and puffy red skin. Really, no more crying, give yourself a chance. So no more tears, alright? Get on with learning to love one another."

"How old is she Shaun?"

"Old enough, she might appear to have the answers but she could really do with your help Siobhan."

Chelsea gave a bewildered look. "Chelsea, you're not going to believe this, but, Siobhan has heaps of contacts with agents. Let her help you."

"Really?"

"Yes… right Siobhan? Siobhan flicked her long lashes and breathed a conciliatory acceptance. I knew that getting her mind off herself would be the best medicine, "Anyway, I'm going outside to relax, drink champagne, eat lobster and when you two are done… come out. No rush."

The fiasco with wronged seating had proved a blessing, I had met Chelsea who had helped me, Siobhan, and now Siobhan could help Chelsea. When they emerged from the 'holding cell' both looked drawn with red eyes. Siobhan sat next to me, Chelsea the other side. First class, wow, an instant upgrade for Chelsea.

"All done?"

"All done," Chelsea and Siobhan said together. A little smile rippled Chelsea's face and Siobhan looked amazed, they giggled simultaneously. This was becoming a better day, better than yesterday, which was tomorrow, or was it today?

When Chelsea excused herself to visit the bathroom, Siobhan announced, "She's a remarkable girl Shaun, I can see why you connected. I would like a soul mate like her – you're lucky."

"I'm available any time."

"You're going to be more, just… I need to go slow."

"I understand. Are you alright with everything?"

"Yeah, but we will need to talk."

"Maybe in a few days then?"

She nodded, but added, "Nothing but talk, okay? When the time is right I want details, every little morsel of information that will help me remember."

Before landing I reflected… my relationship with Lyn was a blink in history. It was better than no blink but still, it would have been nice to have a normal relationship, however was I deluding myself, Lyn was a spirit, I was a mortal, nothing could bridge the gap – except death. How she had accomplished this was beyond comprehension. Even now I was having trouble believing.

Chelsea returned, having had the foresight to retrieve her on-board luggage. She snuggled comfortably into her first class seat. I gave her more details of Lyn's death and my involvement. We exchanged phone numbers and pledged our support. I wished her luck with the press conference. She seemed excited and promised to give me details when her life settled.

The plane finally touched down. Chelsea was ushered to the media room and Siobhan and I followed the straggling array of weary travellers heading in the opposite direction. There were thousands of people in the Custom's Hall. Nudging was the order of the day and tiredness flowed to frustration. We hadn't spoken about the real issues and on the far side of customs Siobhan's tears started again. When we exited the airport, we were both unsure what to do. We separated, Siobhan to one taxi while I another. It was then I realised my mistake. I closed my taxi's door after leaving a ten-dollar tip and raced to Siobhan's. I slammed on the taxi's boot lid just as it was driving off. A screech of brakes brought it to a screaming halt. I put my head in the window and insisted, "Siobhan, I'm staying with you, we need to talk."

CHAPTER 28

LOST LOVE

The trip from the airport proved uneventful, we sat in the taxi nurturing our thoughts.

When the cab pulled outside Siobhan's house I was stunned. It was of modernistic design far beyond the humdrum shapes of suburbia. Siobhan saw my surprised face and explained, "This whole estate is an experiment in planning."

"Wow, it was dark when I was here last, I never realised."

"When was that?"

"You don't remember?"

She shook her head.

"When the cab picked you up to go to the airport," she gave me a distant look.

Siobhan's house had no roof line as such, for the concept was to duplicate modular blocks stacked on top of the other and the rendered walls were white with splashes of creativity drawn from deep-pigmented ochre. Somehow, this blended with the backdrop of rolling green hills and landscaped parkways. Whoever designed the estate had worked miracles. There was also a recreational facility which included an eighteen-hole golf course and, most surprisingly, there was an underground bunker in case of emergencies. I felt secure knowing we could go somewhere if there was a gassing or nuclear attack. Was there still a threat? Someone thought so.

Inside this eco-designed house, everything was clean, fresh and modern – my guest room was enormous. It had a giant plasma screen concealed into the wall and the king size bed would be absolute bliss after such a long flight. Interestingly, nothing remained of Tom and I was glad, he was not my favourite person.

The next day I checked on Chelsea, with the exception of jet-lag she was faring better and the press conference had gone well. She had entered the media room with lights ablaze and a new found confidence. She thanked me for balancing her outlook, "See, there is always someone worst off than yourself – you shouldn't grumble should you?"

"Thanks Chelsea, your insight has lifted me to a greater level of uncertainty. What if I can't find someone worse off than me, say I'm the last?"

"Shaun, you're rock bottom but you haven't been there long enough to be a statistic. Hey, you know I'm playing you, don't you?"

"I suspected as much and what's this about us being soulmates, that was a big surprise, I never saw that coming."

"I thought it was a nice touch and appropriate, any objections?"

"No, it's flattering. What happened with Des Rains, the guy who wanted to be your agent?"

"Err... he turned up at the press conference but stayed in the background. He was glaring at me the whole time. It was a bit scary."

"Is there something you're not telling me?"

"How low are you Shaun?"

"What do you mean?"

"Remember when I sat next to Des on the plane?"

"For his debriefing?"

"Yes, well he asked me to do something that was disturbing and this is the reason I dumped him."

"What did he ask?"

"He wanted me to find out as much as I could about you."

"But you said it was…"

"I know, but you were hurting at the time and I didn't want to upset you further. Can you handle the truth now?"

"Of course."

"Des asked me what we had been talking about. That was innocent enough and I kept it light even though the subject was a minefield. You do realise I can manipulate a conversation."

"Of course, that's a given."

"Then he reached into his pocket and offered me a wad of cash. The more information I collected the better. It was to be an ongoing arrangement being a lucrative deal for us both."

"But why?"

"I don't know, I asked him but he refused to answer."

"Why would he want information about me? I've never seen him before."

"He seemed to know a lot about you."

"But how? Even I…," of course, my seating had been altered from first class to economy. I remember Siobhan was distressed and wanted us separated. I had assumed she changed my seating at check-in, which instantly had me downgraded. However, now I wasn't sure.

"He is working for someone, that part is clear. Who would want feedback on you Shaun?"

"Maybe my estranged wife Samantha," I remember losing my temper in the hotel's foyer and telling the private investigator I was leaving London. Maybe he followed Siobhan to the airport… or… what if he didn't work for Samantha! Who else would want to follow me and how did Des Rains become involved? I felt angry. I explained to Chelsea what happened in London, I asked, "And you dumped Des as your agent because of this?"

Chelsea said, "Stupid hey!"

"Depends, how much money are we talking?"

"A lot! Shaun, there is someone you can't trust."

I admired Chelsea's ethics, at her own expense she had stuck up for me even though we had just met. I gave Chelsea Siobhan's list of agents. Chelsea finished the conversation with, "Thank Siobhan for the referrals."

With Siobhan, networking was as natural as washing your hair, however she was at a loss to understand who would be spying. She asked, "Shaun what happened in London?"

"Are you sure you're ready for this?"

She raised an eyebrow, "It's time, I need to know. Shaun, the beginning; start at the beginning." She crossed her arms, frowned and prompted, "I know you think Lyn's spirit possessed me... which meant you had to be physically attracted to me or this wouldn't have worked."

"Well of course..."

She unfolded her arms somewhat relieved, "Ok, what else am I missing?"

"Let's back up. You remember the four of us at the restaurant? Samantha, Tom, you and I?" I recapped the restaurant fiasco, I even analysed her motives to stay at our house.

"You could have stayed at a hotel."

"I wanted to be near you. I told you, I... anyway, it happened, we stayed alright."

"Then you came onto me and with Samantha in the next room."

"I told you, it was no secret, I had been drinking and nothing else seemed to matter – I was yours Shaun. I'm sorry if I embarrassed you and compromised your relationship with Samantha." She hesitantly added, "I'm not like that normally, I've never been that forward with anyone, honest!"

"Then what happened?"

She hesitated, "... you really want to know?"

"I think every bit of information may assist."

"I'm embarrassed."

"Siobhan, I'm thinking there has to be a reason for this union of ours and I'll be truthful if you will, that way we might find an answer."

"... alright then. After Samantha turned on the light and

sprung my clumsy attempt at romancing you, I went to the bathroom and…"

I questioned, "What?"

"Relieved myself."

"As you do."

Her face was reddening, "No, really relieved myself."

"What do you mean?"

"Hell, do I have to spell it out?"

"I think so."

"Christ Shaun… I masturbated, alright! I had to get relief somehow. It was an insatiable urge. I left the bathroom feeling uneasy then I went to bed but couldn't sleep. I went to the fridge for a glass of milk, anything to help me settle. I needed to forget my ineptitude, my embarrassment, the room began spinning and then came the warning to back away from you. It was a terrible experience. The next thing I remember was waking up in hospital."

"You remember Tom coming to see you?"

"Yeah, he never spoke, he just looked at me with a disgusting sneer. I was so over him and I told him we were finished. He appeared relieved. He returned to my room a little later and we formalised the break. Nothing traumatic; we were both glad it was over."

"You don't think Tom was following us in London?"

Siobhan thought for a minute, "No, we were already wrapped up."

"I'm just trying to cover everyone, anyway, when I visited you at the hospital, that second time, you didn't appear as frightened."

"Shaun, I was prepared to fight for you. I wasn't going to be warned off by a… a spirit, if that's what it was! I had already made a fool of myself with Samantha, what did I have to lose?"

"If Lyn gave you a warning, why did she mesh with you? It sounds contradictory, was this a part of her plan? Nothing makes sense!"

"Shaun what was your relationship with this girl?"

"A non-existing one, I was young, completely out of my depth and didn't know how to relate to girls. If I had done things differently she may well be alive. My mother's insecurities nurtured in me. She warned me that girls were trouble."

Siobhan laughed, "They are, she gave you excellent advice."

"I don't know, you have no idea the extent of my brainwashing."

"Shaun, you blame yourself for not doing enough to prevent Lyn's death? You must really love her."

"I do. Although I have no idea why she wants us to be together, it's obvious you are an attractive woman and I could quite easily have a relationship with you but there is this enormous problem... Lyn! Beside me, you are the only person to have experienced her determination. Siobhan, after London, I'm further convinced something special is going to happen and you're an integral part of the process. With her controlling you, I only saw perfection. You two were the ideal combination."

"Mm," Siobhan was not convinced. "Let's say I'm a quarter of the way to accepting this story. What possible reason would Lyn have for doing this?"

"I don't know, maybe she needs me to right a wrong, see justice prevail, there are people responsible for what happened. Maybe you're a part of the process."

"If any of this is true you should help her, if you drift off track, I'm sure she will correct your direction."

"So, you think Lyn's spirit exists?"

"Something happened, I not sure what. I'm trying to be supportive, that's all."

"Siobhan, while on the flight to London you told me Tom was having an affair with his secretary. You never did anything about his infidelity as you were waiting for the right time to terminate the marriage."

"I said that?"

"Yeah."

"Wow, I never told anyone my suspicions." She hesitated, "Shaun, in all honesty... was I good in bed?"

"Magnificent."

She smiled, "No... barriers?"

"Absolutely none, you were a free spirit, sorry, that is a terrible pun, but you were certainly… uninhibited!"

"Great. Now, how did we get together?"

"Samantha walked out on me, but first, let me explain my state of mind."

"Fragile?"

"It's not that simple. Samantha couldn't tolerate my obsession with Lyn's spirit and insisted I get over it. I wasn't to mention her name or even to think about her. I told her I loved Lyn and couldn't forget her. Samantha was bitter because I could never tell her I loved her."

"Really, you never said, 'I love you'. Why?"

"Never… I was scared Samantha would detect my divided allegiance. Besides, Samantha's possessiveness is another story. It seems crazy to admit this after all this time but I do love Samantha, just differently. Anyway, when Samantha left I was at a low point, she had been gone for days, I even saw a psychiatrist."

"Oh Shaun, I had no idea."

"Well, tough times, but I'm guessing Lyn took control of you during my second hospital visit. She saw an opportunity and grabbed it. When discharged you came to our house, mainly to thank us for the support. Of course Samantha wasn't there and you were prepared to look after me, I was a mess. You cooked dinner while I had a shower, then you guided me through these little tests."

"Tests?"

I explained to Siobhan the kissing and eye tests, "Then you duplicated Lyn's exact gaze, another tantalising spell from an equally vibrant seductress."

She blushed.

I explained how with Lyn's guidance she had defined the 'layering of love', love without boundaries, love that was nurturing and fulfilling. She nodded as if she understood. "Honestly Siobhan, I could never stop loving Lyn. I don't feel the least bit embarrassed by telling you that but when you kissed me again it was passionate, raunchy, and guess who had let herself into the house and was watching?"

"Samantha? Oh no."

"Oh yes. Soon after we agreed to separate, it was pointless us continuing, Samantha wasn't prepared to bend and I wasn't forgetting Lyn. Of course you cemented our direction."

"I had no idea."

"Siobhan, I know things have changed but I think we should be there for each other. There has to be a purpose, there has to be a reason."

Siobhan leaned over and kissed me on the forehead. She held my head with both hands and looked me in the eye. She said, "Don't worry, it will be alright, I promise."

I breathed a sigh of relief. Then she said, "Before we finish, I need to know, this is important to me."

"What is?"

"When we were in London… my body was used for…"

"Love."

"I have been candid and I want you to be. What did you do to me and don't say we made love, that doesn't explain a thing. I need details… please."

I explained every passionate moment but only brushed over our last night in London, an hour later Siobhan summarised, "It was what I suspected, I was…"

I interrupted, "The perfect woman!"

"Shaun, can you give me time. I'm still struggling."

"I'm going nowhere, you have my full support. If you get sick of me, tell me to go."

She smiled and held my hand, "We have a chance you know."

"Great," we had survived the first hurdle.

Later that day I tried to rest but memories of Lyn kept surfacing, I remembered our last moments in London. That jar, it was not until this moment I had a chance to reason, that strange state where we flowed into each other's arms. She had wrapped me in a sheet and together we had loved enough for all eternity. Now, it was my test to look after Siobhan, but why? Where did this leave me with Lyn? Was it my destiny to be with Siobhan? Was Siobhan the key to this mystery and who in the hell had me under surveillance?

PART THREE

CHAPTER 29

◄○►

BIG BUCKS FOR NOTHING

It was back to business, researching my book and ferreting out the truth, also asking why someone would pay big bucks for on-going surveillance. It didn't make sense for Samantha to have me followed and Siobhan had dismissed Tom as a suspect. The only link I knew was Des Rains, the guy who wanted to be Chelsea's half-baked agent.

From the phone book I discovered Des lived in a down town area of Sydney where small terraces and businesses flourished together. As I drove into his street I debated what to say but all I could come up with was... WHY? I found the street number by accident and discovered it was a rickety old wool shed made from tin sheeting. It was browned by rust and painted with every graffiti tag imaginable. If it wasn't for the paint reinforcing the two storey structure, I'm sure the building would have collapsed. Then I was worried about the next gust of wind which would surely loosen some sheets and decapitate the surrounding populace, even in this light breeze the tin rattled nervously. The area was run-down and seedy.

I locked the car and kept my hand on my wallet. There were large cardboard boxes at the end of the street where destitute dwellers spent their night and on either side of the wool shed there were vacant blocks strewn with rubbish. The smell of uric acid permeated the air and this being enough to make me gag.

A large metal door hung skewed to its frame, I knocked, it rattled for several seconds and the silence returned. I waited. Nothing! Peering through a gap in the door I could see a metal bar securing the entrance. It was the type of bar that could be removed and repositioned to the outside and bolted down when leaving. This meant someone had to be inside and would have heard me knock. I banged harder, the front of the building shook again. Maybe Des was asleep. There was no response to my second knock so I checked the perimeter. There was no other access, only one bent up sheet of iron which might allow entry but only if given encouragement. The street was still deserted. I gave the iron sheet a healthy tug and it came away in my hands.

Inside, the light was dim, lit by hundreds of sun drenched puncture holes, a reinforcement that the building had been made from second hand material. The dust lay thick over crumbling concrete. There were large wooden pallets and steel containers stacked neatly in rows. I checked each row but there was nothing suspicious. In one corner of this massive shed stood a bathroom facility with an office directly above, a steel stairway led to the office door.

There was nowhere else to search but up the flight of stairs which led to the office. I took each step slowly and was prepared to bolt at the slightest commotion. The place was eerie and supported by a breeze that now whistled the holes and expansion cracks. On the stairway landing I had two options, leave or turn the door handle. Was Des Rains behind the door? Should I start questioning him immediately? But what if he called the police?

It was a hunch more than anything; something was drawing me to confront the bastard. I gripped the handle, twisted it, pushed a little and let momentum do the rest.

Sure enough, there he was, right in front of me, his eyes wide; his arms strangely at his side. A chair had been upended and an electrical cable secured around his skinny little neck. His toes dangled millimetres from safety but in this case, millimetres meant the difference between life and death. He had been dead for some hours. But something wasn't right. I surveyed the room trying to figure it out. I wasn't buying suicide. There was a collapsible bed propped against the wall, so Des did live here. His desk was neat when compared to mine and that raised my suspicions; his wallet was open and fat with unconverted English Pounds, so robbery seemed remote. I used a pen to flick through the wallet. He had a driver's license but there was no car parked outside. I noticed his bags were still packed and they stood upright in the corner. He was unshaven and his stubby growth days old. Since arriving home he had time to freshen up… unless waylaid. How was he going to contact the private investigator, or was it the other way around? I patted his left pocket, nothing, then the right, something. It was a business card, glossy on one side. I handled it by the edges. It was an airport shuttle's pick-up advice. It stated: 11 am, in hand written ink. It had a phone number in case of a delay. I memorised the card and slipped it back into Des's pocket. There was nothing else that grabbed my attention so I backed out of the room to consider my options. I had to let the police know, regardless of how I viewed their investigative skills. I wiped my fingerprints from the handle. There was no rush for an ambulance but there was a need to tell Chelsea and she could alert Siobhan. I dialled 000. I retreated down the stairs and returned the iron sheet to its original precarious holding. There was still no one around and I left the scene driving slowly just in case speed attracted attention. Within thirty seconds I could hear a siren and then a patrol car screamed past.

I called Chelsea and for once she was silent, I told her the police may ask questions. After a drawn silence she asked, "You didn't murder him on my account?"

"Are you serious?" I replied.

"I have to ask, why were you at his place?"

"Gee Chelsea, this guy tried to cash in at my expense, he was the only person I knew connected to the surveillance. I had to pay him a visit. You can imagine how inconvenient this is for me."

"Actually no, it's probably five times more inconvenient for him, regardless of his motives."

I asked her to tell Siobhan what had happened. I wasn't sure if she was playing me or genuinely distressed, "Anyway, where were you four hours ago?"

The phone went dead.

In need of information, I drove to Beaulieu's house. As the security door opened she sprouted, "The leper returns, the outcast, ran away with a girlfriend did we? Left the poor wife to pick up the pieces, have you signed the divorce papers and the settlement agreement? I was the last to know what had happened. How do you think I feel, being used like that...?"

"... USED!" I challenged. "You don't know what the word means. Beaulieu, don't give me the hurt more than thou routine, because you don't know shit!" She took a step back, "Anyway, I tried to phone you at the airport but you didn't answer."

"A telecommunication glitch that had me waylaid for forty-eight hours."

"Well... not my fault."

"You sound terribly bitter. Did the new girlfriend double cross you?"

"You wouldn't understand."

"I feel absolute despair for Samantha, that's all. I feel you've deserted her, left her high and dry. Shaun that's how I feel, and after all, she is family."

"She left me first. Would you prefer I go?"

Beaulieu folded her arms and replied, "Yes."

"Then that's it," I turned to go.

"I would prefer you go but I'm professional and this job has to be completed. If we just understand that this is about the project."

"Fine by me but I need to make this abundantly clear, what happened to me was to do with this project. I don't expect you'll understand, but that's the truth."

Beaulieu said, "Mm… if it has anything to do with this project, you need to tell me. I'm reasonable; the facts will speak for themselves."

I explained my harrowing few weeks leaving out spiritual matters and the exceptional romantic bits. Beaulieu was accepting and surprisingly compassionate, she even shred a tear. Then she said a little prayer for Samantha, me, and finally, one for Siobhan. Although quickly delivered the content was moving. Not since my son lay helpless in hospital had anyone prayed with me, at that time the nurse who guided us was a saviour.

Beaulieu returned to business, "I have something else."

"What …?"

"Debbie Hudson was Lyn Monday's girlfriend. She was sixteen, Lyn had just turned seventeen. They knew each other for four years, school friends and it appears Lyn confided everything with Debbie. You need to find her before you go much further."

"Me… find her? You're the researcher."

"I forgot. I thought I was terminated." Beaulieu smiled, "Problem is, Debbie married, was divorced but then remarried. She is alive however I have no idea how to contact her. This girlfriend of Lyn's is the key to all the little secrets the parents never knew. Debbie exposed Malcolm Shailler to the police, remember he gave Lyn those abortion tablets, and I'll add, without a doctor's prescription!"

"So Debbie was the one responsible, I thought the police had uncovered that information."

"No, this was not their finest moment. The information was dropped into their lap but they still didn't know what to do with it."

"Don't talk to me about the professionalism of the police, you know my experience, you remember what happened to my son Joel?"

"Yes, sad," she exhaled as if to say any more would be pointless.

"Oh Beaulieu, one more thing, I want you to find out about a guy called Des Rains, he died recently."

"What year?"

"Five hours ago. It looks like suicide but I've got a hunch there was foul play."

"What does this have to do with researching Lyn Monday?"

"He was recruiting people to keep an eye on me."

"What do you mean?"

"Sleuths, spying all things sinister and ugly, you better be careful."

"And this is to do with the case?"

"Precisely," I gave her what I had.

I stood to leave. We hugged tighter than expected. Beaulieu asked, "Can I suggest you talk to Samantha and let her know what has happened? It may help the pain. She's hurting you know."

"I promise I will. This has affected us all, but please don't tell Samantha what I've discussed, leave that for me."

She patted my arm and smiled, "I swear I won't. Good then, the air is clear except for finding out who is following you."

I left a nervous researcher, better that than someone uninformed.

As I drove to Siobhan's house I kept going over every facet of the London trip. Not in my wildest of dreams could I have imagined Chelsea's involvement; that went beyond co-incidence or was she a part of the plan. My time with Lyn was a soul retching journey – nothing was achieved except heartache and confusion. Poor Siobhan had lost weeks from her life and nothing seemed real any more. I had no idea what I should write in the novel, 'Lyn Monday', for as interesting as the topic was, I had a start but no ending, I wasn't even sure the chapters from 2 to 32 had anything to do with the books direction. In fact, the story line had everything tossed in like a Cajun Jambalaya, there were so many flavours all simmering against the heat for supremacy and now Des Rains was dead.

Twenty-four hours later there was still no change with Siobhan. She was still recovering from jet-lag and loss of freedom issues, so it was easier for me to buy take out and return with take in. I also visited the cleaners and the Chinese girl gave me a docket stamped PAID, with a warning 'Don't loose under any conditional'. The docket number was 306, the same number as our hotel room in London, memorable! I walked back to my car and remembered the hotel account was still in my trousers back pocket and that Chinese girl was eager to clean. I panicked. Here was further evidence of our trip. With so much happening I had overlooked the account. I raced back to the cleaners only to find the Chinese girl grinning, I think her name was Mekong, maybe she was Vietnamese and her last name was Delta, she seemed experienced going through pockets.

"Mister, you leave something?"

"A piece of paper."

She grinned innocently and handed me a folded A4 sheet from a little box labelled, 'Losed Properly', "Thank you so much Mekong, you have no idea how important this document is."

"My name is Me-long not Mekong."

"Me, is very grateful," I said with an accent towards transla-tion hip.

She giggled, "That is alright... Me."

I bowed for full affect.

She bowed a little lower, a sign of respecting your elders. Why couldn't our young Australians show due courtesy like this young girl, a little nodding here, a little bowing there, a lit-tle acknowledgement of your name... 'Me'.

I thought of Lyn – Me: You: Forever.

Then I thought of Siobhan and her distressed state in Lon-don, then our abrupt whirlwind return. Anyway, I had the hotel account in my tight grip but once I perused the form I was be-wildered. The invoice was made out to...

Australian High Commission Diplomatic Services

Attention Mr. Fourever – Accounts Department

Each day was efficiently itemised and prepared for the Dip-lomatic Services, Account Department's reference. The invoice number, the account number, the room number and the cleaning docket were all numbered '306', which was the same room num-

ber where my son had been held hostage during the hotel robbery. I needed to think this through but my first consideration
was that some form of check and balances were in order. Was I
ripping off the government and all because I had a romantic two
weeks? I could see my photo on the front page of the newspapers
exposed in the fraud. The headlines ruthless and biased – how
could I explain what had happened? I returned to Siobhan's
house with another predicament. How could I explain her part
in this government-funded holiday? At least I had paid for my
ticket. My name wasn't mentioned on the account nor was there
any mention of Siobhan. Maybe I shouldn't say anything, but
why were we on a free junket and our hotel bill on the Australian
Diplomatic Services account? Then I remembered the hotel receptionist saying my wife had finalised the bill and there was a
zero balance. Maybe she thought Siobhan was my wife; there
was no way Samantha would pay. Nothing added up and the account was to the attention of Mr. Fourever accounts department,
my head ached, the more I thought the stranger things became.
One contradiction led to another.

My test was tomorrow, I think Chelsea was right 'Tomorrow' never came, I was stuck in trouble and no matter what I
did it would always be the same. I spent an agonising few hours
but decided to break the news to Siobhan.

"Oh my God Shaun, I never thought about paying for ac-
commodation and I didn't tip for baggage, even though the
concierge went beyond the call of duty."

"I just bet he did", I queried further, "Did you pay for your
taxi fare?"

"Now that you mention it, no. I had no money. You know I
was transported against my will to a foreign country where my
body was defiled."

"Be serious."

"I'm trying but it's hard. I can't imagine I have to pay for
what happened to me."

"No, of course not, but what I'm suggesting is that you will
need to declare the fringe benefits on your income tax."

"Why?"

At this point, she had no sense of humour, I persevered, "Obviously, the government has records of these comings and goings, for example your passport notations, which proves you were in London."

"Shit Shaun, you are such a miserable person to be around. For a moment, I thought this might be a day to escape the past, but no, you take care of that by destroying everything. I suggest you get this worked out and quickly. I'm not declaring anything; I was oblivious to what happened!" She raised an eyebrow, challenging me to rebuke her statement. I shrugged. I had seen her at her finest, she just needed time.

I decided to go to the source and made a call to the London hotel. Within five seconds an enthusiastic accountant manager bubbled down the line, "Welcome to accounts, great day isn't it?"

"Not from where I'm sitting. I was wondering if you could help me."

"This isn't about the account for room 306 again is it?"

"Well yes." Again?

"Do you need me to go through that one more time?"

"I don't…"

"Understand," he interrupted with a sympathetic tone.

"Yes."

"As explained, there was a mistake, I apologise, and we need the money transferred into our account today, 5016 pounds please. Please hold," I did the conversion figure… wow! That was a lot of money,

"Thanks for holding."

"You said you have spoken to someone else about this account?"

"I thought you were the same person contacting me from the Australian Government but obviously not. Your accents throw me. You're not from the government? You're not Mr. Fourever?"

"No, I was the guest. I just need to understand who made the booking and why the invoice was made attention to Mr. Fourever."

"Oh, I'm sorry who am I talking to?"

"Shaun Reece."

"Yes, I have your details on our records. Oh… it's already been finalised, your account shows zero."

"Really?"

"Yes, a transfer has been made, wait a minute… it's changing, you have a credit. We need to refund you 8000 pounds."

"Who transferred the money?"

"The Australian Government, High Commission apparently, you are well respected sir. Thank you, the money is being redirected as we speak."

I called out, "Siobhan, the trip is paid for and apparently I'm a spy! Forget declaring anything on your income tax."

CHAPTER 30

THE LAST WORD

The money kept arriving, totalling $35,099.10, all over-payments from our London holiday. The excesses represented cab charges, car rental and detailing, a restaurant credit of five thousand pounds and of course, a first class kickback with the airline. That was for twelve thousand dollars. There were further irregularities and as a consequence I formed a trust account and waited for someone to contact me, but nothing happened, it was as if I was released from spy duty. It was intriguing how Lyn had pulled this off, the sheer audacity to access the country's mainframe database and have me the recipient. I guess where Lyn was now, money wasn't such a big deal but I was flabbergasted that Mr. Fourever, pronounced Foo – river actually existed. There were too many strange events for me to be concerned. These had to be a signal from Lyn, finally I just accepted my life was different and all the better for having crossed Lyn Monday's path. I missed those times in London. The only thing I wanted most was for Siobhan to return to normal, only then could we resurrect our lives.

I kept in touch with Robin, Lyn Monday's aunt. I checked how Bess Monday was handling my research of her daughter's death. All reports indicated she was comfortable with my involvement. I would love to meet her, if for no other reason but to tell her how special her daughter was. Over the coming weeks, I led Robin closer, never revealing the facts nor concealing them. I was surprised when I sent her a draft detailing my first encounter with Lyn. Her comment was, "You would be most fortunate to experience something like that."

I was, but completely unfortunate that I had lost a second chance.

I began to think of Robin's comment, 'most fortunate', was she a believer or was she humouring me, had she experienced something herself? Had Lyn been in touch with her also? I should explore that option later but first I needed to talk to Steve, her husband, the person responsible for advising Malcolm Shailler of Lyn's death all those years ago.

Steve had a vibrant personality, open and earthy and said he ripped shreds off Malcolm on that fateful day. He described how upset Malcolm appeared and had literally cowered during Steve's five-minute barrage. Was it an act, or was Malcolm really shocked? There were inconsistencies with Steve's recollection of events; he thought Lyn died from overdosing on the abortion tablets as opposed to that red mixture 'Mickey Finn'. This led me to believe Robin, his wife didn't know all the details. I phoned her and said, "I'm sorry to rehash the past but I assumed you knew every detail of Lyn's death. It was a long time ago and I shouldn't have taken that for granted. I'd liked to send you the Coronial Inquest's transcript."

After several days, she responded and said she was shocked. Until this time she never knew the real story and thanked me for keeping her informed. I asked her to check the Inquest's transcript and the Police's statements for inaccuracies, especially Malcolm Shailler's evidence.

As promised to Beaulieu, I plucked up the courage to see Samantha. When I arrived, I noticed the lawns were in need of mowing and the hedges, always sculptured now in need of a trim. Even the porch looked dusty. Little things that we had helped each other with now appeared too painful to tackle.

"What do you want?" Samantha said sourly. This was an attitude I had seen a few times over the years but her resolve now seemed doggedly determined.

"To make sure you're alright."

"Huh, as if you care."

"You may not think so, but I do care. Regardless of what has happened. What we had was special."

"You sound robotic as if you've been practising the lines."

I dismissed her grating comment and asked about the private investigator, it was a long shot but I needed to eliminate everyone, "Samantha, do you have something to tell me?"

"No; what?"

"Something you may now be regretting."

"Yes, marrying you. You know our children are mortified that you've taken up with that bimbo, her of all people. Are you having a mid-life crisis? Tell me so I can understand what has happened."

"I'm thinking of a third party, someone you paid?"

"My solicitor?"

"Mm… anyone else?"

"What are you on about? Are you going to explain or not, what happened, are you still hooked up with her and dwelling on spirits each day?"

What could I say, I had been contacted, drawn, spiritualised. "Siobhan is not like you think, she's different and I'm different."

"All very well, I'm traded for a newer model. Now I'm different too, I'm bitter and a hard nose bitch and with each hour passing making it worse. I'm hard pressed to resign myself to this situation and that is being kind."

"Samantha, please."

"Did you enjoy yourself vacationing in, where was it…?"

She knew very well, she just wanted me to say it, to hear the disappointment or the exultation in my voice. I spoke in a level tone, one mid way, one she found hard to interrupt, "Oh, yes London, mm, yes, it was nice but it rained a lot."

How could I explain I'd been locked up in a hotel room for

two weeks. There was no way she'd buy Lyn Monday was there, or that Siobhan had no memory of events. Samantha would probably think I drugged her or she drugged me. Whatever reasoning I gave, I knew it would be wrong – so I shut up!

"I never received one of those pictorial postcards we always send friends." The comment was snide, sarcastic and bitter. She was determined to find the crack and prise it open, "Samantha, can I come in and talk? You owe me a couple of minutes."

"I don't think I owe you anything Shaun, but I grant you five minutes."

She left the door unattended and walked to the sitting room, an extension we had built some ten years earlier, this allowed the sun to stream in and most times through summer we drew shades to reduce the heat. Today it was stifling hot and unshaded or it may have been because I was under intense scrutiny. Samantha didn't offer me anything to drink so I assume my five minutes was that and already counting. There was a pause between us.

"You're having trouble starting. Tell me Shaun, you want us to get back together?"

"No, it won't work."

"What does that mean?"

"It means, I haven't changed, not the way you would want me to change but I think we could be…"

"What friends? Is that the reason you came here."

"Samantha, we have a chance to right the past, I will always love you."

"Now you say the word LOVE but it's said conditionally. You will love me while you also love Siobhan and your spirit girl, all equals, we can all co-exist in perfect harmony. Is that the plan? This is a win-win for you, isn't it?"

"Samantha, you love our children, you loved your parents when they were with us, even that brother of yours, you loved him, even if you don't want to admit it. We don't have to stop caring for each other. You can love others, it's natural, it just that you want a possessive relationship."

"But you cheated on me and here lies the deception. I can't trust you, especially now that you've been with Siobhan."

"I didn't cheat on you with Siobhan, I told you before, I cheated on you with Lyn Monday."

"You're mad."

"Samantha, that's the other thing, I thought I was off the planet too but I'm not, a psychiatrist confirmed my stability."

"What in the hell are you talking about?"

"Remember that psychiatrist you wanted me to see, well I saw her. I'm as normal as any other red blooded male, not a glowing credential but accurate. Samantha, I didn't come here to win you back only to explain and hope you'd understand. I'm hoping we can be there for each other."

The tears rolled down Samantha's cheeks and a lump formed in my throat, I ventured, "Sorry."

She wiped her face with both hands, "Just so I can understand, you're telling me you're in love with a dead girl and Siobhan is happy with that."

"This is complex. She understands. She has changed; I never thought I would say that. I hope you can understand what I've gone through. I never expected this. I never wanted to hurt you."

"Well you have. Now that leaves me in limbo doesn't it, what happened to death do us part, in sickness and in health. Do I need to go on … Siobhan is playing you, be warned!"

"Well that's just it, I'm not talking about love without you, I'm referring to love with you, we could still be close."

"That line again? You're both sick or drugged out of your minds. What is it Shaun?"

I knew it would come down to this, I pleaded, "Neither, please Samantha, see this from another perspective, what if this was happening to you?"

Without thinking she stated, "I'd rebuke the demons and remain loyal to you and that's what this is about, something dark and sinister has grabbed hold of you and you refuse to do anything about it. A part-timer is no good to me. It's all or nothing."

She was determined, there was no room to discuss the 'layering of love'; regardless, I did love her, always would. I kept a strong face for fear of losing it. Samantha was terribly bitter, I couldn't blame her but I kept in the back of my mind Doctor Roberts's advice… 'Me time'. God that sounded so selfish.

"Would you do something for me Samantha, and I have no right to be asking you this."

"What?" she snapped.

"Could you pray for us? I pray for you each night, could you please try?"

"I'll think about it, but I won't pray for that flaming red-haired harlot, your time is up."

"I'm sorry Samantha, can you ever forgive me."

To which she responded, "No Shaun, I feel like I've been a reserve wife, one that was filling in until the right one came along. Shaun, you have never loved me like you loved Lyn Monday and the biggest betrayal was that you kept her a secret for all those years. It might be a small point to most people but I know you, this is a major issue. I just can't get over that deception. All those years you kept that lie, it must have been eating you up. Tell me Shaun, besides Lyn Monday what do you and Siobhan have in common?"

"I honestly don't know Samantha, it just feels right but I guess you don't want to hear that."

"Christ no. Why would I want to know it 'feels right'? I'm miserable and bitter, especially that you have someone else. I could run a knife through you and twist it until your last breath drains from your stinking body, that's how angry I've become."

Again I went to say sorry but caught her looking towards the kitchen. There six long blades sat ominously sheathed. I remembered my mother's attempt to kill my father with a knife, it was then I saw Samantha hesitate, was this history repeating itself? Her body shifted before collecting itself, she spat out venomously, "Don't push me further," then her eyes welled, "I never want to see you again… now go!"

This had to be the worse moment to ask, but I needed to know, "Samantha… have you ever heard of a person called Des Rains?"

CHAPTER 31

THE TEASE

Samantha refused to answer my question, instead she slammed the door in my face. She was bitter alright but not that bitter to employ Des Rains. So who was paying him?

My phone beeped, it was an SMS from Beaulieu... 'Des Rains was murdered'. I was not surprised I had even suggested the possibility. I scrolled the rest of the message...

'Des never used the airport shuttle. Maybe the murderer picked him up from the terminal. Now cautious – B'

Des murdered? Now what? I had little faith in the police's ability to solve this crime, my son's case was a typical example of their incompetence. I hated myself for being this simplistic but regardless I had an excellent excuse to feel bitter. There had to be a link to the murder and the person following me. I phoned Chelsea at the same time she was calling me, it just happened she was marginally quicker.

"Hi Chelsea."

"Shaun, I hung up on you when you questioned me over Des's death. At the time I was shaken but can understand why you would be suspicious. I would like to explain this in person, especially seeing Des tried to recruit me. You must doubt my integrity?"

"It had crossed my mind. You know Des was murdered."

She coolly remarked, "Have the police announced how he died?"

"No, it was only minutes ago I received the news. Chelsea, I'm gathering information for my novel, do you want to tag along?"

"Is this a memory lane thing, should I bring a camera?"

"You can bring what you want. I'll see you in twenty." If nothing else, having Chelsea along would give me the chance to quiz her. She had to know more about Des Rains.

She was waiting on the footpath outside her house and hailed me like you would a bus driver. Her first sentence was, "Guess how much Des offered to pay me?" but I countered, "The amount doesn't matter, it's just the fact he wanted to pay you. Anyway, how much?"

She countered, "Your right, of course the money isn't important. I've been trying to work out who would commit this murder and spy on you."

"But why?"

"Because I'm figuring you're suspicious of everyone."

"You're not half wrong."

"Shaun, I would like to remain your friend especially now you haven't many."

"You sure know how to lift my confidence."

"How can you trust me, I'm like a Santa Anna who just blew into your life."

"How do you know about Santa Anna's?" I looked at her puzzled. It was a wind that blew with fury into the South Western United States, not many Australians would know of this Mexican General's reference.

"I know a lot about trivia,"

"Well trivia is one thing, but if you knew I lived in California that would appear more than a coincidence."

"You lived in California? I didn't know. Well that makes what I'm about to say more difficult. Am I trying to win your confidence or just being honest? Am I a double agent Shaun?"

"Double trouble maybe," Christ, she was only eighteen, too

young to be involved but regardless I would ask Beaulieu to run a background check.

"Ok Shaun, let's make a list of suspects, I've got Samantha, Siobhan and her husband Tom."

"Keep Tom on, cross the other two off."

"What about that research person you've been working with?"

"Beaulieu... Samantha's niece? She is sometimes a little wacky but no way!" Chelsea wrote her name down anyway.

"What about someone from Lyn's family. Maybe they have something to hide."

"Wow, I never even thought of their involvement." Chelsea added them.

Then she asked, "What about that friend of yours, the one you said was acting suspicious, what's his name?"

"Josh Freemont, he's a possibility."

"Lyn's boyfriend, that pharmacist?"

"Malcolm Shailler?" for some reason I shivered and Chelsea picked up on the tremor.

"Have you spoken to him?"

"No, he wouldn't know me." Then I wondered if Beaulieu had innocently alerted him, "Better add him to the list."

"What about Lyn's friends, any possibility someone might be irked by your involvement."

"She had one close friend, her name is Debbie Hudson and that's the reason for visiting my old stomping ground."

"Anyone else? Although I think we've covered the serious possibilities."

"All, with the exception of the most obvious."

"Who?"

We made eye contact, she didn't blink then I added, "You!" There was a beat of two seconds before she said, "See... I'm already here," without further discussion she crossed her name off the list as if it was expected.

"Crossing your name off the list doesn't prove a thing. You don't want to discuss your involvement?"

"Nothing to discuss, it wasn't me that killed Des and I wasn't recruited to befriend you on the plane."

"What happened at Heathrow Airport? Was Des acting strange?"

"He had a lengthy phone call which seemed to excite him and then a guy delivered an envelope, probably the money!"

"Can you describe him?"

"The only thing I remember was his squashed-in nose."

"It sounds like the same guy who followed me. I sprang him at the hotel just before leaving London."

We drove in silence, both deep in thought.

Twenty minutes later we pulled to a stop outside Debbie Hudson's last known address. Chelsea asked, "So this is where she lives?"

"I hope so."

I felt sad, she had been Lyn's best friend, their closeness apparent. Even Debbie's name was inscribed on Lyn's headstone, her loyalty undeniable. She had provided us with a challenge and I knew Beaulieu would be anxious to finalise this part of her research. Did she still live here? With each passing second my hopes were dashed – there was no answer.

As was frequently the case, I looked for a signal. Sure enough, opposite Debbie's house was a lady who would be in her eighties. She walked with a sprightly step and disappeared inside. I gave her a few seconds before knocking. Seconds later she opened the door. I introduced myself, then said, "I'm trying to track down Debbie Hudson, she lived opposite."

"I'm Helen, I've lived here for fifty-one years and knew the Hudsons."

"I'm trying to find Debbie. She was a best friend to a girl I knew. You don't know where she lives?"

She replied, "No. She hasn't lived here for awhile, you know she married."

I added, "Then divorced."

She countered, "Then remarried..." She thought for a second, "Come with me," and we strode out of her front yard and down the street. I did a half run just trying to keep up. We passed Chelsea who was pre-programming my car radio. Our destination was a neighbour's weatherboard cottage some six houses away. Helen asked a short plump woman in her late sixties, "I thought you might remember the people your daughter purchased their house from?"

The woman spoke little English and couldn't remember a thing, more for convenience. Helen turned to me and explained, "Her daughter bought Debbie's old house."

"Oh, I see."

The woman cut her off, "No, no, sorry, can't remember." It reminded me of when the Soviet Bloc controlled Eastern Europe and everyone shut-up, more for self-preservation. Undeterred, Helen was off again, striding up the street to a house two doors from her own. A short balding man tried to help but could not remember Debbie's married name, all he could remember was her father who had worked as a chauffeur. There was nothing else of significance, except he said, "Debbie's next-door neighbour could have helped."

"Really?"

"Oh yes, he knew her well, unfortunately he died three years ago."

Regardless of Helen's growing enthusiasm, no one else was home. She appeared frustrated, "I'll try to track her down. Maybe I should take your phone number."

We exchanged numbers. Before we parted Helen said, "I think she moved to Seven Hills. She married a pharmacist, although I'm not sure if that was the first or second marriage."

My heart skipped, "A pharmacist?" Chelsea was within earshot and I saw her add Debbie's name to the list. Did she marry Malcolm Shailler? Christ, that would be bizarre! The task would become more difficult if she had married him. From here on I would have to be careful.

As we went to drive away, Helen suddenly turned, "Did I mention I saw a strange man walking around Debbie's old house. He was peering into the windows. That was only yesterday."

"Can you describe him?"

"I didn't have my glasses with me but he was of medium height and was wearing a black jacket. The collar was pulled up around his neck and he wore a baseball cap. He looked agitated so I kept inside."

"Thanks Helen, you're a gem."

As we drove away, Chelsea said, "That's bizarre, someone else is looking for Debbie," a second later she added, "If Debbie married that bastard, Lyn would turn in her grave."

I nodded, "I have to make a call," three seconds later Beaulieu answered, "Just ringing with an update. Yes, I received your text, no word on how Des died? No, ok. I just found out something, someone else maybe looking for Debbie and to make matters worse, are you sitting down, she may have married Malcolm Shailler." There was a gap in the conversation. "You better be careful, also could you do a background check on Chelsea Melton, she is supposed to have won a debating championship in London, it was some minuscule event, check her past, she had a connection to Des Rains, she's giving me bad vibes, some-thing's up."

Chelsea gave me a retaliating look, then crossed her eyes contemptuously. She was after all my main suspect and I needed to know her past.

I slowly drove through the suburbs of my youth, only speaking when a poignant moment needed explaining. My house and the tree I had climbed when young was still there. It looked like my darkroom, 'the black hole', had survived the years but was now a laundry. Thirty seconds later, Chelsea was panicking, she asked me to stop the car. She needed fresh air to prevent motion sickness. She couldn't have imagined the look on my face once I turned off the ignition. We were at the very steps of the church where Lyn's coffin would have been carried from the service. When I told her of the significance, she said, "I'm sorry Shaun, I didn't realise." I tried to dismiss this as being coincidental, "A lot of things happened in this church besides funerals."

"But still, what were the chances at this very spot."

Thirty minutes later we drove past the shops in Berala, I pointed, "This is the pharmacy where Malcolm worked and there is the milk bar where I first spoke to Lyn. That shop there, is the surgery where Lyn worked as a dental nurse."

"Oh Shaun, do you realise the significance, they were working close to each other, but look what happened, that milk bar is dead set in the middle. You divided them."

The milk bar had to be the midpoint. I had never considered that, had I divided what they had, had my energy lingered enough to cause a disruption. Each day on her way to see Malcolm, Lyn would have passed that milk bar where she asked, "Do you like me?" And of course I said I did but had walked away too shocked to continue. There was no way Lyn could bypass that milk bar. Uncharacteristically, Chelsea looked teary. Her story had a neat fit but her theory was riddled with questions. I sensed a spirituality about its concept. I wanted to believe more than anything but knew how improbably this was in a real world.

We drove further, to Josh Freemont's old house and I pointed out the backyard where his brother had his 21st birthday party. I also explained the disastrous bonfire celebration that night, "Some idiot placed a bunger into a glass bottle and it showered everyone with glass. It was here I spoke to Lyn for the second time and what turned out to be the last."

"Except for London," Chelsea reminded me.

"Of course, except for that surreal London trip. It seems so long ago – unbelievable."

"Is Siobhan accepting of what happened?"

"She's sceptical and I can't blame her, although as each day passes she appears more relaxed."

"What about Samantha, no chance of a re-conciliation?"

"None. And Chelsea, how are you? Are you still reeling from Des's death?"

"We weren't close, he was an opportunistic bastard but one of God's creatures. We're all here for a purpose, so I guess I'm accepting, but over all, I'm probably too young to be that understanding."

"So how come you're hanging out with me, rather than living your own life?"

"You've got me Shaun, I really don't know."

Later that day when I returned to Siobhan's house there was an email from Beaulieu.

'Call Debbie Hudson on the attached number but beware – the dog's bite!'

She had found her but why the mystery? Beaulieu was always trying to achieve a reaction. Then I noticed an emoticon flashing at the bottom of the screen. It was a picture of a bulldog holding a bone in its mouth; which it dropped and picked up repeatedly. Beaulieu had the weirdest sense of humour.

I phoned Debbie Hudson, but her answering machine kicked in, "I'm either out, or on another call." Then there was a pause… "Or another option… I just don't want to talk to you… leave a message and I'll work out your status eventually."

I hung up. What I had to say was far more important than an answering machine's introduction.

I called Beaulieu, "What's the reference to the dogs biting."

She projected through the phone, "She has dogs, it's simple. Shaun… I don't want to say any more. You know what I mean?"

"No."

"The bugs are listening."

"Would you like me to come over?"

"Yes."

In less than an hour, Beaulieu's door was opening, "Good, it's you." She invited me in and I could hear Indian flute music playing hauntingly along the corridor. We sat on her sofa. She was dressed to go out and her make-up had been applied with care an artistic endowment to an already beautiful face. She spoke mere centimetres from my ear. I considered her revealing top and 'oil esénciala' excessive, although I was surprised when she said softly, "In case of the bugs!" Then I thought, 'why would bugs influence her plunging neckline and the way she smelt'. I adjusted my thinking to consider the bigger picture and realised the music was her reference to drowning our voices from a listening device.

"From here on, be careful, I'm sure the phone is tapped and the house is under surveillance.

"Are you sure?"

"Am I normally paranoid?"

Beaulieu was still close, "Why are you wearing that top? Are you going out?"

She looked down, flushed for a few seconds and heaved the material higher. Then to distract me, she pulled out a folder. I asked, "What's that?"

"A report, summarising your novel's research, I have also included some suggestions." There were colour tabs running its edge but most amazing was the sheer size of the production, it must have taken weeks to complete, "Your copy, keep it safe. Once you have read it, contact me. Also, I need to increase my hourly rate. This is a stress related environment, maybe a further ten percent?"

I would now be paying her $5.50 per hour, "You can forget researching anything else. Your rates are excessive."

She sniggered, "You'll be back, you love me."

She queried, "You spoke to Samantha?"

"Yeah, just as you asked."

"And?"

"We have agreed to be good enemies. She's as bitter as a double Campari, nothing will pacify her. That last meeting was final. She even rallied the kids against me. Joel refuses my calls. Tamara the same, and Kem, God bless her subtleness has sent me a book on 'How to Win Friends and Influence People."

"We all need time, there is hurt, I know how things work in the Universe, I've studied cosmic forces, they are out there and eventually everything meshes to form harmony. You have to have faith. As for Siobhan, how is she faring?"

"Coming to terms with her new life, she is certainly different from the old Siobhan."

"I wish her well."

"Beaulieu, before I go, Debbie Hudson… do you think she married Malcolm Shailler?"

She laughed, "Absolutely not, I checked, although she did marry a pharmacist by the name of Judd, just a coincidence, but what a horrible concept if it was true."

"That's a relief."

Beaulieu continued smiling, an unusual occurrence these days, most times she buried herself in research and fed off her own company. She looked different, there was even a sparkle in her eye, I queried, "When was the last time you went on a date?"

She looked away, "This is different… it's business!"

I couldn't resist, "Sure… of course it is, male or female?"

She wouldn't answer but I knew that top wasn't for business… unless funny business!

My return trip to Siobhan's was one of reflection. My thoughts were scattered, Chelsea had felt car sick at the very location where Lyn's funeral was conducted. This had emotionalised Chelsea and I detected tears and an understanding not previously apparent. I felt Chelsea was here for a purpose, not someone on the outside looking in. But what could an eighteen year-old possibly do that would make a difference? In a way I regretted asking Beaulieu to do that background check on her.

Once home I found Siobhan resting. I massaged her feet and she purred. I reminded her she had offered to massage mine whilst I wrote my novel but she stated she wasn't in control at the time, so all offers were null and void. I continued to massage her feet with nil expectations. She did kiss me on the crown of the head once I had finished.

An hour later, I redialled Debbie's phone, "For an automatic transfer to my mobile, press 1, for information regarding your next appointment, press 2, to leave a message, press 3."

One sounded the better option. I left my finger on the button for a full second to ensure her system recognised the tone.

"I'm sorry, your touch phone system is incompatible."

The connection was terminated. What type of system did she have? Would it be best to leave a message? I resigned myself to call in the morning.

I read two pages of Beaulieu's report and fell asleep.

After 9 am the next day I felt confident. I punched in Debbie's phone number and was surprised to hear, "Julie's Day Care."

"I'm sorry, I must have the... Debbie?"

"Who wants to know?"

"My name is Shaun. Are you Debbie?"

"Maybe, this is important, how old are you Shaun?"

"One year older than you Debbie, so that would make you..."

"Alright, it's me, just don't mention my age."

"Why the confusing messages?"

"Some guy has been harassing me. Beaulieu said you may phone but I need to screen each call. She told me about my good friend Lyn is a part of the action, right!" She went quiet before divulging, "We had some good times."

"Lyn's the reason for my call. Incidentally, Helen sends her regards."

"Oh, my neighbour where I grew up, she is such a cutie, how old would she be now?"

"82."

"Wow."

"Can we meet up and talk?"

"Yeah, just drop by any time."

"Okay, where do you live?"

Instead of answering she cautioned, "Come by yourself Shaun. Just you and me, I won't bite, I promise."

"Really?"

She gave me the address and the phone went dead.

CHAPTER 32

DOGS BITE

All I could think of was the infamous Debbie Hudson. What would she look like? What should I say?

I set the GPS finder for her address and arrived an hour later. This had to be the weirdest destination known to man. There was no possibility I could have stumbled upon it for it was a private road named after a brickwork owner, a Trudeon McFalter and the lane way stopped at the lip of the Sydney Harbour. Then I remembered the reference to biting dogs, what was that about? As I stood pondering the question and at the same time admiring the harbour foreshore, a woman called out, "Shaun Reece, over here," I turned to see a beautifully matured woman, fittingly attired in a long flowing dress. Her hair was shoulder length and had a haloing sheen that supported an auburn tint, "Come on, the kettle's boiling." Her scarf lifted in the breeze, she smiled and beckoned me to follow, without notice she disappeared into the cottage. A rusting sign above the door displayed the word… CARETAKER

The caretaker's cottage belonged to the defunct brickworks which had made custom designed blocks for heritage houses. The setting was magnificent with a winding gravel road leading to this beautiful harbour vista.

As I entered the door she said, "So, here we have Shaun Reece. Yeah… Lyn would have been pleased with you; you survived the harsh Australian climate with a combination of good genetics. What age did your father's mother live to?"

"Until she was 99, almost made it for a telegram." She smiled and I added, "The elusive Debbie, we probably crossed paths at high school, especially every Monday afternoon when the girls and boys schools met for dance lessons."

"Yes, I remember that, so here we are again."

We said together, "Sorry, I don't remember you," and then laughed simultaneously.

We were silent for almost a minute.

Debbie broke the silence, "It upset me no end. She didn't commit suicide you know."

"I know."

Debbie was silent again. There was no rush, I had the rest of my life to ask her questions and there was some rapport happening. It just needed time.

She asked, "Tea? Scottish Breakfast?"

"I haven't had one since London, great."

"Were you in love with her."

"Still am."

"God knows I tried to talk Lyn out of that relationship with that pompous smart-arse pharmacist. Admittedly, he was good looking but he was playing her, I could see that but she couldn't. How do you tell your best friend she has made a mistake? You test your own relationship, bordering it on the brink. She was possessed by the illusion."

All I could muster was, "Yeah," seconds later I spat out, "Malcolm Shailler was a real piece of work."

"No argument there."

"Debbie, tell me about your life."

"Married twice, divorced twice, I'd do it all again given the outcome."

"Outcome?"

"Yes, those marriages produced two great children who have

gone on to spectacular careers. Now that they have left home, I'm stuck in these wandering years and all on my lonesome."

"Just so I'm clear on this, you married a pharmacist?

"Oh, John, yes."

"That's a relief at one point I thought you had married Malcolm."

"Even if he was the last person on earth, it would be an empathic… NO."

She went to say something but my question cut her off, "Debbie, did Lyn ever mention…"

"You."

"No, a Josh Freemont."

She thought for a moment, "The name is familiar. Give me a clue."

"Same age as you, one year younger than Lyn, he claimed to be her boyfriend, although it appeared a well-kept secret and hidden from me for forty-five years."

"What are you saying that he was seeing her at the same time?"

"It's a possibility. When Lyn had an argument with Malcolm, they broke up for a while, he may have slotted in as her new boyfriend."

"I'm unsure. The name is strangely familiar but I would only be guessing if I said I knew him."

I sighed, "Time is a killer for memories."

"Except some are too ingrained to be erased."

"True."

I asked, "After reading the Coronial Inquest transcript I was surprised the police never called you to give evidence?"

"I was relieved at the time but now I feel cheated at not having the chance to stand up and protect Lyn's reputation. Do you know what happened? No one ever told me."

Forty minutes later, I had divulged all I knew.

"Debbie, you were the only one who had the guts to stand up to Malcolm. Without you, there would not have been an inquest. The police handled her death badly; they over looked so many things. I'm sure his family's influence allowed him to get off, you know what I mean?"

"You're kidding? It is so sad. And you want my help to write your book."

"Besides other things, I'm not sure where this is heading. Sometimes I feel I'm stirring everyone up. I have no idea how my book will help, it just seems the right thing to do. You could never believe the coincidences and events I have experienced since I started. Sometimes I'm overwhelmed by everything and regardless of where I go there are signs reminding me of Lyn. What would she want me to do?"

"What a shining knight, where were you when she died, were you at the funeral?

"I found out she died two weeks later."

"Oh really, no closure, all by yourself and with no one to talk to, I know your predicament. I tried to keep in touch with the family but it was hard, Lyn's father died and every time I called her mother she became upset. Is she still alive?"

"Yes. She would like you to call her. I'll give you the number later."

Debbie stood and wandered into the kitchen. On the stove was a simmering stew that smelt divine, "Another half an hour and we can eat." She stirred the pot and I saw carrots and potatoes trying to escape.

"Smells good."

"My mother's recipe."

"Your mum and dad both gone?"

"Yes. Tell me about your life Shaun."

"I'm separated from my wife, I'm sure Beaulieu told you that, I have three kids, all grown up – two girls and one boy, my son has a brain injury."

"Who do you spend your time with, your son?"

"Yes, well I used to. Now I don't see him. My children refuse to accept my new girlfriend."

"Ahh, the one that split up the marriage, Beaulieu did explain that."

"I'd doubt she gave you the right information for this is the most bizarre situation."

"Oh, I think she grasps what happened precisely. A family man is living his life, a day at a time when suddenly a friend makes a move on him."

"Close, but not right."

"What then."

"This was orchestrated by Lyn."

"Lyn, our Lyn?" She looked amused.

"Why are you smiling? It's true."

"That's Lyn, she had a wilder side, and some people thought I was the rebellious one, more worldly, but she was the one instigating all the moves and I was the one getting the blame. I'm intrigued, tell me more."

"Lyn may well have whacked me over the head with a sledgehammer for I ended up in hospital after a panic attack. She came to me asking for help." Debbie looked amazed. She stirred the pot with consideration. She wanted to say something but bit her bottom lip. As she pulled her hair back behind her left ear I reinforced, "I know, it sounds ridiculous."

Debbie nodded, "It is…"

"But?"

"Things go missing here, later I find them in the most unusual places."

"You think Lyn is trying to contact you?"

"Or the original owner Trudeon McFalter, he was murdered in this cottage."

"How long has this been happening?"

"About a month."

"The timing is right for Lyn. My friend Siobhan experienced a similar attack to me. Anyway, I don't expect you to believe this, I'm still having trouble unravelling what's fact and fiction. My mind's in denial."

"It's obvious you experienced something, you need time."

"I doubt it, I'm pretty much stuck in limbo, realising this happened and wondering where I'm heading. What could Lyn possibly want from me?" I didn't dare mention that Lyn had merged with Siobhan during our London holiday. Already I had overloaded Debbie with information.

"Shaun, the subject of Lyn Monday is a heavy one; we are possibly the only two with the same outlook. I think of her constantly." Debbie uncorked a bottle of red and filled our glasses.

"A toast, to a good friend, I loved you Lyn. Life hasn't been the same since."

"I... I... can't toast to that."

"Why, what's wrong?"

"You said... loved. I don't consider her in the past tense. She's here now!"

"That would be nice, a little scary though."

"No... she is, honestly, I can feel her."

"You're not just saying that, you're not going all weird on me, are you?"

"I can feel her. This is the hardest thing for me to accept. I can understand you're scepticism."

"Well Shaun, you present the toast."

I raised my glass, "ME: YOU – FOREVER – I love you."

"Lyn," We said together and clinked the glasses.

Debbie looked at me puzzled, "You say love, I said loved, there's the difference, you haven't let go. That's ridiculous after all these years."

"Exactly."

"If you don't let go, you'll always be caught up with her."

"I'd be happy with that."

"She really made an impression, didn't she? No more Lyn until we eat."

She returned to the kitchen and called out, "Hungry?"

"Famished. Can I help?"

"No, sit there and relax."

"Anyway, we have heaps to talk about. Tell me more about your son."

I explained how similar Joel's story was to Lyn's but how he survived – however at an enormous cost. "He has shown improvement although every change takes time. The most significant moment after leaving hospital was the re-instatement of his driver's licence. The strange thing is, he was busting at the seams to get it but once he procured it, driving wasn't that important. He's mainly a home body, it's safer at home, no chance of being attacked."

"I'm sorry Shaun, at least you still have him."

"Yes. I have him but I don't, I'm sorry," I reflected on my life and sipped the Shiraz.

We enjoyed rambling along and reliving the past. After dinner, there were flashes of 'Mondayism'. It was as if Lyn was sitting with us and had orchestrated the whole meeting. My body felt a gentle pressure and I closed my eyes unable to stay awake.

It must have been 4 am when I stirred, the fire was still crackling and I heard an occasional whimper from outside. Strange, I had not seen any dogs on arrival. So Beaulieu was right, there were dogs. Their whimpers suddenly converted to growls then barks, their incessant barrage coming from the front of the cottage. Debbie was on her feet and before I could ask what was happening she began peering through a small window to the rear of the cottage. There was a flash and a bang followed simultaneously by a zap of metal against something brittle. It sounded so precise, an unrealistic 'whack'. It was the pane next to her shattering, spotting her face with stained glass flecks. She fell to the ground holding her face and crying out, "Oh shit." I dropped to the floor and scrambled to her assistance, she managed, "Hit the light switch… quick!"

I backed up the wall and flicked the switch. A flood of light hit the shadows. A wire meshed fence was restricting the dog's entry to the rear. I could see someone crouching, taking aim again, a mere eighty metres away. Before he could prepare, one dog scampered the fence and charged him. He rose in a panic and leaped at the retaining wall some metres to his rear. He was seconds from a mauling. The rest of the dogs continued barking as he climbed the upper wire to safety.

Debbie distressed, asked, "Is he gone?"

"Yeah, what a bastard!"

"My face Shaun, he shot at my face."

"I'll call for an ambulance."

"No don't!"

"Why not?"

"I'm not allowed to run the dogs. If an ambulance comes they will create a commotion. Either way I'm screwed."

"But this guy nearly killed you."

"Forget him, my face Shaun?"

"Sit up Debbie. Hold you head towards the light."

The globes were energy saving little suckers and next to useless. There was no bullet hole per se, but there were numerous glass slithers sitting in blood stained skin. Each was raised above the surface and accessible. Her eyes had missed the shrapnel and nothing was to be gained by biding hours in emergency, I volunteered, "If you have tweezers I'll operate for free and that will save you megabucks."

I could tell she was worried, "Will I be scarred?"

I joked, "No way, just little nicks which will give you some character lines."

"Shit, its serious then. I don't have many options do I?"

I plucked and sterilised each wound and used fine strips of tape to close the nicks. "I'd see a doctor tomorrow in case I've missed something. This light is atrocious."

"Sorry."

"Not your fault. Who has a grudge against you Debbie?"

"Two ex – husbands, neighbours, you understand there is a barking problem, I owe some money, a lot, I've had those crank phone calls, the landlord would like to see the back of me but his hands are tied by some piece of legislature preventing eviction and then there is that bastard…"

"Alright, I get the picture. It sounds like the dogs are a necessary form of protection. How come I never saw them when I arrived?"

"A security company utilises them during the day and drops

them back about midnight." She looked somewhat sheepish, "It's the only way I can make ends meet."

I offered, "You know you can stay with me until everything settles."

"Thanks but the dogs will be hyper-alert now. With them I feel safe."

"Well watch yourself."

She nodded and rose from her seat. She went to a broom closet and withdrew a 12 gauge shotgun. She loaded the gun as I asked, "Do you have a license for that?"

She smiled wickedly and said, "I don't need one here, I'm immune from prosecution. Don't you just love those old laws?"

"Where were you?" Siobhan scolded, "I couldn't reach you."

"Sorry, I forgot to turn the phone back on."

"You were gone all night. Where were you?"

"At Debbie's, we were talking and I dozed off."

"You slept there? Is Debbie good looking?"

"Somewhat, but no... I never... I was just resting my eyes. Look... we both nodded off, but honestly nothing happened."

"You slept with her? Shaun?"

"No, no, really Siobhan... we were zapped... discussing Lyn was draining. You're not jealous are you?"

She assessed herself, "Yeah... a little."

"That's good then. You must be getting better."

"She's dead meat if she slept with you."

"You're cute."

"Why say that... jealousy isn't cute, it's ugly."

"Not when you're so open about it, you have nothing to worry about. We talked, that's all."

There was a huge gap in the conversation while we both pondered what had happened; I was trying to defend my actions while Siobhan had been clearly threatened, all innocent, but enough to show we cared for each other – I figured a good start!

Minutes later I informed Siobhan, "Remember Beaulieu's warning, 'the dogs' bite', well Debbie runs security dogs on the property however I must tell you what happened. Some guy took a pot-shot at Debbie."

"What? Someone shot at her?"

"Yeah, but he escaped over the fence just before a dog reached him. It was funny seeing him scamper off like that."

"But why would any one shoot at her?"

"I'm not sure."

"Do you think this has anything to do with you being followed?"

"It had crossed my mind."

"Can you describe him?"

"It happened so fast and all I remember was him taking a giant leap at the fence, if anything he was athletic. The distance was too great for a description."

"Do you think the police should be notified?"

"Debbie has too many problems to involve the police but if he turns up again she has a surprise."

"But what if he was after you, what's your surprise?

CHAPTER 33

—◄○►—

SPLAT!

It was early morning. The sun found a crack in the blinds and doused me in limelight – unnerving, a strange feeling and I knew today would be remembered.

I headed to Siobhan's room. Her door was ajar. She lay peaceful and oblivious to my concerns, her curvaceous lines cocooned in the finest of charcoal coloured sheets. On a crisp contrasting pillow, white and stark, her red hair laid perfectly aligned, not a wayward strand and nothing encroaching upon those curvaceous shoulders, except... those thin pink satin straps... so sexy... just sitting there, virtuously defending her body.

She opened her eyes and drawled, "Shaun... darling."

"Hi, go back to sleep."

"No, sit here next to me, keep me company." She moved over a little, just enough for us to be close.

I leaned forward and whispered, "You look beautiful." She stretched her arms and yawned. I asked, "Can I get you breakfast?"

"Later maybe, talk to me first, tell me what you're thinking?"

"Just thoughts about you, I miss London, we were close."

"I understand, we're almost there, the worst thing I could do is rush. I need to ease into this relationship."

"Siobhan, I know, but it's difficult, especially when we were the ultimate couple and then by sunrise our relationship had vanished. We had to start all over, only this time you're full of apprehension and seeking assurance. You know my theory about Lyn, trust me this is something good."

"Well then, maybe you should do something for me?"

"Anything."

"Kiss me Shaun, a passionate kiss, something that will kick start my motor."

"What then? Am I to leave you alone for another week? This is tough."

She placed her finger against my lips. "You're thinking too much," and she raised herself onto her elbow and closed her eyes before positioning her mouth for contact. I touched her lips; the finest skin of the body – the passion from past week invaded my consciousness. My hand rested on her shoulder, her warmth obvious, her body twisted a little, suddenly we were into a fevered embrace and anxious for each other.

Ten minutes must have passed and I had nibbled her neck and caressed her beautiful hair, she was breathing heavily and just when I thought we might go that 'extra mile', she said with a palm against my chest, "Breakfast in bed sounds great."

"Ok," I tried to maintain my breathing.

"Will you eat with me?"

"Is your motor started yet?"

"Purring along just before I hit the hill. I'll need big revs for that!"

Upon leaving the room, she called me back. She didn't say a word, she didn't have to; it was where she positioned her eyes that said it all. She just smiled and I felt a little embarrassed.

I was preparing scrambled eggs, whipping yolks and wrestling arousal. I spat bacon in a fry pan and produced something I thought may tantalise her palate. It was a non-alcoholic Julep and I had just added fresh mint when my mobile phone rang. I checked the caller identification. Why would Samantha call? She questioned immediately, "Who is Chelsea?"

"Nice to hear from you Samantha, how are you?"

"Who in the hell is Chelsea?"

"Why do you want to know about Chelsea?"

"Who is she Shaun? She rang me."

"Someone I met recently."

I knew Chelsea would have an excellent excuse to call but I couldn't think of one, "What did she say?"

"So you know her… well?"

"Yes, I know her."

Samantha became conciliatory, almost believable, "Ok then and you're alright?"

"Well yes; as well as to be expected considering the circumstances."

"What are you doing?"

"I was just reaching for my medication," to be precise, my cholesterol lowering tablets. Without further ado she huffed and hung up.

Siobhan called out, "Who was it Shaun?"

"Hang on, I'm coming, sit up. It was Samantha. She wanted to know…" when I saw Siobhan, I almost dropped the tray. She was naked and sitting upright in bed. I cautioned her as I approached, "Don't spill the coffee, it's scalding hot." I settled the tray with a gentle softness admiring her figure at the same time.

"And where's your breakfast?"

"Coming, I have a separate tray." I raced to the kitchen and returned quicker than a bounding cheetah.

"Take your pyjamas off, let's have a nudie breakfast."

"Great," she tossed my pyjamas somewhere.

"Let me feed you," and with crisp strips of bacon I took a bite. In return I balanced a fork full of crumbling eggs into her mouth, she giggled as some avalanched across her breasts.

"Try this," I said raising the dew encrusted glass to her lips.

She sipped, raised her napkin and patted her moist lips, she smiled, "Your full of surprises, aren't you? Julep?"

"Shaun actually, the drink's Julep."

"Shaun seriously, I've passed the first hurdle, the attraction is still there and I'm sure we can jump each others bodies without hesitation." She leaned across and kissed me, "Shaun this is my first time with you, you realise that, you know me far better than I know you. Gosh, it strange talking like this," she raised another strip of bacon for me to crunch. "I only have one hurdle and that's to account for Lyn within me. It's that part that has me struggling, can you be patient while I work that out?"

I sighed at the delay, she added, "Hey, I'm not asking you to stop paying attention. I want to be stimulated, can you still do that?"

I placed my hand on her leg. I felt her muscles relax and the softness of her inner thigh. She placed her tray on the bedside table, I did likewise. She giggled. My hand ran up the inside of her leg. I cupped her breasts firmly and nibbled aggressively at her neck. I raised her hair to resemble corded twine, tugging it tight and letting it fall to the pillow. I turned her onto her back and ran my tongue the length of her body. She tightened her legs where I lingered way longer than expected. She sunk into the mattress totally gripped by the sensation.

It was then the phone rang.

It rang again.

Once more it repeated its ten ring cycle.

"Shit, turn it off," she said.

I raised my head, "Maybe it's important." She massaged my head, I ignored the constant ringing.

Finally it stopped.

"Whoever it is will leave a message. Don't stop." Then, as if removed from the action she said, "You know I clean the house in the nude."

I raised my head, ever curious and asked, "Really, why?"

She rested her head back, "I feel free, there's something about the concept of nakedness, it's totally uplifting."

I encouraged, "Any time you want to clean, go for it, drop whatever you're wearing and I'll be your devoted cheer squad." I dropped my head.

"You wouldn't help me?"

I raised my head, "Maybe, but not in winter."

At the mere suggestion of chill, she pulled the covers over our heads and started mumbling. "Siobhan, what are you doing?"

"Nothing."

"No you're not, your doing something. You're mumbling for starters and you're way too close for innocence."

"Are you going to make love to me or are we going to talk all day. You're way bigger than I expected."

"If this is sex talk, you have a strange way of … ok… ok…"

We were about to 'knowingly' consummate when we heard a loud banging at the front door. It was persistent. It shook Siobhan from a woman lovingly possessed to a woman brimming with frustration, "Can't they give us a few minutes."

The banging persisted.

I asked, "Where are my pyjamas?"

"I threw them in the laundry chute; it's too late for them."

"They're gone?"

"You were going to help me with the nudie cleaning."

"No, to watch only – who is that knocking?"

"Shaun, for Christ sake, take my robe and answer the door."

I wrapped the satin material around me. When I opened the door I was surprised. It was Tom, Siobhan's husband. His eyes gathered with a wild and furious look and then he hesitated, confused at my presence. He went to speak but a gust of wind hit my face. I pulled back. He brushed at something – a fly perhaps. I heard it buzz by. Then I saw a red dot appear on his forehead, like a boil due for discharge, then his eyes widened with shock. Everything was happening so fast, it was weird. He spat in my face, a disgusting show of respect. My finger went instinctively to the runniest of drops. It was warm, red and sticky. Tom's knees bent slightly and he staggered backwards before falling onto his face. It was then I noticed a small bullet hole at the back of his head. The blood pooled too quickly to be superficial. He was dead. I looked around but there was no one, not even a car, I slammed the door and screamed, "Siobhan, Siobhan, take cover," and instantly another round shattered the cedar entry. There were five more shots then silence.

Siobhan yelled, "What's happening?"

"Tom's been shot."

She crawled on her hands and knees towards me and looked at my blood splattered face, "Is he…?"

"I think so, call the police."

Of course the police came and surprisingly fast. They roped off the crime scene with blue and white flapping tape. They questioned Siobhan first, then she made cups of tea for three detectives, four forensic specialists, three perimeter security guys and a media representative in case Tom's death attracted reporters. In every case the china rattled nervously as Siobhan settled cups on saucers. Of course we had dressed by this stage and Tom's body was bagged and trundled unceremoniously to the morgue's van.

My intense interrogation was to be expected. I was the eye witness, although I was unsure how to help. My predisposition towards the police hindered an otherwise cordial rapport. Senior Detective Lance Petersen, a tall guy with close cropped hair and bulging biceps asked, "And what type of relationship do you have with the deceased's wife?"

"We're friends."

He looked at me for several seconds weighing up the age variance. I looked at him trying to figure how some one so young could have experience adjudicating on matters of life and death. It was at this point we considered each other as equals, he had his job and I had some of the answers.

"And you were standing where when the deceased died?"

"In the doorway."

"How far was he from you?"

"Close, so close I was splattered with his blood but of course you have my robe as evidence."

He coughed.

"Well, it was the only thing I could find to put on. He was knocking incessantly."

"Would you say he was agitated?"

"Maybe, I don't know, his knocking appeared aggressive. Everything happened so quickly."

"Did he say anything?"

"No, the bullet stopped him in his tracks."

"Did you hear the gun discharge?"

"No."

"Just so I'm clear on this, if you were standing facing him, so how did this projectile miss you?"

It was then I remembered the gush of wind just before Tom was shot. It was enough to unbalance me and I assume miss the bullet. "Lucky I guess," I thought of my guardian angel Lyn. Was I the target?

"Now considering everything prior to this tragedy, what were you doing?"

"Trying to have sex."

"With Tom's wife?"

"Yes. They had split up, an amicable agreement."

"And you had split with your wife?'

"Yes."

"Was that also amicable?"

"God no."

"Her name?"

"Samantha Reece." I gave him Samantha's address but added, "If Tom's death was gun related then you can forget Samantha's involvement, she emphatically hates guns."

Senior Detective Petersen replied, "From what you're telling me, the killer would have used a high powered rifle with telescopic sights and had the benefit of a silencer. Samantha Reece may emphatically hate guns, but it sounds like she hates you more."

I considered her both hates, "Maybe."

"And what was your opinion of... Tom?"

"Is that relevant?"

"Of course."

"I didn't like him, it no secret, I would have liked to have killed him but I didn't. I suspect he had a girlfriend but I have no idea who."

"Was there anyone else who would want to harm him?"

I thought for a second, "Maybe…"

It was the golden rule with cops that every interview should produce a lead. I had given him three. Unfortunately Samantha was one of them. He concluded the interview with, "I may need to ask more questions, don't go on holidays."

Although I had lost patience with the police's ability to solve crime, I was nevertheless sympathetic to their cause for they bore witness to the vilest acts and now, so had I. With so much happening, I had forgotten my phone; there were four messages which were to raise more questions than answers.

CHAPTER 34

◄◦►

HI, I'M CHELSEA

Siobhan and I were finally alone. We felt terrible, Tom's death being replayed a thousand times over, each time a different nightmare but eventually we would accept the truth, this shocking waste of life.

Words seemed irrelevant, as was my phone messages – the silence roared!

It was hours later...

Siobhan looked pale, when she spoke it was accompanied with a vacant stare, "Shaun, I feel absolutely gutted, I'll never see Tom again. As much as I detested him he was after all my husband and we did have some good times. I'll need to mourn him, I hope you'll understand."

"I understand more than you realise."

Later, as if the compass had spun full circle, Siobhan lashed out oblivious to our time frame, "Shaun... couldn't you have turned that stupid phone off?"

I retaliated, "That wouldn't have stopped Tom being killed. Anyway..."

She cut me off, "I'm too upset to discuss it right now!"

"Of course you are; I'm sorry. Siobhan, truly, I don't want to upset you."

She hesitated, "I know… we are starting to argue over things beyond our control. You know why that is don't you?"

"No, not really."

"It's the shock setting in. You know there is nothing we could have done to prevent this catastrophe."

"Come here," we hugged and sensed the ordeal confronting us. Siobhan began shaking, her sobbing relentless, she nuzzled my neck, wetting my shirt as her tears rolled freely. She managed, "Tom's death will change me forever." I held her close. It was then we realised the comfort we gave each other, we were able to communicate and decipher our problems, the whole world may have gone mad but together we were immune to its intrusion. If anything felt right, it was this moment. We lingered in that tight grip for ages, finally I asked, "Why do you think Tom came here?"

"Maybe he needed a safe haven, or he wanted to talk of our divorce, maybe he wanted to make amends. Who knows? It's such a terrible way to die, one second he's with us and the next gone. Shaun, how did he appear to you?"

"His eyes were dancing wildly but then he appeared confused."

"Shaun, normally he would push past you; he was such an arrogant son-of-a-bitch, so to be confused and linger at the door seems strange. There have been two deaths now, I wonder if there is a connection?"

I finally listened to my phone messages and was astounded.

One was from Samantha who apologised for her rude phone manner – now that was a first!

The second was from Chelsea who said, "Guess who I've been talking to, call back when you two get out of bed."

The third was from Beaulieu who wanted to know if I had finished her report, she had something important to tell me – maybe about her date.

The fourth was from Tom, "I need your help old man, got myself into a spot of bother actually, my friend is also in a pickle. You and I need to meet up urgently. If I don't get your call by 8:45 am, I'll wait at Siobhan's until you arrive."

I replayed the messages for Siobhan, she queried, "'my friend'…?

Tom must have meant his secretary, the one he was seeing behind my back."

"I've got a horrible feeling about this. I need to notify the police. Siobhan, I haven't had a chance to tell you, something happened when I opened the door."

"What?"

"I was buffeted by a strong breeze, it forced me sideways, several centimetres in fact."

"What are you saying? That this saved your life?"

I nodded.

"You think…?"

I caught her gaze, "It's a hunch, that's all. Someone wants me dead. Regardless, that gust of wind saved me otherwise I may have been killed as well."

"Who would want to kill you?"

"Who has the most to lose?"

"Someone you stirred, someone with a guilty conscience?"

"Maybe I didn't stir anyone, maybe Beaulieu has, she may not even realise."

"That would make Tom, what… someone luring you to a killer? If he didn't know you were living here, it's no wonder he looked confused, especially when you opened the door in my dressing gown. Whoever the murderer is would have had a perfect shot … but from where… the bushes? That would be one hundred metres away."

Siobhan's tears continued to tumble, she was distressed beyond reason, "Oh Shaun, that bullet hit Tom and then lodged into the wall. It was meant for you?"

"If not, the other shots certainly were."

"Tom could probably identify the killer and became expendable. Shaun, I don't feel safe here."

For fear of upsetting Siobhan, I didn't tell her what I told the police, they asked who would harm Tom, and I replied, 'Revenge maybe'. It was a long shot but worth investigating. Tom's car accident, several weeks ago had undertones of ethnic violence and I wondered if there was a connection.

I called Detective Petersen and advised him of Tom's phone message. Without hesitation he demanded my phone. I spluttered, "What… whatever for?"

"It's evidence in a murder investigation, of course I want it. Mr. Reece, I have already despatched a patrol car."

I thanked him for his consideration and quickly deleted everything of a personal nature. I left Tom's message as the police's only evidence. The patrol car arrived promptly and with them my replacement phone. They insisted I pay a $100.00 security bond. Then my phone was swallowed into an evidence bag. It was tagged, zipped and carted away.

I called Chelsea on my new entry level phone, it appeared to be working perfectly, she said, "Some marathon; did Siobhan pull up alright?"

"What do you mean?"

"Was the sex good?"

"Christ Chelsea, not everything is about sex. I've been busy, something terrible has happened but before I tell you, where were you about nine this morning?"

"On the phone to Samantha, what has happened?"

"That's a neat alibi. Were you using your home phone or your mobile and don't lie to me? So far I've kept your name out of this, so providing you tell the truth, you're safe, trust me!"

"Shaun, you're terrible at bluffing but I love how you mess up your own head with the lie," she giggled, "Anyway to answer your question, a home phone of course. I haven't got one of those super-duper phones where you can talk all day for nothing."

I lamented, "Neither do I any more."

"Anyway, what happened?"

"Chelsea, Tom was murdered."

"Shit. Where were you Shaun when this murder took place?"

"I was with Tom, I saw him die, a shot to the head, the murderer was some distance away, and Tom's secretary may have been killed as well. That puts the toll to three. I suggest you be careful."

"How did she die?"

"I don't know if she has, I'm just assuming she's dead."

"So maybe there are only two."

Somewhat frustrated with the discussion I changed direction, "Chelsea why did you ring Samantha?"

"Remember when you dropped me off the other day, one of the last things we considered was who should be on the list of possible suspects. Then I realised I had forgotten someone important."

I sighed, "Ok, who?"

"You."

"Me?"

"Yep, shit yeah."

"Why?"

"You found Des."

"That is ridiculous."

"Who found Tom?"

"Just because I was there doesn't make me a suspect."

"I don't know. You suspect his secretary has died?"

"Chelsea, it's all just a coincidence... I'm..."

"Maybe, but you're more a suspect than I am. Anyway I'm on your list."

I reminded her, "You crossed your own name off."

"Not on your list, that was my list. Remember Beaulieu was going to do a background check on me. What did she discover?"

"I haven't spoken to her."

"Oh, anyway, I decided to do my own check. If it was good enough for you, it was good enough for me. I started with Samantha and that was an interesting phone call – shit yeah!"

"Why do you swear Chelsea?"

"For reinforcement, everyone knows that."

"But you argue with such clarity you don't need to."

"Alright Shaun, I promise to curb my behaviour."

"Chelsea, what did you say to Samantha?"

She tentatively answered, "Am I in trouble?"

"You're not in trouble."

"That's a relief. I didn't talk for long."

"I don't believe you."

"It didn't seem that long and I think I helped your situation. What I did probably saved you days, weeks or maybe months of negotiations."

"Shit Chelsea, there was nothing to negotiate."

"Now I've got you swearing, see how contagious it is."

"Stop changing the subject and what did you say to Samantha?"

"She was willing to listen."

"I bet."

"How did you introduce yourself?"

"As your soul mate."

"Shit... that would have attracted her attention."

"Shaun really, the swearing."

"Do I have to draw teeth to find out what you said?"

"Are you threatening me?"

"Not yet, but you could have warned me."

"I told Samantha you had a problem."

"What sort of problem."

"Well that's it, I didn't say exactly, I kept talking, keeping in mind this was my investigation. I said you needed help, like you were desperate, at the end of the line type of desperate. I was referring to you being followed and how frustrated you were but she wasn't listening to that. She may have misconstrued what I said; I can't help it if she interpreted what I said as a terminal illness."

"Shit, Chelsea, she thinks I'm dying?"

"There you go swearing again. Initially Samantha appeared elated you maybe dying but when she thought it through she seemed more perturbed than anything, I added, 'It's a shame his life has been so turbulent, he gets to this point and has no answers only obstacles. Damn shame'. Shaun, I wouldn't be surprised if she allows you to see the kids, even the grand kids."

"Chelsea, you're out of control, the power of winning the World Debating Championship has gone to your head."

"That's what I thought when I got off the phone, strange how we think alike. Anyway, she promised to contact you and adjust any imperfections or complications brought about by your relationship breakdown. Happy now!"

"Well she left a message on my mobile saying sorry, so that was a first. Chelsea, how long do you think you can get away with this type of behaviour?"

"Until I'm in a nursing home."

I imagined she wouldn't stop there.

"Shaun, by the way, did the meeting work out with Debbie?"

"Yeah, we are going to stay in touch. She tried to keep in touch with Lyn's family but each time Lyn's mother became too upset. Eventually she gave up. She had the same problem I had, no one to talk to, at least she accepted Lyn's death, whereas I never did."

"How long did you stay?"

"All night, I know your next question and before you jump to conclusions… I slept on the sofa!"

"Is she good looking Shaun?"

"Oh, reasonably good looking. Why?"

"You didn't compromise your relationship with Siobhan?"

"Of course not. What is with you women, always worried men are going to compromise something?"

"We know the lengths our species will go to procure a mate. It's a jungle out there."

"Apparently."

"So, you are happy?"

"Yes, all my questions have been answered but my answers are under question."

"Shaun, if it's any consolation I don't think you killed those three people."

"And apparently you're off the hook also," although being on the hook had created a nightmare with Samantha. Explaining my health would now create aggravation beyond description.

"Oh Shaun, there is something else."

"What? I've got a bad feeling about this."

"Samantha wants a meeting."

"She wants to see me?"

"No, Siobhan."

"Why?"

"I don't know."

My mind was reeling, what could Samantha want with Siobhan?

CHAPTER 35

◄○►

THE SUBWAY

Samantha had requested a meeting with Siobhan – not likely! I knew Samantha was bitter but a meeting with Siobhan would be a nightmare, and as for Chelsea, what a conniving little bugger, she had ended the call with, "Of course your expiry date isn't up, it's just Samantha's interpretation, but of course your used by date is a completely different story." She was a master of double talk, it was no wonder Samantha thought I was dying.

Siobhan and I decided to move house in case the killer returned. It was then Siobhan surprised me, she produced a key, encrypted with high-tech coding allowing entry to the safest of houses. It was the 'bunker', a security shelter situated on her community estate. I remember Siobhan mentioning it on our return from London. At the time it seemed bizarre to be talking nuclear fallout, terrorists and survival, but now I wasn't sure. Siobhan explained how the key opened and sealed two chambers. The first allowed entry and then shut using a scanner to detect weapons that may be smuggled into the bunker. The key was then used for the second stage where a dusting process removed dirt and loose fibres, then a detoxifying solution was sprayed into the air to remove bacteria and a check was made for radiation poisoning. I thought this should have been the first stage but I wasn't an expert.

Nothing would be left to chance and of course this sounded a better alternative than waiting for the killer, but a fallout shelter, that seemed like overkill – I couldn't wait to see it!

Siobhan packed up a few things while I made phone calls, "Hi Beaulieu, Shaun here."

"Shaun who?" I remember our conversation started like this weeks ago, "Oh, that Shaun. You owe me heaps; the tab has reached $43.00. United States dollars," she reinforced.

Before she could say another word, I said, "I've read your lengthy report, I don't know how you do it, the best I can write is a chapter a day and somehow you were able to condense five hundred lives into three hundred pages and with single spacing to boot. What was it, 150,000 words?" I flicked to her summary and scanned the pages as we spoke. Of course I was exaggerating, for there was nowhere near five hundred people in this report but there were that many questions. I was glad I hadn't read her compilation, jumping to her conclusions was far easier.

Then she shocked me, "Forget the report, that's obsolete... Shaun... Chelsea has a secret..."

I had a sinking feeling about my new phone company, courtesy of the police. I interrupted, "Maybe we can meet up and discuss the details, however before I go, I need to tell you what happened. Tom was murdered. I witnessed his death. Beaulieu, you need to be very careful."

"Shaun, are you feeling ok?"

"Yes."

"Are you sure?"

"Word travels fast."

"What word."

"Samantha's word."

"What did she say?"

"You haven't spoken to Samantha?"

"No, but I'm worried for you. Witnessing Tom's death must have been terrible."

"I'm alright, I'll explain everything when we meet up."

"But still, everything is so finite. I worry"

"That is really nice of you, but don't." I asked lightly, more for a reaction, "Beaulieu, how was your date and who did you go out with?"

She hesitated, a strange response, "Err, I …"

"What?"

"Nothing, nothing. Let's talk when we meet up."

"Was it related to our research?"

"I don't think so."

"But you're not sure?"

She said determinedly, "I said when we meet up."

I was playing her, making her squirm like she had done to me in the past, "I'm feeling unsettled with your response, after all I'm paying you the big bucks and then I find your report is obsolete. This gets me thinking you have made mistakes."

She heaved frustration, "Alright, alright, I'll take $20.00 off your account."

She hissed like a kettle coming to boil, it was then I heard a voice muttering in the background.

I queried, "Beaulieu, are you alone?"

She said goodbye and hung up quickly – strange? Who could be making her react like that? That little whisper, sounded like, 'hang up, hang up!'

I reflected: Des and Tom had been murdered. Siobhan was restless and Chelsea and Beaulieu had secrets. Tom's secretary may have met foul play. Josh Freemont had lied and someone was trying to kill me. Was any of this connected to Lyn, or was my imagination in overdrive? Then, to add a touch more drama, Samantha thought I was dying. I phoned Samantha but her answering machine kicked in, in a way I was glad, how to explain that dying wasn't an option especially seeing her expectations had been raised; anyway, what I really wanted to tell her was that Tom was murdered and she was part of the ensuing investigation. At the end of my message I said, "I think you're a suspect!"

Siobhan's choice of security house surpassed my expectations. It was nothing like a bunker, although it's was secure enough to withstand an atomic blast, a gassing, even an assault by a small army. It was exactly as she described, roomy, modern and secure from all catastrophes. The air was triple filtered and oxygenated, ensuring the correct temperature and sustainability for months. The only drawback was the food. There was nothing fresh, nothing frozen, there were only freeze dried packs that required water to expand. I was fascinated that an apple crumble could be deflated to a quarter of its original size then swollen back to look authentic. There was a television but no cable. Our bedroom had double bunks and Siobhan pointed to the top to indicate my bed. At least she would be close. The outside was monitored by security cameras so we could see someone approach. Warning bells would kick in if someone tried to breach security. The first indication that things weren't right was when the security doors refused to lock. Siobhan explained, "The locksmith must have overlooked something, don't worry I have his number."

She dialled 1300 DoctorLock. I was worried. When he pulled up, his small mini van carried a sign showing a stethoscope attached to a key. Great advertising except for the dilapidated state of the vehicle, he was eccentric to detail and laid his tools onto a red felt mat. Regardless of this pre-operative preparation he had made a mistake, so I asked, "Doctor?"

"Yes," he said cautiously.

"Is there a master key?"

"Yes."

"Could anyone besides you access that key?"

"No, it could never happen. I abide by a code of ethics."

"Would holding a gun to your head be enough incentive to break that code?"

Flustered, he quickly replied, "No... no... never."

"Mm, interesting, just thought I'd ask," he gave me a discerning look knowing I didn't believe him.

Within twenty minute we were able to lock the vast doors and with the hope we were secure.

Samantha phoned and blurted out minus an introduction, "The police paid me a visit."

"Hi Samantha, how are you?"

She ignored me, "Couldn't you have warned me?"

"I did."

Furious, "No you didn't."

"Yes I did, check your voice mail."

There was a pause while she checked, "Nope nothing."

"I've got a new phone, maybe there's a glitch, and anyway this call was diverted so it must be working. Well Samantha, did you murder anyone? Are you out on bail?"

"No, my frustration is with you, not others, if it wasn't for your…" She fell short of mentioning my terminal condition, "I swear I could rip your head right off. I need to see Siobhan urgently."

I explained that Siobhan had no desire to speak. Samantha hissed liked her niece Beaulieu, which reminded me of a carpet snake ready to strike. She replaced the receiver but there was a strange beeping that followed, it wasn't an engaged signal and no matter what I did I couldn't get a connection. I took the battery out to reset the phone but that didn't work. I figured the police would fix the problem, especially if they were keen to eavesdrop on my conversations. Anyway, I could really do with a break.

Siobhan queried, "Didn't go well with Samantha?"

"She's hostile but she still wants to meet you but I said no."

"Good, that's it then."

"I don't think so, Samantha doesn't take no for an answer. Are we all locked up?"

Siobhan said, "Yeah, now it's only DoctorLock who can gain access."

"I don't trust him."

"Relax, not everyone is trouble."

"How much did this bunker cost?"

"Twenty thousand extra per unit holder which would bring the total to $2.6 million."

"Incredible," it was cheap if it saved lives – ours in particular.

My phone was still off line. There were old movies stacked on a shelf. Siobhan flicked the Cary Grant classics until she found 'Charade'. She cried as I massaged her feet. The movie finished with black grainy dots invading the screen.

Siobhan said, "This has been some day, who would have thought."

"Are you alright?"

She nodded, "I'm more disgusted with Tom than anything, isn't it strange how emotions can change, especially when you're aware of someone's deception."

"Just desserts I think."

"Exactly. I can't believe we are holed up here for protection, you know we can't stay forever."

"It would be good if we could, just you, me, and no one else to worry about. I can see why humans become reclusive; Howard Hughes had some insight."

"He had nothing without others, he died lonely. In hindsight, the range of emotions we've experienced should have been spread across a lifetime."

"I'm feeling it to, too many highs and lows, it's just not natural."

"This is unique."

Siobhan queried, "What?"

"That we can talk through our problems, weeks ago we were both stuck in relationships where others refused our point of view. It feels good to talk, I feel comfortable with you, and you don't have an agenda other than to be yourself. "

"You mean, I don't want to change you, I'm sure you'll find my flaws over time, we all have them."

"But we're able to communicate, take today for example. You could have lost it and I wasn't the most congenial person to be around."

"You did say sorry. I haven't heard a man say 'sorry' for so long, it surprised me. It takes a lot to apologise. I admire you for that."

"You're good for me. I might be blinded by affection but I sense something important, it's as if we have a unique connection."

"I know. I'm glad I'm with you. But admit it, these are strange times and strange circumstances."

"It's all fantasy, I'm sure none of this is happening we'll wake tomorrow and find it didn't."

"It's total fantasy… you know, if I was going to have a fantasy forced on me… it should be about you and this bunker."

I smiled, "Do you want to discuss it?"

She smiled coyly, "I said, 'if I was going to have a fantasy forced on me', what we are experiencing isn't real, even if it turns out to be."

"Close your eyes and let your mind wander." She could have refused to play, instead she shut her eyes, "Have you ever experienced something so sexy you can't share it with anyone?"

"Yes," she giggled, her eyes were still shut.

"Well, now is your chance, tell me, let me share it with you."

Without further prompting she said, "Well, it's a train station…"

"You're really going to tell me?"

"You asked… anyway, it's a fantasy, not real, I'm at a train station, a subway exit to be precise… underground, loads of people passing when all of a sudden a man stops. He is handsome with black wavy hair, a chisel chin and eyes set deep. He stops and looks at me leaning against this tiled wall. Now, why would I be leaning against a tile wall and in a public thoroughfare? No time for answers but I realise where I'm leaning is white and stark. I'm dressed in black – slinky black, a material you need to adjust constantly and my high heels match, but they are like stiletto towers. This guy ambles over and stops. He looks me in the eye. He keeps looking, not a word. It's like I can sense what his thinking. I know he can read my thoughts. I blush. How embarrassing. He smiles at my naivety. I adjust my dress around my breasts and down around my legs. His eyes don't waver. Then he moves closer, so close it's like a wafer divide, we don't touch. He takes a deep breath and exhales; I can feel this zephyr like breeze. I suck in what remains. Instantly I must have him, to sense him, savour him, but there are so many people around. This closeness is driving me crazy – he is perfect. My legs go weak. My heart begins to race. I can feel the blood course my neck and my metabolism goes off the scale. I go to speak but he places his finger against his lips. No talking. A word spoken will change history. Still something must be said, we are so close and he is so handsomely divine. My hand reaches out and he takes it. It's cool, no cold, iced – mine's hot, it's like ice cream and coke, they don't mix but they do. I'm his effervescence, his sweet, coke in black; I'm ready to pull him to me and complete this chemical union. I hear a cough somewhere to my right. I look and it's another me standing there and beckoning him to come. He takes a step back. Oh no! He turns and waits for this other me to catch up. They hold hands and join the scores of people exiting the subway. I watch bewildered. So close but so far, so hot and so cold. We could never exist for long but a minute would have been all I needed… anyway, he did choose the right woman, didn't he?

"Wow… you're hot."

She flushed a little, a lot, she opened her eyes, "I'm not hot."

"You are, trust me."

"Your turn, can you match my fantasy?"

"Oh… the way you told that story I thought you had experienced it first hand."

"No silly," I hadn't heard her call me 'silly', an affectionate term since London. I breathed a sigh of relief. I ventured, "A fantasy, can I match your raw uninhibited zest for life?"

"Go on try."

"Ok. It also has to do with rail travel. I'm not sure you can handle this."

"Of course I can."

"Alright but this is a dream… I knew this girl who…"

"What?"

"She… a girl in her early twenties was returning from a work's party. Not necessarily a memorable night for her boss had 'hit on' her. She said 'no' and was instantly sacked. It was late as she boarded the first of eight carriages and at the next station, these men, three hulking types, board the train. They look in her direction, she suddenly feels vulnerable. They keep looking at her. Not all at once, it's like they take turns. She feels sick to the stomach. The train is empty so she decides to move to the guard's compartment which is at the very end of the train. As she stands she notices the whole three looking at her. She has never felt this uncomfortable. As she passes through each carriage her pace quickens. She looks back. They're following. She is in a panic. She wishes she was wearing something less revealing and these high heels are killing her. She tries running, barely keeping ahead. She envisages them tackling her to the dusty carriage floor where flickering neon's will be her only company. Then she realises this is a non-stop train to the city and the guard is the only one who can defend her honour. Upon reaching the guard's door she frantically knocks. As he opens the door one of the men shouts, 'Hey wait, your handbag, you left it'. She sheepishly thanks them. They return to the front of the train. The guard advises her to stay with him and he closes the door. Suddenly, she has the strangest of feelings. The guard's hand is over her mouth and all she can see is the flash of red track-side lights as they disappear into the distance. His grip is like iron and he wrestles her to the floor. She tries to struggle but his weight is overpowering. He is tearing her clothes. Without thinking her hand goes instinctively to her hair where she is able to retrieve a hairpin – her grandmother's. The pin is long, sharp and without hesitation she shoves it into the guard's neck – his body spasms. She watches amazed. She has never experienced emotions this strong – a powerful turn on, finally she has control. It's like she has killed Goliath or climbed Everest. The train nears its destination and stops. She exits, unsteady on her feet. The three men are standing on the platform and note her appearance, she tries to adjust her dress but her shoulders remain bare. Her hair is dishevelled. The guys ask if she is alright but she just looks at them with a vacant stare. They offer to buy her a drink, she nods, she doesn't speak, one puts his arm around her and the other two stay close, really close and you can imagine what comes next?"

Siobhan said anxiously, "What? What happened?"

"I don't know, I woke up?"

"Gee Shaun, that is such a bloke's story, I'm going to bed."

We lay on our bunks, silent, the light off, but still a low intensity lamp lit the walls as a security precaution. Its filament jumped every second or so, reminding me of transient shadows etched wildly onto calico tents.

"I'm sorry, do you want me to tell you the story about my cousin before she married?"

"Does it have anything to do with trains?"

"No."

"Maybe later then."

"It's best I hold you."

"Why?"

"I know you have questions."

"Mm, ok." I changed bunks, she held the covers back and snuggled me in. She was warm and soft, just what I needed. She whispered, "What do you think happened to that girl on the train, did the police question her, did the three guys help her or take advantage of her, they may have got her drunk and raped her? If they were decent guys they should have taken her home or at least to a hospital. It was attempted rape by the train guard." She paused to think, "For her to feel in control, a person has to die? I can imagine it happening. What was she like, was she beautiful Shaun?"

"Gorgeous but now she's a killer with power."

"But doesn't his action justify her killing him?"

"Maybe she found a way to kill those other guys, or maybe she walked away after the first drink and the authorities are wondering what happened."

"Did she withdraw the hairpin or leave it in the guard's neck? After all, that was her grandmother's. I bet she withdrew it, wiped it clean and pushed it back into her hair."

"Siobhan relax, its just fantasy."

"I know but every woman has that nightmare locked inside her, we all dread these moments being told in a story like this, although thankfully most of us will never experience the drama."

"What is your concern, that she was nearly raped, or she took a life, or that some guys were going to have her?"

"No, it's not that, the problem is the story, there is no ending and now you've passed it onto me to be its keeper. I can only let it go when I tell someone else but then they'll be stuck with it."

"You women, sleep, don't worry so much. Anyway, tell me the truth, was that really you in the subway tunnel?"

"Fantasy only, you don't think less of me do you?"

"Actually, you are more exciting than I thought possible."

We held each other tight, then exhaustion hit. I knew she'd be dreaming of trains and I would be thinking of subway tunnels, a better alternative than dwelling on Tom's subterfuge, within seconds we were asleep.

CHAPTER 36

MAPLE AND BLUEBERRY SAUCE

With the exception of London, yesterday was the closest Siobhan and I had been. We were into each others minds, unravelling mysteries and trying to solve murders but besides all that we could communicate without aggression. Was that what Lyn wanted? Then yesterday with a mere gust of wind, Lyn had saved my life from that bullet, she was difficult to ignore and now Siobhan was a part of the process no matter how I rationalised differently. I didn't dare bring up the subject of Lyn; I resigned myself to let nature take its course. If something was going to happen it would.

I lay awake thinking, trying to find a link, who would want to kill me and why? People were being recruited to spy, in Des's case he had become greedy and Tom had been persuaded to lure me to the killer. Why? Were Siobhan and I really safe? My mind was running rampant trying to beat the system, how could anyone defeat the 'bunker'? Brilliant minds had spent years fathoming foolproof methods to keep it safe but still I reckoned there had to be a way. Already I knew DoctorLock was not invincible.

Siobhan stirred and stretched. She said, "I slept like a baby, and you?"

"I managed a few hours, it was nice lying next to you."

"Shaun, what should we do today?"

"I'm meeting with Beaulieu at noon."

"Should I come?"

"If you want, but I must warn you, meeting Beaulieu will be an experience."

"Why, what's she like?"

"Eccentric but not wacko eccentric, she is attractive, tall and loves stirring, however and bottom line she does a great job and charges next to nothing for her research. But always remember, she is Samantha's niece so we need to tread carefully."

"Blood thicker than water, hey!"

"Regardless, I think you will like her. She presents as a stirrer but she has a heart of gold."

"Not a boring individual it sounds."

"No."

"But where and how to meet her, if we leave the bunker we will need to organise a security company. Not much point going to all this trouble only to find the sniper is waiting outside."

"I think it would be safer for Beaulieu to come here, we would be less exposed."

"You're right. If my phone is working I'll call her later and make arrangements. Would you like breakfast in bed again?"

"Not if your phone is turned on?"

I replied from the galley, "The phone has a signal but I've switched it off. What would you like? There are powdered eggs and reconstituted bacon made from nuts?"

She called back, "I saw a pack of pancakes which look like crepes. Pour plenty of blueberry sauce and maple, it may disguise the taste."

"But what do I pour over the berries and maple to make them real."

"They are real for people in shelters. Anyway hurry, I need to talk."

"But we are talking."

"No serious talk."

"Oh."

After several microwave pings our pancakes were steaming, I added the trimmings and carried the tray to Siobhan. She was still in her pyjamas. I settled the tray and added milk to her coffee.

"Thanks, and you have a separate tray again?"

I nodded.

Compared to yesterday, I returned with a lethargic approach. We sat on the bed, she one end, I the other, "Delicious," she said.

"You're lying?"

"I didn't want to hurt your feelings."

I prompted, "And you want to talk?"

"You know how we were going to mesh into unbridled love yesterday. I need to discuss that."

"Siobhan, this isn't something you talk through, it's just accepted with couples."

"But we're different, ours is the strangest of relationships, everything is back to front. I told you I loved you when Tom and I stayed at your house but now I realise that wasn't love, it was more to do with..."

"Lust?"

"Yeah, I wanted you bad, don't be embarrassed, it's time for honesty. Then I had that fit and you think Lyn orchestrated that and my memory loss. I'm sorry Shaun, I don't. I don't think your theory will ever sit comfortably with me. If Lyn's spirit does exist and she keeps you safe I'll be delighted. You see, I'm really in conflict with your beliefs."

I wasn't sure what to say, except, "Siobhan, what happened in London was good, I'll never forget that time, but how do you explain your memory loss?"

"The doctor said, 'temporary amnesia', let's not read more into it."

"It's not that simple... you have to ask yourself why?"

"Things happen, I had just come out of hospital."

"But you were warned to back away. Remember saying that to me in hospital? There has to be a better explanation for what happened?"

"Well, maybe I dreamt it, maybe having a fit does strange things to a person. Maybe it was a fever making me delirious? Maybe they gave me drugs to control the seizure…"

"Siobhan, there are too many maybes, you're in denial and I can understand that."

"Well I'm sorry; I just can't accept that Lyn's spirit controlled me. So where does that leave us?"

"Siobhan, I have already committed to you."

"When?"

"In London, I vowed myself to you. We became one."

She protested, "But that was Lyn."

"But you don't believe she controlled you, so it had to be you. You can't have a bet each way."

"If you love me, tell me. Tell me what you said."

I reached over, holding the back of her neck, then I drew her forehead to mine, I whispered slowly, "Me: You – Forever." She cried, first a gentle tear slipping her cheek and then another. We kissed, moving our heads slowly, insisting on enough pressure but not that much to be demanding. She wrapped both arms around me and simply hugged tight. When we parted, Siobhan said, "Then we continue as…"

"One. We have something special you know."

She sighed, "We do, don't we? I'm loving you Shaun, even though we have a different point of view."

I could understand Siobhan rejecting my theory – it was kind of 'out there'. The premise that Lyn took control was not backed by proof, only assumption. A rational person could never accept that, so that left me the only believer – it only needed one!

We finished breakfast and read twelve month old gossip magazines. Nothing had changed, with the same actors having the same dramas. Siobhan and I were quietly happy, we had cleared the air but still there was a restlessness hanging over us. Was it that someone wanted to kill me or did Siobhan feel unsettled because my theory contained a smidgen of truth?

At 9 am, I switched on my phone and called Beaulieu. She was favouring Spanish for lunch and at her favourite restaurant however when I suggested the 'bunker' with freeze dried food her curiosity was raised.

I called the security company and we monitored the closed circuit television for their arrival. The plan was for two guards to scout the area and wait for Beaulieu.

When Beaulieu arrived she was carrying four large bags. Over the intercom I questioned, "What's in the bags Beaulieu?"

"A culinary feast, if Mohammed can't come to El Cid's, then, El Cid's will come to Mohammed."

"What's an El Cid's?"

"My favourite Spanish restaurant, how much longer am I going to be held here like a Guantanamo Bay inmate? Let me in!"

Of course, Beaulieu's discomfort lasted a minute and when she emerged we could smell the tapas and tortillas wafting the air. I introduced Siobhan. Both shook hands, Beaulieu nodded, Siobhan nodded back. Both conversed through eye contact a pleasant enough exchange until Beaulieu broke the silence, "Remarkable."

"What's remarkable?" I asked.

"You complexion Shaun, you're ruddier than a radish."

"What?"

"Are you under stress?" she asked.

"Of course I'm under stress, seeing you is demanding."

To change the subject, Beaulieu described El Cid's as a two story building having stark white walls with tanned Mediterranean roof tiles; a large sign depicted a warrior on horse back. She described it as an impressive Spanish restaurant with menu pricing similar to Yum Cha, then she added, "We must go there sometime." Trust Beaulieu to find Chinese value with European flair but all we could do was look at the plastic bags. Real food was only metres away and she questioned, "Do you two want to start?"

Siobhan ushered our guest to the galley where she poured the wine Beaulieu had purchased. In the meantime Beaulieu served up the food onto six oversized plates and 'pinged' the microwave to moderate heat.

Siobhan whispered, "Beaulieu looks nothing like I imagined."

"No one ever does. Pre-empting people's profiles is a waste of time."

We sat and drank unauthenticated Sangrias.

I asked Beaulieu, "You weren't followed?"

Her eyes went directly to the monitors. She shook her head sheepishly and with a shake too quick to be convincing, I insisted, "Were you followed or not?"

"Err, what am I, a super sleuth with eyes in the back of my head?"

"Beaulieu, it is better to be careful then to repeat Siobhan's husband's mistake." She looked guilty but tried to cover up, "I'm sorry, I'm not myself."

I questioned, "You're distant today! Is it because Siobhan is here?"

"No… no… of course not, it's just, I've found out something that blows this case wide open."

"Is this to do with Chelsea?"

"No, though she's an interesting girl that one, I'll tell you later."

I exhaled, somewhat exasperated, Beaulieu was as manipulative as Chelsea.

I received a call to my mobile. It was one of the security guards. With him was a woman. I checked the monitor. It was Samantha. I asked Beaulieu, "Did you invite her?"

"No, she found out we were meeting up."

"How? Why is she here?"

"I told her where I was going, she is after all my aunt."

"Shit Beaulieu, we're trying to have a meeting, not a meltdown. This is a secure bunker. Did you explain the risk?"

"She doesn't want to talk to you, she wants Siobhan. It'll only take five minutes."

"I'm not letting her in, this is ridiculous."

Siobhan interrupted, "Shaun you must, she can't stand out there, it's too dangerous."

I instructed security to bring her to the shelter's door. They searched her for weapons. I could see her agitation. Once the first door closed and regained its pressure I went to open the second only to hear an alarm flooding the bunker.

Beaulieu questioned, "What's happening?"

"Samantha has breached security." I was amazed, Samantha was moving through the next door and without the slightest degree of difficulty. When she stepped inside she used a key, which amazingly stopped the alarm. I looked at Siobhan who looked surprised. I asked, fearing DoctorLock's involvement, "Where did you get a security key from?"

She looked at me as if that was a stupid question, "Toyota."

"Toyota?"

"It's my car key."

Siobhan shook her head. As Samantha approached, Beaulieu rose and embraced her, a hug that lasted ten seconds. It was a reminder how close they were.

Samantha broke the hug and said, "You look ok Shaun," to which I replied, "Hello Samantha," she responded by lifting her head, a form of acknowledgement which was quickly followed by a nasal sniff, just the one snort. "I'm here to speak to Siobhan, I was guessing she would be here. Siobhan, would you mind if we move to another room? What a strange place, is this your house?"

Siobhan answered, "Part of our community estate."

"Right, of course," she shook her head, knowing but dismissing, "I need you for a few minutes. It won't take long and while we're talking, Beaulieu and Shaun can unravel their mysteries." She smiled a false gift, even her tone proved demanding and designed to denigrate the meeting. Beaulieu looked anything but impressed.

"Samantha, Siobhan is a part of this meeting. I already went through this. Siobhan is not interested in speaking to you."

Siobhan interrupted, "Its ok. I'll do it."

Samantha smiled; another battle won, proving those who persisted got their own way – Samantha knew the angles.

I said to Beaulieu, "They're completely out of earshot and

unless they start screaming we will never know if they're killing each other."

Beaulieu encourage, "They'll be fine, their grown women."

"I don't know, I just don't know."

"Relax, if their discussion heats up, we can interject."

In the Galley

Samantha sat first and sighed, "As you can imagine Siobhan, this is not the most pleasant of times but we need to talk, putting our differences aside."

"Ok," Siobhan replied.

"How is Shaun?"

"Ok."

"Good. That's good. He must be worried."

"He does have a lot to worry about."

"Precisely, you see Siobhan, there is more at stake than just you and I. We need to prepare, there are arrangements being attended to by our solicitors, amicable arrangements I might add, and I have no idea when they will be finalised and most importantly, when Shaun may go – any indication?"

Siobhan didn't answer.

Samantha continued, "Of course, the children need consideration and as for myself, I'm happy with what's in place. Could we discuss where you see yourself in this complicated arrangement?"

"Why?"

"I thought that would be obvious."

"Not to me it isn't."

"Well, let me spell it out for you. When you have a de facto relationship, you, as the unofficial spouse have rights. Strange, I know, but believe me Siobhan, I have sought this information from learned professionals and they advise me that you have a claim once Shaun goes. I'm trying to circumvent the pain and misery for all concerned. Can we come to some form of agreement so our affairs will be in order and we can continue our lives with certainty?"

"Well I…"

"Alright then, excellent. What I have in mind is for you to receive twenty percent of Shaun's estate, because there are three children, myself and you as the de facto, will work out to be a fair distribution system."

"I see."

"I know, this appears heartless but in view of the circumstances, it is better to be prepared than be sorry. I've given a great deal of thought to the matter."

"I can see that."

"Now on a personal note."

"Yes."

"The arrangement."

"Arrangement?"

"Yes, I never want to see Shaun again. To be fair to the children and grandchildren it might be nice for Shaun to see them one more time before he passes. You know, say goodbye, I think that would be nice, don't you?"

"Samantha, you talk about your children being allowed access to their father. Christ Samantha, they are adults, surely they can make up their own minds."

"Well I thought…"

"That's it, you think too much. Shaun can decide what distribution there will be from his estate; although I can imagine very little, leave the poor guy alone. Let him live without your interference. I don't know what changed you into this abominable creature, because all I'm seeing is an ugly person trapped in a beautiful body. Incidentally, Shaun isn't dying."

"What do you mean? He isn't dying?"

"There is nothing wrong with him."

"Well, what was that stupid little girl on about?"

"Oh, Chelsea? She never told you he was dying, just that he was at the 'end of the line' together with some other inferences, like 'needing help', 'slow and painful'; does that sound familiar? Chelsea may have summarised his life by saying, 'It's a shame his life has been so turbulent, he gets to this point and has no answers only obstacles'. You misinterpreted Chelsea's conversation. Maybe you desperately wanted to hear those words."

Samantha looked embarrassed but responded quicker than Siobhan could have imagined, "If he's not dying, I want him back, get your claws out of him and walk away. I won't tell you again."

"But you said you never wanted to see him."

"I've changed my mind."

Siobhan responded, "Samantha, he is with me by choice, we don't have a relationship built on fear, what we have is an open door policy, if he wants to return, he will, and with my blessing. Why don't you ask him? He has no idea what we spoke about so this would be an excellent opportunity to explain yourself."

Samantha rose and Siobhan's heart skipped a beat, was she really going to ask him? Siobhan's mouth went dry and her hands felt clammy. Samantha had a fantastic figure, attractive, with long shapely legs, the equivalent of a twenty-year old, a neat tempting package but would Shaun fall for it. Siobhan had to trust him but she knew the kind, Samantha was manipulative. Suddenly Shaun rose and took hold of Samantha's arm. They headed to the exit. Siobhan could feel the emptiness and knew what would follow – the lowest of ebbs. Her wine refused to digest. She stood panicking, this making her condition worse, she rushed to the bathroom and vomited, her whole world was spinning. An 'open door policy' was crap. How did she dream up such shit? She wanted Shaun desperately. Was he leaving? The security door opened and within thirty seconds, closed. Siobhan couldn't bear to look.

CHAPTER 37

FORGET THE SECURITY

I was rocked when Samantha asked me to return home. I was further shocked when she declared, "No questions, no recriminations." I doubted she could contain herself for twenty-four hours let alone twenty-four more years. Even Beaulieu lifted her eyebrows. Without taking stock, I blurted out, "How?"

"Just walk into the house and we can resume as if nothing happened, you had a fling, it happens, you made a mistake, we move on, you learn. I'll forget how you hurt me."

"Samantha, you are not going to forget, you never do." For a moment I considered Samantha and then Siobhan, and as ridiculous as the story was, I decided to tell my fantasy. "I knew this girl who…"

She snapped, "What?"

"She… was on a late night train. She was on the first of eight carriages when suddenly these men, three hulking types, board…" Beaulieu remained motionless as I finished the fantasy word for word; both were gripped until my anti-climatic ending. Samantha's frustration peaked and announced, "And that's it?"

"Yes. Tell me what you think."

Samantha huffed and shook her head, "Is this a test?"

I nodded.

"Forget it, you're the one at fault, I don't have to prove a thing, I should be testing you."

"Samantha, I love you but not enough to be vetted constantly. I've made plenty of mistakes and I'll admit that. I'm sorry but you never forgive. What's more you can't forget and you certainly have no understanding of how my life has changed."

As I walked Samantha to the door she said, "You'll be sorry Shaun, this is your last chance, a small window of opportunity and not on offer again," she paused, I shook my head, she queried, "What sort of life will you have, burrowed up in this warren. Last chance!"

"You know I love you Samantha, which is the very reason I can't come back. Any affection I have will be destroyed. I'd rather keep what remains, although that's in a fragile place."

"Shaun, I'd work on your security system, although I loathe you I don't wish for your brains to be splattered."

I kissed her on the cheek, it was at this moment she realised her role, her dominance mixed with my inflexibility – we were both responsible.

When I returned to Beaulieu she said, "I think you've done the right thing Shaun, continuing the facade would be counter productive."

"Do you really think that?"

"Yes, it was going to be a band-aid solution at best, however now I'm in a pickle, I'm stuck with your story's ending, I'll never be able to sleep realising that girl killed the train-guard. You're such a nightmare to work with."

I managed a small laugh and went to Siobhan who was still retching in the bathroom. She turned her head and in between the upheavals she tried to hold my hand. Instead I gently rubbed her back until her vile purging subsided. She advised she was going to bed and I returned to Beaulieu who was already eating Spanish tortillas and chicken.

Beaulieu stated the obvious, "Great security you have here. Do you think we are safe?"

"I don't know, anyway, we'll keep the security guys posted just in case."

She responded with a sly look, "Are they the ones who frisked Samantha?"

"There were no complaints, do you think I should apologise?"

"I doubt the security guys will be interested in your apology."

I corrected, "No… I meant apologise to Samantha."

"No way, let her have her memories."

"You're wicked." This was a different Beaulieu, most times she was blatantly 'Samantha' but now she had become fair minded and conciliatory, something was different.

She ordered, "Back to the research, I've stumbled onto something important. Ever since I told you about Malcolm Shailler the pharmacist and your high school friend Josh Freemont being neighbours, I have been trying to establish why? I've ruled out coincidence so that left me wondering about a mutual arrangement or there was one party manipulating the other. Anyway, one thing led to another and then a name cropped up. Do you remember Chantal Witherspoon?"

"Chantal… Chantal Witherspoon? Of course," I was shocked to hear her name. I remembered her love letter and my dismissive lying on the dusty steps of the Berala train station.

Beaulieu said, "A troubled girl that, she left high school and within two years married, she had two children and ended up in a mental institution for years. A complete lack of confidence is the report. But here is the thing, she is somehow connected to Josh Freemont. He witnessed her marriage certificate. You need to see her as soon as possible." Beaulieu handed me a slip of paper containing her address.

"Great, just what I need," I remembered Chantal's public outburst after playing that party game called 'Captain Blood'. I still had an etched memory of tomato pulp dripping from her stiffened finger.

"So tell me Shaun, how do you know Chantal?"

"We went to the same school and church. We were also at a party along with Lyn. Lyn died soon after." I hesitated, smothered by memories, "You're not suggesting something suspicious?"

She shrugged, "Keep it in mind. That's all."

I continued cautiously, "That party was for Josh Freemont's brother, so Josh had to know Chantal."

"It appears so, was Chantal religious?"

"Every Sunday she would be there, never missed a beat."

"I suggest you speak to Chantal, and then see…"

"Don't tell me… Josh Freemont."

She nodded, "Shaun, you need to be careful, there is a murderer on the loose."

I was silent for sometime, reflecting on the link between Chantal Witherspoon and Josh Freemont. Unlike Chantal, Josh never went to church but he did live close to her. It was then I remembered Lyn and Chantal lived in the same street, some fifty metres from each. I didn't remember them being friends but there had to be a connection, and why had Josh Freemont witnessed Chantal's marriage certificate?

"I have to make tracks Shaun."

"What, leaving so soon?"

"I'm meeting someone."

"But what about Chelsea's secret."

"Yes, how silly of me."

"Your mind is elsewhere?"

She ignored my question, "Chelsea did win the World Debating Championship but by default. Her opponent came down with food poisoning. Regardless, she went into the finals as the clear favourite. Her background looks legit except…"

"What."

"Her father is an Olympian."

"An athlete?"

"Of sorts. He won silver for trap shooting."

My mind raced ahead, "A shooter?"

"Yeah, a good one, I'm sure there is nothing to be perturbed about. No connection I can see. Anyway, I have to run."

"Beaulieu, do you have a date?"

"Sorry Shaun, nothing to do with your research. You're not paying me for gossip. I have to go. Open up the security doors or I'll use my Hyundai key and really embarrass you."

"Are you happy Beaulieu?"

"Actually I am, so no more questions. Say goodbye to Siobhan for me."

She slid between each door and was out of the bunker quicker than a surfer riding a tsunami. Siobhan popped her head around the corner and said, "What a nightmare."

"Sorry Siobhan, Samantha can be painful."

"Kind of, but I'm talking about my ability to keep vomiting, hang on, here I go again." She rushed to the bathroom.

Once Siobhan settled, we discussed the vulnerability of the bunker, Samantha had desecrated our view of 'utopia' however she did prove how defenceless we were – tomorrow we would have to find some place safe.

Siobhan slept peacefully, however it was all my brain could do to maintain order. I tried to sleep but there was too much happening, an unsettled time filled with apprehension. I sat up, restless. I noticed the air vents delivering a misting air. The fog settled with intensity. Was this my imagination playing tricks? It was freezing and I estimated the temperature to have dropped ten degrees. Shivering, I tried to stand but something prevented me – that pressure I had noticed previously, gentle but enforcing. Within this gathering miasma of dewed particles I could still see Siobhan sleeping peacefully. The cold was something else... maybe three degrees cooler now, however and mid centre of this fog strewn scene was something weird... a flickering old projector screen was playing old movies. The film was scratched and dirty and its sound effects crackly. Up flashed Josh Freemont who jumped excitedly around, he was about to race me to the finish line and swiftly bent to start. My heart pounded, before I knew what was happening, we were off. I got a bad start, strange, however I was gaining. He kept looking back, something runners, good runners never do. He looked confident and as usual he crossed the line

before me. He had an insufferable grin with arms raised trium-
phantly – I hated his arrogance. As I crossed the line I saw a
young Chantal Witherspoon, she was cheering but I wasn't sure
for whom. I could also hear the sound of the projector running,
'clickkkk-clackkkk-clunkkkk', or was that the sound of a rifle being loaded. I felt sick. My stomach churned and a sweat invaded
my skin to produce a glistening slick. The misty air intensified, it
swirled and plummeted from the vents as if announcing a new
arrival. The bunker lights dimmed to a tenth of their capacity.

I was really losing it.

Another race was starting. There were two runners – I managed to see their faces, it was me... and that despicable
pharmacist... Malcolm Shailler. We were both on the starting
line. Why? I had never raced against him. What was even
stranger was a shimmery image some distance off, it looked
like... Lyn! Lyn was holding the starting gun, however she refused to shoot. She just kept looking at us, she held time
preciously, gun raised and the only movement was her trigger-
finger, it twitched incessantly! I shook my head to clear my
thoughts – it was only then that everything reversed. The images rewound and the fog sucked to the vents. The temperature
rose along with the lights, here was my chance, I pleaded before
it was too late, 'Lyn... Lyn, what do you need help with?'

There was no answer.

My shaking slowly subsided. Another encounter, nothing
said, nothing obvious – a warning nevertheless. When I could
move, I shook Siobhan from her deep sleep. She looked refreshed and surprisingly warm, "Are you alright?"

She stretched, "Yes, the nausea has passed. How long did I
sleep?"

"I'm not sure, I imagine twenty minutes."

"Really? It seems like hours." Her hand reach for my arm,
"You feel so cold."

"Yeah, I need a sweater," she held me close instead. I diverted
Siobhan away from what had happened, what had happened
anyway? I asked, cautiously, "What did Samantha have to say?"

"Shaun, it doesn't matter."

"Yes it does. She upset you." She nodded and I replied, "She's good at turning everything into her own drama, anyway we survived. I told Samantha and Beaulieu 'the girl on the train fantasy'."

"Whatever for?"

"I had to prove something to myself. That story reflects the soul of the listener. I needed to know Samantha's answer."

"And?"

"It reinforced my belief that I'm doing the right thing," Siobhan went quiet, "Beaulieu thought the same as you, while Samantha refused to comment. Her lack of participation reflects her self-centred approach to life. Siobhan, this is really important, what would life be without me?"

Siobhan gazed at the wall, she swallowed and her eyes welled, "Impossible... if nothing else Samantha proved how much I care for you, she produced a panic. But you rejected her based on that train fantasy?"

"No, I've never rejected Samantha, never will. I know she loves me, we just can't live together; our marriage is over but not our love for each other. That fantasy was dumb but it allowed Samantha a moment to evaluate."

"You said you're doing the right thing. What's that?"

"Look me in the eye and tell me what you see."

Siobhan placed both hands on my cool face and drew close. That wafer subway closeness, she smiled, "Us, forever."

I nodded.

"Shaun, I want a real life fantasy, one about you and me."

"I'm not sure you can handle something so raw and uninhibited."

"Oh, I can handle it, however I have something in mind."

"Really? Ok then, no holding back, no caveats, nothing artificial, just raw unadulterated love. What?"

She teased, "If you give me what I need you can do what you want with me."

"A condition, what?"

"Try and guess."

I figured I should start somewhere. I unbuttoned her blouse; a red bra lay beneath, laced finely, holding voluptuous breasts, rising, falling, silky skin, warm as the summer sun.

"Not so quick."

"Quick?"

"Stop pilfering my time. I want to experience that stolen moment, think of what I want most."

"I'm trying."

"Look at you, you're half into it and we haven't even kissed." She removed the blouse and left her bra in tact, "Romance me with the best story... you know what to do."

I swallowed trying to think, "I could whisper to you."

"Try that."

Her ear was covered by flamed hair. I brushed it aside to expose a pink tender lobe, fleshy, ready for whispers. She nuzzled close, my breath hot within an echoing shell, I nibbled the soft lower portion, that floppy bit where sensors dwell, I moved to her slender neck. She shivered a little, then purred, I ventured, "Have I found a soft spot?"

"Every spot is soft, go on, whisper to me. Tell me what I want."

"You're beautiful."

"Mm."

My lips caressed her shoulders but were stopped by barricading red straps. I edged them down and waited for the protest. Nothing. They hang limply around her arms but her brassiere remained defiant. It was only that little clasp preventing freedom, two little silver hooks, teenage boys practice snapping those in their dreams; I edge my hand to the clasp but she said, "Not yet... take me to that special place."

CHAPTER 38

THE LIE CORRECTOR

Siobhan stood seductively in hip hugging jeans and a red lacy bulging bra, I had almost unclasped the device to provide free fall but then she quashed the idea, instead there was a condition, "I've been thinking about what you said, remember you described that last night in London being the most passionate of experiences. You fell short of detail, something was missing. I want that type of romance; if you give me that you can have everything of me, London... last night please!" She held her hands to her back ready to unclasp the bra. All I had to do was nod.

I almost cried. London; that last night was beyond ecstasy! The dusting, wrapped within a sheet, we were literally cocooned and it was such a profound lead up, first Stonehenge, the Cavern of Dreams and then the Thames. Nothing could replace that time. There were no equals, no catch up. How could she understand the significance? How could I explain that? How could Siobhan understand that Lyn was there, within her, with me, while at the same time it was her, Siobhan? Romancing was beyond the equation, whichever way I looked at it I had lost someone. There could be no replication, no counterfeiting of time.

"Well, am I stripping?"

"Come here, put your top back on."

"Why? What's wrong?"

"You're right. I did explain most things that happened in London… except that last day. Siobhan, have you ever studied the ancient ruins of Stonehenge? Say at school?"

"No."

"Well Lyn had."

"What are you saying?"

"She knew a back way into the reserve; she guided me like she was following the back of her hand. Why I'm saying this is because I cannot duplicate that last day, please understand how special it was."

She said hurt, "Except, it was with my body – you used my body Shaun."

"Siobhan, I don't know what to say."

"What about showing respect for me?"

We lay on our bunks, she the bottom, me the top. I knew she didn't sleep well, it was a restless night but I couldn't sacrifice Lyn's memory, if there was a stand to take, this was it.

Next morning we left the 'bunker' under the distant eye of security. There hadn't been a sighting or report, nothing suspicious. Once outside Siobhan clasped my hand and turned me around. She drew me close and whispered, "About last night, I'm really sorry. We can do our own romancing and create our own memories."

I sighed, an understanding breath but peppered with frustration and sibilance.

I drove Siobhan to her cousins; 'someone trustworthy' was her assessment and then I continued my journey to Chantal Witherspoon's house. Direction became a secondary concern. I arrived and killed the engine. Why was I here? Did I really want to revive the past? I hadn't prepared and I was as vulnerable as when she confronted me on the steps of the Berala train station. I knew my lie had hurt and since then my guilt had multiplied. Her love letter was touching, how could you ignore such honesty? On my mother's advice, I told her I hadn't received her letter. That little white lie had become a major, I could apologise but would she accept the truth? Would her mental condition allow such brutality?

I sat in the car trying to understand. I ached for renewal, amidst these times was Lyn and with that my problems fixed, if only I had spoken to Lyn in that milk bar, maybe none of this would be happening. Would Chantal remember me? I certainly remembered her letter:

> *Dear Shaun,*
> *I may be stupid for doing this as all my friends have advised against writing. I can't stand it any longer and want you to know – I love you!*
> *I lie awake at night unable to settle. My body burns when I think of you. Please let me know if you feel the same.*
> *My Deepest Love,*
> *Chantal Witherspoon*

Unless you hated someone, a love letter had a way of attaching itself. You had to admire the writer's courage. I closed the car door and opened a picket gate. It squeaked a rusty sound; more liked a bird in trouble. The paving stones were uneven and moss grew as grout. I climbed three wooden stairs which barely contained my weight. I knocked twice. Three seconds later.

"Chantal?

"Yes."

"You may not remember me, I'm…"

"Shaun Reece, what are you doing here?" Standing before me was a woman the same age with strange worry lines that embraced her forehead. They added character if nothing else. She wasn't bad looking, had a smart figure and utilised do-it-yourself hair products. Those blonde tips and dark roots were sadly due for maintenance.

"You remember me?"

She replied slower this time, "Yes, I remember."

"I want to talk. Is this a good time?" She nodded, "The last time we saw each other you called me a f...ing liar. I just wanted to say I'm sorry for being dishonest with you. You had every right to be hostile."

She managed, "Shaun, you destroyed years of admiration within seconds."

Her eyes locked onto mine, they were moist, and then the dam broke, I said, "I'm really sorry."

Her head drifted back, she sniffled and used both hands to clear her eyes, "Come inside."

I followed her to the lounge room, it was a dim lit room hanging with musk. She turned and perused me closely, taking in more than my appearance, it was as if she was drawing from me, a scent, energy or maybe her ability to read my mind, maybe all three. I could feel sweat running my back. I looked around the room which featured old collectibles, hundreds of them and each crammed against the other. An old piano carried its share. To divert her fixation I asked, "You collect figurines?"

She replied quickly, "No. They were my mothers; when she died I didn't have the heart to throw them out."

I sat opposite her, a silence brewing. Her eyes returned to me, deep blue with large pupils, "What can I say?"

Her head cocked to the side as she pondered my question, after several seconds she demanded, "Did you receive my... my letter?" Those last words came with attitude.

"Yes," I swallowed.

Her eyes tightened. She sat back on the sofa and licked her lips, "Why did you lie then?"

I swallowed, "My mother told me to."

She looked shocked, her eyes widened and danced crazily, like a yo-yo going horizontally. She leaned forward and snapped, "Your mother? Your mother?"

"Yes, she steamed your letter open and warned me off before I had a chance to read it."

She spat out, "That's despicable!"

"I know. I've regretted it ever since."

"What, so all this time you did love me?"

"I regretted the lying part, I'm sorry Chantal; no, I didn't love you."

"You were into Lyn, weren't you? I should have realised. I feel so stupid. Time doesn't heal a thing. How long has it been Shaun?"

"Forty something."

"Christ, and forty years on I'm still plague by your rejection."

"But now you know I feel as bad as you do."

She continued studying my face, an uncomfortable feeling, something was brewing, I just couldn't understand what, "And why after all this time have you decided to come forward and confess to me?"

"I have some questions."

"So you want something from me, something besides my heart rendering emotions? You're a piece of work!"

She had a volatile nature, no different from when I had known her at school, "Chantal, people are being murdered, I'm not sure the killer is going to stop."

She said surprised, "What do you mean? You are the target?"

"I think so."

"What a strange situation this is Shaun, you're forced to apologise with the hope I may help."

"You're right. I'm being a proper bastard, completely insensitive, I should go."

I rose and headed to the door, she called out, "Sit." I returned to my seat feeling akin to a canine. She continued, "I might be singed but I'm not unchristian. We did go to the same church, something rubbed off and I'm determined not to be that unscrupulous," I kept in mind her stability, it was definitely borderline.

"If Lyn Monday hadn't been around, would you have paid me any attention?"

"No, I'm sorry."

"I had no chance."

"None."

She sighed, "Well Shaun Reece has learned not to lie. It hurt me Shaun. That lie was painful, more painful than your rejection. Anyway, what do you want?"

"First off, are you alright? I heard…"

"Mental, deranged, paranoid, suicidal, schizophrenia, any of those?"

"I heard you had a rough time."

"I lost everything, except I never lost faith in God and that my life could get better. Today is an example."

"I admire you Chantal, maybe we were closer than you realise."

A little smirk creased her face, "I was close alright, and every Sunday I'd be edging out someone so I could sit next to you in church. You didn't even realise, did you?" She went to say something but stopped.

"You know I was flattered by your letter, most people wouldn't have the courage."

"Thanks, better to hear it late than never," she sighed a painful breath as if her lungs had expelled the last trace of air.

"And you lived close to Lyn?"

"Yes, about ten houses away. We weren't friends, just acquaintances."

"How come you were invited to the Freemont's birthday party, you remember the bonfire?" I purposefully sidetracked the Captain Blood Eye game.

She swallowed before answering, "I was really pissed off with you and wanted to make you jealous. I became friends with Josh's cousin."

"Is that the person you married?"

"Christ, you didn't know?"

"Know what?"

"I married David Collier."

I scrambled for recognition and suddenly the gears meshed. David had been in my class during primary and high school.

Chantal said, "He was the idiot who placed the bunger into that glass bottle and blew its splintery shards at everyone."

"Shit really? That was him? Look at the scar," I said showing her my hand.

"He was a dickhead then and even worse now, he drove me insane but I think he is more off the planet than I am."

"I don't think you're that bad," I was being kind.

"You don't know the half of it."

"Chantal, why did you split with him?"

"Necessities of life, I can't fight him any more and I've run out of money."

"What went wrong? Why fight him anyway?"

"We disagree over everything. I'm exhausted while at the same time he becomes energised from each confrontation. We're such a bad mix."

I asked, "And of course the Freemont's were at your wedding and let me guess, Josh was the best man?"

"Yes."

"And are Josh and David close?"

"Sickeningly close until recently, then, they had a huge argument and stopped talking."

"What was the argument over?"

"A family dispute. They'll patch it up eventually."

"Did you know how Lyn Monday died?"

"Suicide wasn't it?"

"That was the rumour." If I went further I'd be sidetracking the real issues.

"Sad for someone so young, you know in high school she told everyone she was going to marry you and have your baby."

"What? She said that?"

"She was convincing but then she went quiet on you and I saw my opportunity. I should have paid more attention." This time she flushed and her eyes looked at the floor.

I tried to lift her spirits, "Honestly Chantal, I was impressed by your openness."

"Really?"

"Yes," however she went teary again. Then, as if the wind had changed direction, she announced, "You know Josh went out with Lyn for awhile."

"For how long?"

"Long enough for him to walk around with a supercilious grin for a day; something happened between them, I have no idea what, but that lasted a millisecond."

"Don't you like Josh?"

She wouldn't answer. Strange, those eyes had shown each emotion but now they were vacant. I prompted, "Chantal?" her eyes blinked and darted the room. It became uncomfortable to press the point. I hesitated, letting her settle and allowing time to think. Josh's deception was still unexplained. I changed the subject, "Chantal, can you forgive me?"

She stood and moved close. I rose from my seat and expected to shake her hand, instead she took my hand and declared, "Forgive you? Maybe, but as you want something, I also want something."

"Anything."

"Do you have someone in your life Shaun?"

"Yes."

"Good then."

She surprised me when she wrapped her arms around my neck, "What are you doing?"

Her cheek brushed mine, I stiffened, "Chantal don't!"

I could hear her breathing, exploring my scent and then she kissed me. Her grip was intense. When we broke seconds later she was smiling, "You owed me something for lying. Explain that to your woman!" It was a double edged challenge and she knew the only way out was to tell the truth. She teased, "No feelings, no arousal Shaun?"

I shook my head. She waited for more but I was only delaying the inevitable, "Sorry, nothing."

She recovered well, "All I get is a lie and then the truth, they both hurt," then as if grasping for a common denominator, she ventured, "You know we have a special bond?"

"How?"

"We went to church together. You won't remember, but I was beside you during our confirmation. Shaun, I have thoughts of you every…"

I protested, "Chantal, I have to leave."

She looked disappointed, "I'm sorry Shaun, take care. Can we stay in touch?"

We exchanged email addresses.

I sat in the car trying to recover, I could have broken her embrace but that would have created more problems. I came away feeling sorry for her. I couldn't drive, not yet. I knew those guilt ridden years had been addressed but they hadn't and now I suspected my visit had made matters worse. It was then I heard a gun discharge. I instinctively ducked. That sickening feeling returned. That shot had come from Chantal's house.

I raced to her front door, it wasn't locked, she was sitting in the same sofa chair. There was a gun resting on her lap. Her eyes wallow, dark and depressed, she said startled, "Shaun... your still here? I thought you had left. Hey, I missed first time, watch me try again."

She straightened her arms with the gun facing towards her; it was shaking wildly, "Chantal no, put the gun down."

"Not much point Shaun, I've got nothing left, I'm bankrupt. My spirit has gone."

I stammered, "Chantal... Chantal..."

She smiled and cocked the gun, its metallic click sounded smooth and well greased almost tempting the holder to pull the trigger. Suddenly she changed positions, "I remember now, shoot the side of the head, women rarely shoot their own face, no wonder I missed, vanity in death," she laughed hauntingly and with one hand she raised the gun to her temple.

Without thinking I blurted out, "Chantal, let's visit the Berala train station."

"What?" the gun dropped slightly.

"Let me do this right. No lies. You deserve better."

A strange look came over her face; I could tell it was an enticing offer. The gun dipped some more, I grabbed it and secured the safety, she said, "Really, the Berala train station and will you say the right things to me this time round?"

"I'll only tell the truth. Shit Chantal, I don't want you to die, you're coming with me, pack a bag. Where did you get the gun from?"

"From the library."

I left that answer alone, to mention guns any further would be counter productive.

As Chantal packed, I made a phone call.

We drove for some time with the radio playing; the only thing I detected was a change in Chantal's mood. She looked content and began humming to the music. The wind whistled her hair and occasionally she glanced at me with a smile, her spirits had definitely lifted.

When we arrived at Berala, parking spaces were at a premium and I had to park in front of our old church however this meant we had to walk the entire shopping centre. I held my breath as we passed the dentist where Lyn had worked and the milk bar where I couldn't speak to her and then there was the pharmacy where Malcolm Shailler had worked. Opposite was the train station, the stairs, the dust, my memories and that lie still bounding off those solid brick walls.

Chantal recalled, "I was at the bottom of the steps and I sighted you coming, I was with my girlfriends and they nudged me to talk. So up you go, when you come down I'll be on the middle landing." She remembered the exact spot. "Go. Do it properly."

I climbed the stairs to the very top, a total of thirty-two steps where I understood her pain. Once I turned I saw her face full of expectation, no different to all those years ago. I slowly descended, I remembered I was on the left side, she came up the middle.

We stopped on the landing, "Hi," she said.

"Hi."

"Did you get my letter?"

I swallowed, déjà vu flash backs had nothing on this moment, "Yes. I received your letter."

"And?"

"I didn't know you cared."

She nodded.

"Chantal, I've been spelled to another and there is absolutely nothing I can do about it. I don't want to lead you on but I would like to have you in my life, somewhere special. Could you be there for me?"

She spat out bitterly, "Who spelled you?"

"Lyn."

"But she died. She's dead!"

"It's a long story."

"Then tell me, I need to know Shaun."

I told her I wouldn't lie and I didn't. I had no idea if she believed my story but she seemed content there was one. She gave me a hug, "You to have had it rough and now I'm your... what am I?"

"Someone special."

She bitterly replied, "Don't patronise me. You make me sound disabled. I have feelings Shaun, I'm human you know."

"I know, you're right and I'm sorry, this is an awkward moment for me. I don't deserve your tolerance. Maybe in a few weeks we could go to church together?"

She looked puzzled, "Communion?"

"Yes, but don't spill your wine on me," her eyes sparkled with mischief, "Chantal, I have a surprise for you but you have to be strong."

CHAPTER 39

DEVIATES ANONYMOUS

When Chantal raised that gun for a second shot, my heart sunk. I had lied to her and that lie hurt, not only for her but for me. I knew exactly what she was experiencing, a gut retching rejection with no way out. Now I vowed to look after her – whatever happened!

Earlier, Samantha had accepted my call with a cool cynicism. When I asked for a favour she said, "No," so I asked again, adding that it wasn't for myself, it was then she mellowed. I explained that someone from my church needed watching and in typical Samantha style she queried, "When was the last time you went to church?" I proudly announced, "Today actually, got a great parking spot right out the front. Anyway, please watch her, I'm talking suicide. Her name is Chantal Witherspoon and I owe her one." Samantha knew of our security concerns so it was pointless rehashing that story but I did give her enough information to keep her on guard. Also, I had warned Chantal to be strong but this was more a reference to putting up with Samantha, however I didn't labour the point. The questions these two could muster would cancel any attempt to take her life and besides Samantha needed company.

Then I got to thinking, was Chelsea's dad a suspect? Although with Des Rains' murder that was concealed to look like suicide so that didn't fit an Olympic sharp shooter's profile, regardless, I called Chelsea, she replied, "Yeah, dad went well until arthritis stopped him shooting, his hands are crunched up a bit. So why the sudden interest in my father?"

It appeared her father was off the most wanted list, so I just replied, "I admire our sporting greats, I was just interested, that's all. And you had a dream run into the final of the World Debating Championship?"

"I gave all the contestants contaminated food but it was only the last one who had a reaction."

"Really?"

"No Shaun, of course not, you know I could have won with my tongue tied behind my back. Is this the level of Beaulieu's research? I'm much further advanced with my investigation, maybe her mind isn't on the job. You know she's sleeping around."

"Chelsea, have you been spying on her?"

"Yes."

"Is it a man or woman?"

"Or why not both Shaun! You really are becoming desperate for information."

"I think I have information overload."

"I suggest you contact Josh Freemont to keep your mind on track, be careful though, there is something fishy going on."

"What?"

"It wouldn't be fishy if I knew? Not everything adds up."

I warned Chelsea, "I think you better stop your investigation, this could get dangerous."

"Do you want me to find out what Beaulieu's up to though?"

"Of course, that would be alright. As soon as you find out something report back to me."

"Shaun, you know you're a deviate."

"Thanks."

I met up with Siobhan at a pre-arranged hotel, a quaint establishment that offered privacy. I suspected the privacy were for people interested in preventing spouse tracking rather than putting their necks on a chopping block. Anyway we were here and safe for the moment.

Once settled, I explained to Siobhan my relationship with Chantal, her love letter, her kiss, her suicide attempt, the steps of the Berala train station and an apprehended violence order which she had served on her husband. Samantha was now looking after her. Of course when the truth was revealed, Chantal was easily explainable, however Siobhan's questions reminded me of Samantha.

Siobhan asked, "You kissed her?"

"She kissed me, no big deal."

"No big deal?"

"Remember this was a sensitive moment, she's fragile, and since then I've made it quiet clear I'm devoted to you."

"Via Lyn." I nodded, "And everyone is settled now; everyone knows I'm the one."

"Absolutely. Oh, one other thing."

"What?"

"I promised Chantal I would take her to church."

"This won't turn into an orgy of worship?"

"Nah, just communion with a little wine."

"Best I come then."

I decided it was time, Josh Freemont's time. It was a time for answers, a time to put aside doubt and make sense of the past. Why couldn't he tell me he was Lyn Monday's boyfriend? It was deception at its finest and the secret could have gathered dust for another forty-five years, however to be a good liar you needed a good memory and if Lyn had not presented herself I still wouldn't have been any the wiser.

I called him, realising he would be reluctant to meet up, "Josh, Shaun Reece here."

"Hi, I was just thinking of calling you."

"How was the Moroccan holiday?"

"Spectacular, we had an unreal time."

"That's really good. When I told Samantha your family were spending time in Morocco, she said, 'lucky bastards'."

"How is Samantha?"

"Good but something happened while you were enjoying the good life. I went to London for a few weeks. What I'm trying to say is, I left Samantha and I have a new friend. Her name is Siobhan, she is gorgeous."

"Really? You split?"

"Yeah."

"You have a new... girlfriend?"

"Yeah, she is stunning. Are you still interested in catching up? Rebecca will have someone to talk to."

"You split with Samantha, why?"

"We decided we were incompatible. It was an easy decision when she caught me 'snogging' the opposition. Anyway, she amicably accepted my departure. She got the house, the kids, although they're all grown up, the furniture, car, bed and cat. Yep, she got most of it... it was a good deal, especially for her... everyone gets on famously if I pretend I'm a leper, unfortunately she treats me as someone with a communicable disease. Josh... I'm only kidding; I'm as healthy as a charging rhino." I laughed at my own joke, anything to keep the tension from my voice.

We made a time but I could feel his trepidation, I kept talking to prevent him going back on the meeting. I finished quickly with, "See you tomorrow then."

As I replaced the handset, I asked Siobhan, "Did you hear what I said?"

"It sounds like he has no sense of humour."

"He's uptight; I could tell he was reluctant to meet. However, he won't be able to resist the bait."

"The bait?"

"Yeah, you, my gorgeous girlfriend, I guarantee he won't cancel, his curiosity has been raised."

"You know him that well."

"Oh yeah, but not well enough to realise Lyn Monday was his girlfriend. This will be an interesting get together."

The phone rang, it was Samantha, "Shaun, you never mentioned Chantal was an integral part of your teenage years."

I whispered, "Is she nearby?"

"Yes."

"Then don't call me until you are alone. Think outside the square on this one and don't let her out of your sight."

"I'm sorry, you're busy. Have a good night."

Siobhan asked, "That was Samantha?'

"Yes."

Siobhan questioned further, "How is Chantal?"

"Ok, I think, as long as Samantha doesn't get carried away with her responsibilities.

I should have called a doctor but just knew Chantal had had a gut full of professionals. Christ Siobhan, Chantal's finger was tightening on the trigger for a second shot. It was a split second decision and I had to run with it. I hurt her Siobhan and just maybe it started her decline. I'll never know."

"From what you told me she has tried to take her life previously."

"It is so sad, she has nothing left and I feel responsible."

"Shaun, you need to relax, with each drama you're taking on more responsibility. Sometimes others have to be responsible. Take me for example…"

"Really?" I said interrupting, "I'd like to do that."

"Shaun concentrate."

"Sorry, that just blurted out. You're very tempting you know," I smiled sheepishly, "Pleaseeee… can you forgive me?"

Siobhan laughed at my use of vowels but it was no way as enticing as her manipulation of the English language, "Shaun, seeing we have changed direction, I need to apologise. I'm torn over placing a condition on sex, I should never have said, ' I want that type of romance… London – that last night please!' I'm so, so, sorry."

"Accepted, but 'torn'… really?"

"Yes, torn is an expression that means…"

"I know what it means. I'm sorry too, it was just as much my fault, I overreacted. It was such a shock to be confronted with that problem, you were in London but you weren't, Lyn was there but she wasn't. Regardless, protecting my memory of Lyn seemed the right thing to do."

Siobhan replied, "All I've been is negative when it comes to that trip. I remember waking and panicking and that's all. I know you were there for me, you'd never hurt me. How many weeks has it been?"

"Maybe five, going on six."

"We've become close." She meant really close but not intimate. I smiled.

"Bed then?"

We lay naked, we kissed and petted. She nuzzled my neck and I caressed her breasts. I ran my fingers over taut, knotted muscle, I poured warm oil from a height and as it ran the small of her back, little sighs became her only conversation. It was then she fell asleep but with my hand in the most relieving of positions.

Next day I called Samantha, "Can you talk?"

"Why are you whispering?"

"Siobhan is still asleep."

"So is Chantal. She needs her rest. So what I asked last night, was she?"

"What, that Chantal was an integral part of my teenage years?"

"Yes that."

"No."

"She seems to know a lot about you."

"We went to the same primary school and church. She sent me a love letter which I disavowed knowledge of. Other than that, there is nothing. She's not well Samantha; you need to monitor her constantly. She's intensely obsessed."

"And with you."

I sighed, "I know, it's not healthy."

"I'll say."

"You know we are starting to agree on more and more things. It's a worry."

She ignored my attempt at conciliation, "I'll keep an eye on her and how are you going with your research?"

"I'm seeing Josh Freemont today, actually we are having dinner." Siobhan stirred and smiled sleepily.

Samantha wrapped up the conversation with, "Keep safe then."

"Thanks, I …" almost saying, 'I love you', but fell short of stirring up that hornet's nest. I hung up.

Siobhan turned onto her side, "Did you almost say, 'I love you'. And that was Samantha wasn't it?"

"Yes it was Samantha. I know, it nearly slipped out, can you believe I almost said that."

She nodded but then realised her nakedness, "Did we do anything naughty?"

"I did but you didn't."

"Oh… what?"

"Next time stay awake, in the meantime, it's my secret, incidentally you were very relaxed." She pouted disappointment.

I called Beaulieu, "I'm off to see Josh Freemont soon, any update?"

"Do you have Chelsea following me?"

"Err… why would I have Chelsea follow you?"

"Well, when I cornered her at the end of the cul-de-sac she declared she was following me on your instructions."

"I bet she wormed her way out of that by offering you a plausible excuse."

"Yes, she said she was following your instructions. What part of my answer are you having trouble with?"

"Beaulieu, I'm concerned. There is a killer on the loose and you seem blasé to the ramifications your associations could have."

"My personal life is none of your concern; anyway, Chelsea has approved whom I'm seeing."

"And who is that Beaulieu?"

Beaulieu hung up on me.

I guess Josh Freemont wasn't her highest priority. I rang Chelsea.

"Hi, who is Beaulieu seeing?"

"Shaun, this may be difficult for you to understand but Beaulieu and I are working together. Whom she is seeing is inconsequential."

"Working together? Whatever for? How does that work?"

"It means we will vet all information handed to you."

"Why?"

Chelsea hung up on me.

Siobhan had been listening, "You didn't say, 'I love you' to those last two calls. No layering there I guess!"

CHAPTER 40

――――◄O►――――

CONTRADICTORY BINARIES

I laughed when Siobhan reminded me of 'layering', that theory where care was enhanced with multiple forms of loving. I had told Siobhan it was 'love without boundaries, love that was nurturing and fulfilling' and I had spoken of how Lyn, during her merging with Siobhan had ventured this theory, now 'layering' was working for me; just by Beaulieu and Chelsea working together proved they had my interest at heart. On the surface it appeared they were plotting and devious, which was pretty much the case but more importantly, their focus was positive – I was likewise caught up with their antics. Again, Lyn's involvement crept to mind. I asked Siobhan, "Layering? Do you believe that theory?"

"What's not to believe, you know I was messing with you?"

"Oh, I know," I moved close, held her hips and perused her faced. "Good, it's back."

"What?"

"That imp!"

I placed my forehead against hers, we lingered, as if thought transference needed time, a download where words were re-dundant. She closed her eyes and sighed gathering my direction, she stated, "We need intimacy, but first we need to sort out Lyn."

I swallowed, it was the best I could do for a response. I ached for Siobhan's acceptance. She was quiet for the next few hours, I didn't push for answers.

I sat on the sofa, a comfortable hotel lounge made from deep brown suede, a bed of delicate rose petals crossed my mind. Siobhan adjusted a pillow behind me; a contrasting blue throw-down, vibrant and uplifting, then she wrapped her arms around me and said, "I do love you."

I smiled acceptance and squeezed her hand, she snuggled up close, her skin warm against the Arctic burst of the air conditioner, "You're thinking of Josh Freemont?"

"Yeah, I need to be at the top of my game, so much has happened since he told me Lyn died. It'll be a nightmare trying to sift relevance into our conversation, most of all I want to expose his lie, an apology would be nice and why he neglected to tell me Lyn was his girlfriend."

"I'll think up something to drag Rebecca away, that way you'll have some privacy."

I revealed, "I do you know."

"What?"

"Love you."

The car had a southerly wind to its rear and we were making excellent time, too quick to gather my thoughts, even though I had stewed all morning over the subject. I tried to collate what I knew, what should I say, obviously not tell Josh everything. At the time of Lyn's death, Josh told me she committed suicide but recently he said he wasn't sure Lyn had died, he said, "Mm, might have," as if. Maybe Josh didn't know Lyn was pregnant but why was he now living so close to her other boyfriend, the pharmacist... Malcolm Shailler? I couldn't wait for that answer. And then I had a bad feeling, maybe we were heading into a trap. I had become so excited to hear his confession I had forgotten the basic steps of survival. When I discussed my safety concerns with Siobhan she said, "What, we're ten minutes away and you think it'll be too dangerous?"

"Well come along, but be careful."

"Careful will mean zilch if he's the murderer."

We cruised past Josh Freemont's palatial mansion and Siobhan whistled. It was very different from his humbled upbringing in Berala where weatherboard houses and tinned roofs dotted a humble landscape. His home spread across the equivalent of three normal house allotments and at the rear, it had its own lake access. I surveyed the area and was surprised to find Malcolm Shallier's house being the reverse image of Josh's and although one house separated both at the front, both properties were 'L' shaped and joined at the rear. In essence, Josh and Malcolm were lake front neighbours.

Siobhan said, "I'm nervous, I'm not sure I can do this."

"I need you and if it's any consolation, I'm ten times more nervous than you are."

Were we doing the right thing? Were we stupid? Was there a reckoning required? A chance for the truth in return for some information, anyway I was assuming he would tell the truth. I locked the car and walked the drive; Siobhan was two paces behind me, an ideal position if we had to make a run for it. I noticed Siobhan wasn't wearing stilettos, more a shoe for all occasions, like sprinting, hedge jumping or wading through the water. I took a deep breath and rang the bell.

When the door drew open I was surprised to find Josh standing there. He had lost most of his hair except for a rim of growth bordering his ears. This surviving grey outcrop was doing its utmost to escape the daily brush. "Shaun," he greeted and shook my hand, "And you were right, this lovely lady is gorgeous."

"Hi, I'm Siobhan," and at the same time, she leaned forward to kiss him on the cheek.

"Josh…," he faltered, somewhat flustered, it was evident he had thought long and hard about Siobhan and how she may look. He seemed stunned by her radiance. Rebecca, his wife appeared, taking off an apron and flicking back shoulder length hair revealing a face of tension and calamity all mixed into the one. "Hi everyone, I'm Rebecca," her voice didn't fit the face but her body was just as rounded as those vocal cords. Josh recovered first and studied my face; he raised a gentle smile, one I had not seen for forty-five years. "You old devil," he ventured, "You haven't changed that much. Can you still run 100 yards under 10.5 seconds?"

"No, because they only have the 100 metre race now and I refuse to go metric."

He laughed. "Sorry Rebecca for not saying hi, but I was…" what was I? "Err, intrigued." That should get me out of trouble.

"Intrigued?" she questioned.

"Yes, where did you get such an incredible voice, do you record or do voice overs?"

She giggled and took it as a compliment, which I belatedly meant.

"Only for the Education Department and Josh's special projects."

"You should venture into the commercial world, that's where the big bucks are."

She grinned at the compliment but her face had such a conflict of expressions it was difficult to know which one dominated.

Josh said, "Come, let me give you the grand tour."

We lingered at the family photos and each child was aged identical to my three. All had left home. We moved through the house. The ceiling would have been three metres high except for the sunken lounge room where I estimated the height to be another metre. Siobhan announced, "Rebecca, the house is magnificent," Josh accepted the compliment as well and both smiled.

Rebecca responded, "Thanks, we designed it and had a builder complete the project."

I couldn't let this opportunity slide and asked, "I noticed your neighbour's is similar, reversed or a mirrored plan I think they call it."

"Yes," they said together, and Josh added, "That was our plan, both houses were built together. At the front we are separated however at the rear we are lake front neighbours."

"Who lives there, is it family?"

"We sold it to pay for this one. I believe an older guy moved in three months back, I haven't met him yet. I think he just retired but he keeps to himself. He does have a wife or she maybe his girlfriend, we don't know, he purchased the house from a work colleague."

Siobhan said, "They are magnificent houses, it's a credit to the both of you."

They smiled.

We settled onto the lounge, "I've been doing a lot of research on neighbourhoods and I've found that people living next door to each other, some for over thirty years are still strangers. It's a strange phenomenon, so you don't know his name then?"

"No," he answered quickly.

"So, you've never spoken to him?"

"No."

"But you have seen him?"

Rebecca answered, "Yes, briefly."

I asked, "How long ago?"

Rebecca answered again, "When he first moved in three months ago."

Josh asked cautiously, "Why so many questions about our neighbour?"

"I read somewhere that when two houses are identical and within close proximity to one another, what affects one family, often affects the other. A balance of the universes, I'm trying to think what this theory is called… remember Newton's law: For every action, there is an equal and opposite reaction. With two 'identical's', neither has a status above the other and this is called, 'Binary'… that's it! Contradictory binaries cancel and confirm each other, as do Nothing – Something and Ying-Yang. Binaries however are meshed as one. In the meantime, you need to be mindful and caring for these people; their lives are intertwined with yours. Tell me Josh, why did the previous owners sell up?"

His eyes widened and he cast a look at Rebecca to keep quiet. He glanced back at me and wet his lips. He curled his bottom lip inward and bit down with his teeth, not hard, just enough to send it white. "A work transfer, we didn't know them that well, it all happened so suddenly."

Rebecca looked puzzled, "Yes we did."

Josh explained, "Well a little, an occasional barbecue." He changed the subject, "Who would like a drink?"

All nodded and Josh rose and strode to the bar.

Rebecca said to Siobhan, "While Josh mixes the drink I'll show you the garden. The boys probably have a million things to talk about."

Josh nodded and kept pouring, I sat opposite him on a tall bar stool and he handed me rum and cola which tasted more like bourbon and coke. He asked as the women disappeared, "Have you been in touch with anyone else from school?"

"No, just you."

"I'm flattered."

I smiled. Mounted in a glass frame above the bar was an old AK47, a Russian designed automatic rifle. It had a huge canister attached which I assumed was a continuous feed device. "Where did you get an AK47 from? Aren't they illegal?"

He looked up, "Oh, that's the first machine to come off the production line, a collectors dream, although it has no firing pin. I estimate its value at one million."

I whistled, "You like guns."

He surprised me, "Yeah, I'll shoot the bugger out of anything. I'm in a shooter's club, we collect guns, attend conferences and train for problems, you know?" and he smiled knowingly.

"No... I don't, not really. When you say you train for problems, what does that mean?"

A sly look encroached his face, "You're away with the birds if you think the police or military will defend you. They're under trained, under equipped and understaffed. Its groups like ours who will be the mainstay behind an attack. There are hundreds of clubs out there, all fully equipped and ready for action. We ask the elite to train us, SAS, Counter Terrorism Commands etc. etc. By themselves they could only control small insurgents but with us behind them their strength is a hundred fold."

"And you use all types of guns?"

"A countless array of weapons to choose from, we have a library, all locked away in a security bunker."

"Library?"

"Where every gun is filed and categorised, just like a book library."

Strange, when I asked Chantal where she acquired a gun she referred to the 'library' also.

I used a shock tactic, "Have you ever killed anyone?"

His eyes stopped moving and I detected a coldness in the air, "No… not yet."

I sipped my strange tasting drink and looked at Josh. He did likewise, scanning my face for something. His eyes went back and forth, never stopping. I spat out, unable to contain myself, "Lyn Monday."

"I knew you came about her."

"I know you know. Look Josh, we've known each other too long."

"What, fifty years since we've seen each other?"

"Not that long. A long time though but we haven't changed, we are still competitive but I've come for answers. I mean no bullshitting. Agree?" He nodded cautiously. "This is important. When did you go out with Lyn?"

He couldn't look at me. "I'm sorry Shaun, I should have told you, it's just… I knew you liked her and I didn't want to upset you. Lyn was as special to me as she was to you. Why the sudden interest?"

I didn't answer, only delivering my next question, "Josh, were you ever intimate with her?"

He reeled, "How dare you. That's my business."

"So you were! Don't worry, I haven't come for details, except…"

"What then?" His face appeared red, his breathing rapid.

"When?"

He spat out, "What? You want to know when I had sex. Are you crazy?"

"Yeah, I must be, regardless, when was the last time?"

"You have a nerve."

"I know but try to calm down, this is important."

"You just front up after all this time and want to know about my sex life?"

"Yes!"

"If you must know, it was only the once and six to seven weeks before my brother's 21st birthday party."

"I'll tell you what I'm doing here Josh…. Lyn's been in touch!" His eyes narrowed in disbelief but before he could query my statement we heard Rebecca's voice as she opened the front door.

"Shit," he said.

I also heard Siobhan say, "Of course, if it's important," and then there was a man's voice, which sounded oddly familiar, "It is!"

My body stiffened. It was a moment later when Siobhan and Rebecca presented with Senior Detective Lance Petersen, the very person heading up Tom's murder investigation, and with him trailed his assistant.

Josh stood, annoyed at the interruption. We shook hands, Detective Petersen in particular going too hard on pressure. He just stood looking at the four of us, not venturing a word. Then he flashed his badge. I was used to people stalling for affect but I felt embarrassed by his delay.

Josh said, "Sit." We did, all uncomfortably like Great Danes, except for Lance who preferred to work the room.

I asked, "Did you bring my phone back?"

The detective smiled but didn't answer and Josh looked puzzled that I should even ask about a phone.

Lance asked, "Can you explain how you two know each other?" the question was directed to Josh who answered a question with a question, "Why?"

Detective Lance Petersen said, "How?"

Josh backed up his previous question with, "Why?"

Lance spat back another, "Sir?"

I could see the frustration on both faces so I interrupted with a mediating response of, "Murder. He's investigating a murder."

"Thank you Mr. Reece you have no idea how that has helped."

"No worries."

I thought if he wanted to control the action, he should have split the group. Rebecca volunteered something, "We know nothing about no murder," eloquent and direct for people involved with education. Josh reinforced his wife's comment, "Exactly. Are we under suspicion for something?" Josh reconsidered his question, "Are our friends under suspicion?"

"Everyone is a suspect. How do you know one another?"

I answered, "I went to school with Josh, I could have murdered him each time he beat me in a race. Does that count?" Josh smiled weakly.

"I know your trying to make light of what is happening but we have three murders we're investigating and…"

I interrupted, "Three? So Fiona, Tom's girlfriend was murdered?"

Josh said, "Whose girlfriend? Who is Fiona? Do you two know each other?"

"Sort of, Fiona was Siobhan's husband's girlfriend. Tom her husband has been murdered, I witnessed his death and Detective Petersen is making enquiries, and as for Des Rains, how was he murdered Detective?"

Lance didn't volunteer a thing.

Josh asked, "Who is Des Rains?"

I answered, "A friend of a friend."

Josh shook his head unable to keep up. Lance fidgeted on the spot trying to fathom our lifetime relationship. He asked, "So, how have you two remained friends after all this time?"

I let Josh answer this one, "Err, common interests."

I knew Detective Petersen's next response, "Like?"

Josh refused to answer, instead asking if he was a suspect, followed by, "Do we need a lawyer?"

"If you've done nothing wrong you won't need a lawyer."

Josh surprised me by saying, "The way you are conducting this enquiry makes me nervous. I think we need lawyers." He warned Siobhan and me, "Not another word until we have representation."

I spoke calmly realising what a perfect moment this was, "Josh, I don't think Detective Petersen is pointing the finger at us, he just hasn't got any clues and would like a bit of assistance, isn't that right detective?"

CHAPTER 41

CAN'T REMEMBER

When I suggested the police were 'clueless', it wasn't said with malice. However my assessment of their ability was like watching oil drip, where each drop greased the clues but for whatever reason made it too slippery to grasp the notion. Except for Samantha, their response time sucked, Chelsea, Beaulieu and Chantal had not been interviewed but I found it strangely amusing that Josh Freemont had jumped the queue to be a person of interest. My phone being tapped may have helped Josh's status and I couldn't think of anyone more deserving – this for any other reason than to watch the bastard squirm.

Annoyingly Detective Petersen took my 'clueless' comment to heart and smiled a benevolent grin that proved people loved power. He suggested we should cooperate or be seen to be hindering a murder investigation. Regardless of this added pressure, Josh refused to cooperate and asked the detective to leave. Rebecca became flustered and I could see this perfect moment evaporating. In desperation I ventured, "Alright, let's throw some things around, off the record of course. Will that be alright detective?" Thankfully he nodded and Josh relaxed into his chair. But why interview Josh and Rebecca in the first place? Or were Siobhan and I the prime suspects for these murders?

Detective Petersen asked, "So I'm clear Mr. Reece, what is your relationship with Mr. Freemont?"

I replied, "We were friends at school and thought we should catch up after all these years." He made no comment but gave a nod for me to continue, "We went to primary and high school together, trained for athletics together, worked during Christmas holidays together and liked the same girl, Lyn Monday, although I never knew that at the time."

Rebecca looked at Josh for an answer. It was clear Josh had never mentioned Lyn to her and further more he was unsettled by my recent comment... 'Lyn's been in touch!'

Rebecca asked, "Josh, who was she?"

"There was nothing to it Rebecca, it's not worth mentioning."

I said to Rebecca, "Josh knew I liked Lyn. Isn't that true Josh?"

"Yeah, Shaun liked her for years."

Detective Petersen asked, "And this Lyn Monday, have either of you kept in touch?"

Josh turned to me for the answer and everyone followed his lead, even Siobhan.

I answered, "We went to England some five or six weeks ago but I haven't seen her since."

Siobhan's mouth dropped and Detective Petersen asked Josh, "Did you two fight over this girl?"

Josh hesitated, caught between the pages of history and my fast-forward version of events, "Err, I can't remember, it was a long time ago." Rebecca looked unsettled.

The detective raised his eyebrows then asked, "No fight?"

I explained, "A decision of mutual agreement, a matter of ethics really, we just stopped being friends."

Josh added, "Quite some time ago."

Detective Petersen asked Josh his whereabouts the day of the murders. Josh simply dismissed his question with, "Here, I'm always here, I haven't left the house since I returned from holidays."

Rebecca nodded as support.

"Never left the house once?" He asked.

"No."

"Never drove to the Spartan Gun Club during this time?"

"I don't remember going anywhere."

"What about the 5th of this month, does that help your memory?"

"Err…"

"And the 7th and 10th, you know the gun club don't you?"

"Of course… it's just I don't remember those dates."

"Mr Freemont, I have a copy of a log book, this belonging to the Spartan Gun Club. Is that your signature?" He turned the page so Josh could peruse the writing.

"It looks like mine but I do my 'J's' with a curly loop."

"I see. So is it your signature or not?"

"I'm not sure."

"Mr. Freemont do you know a Chantal Collier?"

"My cousin's ex. Yes, I know her."

"And they lived close to you during the time they were married?"

Josh replied, "Yes. I'm not sure any of this is relevant, can you give me some form of direction here detective? Off the record of course."

"Just curious, some background information always helps the larger picture."

"And do you see me in this larger picture?"

"Not necessarily but as I said, everyone's a suspect."

Josh replied to the detective, "So you're on the list as well?"

"With the exception of myself because I know I never committed these crimes."

Josh whispered, "Of course. Convenient."

Detective Petersen continued, "And what is your evaluation of your cousin's ex-wife?"

"Unstable, she may have committed those murders, anything is possible."

I noticed the detective look for a reaction, he knew far more than I gave him credit. I didn't flinch. My mind was coming to terms with the tapping of my mobile phone calls, especially the

calls mentioning Chantal. The only thing I wasn't sure about...
had Chantal committed those murders?

Detective Petersen asked, "Mrs Freemont, the house next
door, the one similar to this... has recently been purchased by?"

Rebecca seemed surprised to be considered in this line of
questioning, she slipped, "Malcolm Shailler," then she realised
Josh and her had disavowed knowing him earlier. She flushed
at her mistake.

I couldn't help myself, "So you know Malcolm Shailler, Josh?"

Detective Petersen sensing something asked, "Mr. Freemont
can you answer that question?"

He wouldn't.

Detective Petersen again looked at me for an answer, "Josh,
Lyn, Chantal and I grew up in Berala. Malcolm Shailler was Lyn
Monday's other boyfriend. He was also our local pharmacist!"

Surprisingly, Detective Petersen rose and bid us farewell. He
offered his card to Josh, "You need to call this number, good
night and thank you for your time. We'll see ourselves out."

There was a silence, a hovering of minds, caught in rewind
and deliberating. Rebecca finally asked, "Hungry anyone?"

Siobhan coughed and said, "I'll help."

It was an uncomfortable time, Josh advised he had a headache and left the room for aspirin.

When Josh returned he looked distressed. He bungled me outside and closed the door. "What do you mean, Lyn's been in
touch? And that you went to London with her is pure fantasy.
Didn't you go with Siobhan? Why lie? Are you mad? Why are
you doing this to me?"

I ignored his attempt for answers and asked, "Why is Malcolm Shailler living next to you? You realise who he is?"

"A creep," was all he said, he added, Chantal's ex-husband is
in real estate, he organised the sale, a sheer co-incidence. Honest, I had nothing to do with it, it has to be fate. Anyway...?"

Rebecca called from the back door, "Are you guys coming in?"

Josh barked at her, "Christ no. Leave us alone."

She retreated like a dog with its tail between its legs, "Easy Josh, she didn't deserve that." He looked anything but remorseful. I asked, "Before I tell you the whole story will you answer something for me?"

"If I can."

"Did Lyn Monday ever use her eyes on you?"

"What do you mean?"

"To flirt, entice, tantalise and to seduce."

"Not really."

I breathed a sigh of relief, he said, "She had nice eyes but for me it was her neck and when she cut her hair, I was a goner, nothing to do with the eyes. Anyway tell me about Lyn."

"A long story."

"Tell me."

I rather tell you something more prudent, "Lyn was pregnant."

He hesitated, "Was it mine?"

"The baby was either yours or Malcolm Shaillers'."

He appeared flustered.

This time Siobhan slid the glass door, "Dinner, hurry, it smells delicious."

In the middle of Josh and Rebecca's lounge-room sat a lava rock fire, it would always be a talking point. It was warm and hypnotic, drawing us with brilliant swathes of orange and subtle yellows, it reflected against walls of whitewashed render. We ate here instead of the dining room.

Josh was quiet, a subdued reaction after all these years. He remained transfixed with the flames and nodded along with the conversation. There were times when it wasn't necessary to move his head and I wondered if he was alright? Rebecca carried the discussion in Josh's absence. Even though he was sitting amongst us, he wasn't, he participated but he didn't, he smiled at all the right times but I knew something was bothering him. He looked stunned. Three times Rebecca queried his well being, and he finally admitted his headache was getting worse. I asked, "Do you get many headaches Josh?" he couldn't look at me but said, "Only when the wind stirs the lake." I looked out across the vast expanse and sure enough, little white caps shimmed the surface creating thousands of moonlit mirrors. I could have sworn I saw a small yacht tacking back and forth but when I looked back some seconds later it was gone.

"Josh, do you have many yachts sail by at night?"

"No never, they can't, it's too shallow for sailing."

I smiled to myself, thinking Lyn must be close.

Josh was restless, he fidgeted, stood and sat, he moved his legs into a full stretch and twisted his head from side to side, anything to relax his shoulders. All this made Rebecca uneasy and I could imagine their conversation once we left.

We had finished the entrée an hour ago, it was now ten o'clock when we started our main meal which was deep fried salt and pepper squid tossed with a risotto. I jokingly said to Josh, "Did you catch this yourself, to which he replied, "Yes."

"Where?"

"Just outside, let me show you," and he left his meal untouched and exited the back door, again without a thought to wait for me. The women looked surprised. I apologised and joined him. As I closed the door, I could hear Rebecca also apologising to Siobhan.

Josh was standing by the lake's edge and his first question was, "Why?"

"Why what?"

He pushed me.

"What was that for?"

He pushed me again, provoking me to fight.

He snapped, "Why are you doing this? Lyn's dead. I know she's dead."

"Dead for you but not from my perspective, she's very much alive and to let you know, I'm doing this for her."

He swung a punch and I ducked under the hay-maker. I rose from my crouched position and I jabbed my fist into his stomach. He doubled over, his breathe completely gone. He gasped for air and held up his hand to stop me.

He struggled, "Alright then... let's assume Lyn is alive... what did Lyn say? What does she want?" He sucked a deep breath.

"She asked for my help."

"Your help? With what?"

"You tell me."

"Oh, Christ, I should have taken care of this."

"And that being?"

He couldn't look at me. I couldn't trust him but there again he couldn't trust me.

We walked inside and finished our deep fried cold squid, more in respect for Rebecca's cooking than anything else. The pepper gave it artificial warmth. Tension was high, no one spoke and we left before dessert was served. The last thing I said was, "Good luck with the cops!"

CHAPTER 42

◄○►

SWEET APOLOGY

When Siobhan and I walked through Josh Freemont's door there was no plan other than to separate him from his wife Rebecca. Our plan worked quicker than expected. It was worth it to have my moment with Josh and to find the police had included him in their investigation. Siobhan proved an absolute gem as she sensed my every thought and worked with my every instinct, regardless we were both shaken by the visit.

We were returning to our hotel, both silent until Siobhan said, "Shaun, did you have to tell everyone Lyn was alive. I hope that doesn't come back to bite you."

"Siobhan, life and death is irrelevant here. She was there, she's everywhere."

"No Shaun. Honestly, others have no idea the intensity you feel for this subject, if the police check on Lyn you're going to lose credibility."

"Then that's the way it is. Regardless, Josh needed a good shake-up and he got it. I couldn't have planned the night better. Did you see the yacht? It had a billowing spinnaker with racing stripes."

"I'm saying this as a friend Shaun, maybe your mind is justifying these sightings, anything to support your theory. You heard Josh, its way too shallow for sailing."

"Siobhan that yacht was out there, how can I prove this?"

"Maybe you can't and what you saw is for your eyes only or it maybe necessary to look at other options. I've heard that shimmering mirages can be atmospherically transferred to other parts of the world and they look exactly like the original. Maybe there was an eerie mist taking the shape of a yacht, or a new form of keel-less boat being tested. Maybe it was one of those new wave skiers using a sail for creativity. I'm convinced you saw something but what?"

"Maybe Lyn?"

"Maybe Lyn," Siobhan sighed, she reached over and patted my shoulder; it wasn't a patronising touch, rather one of gentle assurance, "You're not mad, just tormented."

I swallowed and changed the subject, "You know I hit him."

"What?"

"He tried to engage me in a fight but came off worse."

"I don't think you should see him again."

"You're probably right."

"When Rebecca and I were in the garden she started asking me the most contrived questions."

"Like?"

"Why did Shaun and Samantha break up? I replied by saying that their marriage had run out of steam but then she asked if Samantha was still in love with you which seemed contradictory."

"And how did you answer that?"

"I told her everyone loves Shaun, he isn't someone you fall out of love with. His wife may not be able to live with him but that certainly doesn't stop her loving him. Then she wanted to know if ours was a physical relationship or one built on sub-stance. Honestly, that question shook me. How could I answer that? It was unsettling, so I lied and said our love was rock solid, impervious to change. In hindsight, what was another lie, after all, they had concealed knowledge of Malcolm Shailler."

"Exactly, anyway you lied to protect us. I guess that was a sticky one but couldn't you say these were early days and we are still getting to know each other."

"I could have but I couldn't think fast enough."

"All strange, anyway, I bet Josh prompted that particular question, was there more?"

"There was going to be but we were interrupted by the police." Siobhan moved closer and rested her head on my shoulder, "You know you're stuck with me. I'm attracted to you in many ways… hey… you're not going to settle… are you?" She sat up and examined my face under the moody gloom of the neon dash light, "You're all hyped up and your shoulder muscles feel like knotted steel. Do you want a coffee to wind down?"

"I know a cute little café on the outskirts of Sydney; we will pass it on the way home."

"Do they have cake?"

"A mile high Angel's Food Cake."

"Fitting."

"Or a sumptuous mountain of Devil's Chocolate Cake?"

We held hands over a small wrought iron table and looked lovingly into each others eyes. We sipped cappuccino's alfresco and spooned cake to each others mouth. We were close to our London moments, where wine and roses, scented soap and starch linen seemed an everyday occurrence, however now; sitting in public had a danger that held the wildest of expectations. A rustling leaf or a slapped shut menu heightened our awareness. A paranoid person wasn't really seeing things, I'd been there with my son and knew it was things seeing you, something was different, something was out of place.

"Siobhan, Josh knows more about Malcolm than he makes out, there's something going on, something bad. I can't work it out. It's funny, every time I went to explain I was interrupted. He must be really confused by the information I gave him."

"You created enough doubt otherwise he would have tossed us out earlier. Shaun, do you think Chantal could have committed those murders?"

"Of course not, would I leave her with Samantha?" Suddenly I felt worried, "Do you think Samantha is safe? It's too late to ring her… right?"

"That's just great, Samantha is put at risk by an uncaring ex – husband, that's something Tom would have done, but still, my money is on Josh being the murderer."

"He belongs to that gun club. The detective sure had his number when he pulled out that log book entry. I wonder how he'll justify that next time round. You know they train with elite forces; I bet he wished he never told me that. What a show off. I despise the character."

"I'm amazed how you had him confused over Lyn. You had me scratching my head and I knew what was going on. You sound very convincing. If you do anything right it's that confusing scenario, you have that down pat!"

"What confusing scenario?"

She ignored me, "How come you got a lucky punch in, especially seeing he trains for trouble?"

"It wasn't luck, I just knew he'd swing high hoping to take my head off, I ducked and came in under his arm."

"You're lucky, you know Rebecca thinks you're trouble, it's like calling the kettle black, isn't it?"

"I don't like Josh. Am I being too critical? Before my initial phone call to Josh, everything was peaceful, now it's a war zone. You know, I have no control over what I'm doing, it's as if I'm on autopilot."

"You stopped being mates when Lyn died. You did the right thing by not seeing him. I wonder if he is making up this relationship he claims he had with Lyn?"

"A possibility but Chantal said they had some type of a fling. She wasn't sure of the details."

Siobhan asked, "But why would he do that?

"That's the big question. Maybe to stir me, maybe to beat me, whatever, he had to keep it a secret. Lyn was at his brother's twenty-first birthday party. He had to have invited her. And I remember her last words to me, 'Sorry, I wish it could be you', that has to be in reference to Josh."

"Or Malcolm Shailler."

I nodded in agreement, "You maybe right, I can't forget

Malcolm as a suspect."

"He probably has the most to lose, especially if the truth should surface. He's definitely a possibility."

"So we have Josh, Malcolm and Chantal as suspects and mainly in that order but there could be someone we have no knowledge of."

"Yes, the wild card."

"You know, I really feel for Lyn's family, I can't imagine how they coped after she died, they would have been shattered. I would even venture they were embarrassed, what people thought during those times were important, Christian beliefs and values were paramount. Cleaning up the pieces would have been difficult. When they had the funeral, it was three days after her death, everything was a rush including the police inquiry and the autopsy. Lyn's parents may not have known the results of the autopsy until days before the inquest, which was five weeks later. They turned up ill prepared but to give them credit they tried, Lyn's father gave Malcolm Shailler a good questioning. I remember reading the transcript where the Coronial Magistrate granted him leave, however there was no hard evidence for the Magistrate to follow up. What the family needed was good legal representation, someone who was prepared to battle for the truth. Malcolm Shailler's statement was full of holes, in the end, the boyfriends and the system let the parents down. Malcolm Shailler may have been blamed for Lyn's pregnancy but there is some doubt as to who the father is. Also Malcolm did the wrong thing by giving Lyn those abortion tablets without a prescription and most importantly I believe he told her to take a large dose of that red mixture which killed her, anything to get rid of the problem. If he did, that would be murder or at least manslaughter, but how do you prove that? So if he took a life then, why not now? He still would be keen to protect his reputation."

"Did Josh appear stunned that he might have been the father?"

"Surprisingly he didn't probe for details nor did he deny it. I'm not convinced that Malcolm Shailler moving close is a coincidence."

"Shaun, you're forgetting Lyn in the equation, "It makes sense if Lyn orchestrated the house sale, stranger things have happened, look at us. According to you, she planned our relationship. You in hospital first, me second and then what, our London love-in?"

"I'm glad she brought us together. It just feels right."

"Shaun, you are the ultimate romantic."

Next morning I rang Samantha, "Is everything ok with Chantal?"

"She's sleeping in, I'll take her breakfast in soon."

"What, you're giving her breakfast in bed? I never got that service."

"She's been through a lot."

"I went through a lot."

"She's here, your somewhere else."

"So, it's all to do with location is it?"

Samantha ignored me and asked, "How did it go at the Freemont's?"

"Not that good, Josh tried to take my head off."

"Really? Why?"

"He's a touch volatile."

"So he tried to hit you, I would have loved to have seen that, are you planning to catch up again, maybe I can come and watch next time."

"Samantha, we could talk all day about your wanton desires but I'm seriously concerned for you. Are you convinced Chantal is…?"

She interrupted, "Straight?"

"Well… not unless there is some doubt in your mind?"

"She's straight Shaun."

"Shit, why interrupt me? Why create doubt?"

"I thought you needed help to finish."

"No… why would I even ask that question. It hardly seems relevant. I wanted to know if she's…"

I could hear Samantha call out, "Chantal, you're awake, what's wrong dear, oh… I have to go Shaun, I have a mini-emergency."

"What's happening?" However she had already hung up.

I said to Siobhan, "Chantal is being served breakfast in bed." Siobhan looked at me bemused, "I can do that too Shaun."

"What... serve breakfast in bed to Chantal?"

"No silly... you!" she picked up the phone and dialled room service.

Later that day I identified the caller on the first ring, "Josh, how are you?"

"Tough times, what is it with the cops, you could have warned me, I handle impromptu meetings badly."

"Really?" That was the whole idea of an impromptu meeting, mainly to unsettle the other party, "I thought you did fine," I rolled my eyes at the absurdity of the comment.

"I'm trying to get my head around everything. What are the odds of all this and I thought pharmacists were like guidance counsellors, a father figure of sorts, you know? They are supposed to be revered, trustworthy. I know for a fact that Lyn was a customer, we all were, so if he was seeing her romantically then that's a breach of ethics – like doctor, patient – teacher and student."

"I agree," I couldn't argue with his outlook regardless of my trust issues.

Josh hesitated for a second, then, "I have to ask you something?"

"Anything."

"Is Lyn dead?"

I clenched my fist, again he was an insensitive bastard, the way he casually spoke of Lyn riled me no end, I somehow managed, "I must apologise. I led you on. That was insensitive of me."

"Oh... right... I accept your apology. Shaun, I'm sorry for lashing out at you. That was pathetic."

"Water under the bridge and we're sweet on everything?"

"Like Golden Syrup."

"It seems Malcolm Shailler is my biggest concern."

"Why?"

"Two ex-boyfriends are now living next to each other and that isn't healthy."

"Is there a reason you lied to me about him?"

"An oversight, nothing sinister, please believe me… you know, I've reviewed the coincidence factor of him turning up and that doesn't cut it. There are murders happening and I've got doubts. Even Rebecca's nervous. She hasn't slept properly since he moved here. I swear if he tries anything I'll take him out."

"Why would you say something like that?"

"It's weird he is living on my doorstep, he must have a plan, what if he tries something?"

"Relax."

"But still I'll be ready, one wrong move and he's dead."

"I don't think this is about you and Malcolm Shailler, where I'm coming from there is something else happening."

"Like what?"

"I wish I knew, this whole thing is bizarre. For me it has been the most arduous of journeys. Really, I'm sorry I contacted you."

"Don't be, it was great catching up." And yet another lie for me to ponder!

A few days had passed when Josh called back, "Shaun, guess who had a stroke?"

It was an obvious conclusion, "Malcolm Shailler?"

"No, his wife, she is in hospital, the report I'm getting is she is in bad shape. To top it off, Malcolm hasn't seen her. I feel like kicking the bastard all the way to the hospital just to force him to see her. What a miserable worm. What a ball-less character."

"Could there be some reason he isn't visiting?"

"The hospital is only five minutes away."

"Have you checked on him?"

"No. Shit Shaun, trust you to make this complicated. I'll go over and check on the bastard."

"Look Josh, why don't you wait for me, I'm only an hour away and we could approach him together."

"I don't know; I'm only seconds away."

"I know but you're likely to crash tackle him or give him a chance to utilise his dental plan. Wait for me."

"Ok, but hurry. You've got an hour and then I'm going in."

CHAPTER 43

THE SHALLOW DEPTHS OF
DESPAIR

I had sixty minutes before Josh stormed Malcolm Shailler's house, I lost two minutes gathering keys and jotting down a quick note for Siobhan. In the car I released the hand brake and planted my foot to drive in excess of the speed limit – I reduced the drive time by five minutes. Josh was already pacing his front lawn, all one hundred and twenty metres of it. He kept walking in an agitated state; I cruised beside him, "What's happening?"

"What? Nothing's happening," his eyes were darting in all directions. He had the appearance of a caged tiger and gave the impression that if one word was misdirected he would attack.

"Josh… let me do this," and I pulled the car to the gutter and killed the engine.

Josh was three steps ahead of me. I caught up and drew equal for the first time in my life. "I mean it, let me approach him, you stay behind me." I paused and listened for the sound of a television, radio or even a vacuum cleaner. There was nothing obvious. The doorbell went through a short canto of Ride of the Valkyries. Loud and annoying. There was no way Malcolm Shailler couldn't hear that. Maybe he had a broken leg or had died in his sleep but there again he may simply be out. After twenty seconds, I rang the bell again.

"Where is he?" Josh said, unable to contain his frustration.

"Josh, are you alright?" He ignored me, I asked, "Could he be in the backyard?"

He snapped, "No, I have checked already."

I suggested cautiously, "Let's case the perimeter anyway."

There was nothing on the grounds to raise suspicion, nor anything to suggest Malcolm's whereabouts. I tried the back sliding door, a door similar to Josh's house. It was unlocked. It glided easily. I called out, "Hello."

There was no response so I edged inside, "Careful," Josh ventured, "It might be a trap."

I noticed the air conditioner had been left on and the room was at least eight degrees colder than the ambience outside. "Anyone here?" A chilling silence confronted me. Josh pushed past me and entered the kitchen. It had dishes piled high and as ever inquisitive, he opened the fridge. It needed stocking but first the leftovers needed disposing of – mould was running rampant. I called out again, "Malcolm… are you alright?"

Josh whispered, "He isn't downstairs. This is definitely a trap!"

"Why? How do you figure it's a trap?"

"Instincts and years of experience with the shooter's club, did I mention we train for this type of thing."

A little sarcastic, "Oh really, in that case, aren't we supposed to be whopping up plenty of noise and knocking down doors, not acting like fairies at a birthday party?"

He ignored me, "I'm going upstairs," and he gave me the hand signal I had seen used on television. Two fingers, two eyes, and then he pointed upstairs. He directed me to stay at the rear.

"Josh don't go up the stairs, let's call the police."

"Ridiculous, why? We can do this. God its cold isn't it?" He pulled out a gun and released the safety.

"Christ, you bought a gun? Why?"

He didn't want to discuss the matter. I swore under my breath.

Josh maintained a low position. He may well have considered a commando roll but I think he was leaving his options open for a quick retreat. At the top of the stairs Josh shut down the air conditioner. The silence became unnerving. When he came to the first room he checked the corridor, his back was against the wall, his gun raised, his eyes scanning wildly. When convinced everything was safe, he rolled his body around the doorway and snuck a peek. He pulled back and nodded an all clear. As he moved to the next room, he repeated the same actions. I just walked behind, if nothing else, intrigued and feeling warmer, still something didn't feel right. I prayed Malcolm was at the hospital or somewhere safe, away from Josh the anti-terrorist vigilante. When there were no rooms left to infiltrate, he offered another option, "Shaun, I need you to give me a hand, this might get curly from here on, so once you lift me, go back and wait in the car."

"Where am I lifting you?" He looked at the manhole cover and put his finger to his lips, "There?"

He nodded as confirmation.

"Why would he be hiding in the ceiling cavity?"

"Trust me, that's a place often overlooked in surveillance operations."

"He will hear you lift the manhole cover."

"I'll be quiet, give me a leg up."

"I don't know."

"Quick, don't think, just do it."

If I was worried previously, now I was contemplating buying him a straight jacket. I relented and cupped my hands saying, "Really Josh, is this necessary?" He stuck the gun into his belt and placed a foot onto my interlocked palms. He was heavier than I remembered and I staggered almost dropping him.

"Steady."

I bent at the knees to distribute the weight. Seconds later the cover was off. As he raised his head into the enemies bunker Josh whispered, "I'm going up, once I'm in, return to the car and wait. If you hear the gun go off, call the police."

"Josh, don't shoot him," although I thought the possibility of finding Malcolm Shailler in the roof cavity remote.

"Shaun, just do as I say."

Humouring him I said, "Alright."

He added, "It just might save your life."

I shook my head in disbelief.

Before he disappeared I asked, "Where is Rebecca?" Calling her might produce a touch of sanity.

He continued whispering, "She's shopping and will not be back for ages, now go," and he pulled himself into the roof's cavity and dismissed me with a wave of his hand. It was like brushing a fly away, "Go," he withdrew the gun and disappeared into the darkness.

Why would Malcolm Shailler be hiding in the roof cavity?

What possible reason would he have to be up there? Besides his age being a drawback, he would need a stepladder for access. I remembered he recently had surgery on his knees which would further reduce his ability to climb. I could hear Josh moving around. Then he stopped. I stayed contrary to his advice, something wasn't right and I hadn't driven this distance to wait in the car. The creaking had an easterly direction, which would place him above the bathroom. He knew the layout of the house because he had designed it. Anyway, how large was the roof's cavity? Surely, he would know if Malcolm Shailler were there by now. I returned along the corridor and stood beneath the manhole. Josh suddenly appeared, "Oh," he said startled, "I thought I told you to go to the car."

"I was worried about you. What's that?"

"Oh, nothing, an old book. Too dark to read up here." He placed it next to the manhole cover but as he dropped to the floor, he left it in the cavity. I helped lever him back up with another interlocked foothold and he replaced the cover. He dusted his hands with swiping claps.

"He's not up there."

"I didn't think so."

"That confirms he isn't in the house, maybe the garage, maybe he's in the car." He appeared excited at this new possibility. "I hope he has the motor running and his lungs have sucked up all the carbon monoxide."

"Josh, our intention is to find him alive, not to wish bad Karma on him." He smiled wickedly. I warned, "These things have a way of coming back to haunt you." He ignored me; his eyes were wide with excitement. He walked to the end of the long corridor and to a narrow mailbox window with salt en-crusted panes. It offered a panoramic view of the lake. He spoke distantly as if the view was a part of the problem, the equation, and the answer all mixed into one, "His perspective is identical to ours, strange, but then..." He paused, distracted, "Shaun what do you think that is?" he said pointing to some-thing in the water some twenty metres off shore.

"Strange, it looks like a towel caught in the weeds, maybe a plastic bag." Suddenly there was a splash near the towel.

"Was that a leg?"

"A fish I think."

"That's Malcolm Shailler," he said excitedly.

Without confirmation from me, he raced down the stairs before I had time to react. I checked again and was convinced it was a towel. As he exited the back door, he hastily called back, "Phone for an ambulance and hurry!"

I hadn't sighted anyone in the water but caved to Josh's evaluation. Within seconds, I was dialling 000 with a tone I hoped removed doubt from my voice. I gave my name, location, nearest cross street and what I thought the problem was, 'an old towel is floating twenty metres off-shore so bring plenty of oxygen', as if. I felt guilty giving a misleading report but Josh seemed convinced. I left the house and scoured the shoreline in both directions but there was no sign of Josh. I had dismissed the chance of seeing Malcolm Shailler. I called out, "Josh."

Nothing, except a gentle ripple caressing the shoreline.

"Josh."

Nothing. Louder this time, "Christ... Josh where are you?"

I returned to the house, maybe he returned without me notic-ing. I ran through the ground floor screaming his name, again there was no answer. I climbed the stairs.

Each room was vacant. Suspiciously, the book left in the roof cavity, now lay on the floor directly below the closed man-hole cover. Had Josh retrieved the book without me noticing? I would have seen him and besides he needed a leg up and why leave it lying on the floor, why not take it with him? I scanned the pages quickly, no time to read the hand writing. I gripped the book tightly. I was about to descend the stairs when I heard someone close the back door. It couldn't be Josh for he previously left each door open. I stopped at the crest of the stairs. The first thing I noticed was a royal blue shirt, the front was unbuttoned and untucked as if hastily dressed. Then I recognised the face... the same face from Beaulieu's identification photo – Malcolm Shailler! He still hadn't seen me but he was holding Josh's gun. I took a step back and hid the book in my back pocket, a tight fit. Where was Josh? Why did he have Josh's gun? I backed up along the corridor some four metres. There were few options, confront him or run, but where? Maybe hide came as a flashing afterthought. I went with the first, I screamed, "Malcolm, are you here? Malcolm, anyone."

He slowed when reaching the landing and I noticed his grey hair was wet. Several droplets ran his forehead and fell aim-lessly to the floor. He pointed the gun at me and a slow smile etched his face, "Well, who do we have here?" He pointed the gun upwards, a move to direct me back.

"Thank God," I said, "Are you...?"

He nodded and smiled. He didn't look the type to be smil-ing. "Mr. Reece, and after all these years we meet again and here you are breaking into my house." He remembered me from the Berala Pharmacy. Shit, what a memory! He was only me-tres away – Malcolm Shailler the guy responsible for Lyn's death. Strangely the switched off air conditioner kicked in and with a hefty rumble, it startled the both of us. I looked up at the vents. I remember Josh had turned it off, suddenly the air felt chilled, although there hadn't been enough time to draft the house, "How did you do that?" he asked.

"It wasn't me!"

Without taking his eyes from me he reached over and shut down the power. The air conditioner squealed a chilling rebuttal, and now his face changed, he appeared too 'knowing' to question further, his eyes now wide, unsettled, different to Josh, different ends of the spectrum, Josh was nervous and twitchy, while Malcolm looked cool with a calculating and superior disposition. I had researched this guy but he had also researched me. I was a threat and obvious he was going to kill me. Was it Beaulieu or Chelsea who had accidentally slipped up, or had I made a wrong turn somewhere?

I broke the silence hoping to stall, "What happened to Josh?"

"He's very wet," was all he said.

I asked, "And what about Lyn Monday?" Again a cool draft suddenly washed the corridor and the hairs on my neck bristled. He smiled, not a blink emanated from those icy eyes. A few seconds elapsed before he spoke, "Mm, interesting girl that, far too popular and you are far too inquisitive. Lyn slipped up once and mentioned your name, from that moment I knew we were finished. I guessed you'd eventually call and cause me grief, anyway, I've been waiting."

"What... what did she say?"

His hand tightened on the gun, "She wanted you, were you having an affair with her?

I shook my head, "Not when you knew her, that came later."

He chuckled to himself, "Of course, in your dreams." That chuckle was disconcerting. He straightened his arm and peered along the gun sight, he then twisted the gun a full ninety degrees.

Stalling I said, "You know Lyn goes sailing out there."

"You're stalling Mr. Reece."

"She's alive you know."

"Alive in your mind, she's gone, long gone."

"Big mistake Malcolm, never underestimate Lyn. Big, big, mistake." He laughed at me as if I was on the loco-juice. I informed, "She may have been gullible once, but not now, be warned! Were you completely incompetent or did you tell Lyn to drink that red mixture on purpose?"

"Your right, a little persuasion perhaps, a little word dropped when she was most vulnerable. What did it matter, I wasn't going to marry her and I certainly wasn't going to father that baby. Did I pour that mixture down her throat? Anyway, her timing was off, the stupid bitch."

"You're a piece of work. And now what, are you going to shoot me?"

"I have a reputation to protect. Call it self defence. I can prove you've been obsessed with me and I have the ultimate excuse, you attacked me in my house."

"This is where you go wrong, this isn't your gun. It's Josh Freemont's, explain that and explain why you're living so close to him."

"Fate draws a strange hand, who would have thought," he smiled conceitedly.

"Can you handle another coroner's inquest, one which will explore my death? Can you lie through that inquest like you did the last?"

He said with a superior air, "But here's where 'you' go wrong, you're assuming they will find your body," he smiled slyly which did nothing for my confidence. Was there something controlling Josh and Malcolm?

"You're nothing but a coward. I dare you to pull the trigger, spit it into my head like you murdered Tom Flanagan."

"Who?" and then he smiled.

I moved towards him at a steady pace, "You're a piece of shit you know, Lyn was better off without you."

He took a step back, "Stop!"

"No shoot."

Another step.

He suddenly looked panicky. He backed up to the precipice of the stairs. If he kept going he was going to tumble. I could see his finger tighten on the trigger and then he fired. A flame erupted from the bore. Strange? The flaming burst seemed to last forever, a snails attempt at slow motion. I heard an echo down the corridor, "Mr. Anderson," precisely as the bullet headed towards me. My mind's thinking what in the hell does 'Mr. Anderson' have to do with anything, he's trying to kill me but it wasn't Malcolm voice it was a character from the movie the Matrix and where ultra slow motion had become chic. Strange! The bullet spun three times to every nanosecond; I bent backwards, the lead steaming hot and searing close to my nose. I had an image of the bullet lodging in my nostril. Everything was weird in this house but that's how it unfolded. The gun blast followed and as the bullet passed me it regained its lightening speed and direction, it hit a steel framed photo of Malcolm's family which was ironically hanging at the far end of the corridor. It hit with a twang and ricocheted back towards Malcolm. It hit the gun's bore and disintegrated it into a thousand pieces. What were the odds? The force pushed Malcolm back. He fell down the stairs with a look of disbelief. There was a sickening crack as his neck snapped. It was quick justice, precise and deadly. I couldn't believe the outcome although I had warned him about Lyn.

What to do next?

Josh.

Water.

Towel.

I raced to the window.

I looked through the encrusted panes and sure enough I could see the towel still floating, then in a moment of disbelief I saw a splash, a flurry of churning water, it sunk away from the bank. Were my eyes playing tricks? Was this Josh Freemont? I could hear a distant siren. I scrambled downstairs half expecting Malcolm's hand to come alive and grab my ankle, but he was definitely dead. I raced to the waters edge and took off my shoes and placed the book inside one. I rolled up my jeans and waded in. The depth was incredibly shallow, no deeper than my knees although the weeds were thick and hard to circumvent. I estimated I was in the right position being twenty metres from the beach. I could see something dark. The water was suddenly cooler. Then I dropped below the surface. I felt something – Josh's ankle. I grabbed it although freezing cold and more intense than the water. I struggled to breathe. The seaweed was thick, long and tangled. I raised my mouth above the waterline. I sucked a breath and prayed. It was all I could do to keep my head raised. Josh slipped from my grasp. I struggled. Something brushed my face… like a towel? Black… intense black! Fading…

The ambulance's siren was my next memory. I looked at the stark interior as the wailing distracted everything; it was such a contrast to the blackness. I felt numb and knew my emotions were critical. There were more tests and questioning by doctors. I had no idea why I had passed out, but there again… Lyn!

I reasoned – I was a good swimmer. I really could have handled the Thames… but the lake… that was somehow different. Eventually, the doctors retreated. I knew they had no answer.

CHAPTER 44

———◄o►———

'62

When Siobhan finally saw me she was as emotional as a funeral congregation. She held my hand and kissed my forehead, I asked, "What happened?"

"I haven't a clue; I thought you might tell me."

"Josh, is he alright? He was acting really weird, he even had a gun! Then Malcolm tried to kill me with Josh's gun."

"Shaun, do you think Lyn had anything to do with it?"

I nodded.

"So that's how he broke his neck?"

I nodded again.

"So swift justice then, but why were you in the water?"

"I was trying to save Josh."

"But the water? Why there?"

"Josh was really losing it, he thought he saw... Malcolm Shailler's body floating off shore but all I saw was an old towel or maybe a plastic bag. I lost track of Josh and went back into the house only to be confronted by Malcolm. With Lyn's help I survived and returned to rescue Josh. I had his ankle Siobhan but I couldn't get him to the surface. It was all I could do to breathe."

"Shaun, you're lucky to be alive, you were found unconscious and floating face down, you nearly drowned. Thank God the ambulance guys arrived when they did. The police are still searching for Josh but what I can't understand is, it is so shallow there, it's no deeper than half a metre."

"I think Josh is gone. I think it was Lyn."

Siobhan went quiet, she swallowed, "Rebecca is beside herself. She is so upset, she blames Josh's disappearance on you. God knows what she told the police. I'm sure they will want to question you."

"I have nothing to hide."

She raised her eyebrows, "Lyn's presence isn't the way to rationalise this."

"I know, anyway who would believe me? They'll probably declare me a confused old man and dismiss my ramblings as dementia."

She shook her head, "You're not that old Shaun but I'm worried, what does Lyn want?"

"I have no idea."

"Do you think what happened at the lake might be the end of everything?"

I shook my head and locked my eyes with hers. There was a moment of silence, still no answers.

"Oh, I almost forgot, the ambulance guys retrieved your shoes and this book. I think you need to read this."

I had forgotten the book. It was some three centimetres thick and bound in rich cowhide leather, it had been heat branded with the words... MY DIARY – M.S. 1962

The spine was cracked but surprisingly the pages held steadfast as if it was their duty to be loyal. I couldn't believe I had Malcolm Shailler's diary. I flicked the pages to 7th July 1962, the only notation was... 'It happened, she's dead!!!!

The next page, 8th July1962, 'Lyn's family hates me and who can blame them. I hate myself. I told her father I always wore a condom but he wasn't listening. He said he would kill me if I attended the funeral. How can I not attend? People will suspect something if I'm not there. The police questioned me. They suspect something already.

The next page, 9th July 1962. The police came again and questioned me about supplying Lyn tablets without a prescription. Another statement was given to the police. Shit, that loud mouth Debbie is a pain. I wish she had overdosed with Lyn.

10th July 1962. Today was the funeral. I drove by the church but didn't have the nerve to get out. After the burial when everyone left, I visited her grave. You know what I noticed most, she wasn't arguing any more. Will I go directly to hell?

A good chance Malcolm Shailler, and Josh Freemont, Lyn was never your girl, not in a million years, you lost this one!

I flicked the diary to the 20th August 1962. A guy by the name of Josh 'something', entered the pharmacy and was screaming at me to come outside. He wanted to fight. I called the police and he went away. I think he was the other boyfriend; maybe it was his baby??? He looked angry, this will not be his last visit, and I could tell by the look on his face – his anger was bitterly entrenched. Anyway, this day proved eventful in more ways than one, I met another girl, a customer by the name of Sarah, nothing like Lyn; I will probably marry this one!!!

I put down the diary and reflected on his words.

A week later, Malcolm's wife died. During that week the lake was scoured like burnt custard from a saucepan, tireless volunteers combed every millimetre, but in the end the search for Josh was abandoned. Josh's wife blamed me for his disappearance; she remained terribly bitter.

I had sympathy for Josh's wife but none for Josh. I read every page of Malcolm Shailler's diary and hated the writer intensely. He was cool and calculating, I doubted his intentions from the beginning. There was now enough information to write two novels.

CHAPTER 45

◄◦►

REFLECTIONS ON A BULLET

Everything had settled and Siobhan and I were heading north on a three-lane motorway, away from the worries of life's drawing vacuum. I felt displaced, numb and running on empty.

Siobhan drove and I closed my eyes reflecting on the past, the good the bad and the peculiar. I thought of my mother, I was proud to be her son, regardless of her warped emphasis on my life. She had been an attractive steadying force in many things except the ones that mattered. It wasn't her fault; she did care and as for my father, I forced myself to dismiss his heart-breaking actions. Better not to dwell on his flaws for I might find traits that were a Pandora's Box of hand-me-downs.

Chantal Witherspoon, my love letter girl now lived with Samantha, a mutually agreeable arrangement. I had planned it as a quick solution but neither wanted to change a thing. I had trouble coming to terms with Samantha being this caring. She had changed for the better and looked energised. To think a love letter could determine such an outcome or was it the lie that made it work. If I had originally told the truth, there would have been a different outcome, should I be thankful for my mother's deceitful instructions? But there again, if I had spoken to Lyn in the milk bar there was no need for such insight.

My children started contacting me; Kem, being the first and admitting she had hit the speed dial button in error, however that conversation lasted forty minutes and the next sixty.

I was lucky to have Siobhan who understood this bizarre story. She was my energy, strange how Lyn had chosen her for me, why? Still no answer. It was just the two of us now, leaving us with memories and a chance for a new life. I knew we would make it and in time be intimate, similar to our London experience, but that was Lyn... wasn't it? Had Lyn played a role in Josh Freemont's disappearance? Had she sent back the bullet to Malcolm Shailler? If anything, I felt settled they were gone. Trust was what that was about. I couldn't trust Josh and Lyn couldn't trust Malcolm, they were both similar and devoid of character. I didn't buy the police's theory that Josh was swept out to sea, the lake's entrance was blocked at the time, but there again I had dropped below the surface of a shallow lake and had almost drowned. Maybe it was possible and as far as I was concerned, Josh Freemont and Malcolm Shailler could go to hell!

I shook my head to clear the repetitive babble, there had to be an answer but I couldn't think of one. The most important question, what did Lyn need help with? Was it all to do with that fateful day at the lake?

No answers, only questions... it had to stop. This break might be all Siobhan and I needed to find each other. I sighed at the possibility, closed my eyes and went to sleep, always restless.

Our destination after this three hour drive was the only asset retrieved from my marriage, a beach house, and it came with its own fat mortgage, a healthy one, more like obese and indecent which would ensure I remained working and not vegetate into oblivion. It was dark when we arrived but Siobhan could see the beach house's potential. We sat on a bench seat near the water's edge.

"Shaun, this is incredible, if I was Samantha I would have taken this as well."

"It was probably the commitment to keep paying that was Samantha's deterrent, besides, she hated coming here."

"Strange, why? What's negative with this place? You have every imaginable appliance, it's contemporary and the view is absolutely challenging. The air smells briny and fresh; she's an idiot for not asking for this."

She spoke in a kind way using the term, 'idiot' as respectfully as possible, it was not as if Samantha was a fool, more like a... yeah, idiot! It was prime real estate.

"It's probably reminded her too much of me and extra baggage, she has a very common-sense approach to everything."

Siobhan raised her eyebrows.

I added, "Maybe she hoped I'd get really screwed and experience a hole in the pocket mortgage. Siobhan, I never did ask, what divorce arrangements did Tom and you discuss?"

"We were selling everything and splitting it down the middle."

"I thought so, see, you are fair."

Siobhan pointed, "Is that a storm out to sea?"

I looked and sure enough there was a small group of clouds with its own voracity for anger. The moon dropped shadowed the whole production and created the most incredible colours of cerulean, magenta and rich Indian ink. Splintering flashes spat from this action cell and circling it was a shimmering glaze where peaceful waters contrasted the turbulence. Unexpectedly a wave clapped the shoreline and shifted my attention, it was a reminder of how powerful nature could be.

Siobhan stood, checked her watch and yawned, "Almost midnight, coming in before the storm?"

"I'll stay awhile, you go ahead."

She kissed my forehead, smiled and returned to the beach house for a shower.

A breeze wafted, lazily, the lull before the storm. A gentle swirl raised the hairs on my neck and I could feel the dampness settling on my skin. I again thought of Lyn and our London trip. I was disappointed, I felt used, how could I ever tell anyone what had happened? Siobhan couldn't recall a thing but at least I had tried to explain. Should I call Dr. Roberts the psychiatrist, that strange stooped woman who knew so much and believed something good was going to happen? But really I had nothing to report.

So here I was, overlooking the ocean, a warm wind blowing just waiting for the storm and I'm looking for a vital link to explain everything. What a nightmare? Nothing was happening, except Lyn was out there, I could feel her, sense her. I'd even walk on water to reach her. Christ, my thoughts were constantly about her. Maybe I was trying too hard but this whole encounter was frustrating, ambiguous, her request puzzling, though not so bad for a free spirited girl who had fused with Siobhan, I smiled to myself...

The storm edged closer. I heard the beach house's door open and when I turned, it was Siobhan. She wore a dressing gown that was sheer and flowing. She smiled and walked towards me. Even in this poor light I could see the front of the gown was... open! She wore no shoes so in essence she was naked except for the gown draping her curvaceous shoulders. Her breasts matched the image I had stored of her, full breasts and perfect figure. Her stomach smooth with a gentle rounding and that encouraged you to touch that velvety skin. Oh, so arousing. When she stopped in front of me, my hands instinctively went to her robe and opened it further. I circled her breasts and came to rest on her hips. My thumbs were forward, rotating below her navel and in large slow arcs.

She gasped, "Oh," I could sense her melting.

"You look beautiful."

There was no reply; her head moved slowly as if an extension of this massage, I removed the robe. It slid away, slowly, then crumpled at her feet. She was exposed, beautiful, she was everything a man could desire and her hands reached out to draw me close. I knelt, aligning with her breasts. She snuggled close and held my head, drawing me to her. I rose, until my lips were millimetres from hers. With the suddenness of a lightening strike, Siobhan spun around, performing the strangest pirouette – her arms flailed wildly. I stood, misunderstanding the signals – she had been hit but not by lightening. She lay on the ground, like a rag doll. Another crack echoed against the storm, definitely not lightening. My mind scrambled for sanity, anything to understand what was happening. I knelt, shock gathering pace, slowly realising she was bleeding. Her head wet, not like her husband's, but sticky at the side. Another shot rang out and my shoulder felt the sting, a nick, everything still worked but a warm liquid was trickling my arm. Another crack out of the dark and this time I recognised the direction, it came from the lifeguard's tower sitting midway down the beach. A total distance of two hundred metres, Siobhan was still breathing. I had to draw the fire. I retrieved my phone and hit 000 turning rapidly and speaking on the run. My voice sounded weird, panting weird. I was sprinting for the tower and regardless of the risk I demanded an ambulance, "My friend has been shot, I'm closing in on the shooter, I'm at the beach, send the cops, hurry, send anyone, I need help fast." I didn't have time to turn the phone off. The only thing offering me protection was the speed of my advance. I surprised myself by this stupid strategy. I did the numbers. Sand and two hundred metres would take twenty eight seconds – minimum. I was crunching the figures. Fifteen to go – another crack spat grit like a sand blaster. I had fifty metres to go when another hail of bullets erupted from the turret. The same shoulder was hit. It hurt like hell. I spun around totally obsessed with regaining my balance. The shooter decided to abandon the tower and quickly descended the ladder. I drove my feet into the slush to gain acceleration. He was only ten metres away. I couldn't recognise him, frightened eyes shining like reflectors. He dropped the rifle and started running. My anger rose, fuelled by pumping adrenaline and within seconds I threw myself into the air with the plan to tackled him. I grabbed one foot but it was enough. I heard a moan as his head hit the sand. I raised myself and used my left fist to subdue him. His head fell sideways. I swung another, only cursing my good arm was completely immobile. Then another, it was the best I could do for quick revenge. The light was poor and I was about to pull him up when the police shouted, "Raise your hands above your head. Step away now!"

'What, they had arrived so quickly?' I tried to explain, "I'm not the shooter," and the guy under me moaned like a baby, I hit him again and another for good luck. The police weren't interested in words, only action. I was hit over the head. It was enough to deliver me senseless. Darkness instantly invaded the night just when I was about to observe the killer's face. I fell sideways where I looked at stars produced from violence and then slow motion spidery sparks which coursed the sky as naturally as any storm intended. Rain pelted my face. Waves crashed and thunder rolled, both sneaking into the background to lie subliminally distant. I heard wailing sirens and thought of my son. I thought of Siobhan. Was she alright? But mostly I thought of black and just a little glimmer of white where I dared not go.

Again I awoke in hospital and this time with Samantha checking my heart monitor, I had forgotten to transfer the beneficiary details of my insurance policy, however this time Samantha seemed genuinely concerned.

"Oh, you're awake? Chantal look, its Shaun back from the dead."

Chantal looked relieved, "Welcome back Shaun," she came close to the bed and let her finger drift on the intricate strapping preventing movement, she asked, "Does it hurt Shaun?"

Samantha interjected, "Of course it hurts, he had a bullet pass through his shoulder," Chantal looked away with moist eyes and then Samantha added, " Shaun, you have the luck of the Irish, I swear. Someone is looking after you."

I knew that already. I asked, "Is Siobhan alright?"

"Our naked Siobhan, the one spread across the front page of the daily news?" She sighed, "Yes Shaun, she is fine."

"Really, the front page?"

"Yes and only a headache for her, but she'll have a scar this long," and she extended her thumb and used her index finger to indicate the length.

"But she's alright?"

"Yes," but there was still a hint of disappointment.

"What happened?"

"As you know you caught him, only…"

"Only?"

'They let him out on bail."

"What?"

"I wouldn't worry, he's dead, hit by a car. Whoever was driving did everyone a big favour."

"Who? Who is dead?"

CHAPTER 46

———◀○▶———

I HIT I RUN

Who was dead? Who had I tackled, and why try to kill me? The questions kept coming but I knew there was only one answer. Samantha looked concerned, "Really Shaun? You have no idea?"

"Was it Josh Freemont?"

"No, he is still missing. The killer followed you all the way to our holiday house."

I queried, "Our holiday house?" being an emphasis on 'our'.

She shrugged, "Anyway..."

"Christ Samantha, who was it?"

Chantal edged close, her eyes teary, "This needs explaining Shaun. My husband was in real estate," her voice trailed with emotion.

"Yes I know."

"Well... David's biggest client... was... Malcolm Shailler... essentially his only client. Malcolm not only owned a pharmacy on the coast but he also controlled forty-eight other outlets all strategically located to price gouge customers."

"Chantal, what does this have to do with anything? There is nothing wrong with either of them seeking business opportunities, that's free enterprise, it's seems unethical at best."

"Think of it this way, if a customer presented a prescription and was overcharged two dollars, then that equates to say one thousand customers per week per outlet paying two thousand dollars too much. You see there was no competitors to make pricing fair, now you multiply that by forty-nine stores and you have ninety-eight thousand extra profit per week, and that's over five million a year."

"Wow."

"Each store ran deals with cosmetic companies who would pay for niche exposure, and then drug companies would throw him incentives to push their generic brands. Malcolm would order in bulk and save even more. Some drug companies paid his staff's wages. He also sub-leased floor space to weight-loss companies or to anyone whose high profiles ensured a healthy return. Each store was a goldmine. There appeared nothing on the surface to raise suspicion… however… something was happening, Malcolm was greedy, there was never enough money. Now for David, his job was to block competitors and to look for opportunities to increase profits. It didn't matter if boundaries were stretched; shops leased to stop others, anything to outsmart the opposition – call him a fix-it-man!"

"That's bordering on restrictive trading."

"But there is more, councils were bribed, I even remember a fire putting paid to a new development, kids were blamed but I know differently."

"Now we are talking corruption and arson. So in essence, David worked for Malcolm."

"Exactly, it was a convenient arrangement for both. No one knew."

"Except you Chantal."

"We all handle stress differently, I blocked my demons with depression and then anti-depressants were used to whiplash them back. I spent enough time in psych wards, believe me."

"Chantal, I'm sorry."

"Don't be, anyway, David would sit in his office dreaming up ways to make Malcolm rich, he received a healthy bonus for each stealthily organised coup."

"When did this start?"

"In 1963, David was fresh out of school. He started working with Malcolm at the pharmacy, however Malcolm moved on. He had a driving ambition to set the world on fire and once he established his first pharmacy he recruited David, obviously he saw some potential and encouraged him to have a career in real estate. David and I married a year later. It was a turbulent marriage. I suffered while he sadistically watched each depressive relapse. He had this callous edge, being similar to a kid pouring petrol on a burning dog or one trying to drown a kitten in a toilet bowl."

I reminded her of the twenty-first birthday party for Josh's brother, "And exploding bungers in glass bottles, that was another favourite, but honestly Chantal, I never realised the connection to Malcolm."

"I haven't told you everything, as bad as David was; he was no match for Malcolm. Malcolm invested in everything, property was one thing and desperate souls another. He was ruthless and corrupt, as long as the end justified the means. He made everyone pay, the more reliant a person became the more he'd screw them. David was a prime example of someone out of his depth, a kid who was playing in the real world. He changed into a clone of Malcolm – pleasing and protecting Malcolm became his highest priority and this made him utterly dependent."

"But what did Josh think? I can't imagine he'd be happy his cousin worked for Malcolm."

"Josh found out the day Malcolm moved to the lake. That made the three of us street front neighbours while Josh and Malcolm properties were joined at the rear. Ever since the house was built, Malcolm was keen to acquire it but had no idea Josh lived next door. David saw it as an easy sale as the owner needed to sell quickly. I remember Josh and Malcolm near the water's edge when they sighted each other for the first time. Both froze, like gunfighters before a shoot-out. It was a surreal moment. Instead of a gun, Malcolm drew his phone and barked at David for action. Josh's face was grim while Malcolm babbled incessantly insisting David remedy the problem. Neither Josh nor Malcolm would take their eyes from each other. Suddenly the wind whipped across the lake and forced them inside, it was a ferocious and bitter change. I have never seen the lake so rough. I'll never forget the intensity."

"Strange for it to happen at that precise moment."

"I'll say, it was totally weird."

"But wasn't David confused, didn't he need to know the reason for such animosity?

"Of course, but he received two versions, Josh's and Malcolm's, he sided with Malcolm which infuriated Josh. Josh couldn't believe his cousin's deception, all those years of kowtowing and sucking up to Malcolm and Josh never realised who he worked for. David and Josh had an enormous fight. David tried to explain but Josh refused to believe in coincidence."

"Couldn't Malcolm move somewhere else, he had other properties?"

"Was it stubbornness or was it something else? I suspect the die had been set, there was nowhere else to go, it was only a matter of time before a confrontation – call it a war of wills! So, Josh greeted each day nervously and hoped for a miracle while Malcolm peered through his window before venturing out. There was an element of uncertainty as each prayed the other would crack. But it was this next piece of information that made me nervous ... I overheard a phone conversation between David and Malcolm, a smattering of facts but enough to raise my suspicions."

"What was said?"

"David said, casually, as if it was an everyday transaction, 'I compromised her, literally'. He laughed a muffled sound as if he had his hand to the mouthpiece, 'The councillor won't be causing any more grief, believe me.' Malcolm must have said something like, 'Better not,' because David had to reinforce his actions, 'My phone is full of photos. Want them? She had nice tits actually, and waxed all the way to Brazil! That stuff you gave me dissolved just like you said and in the end she looked like a crazed whore who needed a football team for company! Pity she stopped breathing, she was going to be a prime example for the others.' I was shocked. I felt sick. I had no idea who she was but it's obvious she was someone stopping their plans. They must have been talking blackmail but it had turned to murder. When I got the chance I checked his phone. My heart stopped. The woman was attractive. Long blonde hair and a face that reminded me of Sharon Tate the late actress, however David had smeared lipstick across her mouth and had unbuttoned her blouse. Her skirt was pulled up to her thighs. Each picture became more revealing. In the end he had her posing... it's too disgusting to talk about, except that last photo... she was dead. My head was spinning; I finally gathered the courage to question him and shoved the phone at his face. He became furious. He lashed out and threw me across the room however I threatened to expose him and our 'illustrious neighbour'. He spat out with a vile contempt, 'She got what she deserved – I Mickey Finned her,' then he laughed. I don't know what he meant, maybe he was referring to sexual performance, really, I'm so out of touch with these things."

"It's nothing to do with sexual performance, he was talking about a date rape drug called 'Mickey Finn', it comes as a mixture and is easily prepared so there are no records required. Lyn overdosed on that same mixture which was also prepared by Malcolm Shailler – old habits die hard. Chantal, what happened then?"

"In a panic, David phoned Malcolm and began talking so fast I couldn't keep up, I was worried. They were discussing what to do with me. I couldn't think. I was scared and ran from the house. It was then I arranged a little insurance."

"Insurance?"

"Our marriage was over so I had little hesitation, I contacted the Pharmaceutical Board with an ethics complaint; the board was keen for information. This was something I should have done years ago. I'll never forgive myself for not acting sooner, anyway I mentioned both their names and the activities I had witnessed over the years. You see the Pharmaceutical Board is obliged to investigate every complaint so I gave them a dozen examples. I could have called the police but knew reporting him would hurt most and besides the Pharmaceutical Board could refer the matter."

"Pity, this all came too late, it should have happened in 1962."

"The Board is a lot tougher these days and can you imagine the turmoil if Malcolm was struck from the register, it would cost him dearly. He was beside himself but knew if anything happened to me it would be viewed with suspicion. Shaun, Malcolm found out you were researching him for your novel… 'Lyn Monday', he instantly imagined the worst and pressured David for results."

"Results?"

"What were the odds of you digging up his past and at the same time as this pharmaceutical enquiry?" They could have dismissed me as a credible witness but you, you were different. He also found out you had two researchers fossicking for dirt. What had they discovered? The pressure was on, what was in your book? How would it influence the hearing? If you kept probing, every unscrupulous deal might be uncovered and this would have been enough to raise a Royal Commission. He could see his 'reputation' and investments disappearing. Silencing you was his only option."

"So it was David who tried to kill me and at the request of Malcolm Shailler?"

"Yes."

"Did he organise a private investigator to follow me in England?"

"It's likely, and if that's the case, Des Rains was also on the payroll, however I suspect Rains became greedy."

"I thought so."

"David used Siobhan's husband in a plan to lure and trap you but that backfired, you were already at the house. I swear David was an absolute idiot. I'm sorry Shaun. Can you imagine how I feel? I would have died rather than let anything happen to you. I'm glad he's gone."

"Chantal, that high powered rifle, did your husband have the expertise?"

"David belonged to the same gun club as Josh and had rifles at his disposal."

"Some thing's been bothering me Chantal… when I first visited you at your mother's house you recognised me instantly, how come?"

"Err…"

"What is really going on Chantal?"

"Err… nothing, no connection to Malcolm and David. Please trust me."

"Chantal? It can't be that bad."

"When Malcolm and his wife moved to the lake, weird things began to happen."

"Like?"

"I'd sew to occupy my mind, God knows I'm not great but I design my own clothes. On the first night of Malcolm's arrival I left the sewing machine on and went to the refrigerator for a drink. It was twelve o'clock when I heard this frantic chatter. The machine was running faster than it had ever gone and when I checked the pedal, it was clear. The only way I could stop it was to flick the power off. I had it checked but nothing was wrong. The next night a tree brushed the side window with an annoying incessant sweep even though there was no wind, but the weirdest event was soon to follow…"

"What happened?"

"The front door kept ringing. It was really late."

"So you took the batteries out?"

"NO!"

"What?"

"I opened the door."

"And?"

"They were standing there."

"Who?"

"That woman on David's phone, the one who looked like Sharon Tate, she was in front of the other, a younger girl dressed in a nightie, I thought I had seen her before."

"Then what happened?" A tear ran Chantal's cheek, she wiped it clear. "What did they say Chantal?"

"Nothing, but I know what they wanted. They wanted me to join them, just walk away from everything. The woman, the one who looked like Sharon Tate reached out but I pulled away... I couldn't do it, not when there was a chance..."

Samantha asked, "A chance of what?"

Chantal's face looked strained, "Being with you Shaun. I've kept track of you over the years and these women support my theory."

"Your theory?"

"Lyn's moving on, Shaun, she's going to the other side, so now you'll be free to choose."

"Chantal?"

She tried to justify her comment, "My problem is no different to yours. We are both stuck in limbo, but with them arriving, I..."

"Are you talking about spirits Chantal?"

She erupted, "CHRIST NO! They were angels Shaun, ANGELS!"

Samantha shook her head dismissively, however I studied Chantal's face with more than a keen interest, she spoke softly now, a little embarrassed, "You don't think my medication was playing tricks, do you?"

"I..." she interjected before I could answer, "Sorry Shaun but the pain is intense, I need to keep track of you, it's the only way I can exist."

"Chantal, have you seen anyone about this condition?"

"Only you," Samantha rolled her eyes. Chantal pleaded, "What am I going to do Shaun? Am I mad?"

Samantha said, "Shaun knows a great doctor who will be able to help, right Shaun?"

I thought of Doctor Roberts, that strange stooped woman,

"Mm, yeah, she'll be perfect. She's not your normal quack and she has her own take on the afterlife, in the meantime, let Samantha and I help." Tears streamed her face and we embraced until it felt uncomfortable to continue. With Chantal, I had to watch that fine line between discretion and discretion and surprisingly Samantha and I were now working together, it felt good... but not that good. And what about those angels... yeah, I believed every word... except that Lyn was leaving me. When it came to Lyn, I couldn't put my faith in anyone, especially Chantal!

Five minutes after they left, Chelsea popped her head around the corner, "Shake, rattle and roll or are you still in pixie land?"

"It's the Botulism Queen of World Debating."

"Your not smart Shaun, I won that title fair and square, it's not my fault Ingrid Bananahead shoved Indian curry down her fat throat and puked up a lifetime of misery."

"Ingrid Bananahead?"

"A metaphor pertaining to her jaundice condition."

"Mm."

"Anyway, I've seen Siobhan, she's three rooms to your left, she not allowed to walk and you're not allowed to talk?"

"Why can't I talk?"

"Because I've got something important to say, you know we should tell each other everything because we are..."

"Soul mates?"

"Shh... yeah, but does that count for things like...? Umm... illegal stuff... you know!"

"Is this something bad?"

"Maybe, maybe not."

"Is this something you could talk your way out of?"

"Of course."

"Well it isn't illegal then."

"I was driving the car that hit Chantal's husband."

"Really, that was you? Was it an accident? "

"No, of course not. I can drive straight you know. It was just... he was crossing the road and heading for the hospital. I was… chosen I guess. It felt right. He was coming for you, he had a look of determination, a killer's lust; anyway, and it's peculiar to be admitting this, but… I'm a …"

"No your not. This is similar to war; you did something to protect others. Don't feel you have to confess, alright? Strangely, I'm immensely proud of you."

She smiled, "I'd thought you'd see the positive side to this, you know I feel better just airing the subject, and oops… it's gone, completely erased from my memory. What were we talking about anyway?"

"We were discussing Beaulieu."

"That's right. You want to know who she's been dating?"

"Yeah, that and other things."

"My father had some explaining to do."

"What? Your father the Olympic champion and Beaulieu, I thought his hands were crunched up with arthritis?"

I exaggerated slightly, anything to remove him from your most wanted list, anyway his hands are not that bad, ask Beaulieu. I'm worried; I might soon be calling her mum."

After Cyclone Chelsea had left the building I settled my feet on cold vinyl and unsteadily walked three doors to see Siobhan. She looked beautiful, eyes shut, just breathing peacefully, breasts rising, head patched. Gosh I loved her. Out of her lips, the ones glossed with pink and pouting, she whispered, "My head hurts and just to let you know, the doctors ran some tests."

"Oh good, I'm sorry, not about your head aching, so everything is normal then? No long term complications?"

She blinked and held eye contact, her lips drew apart with expectation; seconds were elapsing and not a word, then… "Yes, I do have a complication, and you have a bigger one."

"What is the doctor saying?" What is the problem Siobhan?"

"I'm pregnant."

"Oh."

"I'm having your baby Shaun! This happened in London and I have no knowledge of us making love. Say something Shaun."

"I can't think of anything to say, except, how do you feel?"

"Scared, I don't want to do this by myself."

"You don't have to, I love you Siobhan."

A tear slipped her cheek and if she could have, Siobhan would have drawn the energy right out of me, the only thing stopping her indulgent squeeze was the tape strapped to my shoulder, however she enthusiastically bubbled, "I pick the name. You have no say... alright?"

There was little point arguing, she had already made up her mind, "Alright, you have the naming rights."

"Shaun, I need to catch up with this romance, I need to have a glimpse of what happened in London."

"It was good Siobhan, exceptional. I can't believe I'm going to be a father again?"

"I'm already nervous."

"You'll be fine."

"Who would have thought that an innocent dinner date could lead to pregnancy?"

"Well, for half the population, a dinner date is the very catalyst for that kind of outcome."

She perused my face with interest, "Mm Shaun... when I think of all that has happened, you've come out of this looking pretty rosy. Lyn helped again, which makes you look like Superman."

"Well, not really, not with two bullet holes ventilating my perspective. I don't know what Lyn was thinking."

It was a deep breath that gave Siobhan a relaxed look, finally an end to the mayhem, but I couldn't settle, I was wondering – what next? Was Lyn really satisfied? Why had she manipulated so many lives and created such havoc, no one would believe a word. I was writing a novel about love and lost moments, but then a determination for justice, who could blame Lyn for seeking a resolution, my anxiety increased... lost but found, but an angel nevertheless.

EPILOGUE

◄○►

It was true, David Collier and Malcolm Shailler were dead and with them others who had no say in the matter but still something needed addressing, I had no idea what! Maybe as simple as living each day, Siobhan, me and a new heartbeat, although the past would never sit comfortably, I would never forget the moment I fell in love, I could never forgive myself for loving but failing to communicate. This being enough to reek havoc on this mere mortal, I suspect I survived because I continued loving... a girl and now an incredible woman chosen for me, this being more intense than all the A-bombs and all the Chernobyl's meltdowns fusing as one. Although I guess my mother was right, girls were trouble – big trouble!

There was no doubt Lyn had intervened, even to the point of splitting my marriage. I still loved Samantha but we were better apart. But what of Josh Freemont, was he dead? The police thought so but without a body his disappearance was doubtful. I remained suspicious and that weird connection between David and Malcolm, was it coincidence that Malcolm moved next door to Josh or had Lyn drawn them together for a final showdown? I'm thinking Josh was the suspicious one, what with a loaded gun and paranoiac behaviour. In hindsight maybe his actions were justified but not his callous nature. I could never forgive his lack of interest when talking about Lyn.

I was excited for Siobhan, the coming months would prove interesting. If Lyn's spirit lived, everything made sense. I doubted I had heard the last of her. Love was endless and how she merged with Siobhan proved equally amazing, especially her explanation of 'layered love', that was eloquent and simple. It made sense and everything sat comfortably. But she had gone to enormous lengths to make this happen and why want us to have this child? At school, Chantal had overheard Lyn say she wanted to marry and have my baby. Now Lyn was determined to correct the past, and remedy that fatal mistake where she and her baby died. But this new baby, definitely mine and Siobhan's – also Lyn's? Was this the help she wanted? Then in a moment of absolute clarity, I realised this baby was a part of Lyn, someone I could love as much as her, her present to me, she had said in London, "… it's important I give you a present, you must see for yourself that I'm committed. I'll always be there for you. Do you believe me?"

I did! Wow! I had forgotten her promise, her way to stop the hurt; her way for me to continue loving. Lyn Monday lived, although she was dead. I knew she wouldn't leave, especially now and with so much happening I would definitely see her again… my inspiration, my stormy Monday!
ME: YOU – FOREVER

A SPECIAL TRIBUTE
FROM THE AUTHOR

I always knew writing was demanding, but with 'She Refuses To Leave' I reaped more than I gave, I found pockets of reflection, corners where my soul replenished. I experienced people who lied and those who told the truth. I came away with answers, I came away with doubt, I never 'truly believed' until I wrote this novel although I doubt everything still, does that make sense?

Along for this experience was Colleen who vetted my every word and my every action, she knows me better than most, this wasn't an easy subject to write about, even harder to adjudicate. I take no solace that I put her through this trying gauntlet of emotions; this novel was exactly that. Some days it hurt, some days it felt good. Nothing seemed to matter other than to complete this story, (I was driven – but that's another chapter), in essence I was determined, Colleen sometimes reluctant. I'm sure she thought there was a better existence.

And so it finished, we survived and grew, we discovered a new love for each other. I found out things, she found out more. I have to add she knows her stuff, a true professional, I couldn't imagine anyone else this capable.

There are no words strong enough to say thanks, and Colleen, you are amazing!

AN EXTRACT FROM
AN INTERVIEW

An extract from an interview between Hamish Douglas of 'Currently Happening', TVC Glasgow and Australian author Ken Anderson.

Courtesy TVC Glasgow

Douglas: "I'm reading from the back cover of your book which spouts to be written as a 'spiritual romance'… 'Motivated by a true story, She Refuses To Leave is a factionalised account of two people, Shaun Reece and Lyn Monday whose struggle to connect becomes frustrated through missed opportunities. Faith and romance provides an uplifting journey against sadness, doubt and seemingly impossible odds – a powerfully inspiring story for those in a relationship and a timely warning for those taking advantage of love'. Welcome to Glasgow. Let me start by asking, why did you write She Refuses To Leave?"
Anderson: "The $64,000.00 question straight up. I knew Lyn Monday, I still know Lyn Monday."
Douglas: "That doesn't answer the question."
Anderson: "I had to set the record straight. Remember this was the sixties; Lyn was different from most girls for she had an energy that was compelling. Very few passed without feeling involved. Then something happened that was disturbing. There were people who did the wrong thing, others who failed to do their duty – justice just slipped away."
Douglas: "You talk with authority as if you were more than an observer, maybe even close?"

Anderson: "I would have liked to have been Monday's interest in life, most definitely. Strange how someone has that effect on you, but regardless of my feelings, her story is a devastating one and needs exposing. You can say I was a distant observer."

Douglas: "Really? Not the main character in this book, say Shaun Reece?"

Anderson: "Why would you say that?"

Douglas: "I have a research department that swears your life runs parallel to Reece."

Anderson: "That's interesting."

Douglas: "And that's your answer?"

Anderson: (Nods)

Douglas: "Ok… why faction? That's truth and fiction merging as one, isn't that the case?"

Anderson: "Yes, a little fantasy and enough truth – a balancing act of sorts. It's the way I write, it's more real than you may imagine; I make no apology for that."

Douglas: "I'm not asking for an apology just an understanding because this story promotes the hero. So, what I'm suggesting is, did you enhance the story to make yourself look better?"

Anderson: "Mm… you're still assuming I'm Shaun Reece."

Douglas: "Funny that. Anyway, your story telling is dissimilar to most mainstream authors, you have a style that is idiosyncratic but at the same time quiescently challenging."

Anderson: "Thanks, I think." (Audience laughs)

Douglas: "What possessed you to write such an account?"

Anderson: "If I said there was no option, would you believe me?"

Douglas: "Yes, but I wouldn't be satisfied. Something had to be driving you."

Anderson: "Love never dies is my only excuse."

Douglas: "So you loved this girl?"

Anderson: "Of course, many people did."

Douglas: (Holds up the novel for the camera) "Nothing too morbid between the pages?"

Anderson: "It's a love story that simmers away, both are young, they make mistakes, of course there is heartache and yearning, but something unexpected happens and they discover their love will last forever."

Douglas: "And you believe this can happen?"

Anderson: "Absolutely."

Douglas: "How can you honestly say that?"

Anderson: "Love is more than heart palpitations, love is an energy, it's out there and more potent than anything else. It exists during life and after death, it can multiply and lift you to new heights. Previously, you asked if my life ran parallel to Shaun Reece and I'll answer that by saying I've experienced something that shocked me. I wrote that into Reece's character, so yes, there are similarities but at a level most people would never anticipate – a lesson in love, if only you're a believer!"

Douglas: "But this book is spiritually motivated, so you'll need to buy it to find the answer?"

Anderson: "I'm talking about the spirit of love. You don't need a book for that."

Douglas: "Glasgow, we've run out of time and our closing words come from our guest."

Anderson: "I hope I've explained the 'spirit of love' correctly."

Douglas: "No you haven't, because 'love' is a word that defies description."

Anderson: "Well in that case, everyone needs to buy this book." (both laugh) "Thanks for having me Hamish." (Both shake hands)

Douglas: (Hamish turns to the camera) "Loyal viewers, another show ends and as always you remain the final adjudicator. Tomorrow night we have another interesting program for you – ghosts who refuse to leave! We have an expert who will test this supernatural phenomenon, spooky stuff... good night Glasgow, lock your doors and as I always say, pray we see each other tomorrow."

(The director calls, 'That's a wrap' and the audience applauds)

COMING SOON FROM
THE SAME AUTHOR

◄○►

The CONnection

On the West Coast, North of San Diego

Shock waves ripple through the coastal township of Encinitas where a high school student has been brutally murdered. Scott Constable, a classmate, knows the girl's killer but his attempt to expose him becomes thwarted, especially when the killer's family manipulates the local police. The murderer takes steps to silence him.

Meanwhile in *New York*, James Coloradas has a dream, one that will provide his people with security. New York is an unlikely place to be but if all goes to plan he will raise the capital to rescue Apache Junction, a small struggling native community and where his dream of 'Alaskan Crab and Snow Peas' the restaurant chain will become a reality. James plans to commits the township as security but subject to forfeiture if a privacy clause is breached. He knows his people can keep a secret and this deal will ensure their future.

James has no idea that this opportunistic deal will become a nightmare and that Scott Constable's survival will govern his future. Mix in two girlfriends and both lives are seriously complicated.

Every struggle, whether won or lost, strengthens us for the next to come. It is not good for people to have an easy life. They become weak and inefficient when they cease to struggle. Some need a series of defeats before developing the strengths and courage to win a victory.

Victorio 1820 –1880

PROLOGUE

———◄o►———

The East Coast – New York

James Coloradas was carrying the hopes and dreams of his people; a race that was united by blood, tradition and degrading oppression, a proud tribe of Native Americans called… Apache!

It was humbling to think of this ancestry; their courage and fortitude had helped them survive famine, disease, and thousands of murdering intruders but today no one cared for that sentimentality, especially when money became the topic of conversation. James could muster all the pride and courage from the past, but the bottom line, his people needed help. He had a mission – save their birthright and create a township that was financially independent, a tall order considering a trust of bankers were terminating their lease. In six months everything would be gone. He needed money and lots of it to prevent eviction.

James stood on the bustling New York street and looked at the office high rise. Thirty-six levels of amber colored glass, the glazing mirrored similar buildings, which were just as shiny and slick, too slick for a boy from the west.

He went through the plan; he was prepared to haggle but also willing to make concessions, anything to make the deal.

He straightened his tie, a nervous reaction; he hadn't worn a tie since his cousin's funeral eighteen months ago. He felt his shirt stick to his back. In Arizona, the humidity was controlled with the desert ensuring a comfortable ratio, but here in New York the wetness seemed stifling, almost suffocating. He struggled to breathe. Beads of perspiration spotted his forehead and the gastric acids from breakfast began to surface, he regretted having Italian sausage. He breathed onto his palm to detect a garlic scent but considered he was too putrid to be impartial. He formed a fist and hit the side of his leg – hard. He did that one more time, like a prize-fighter spurring himself on, gripping at anything that might make him focus. It seemed to work, he felt more comfortable when there was a little pain.

He crossed the street slightly buoyed by this new determination. He hit his leg one more time, just in case he needed a reserve of self-medication. He received a strange look from one passer-by but in this city most people didn't pay a heed, being safer to mind your own business. He entered the building. On the thirty-fourth floor the sign read...

Kingsley Smith and Partners Attorneys at Law

Expansive views captured his attention and he lingered at the door looking at Long Island. A casket of beads was all it took to purchase that real estate, a mistake his ancestors soon realized; he was hoping he didn't fall into the same trap.

The receptionist smiled, she seemed innocent enough.

"Hi, I'm here to see Kingsley Smith."

"Your name?"

"James Coloradas, I'm five minutes early."

She was young, pleasant and had the eagerness of an intern. She invited him to have a seat and offered him a coffee. James regretted the decision to have three top-ups and after waiting forty minutes, he was advised that the principal, Mr. Smith, would be arriving soon. He had been delayed for personal reasons. James was understanding and took this opportunity to visit the restroom. He chose cubicle number three and released a little flatulence resembling a bugle player's final ten notes of the 'Last Post'. The coffee was as strong as a stampeding buffalo and the garlic from the sausage had stirred up something else.

A minute later, he heard the voices of two men laughing as they entered the restroom. He regretted the smell and hoped the air was filtered.

One man sounded Harvard disciplined, the other had an English suaveness, which he considered similar accented to an old Arthur J. Rank rerun on television.

James remained motionless not wishing to draw their attention, though he couldn't imagine how they hadn't detected his presence.

The Englishman was to his right at the urinal and he heard the sound of a zipper being released. The Englishman then spoke to the other, "I've had no time to brief you but the client insists we close this deal today. What I suggest is that we give this hick from the desert a hard time, offer him a few scraps to keep his interest but hold back to the last moment. The client says three million now, five million when the deal starts to roll, and then forty-nine percent of the net. He does all the work and our client stays in the background silently reaping the returns," he chuckled to himself.

James realized the implications of this. This was a better deal than he had anticipated.

The other man at the washbasin replied, "Kingsley, I don't know, that's an awful lot of money. Are you sure?"

"Yes of course, let me run with this, I think we should let him sweat for say another twenty minutes and then reel him in."

The urinal flushed and they both exited. James noted the Englishman, Kingsley, hadn't washed his hands.

James pulled up his pants, flushed, and quickly washed. He examined his face in the mirror and smiled. He knew he had a deal; he just had to ride out the initial onslaught. The 'hick from the desert' comment should give him the strength he needed.

He returned to reception and waited another fifteen minutes. Finally, two men walked briskly towards him; the taller, middle-aged man was dressed in a charcoal tailored suit that despite the professional's attempt to make it fit was clearly oversized and hanging loosely from his shoulders. His face was narrow with an elbowed chin. The other man was shorter, plumpish and in his late thirties. His beady eyes drew James's attention, being a physical characteristic he found disconcerting.

"James," the tall Englishman said, extending his unwashed hand, "I'm Kingsley Smith."

At this point James hesitated but decided he didn't care if his hand had been dipped in cow manure, as long as the money was coming.

"Come in, I'm sorry to have kept you waiting. Let me introduce you to my associate… Tony Carras."

Tony extended his hand. Some fingers overlapped so the palm wasn't flat for cupping and resulted in a weak pressured handshake. Tony asked, "Would you like a coffee, tea, water?"

"No thanks."

James took a seat, which was positioned facing the glaring sun. His eyes squinted. He had heard about the old west gunfighters choosing the sun at their backs; during a shoot out, it was a distinct advantage.

"As you know," Kingsley said, "I represent a client who wishes to remain anonymous. I admit he's eccentric but that's his prerogative. He wishes, for God knows what reason, to go into business with you and the good people from… where are…?

James prompted, "Apache Junction, Arizona."

Kingsley continued, a sneer of disdain appearing on his face, "Mmm, now you have this idea about selling crabs? A restaurant chain exclusively to sell crab cakes!"

Tony laughed for several seconds and James twisted uncomfortably in his seat. Tony asked, "I know I'm new to this but you can't be serious, you want to sell crabs? Are you a fisherman? Do you belong to a co-operative? Do you have any selling experience? Have you managed a restaurant previously?"

"No."

Tony snapped, "Kingsley, this is crazy, you can't let your client invest in every hair brained scheme that comes along."

"Relax Tony, he wants to. All we have to do is work out the details."

Tony spat vehemently, "Give him five bucks and that's being generous."

James sighed heavily; there was a long way to go before they reached an agreement. Tony was the bad cop, Kingsley the good; it was becoming a cliché routine but nevertheless one where the game had to be played.

James replied, "I didn't come here to talk you into this venture, which has already been done with your client. What we don't have is an amount. Let me tell you what I'm thinking. Ten million now, twenty million on start-up and we get fifty-one percent of the net."

"What? You're wasting our time," Tony protested.

Kingsley replied, "That's a bit rich old boy."

"Take it or leave it," James began to rise from his seat.

Kingsley gripped his grimy little hands together and said, "Hold on, let's be reasonable, what you're suggesting is preposterous. My client puts in all the money, you put in nothing except an idea and a bit of work, and you want instant result. There is no way I can recommend that."

James sat down and demanded, "Write down on a piece of paper your best deal and I'll write down the lowest price my people will accept. Remember we have an ongoing commitment for the rest of our lives, while your client has an initial investment. From there he can see the profit potential before committing further funds."

They wrote their numbers and synchronized the paper swap.

Kingsley said, "You know this deal is happening because my client likes the concept of an Alaskan Crab and Snow Peas restaurant chain, nothing more nothing less. One more thing, my client wants a privacy clause included. You'll need to register some form of security."

James wasn't going to question a thing; he saw the figure and left smiling.

CHAPTER 1

◄|O|►

The West Coast – Encinitas, North of San Diego
Scott Constable's story

It was my final year of high school, a time I would rather forget. Was it fate or bad luck that I ended up with Phipps for math and sex education? He was the head of the math department and the quasi-personal development educator who had landed the position by default rather than raising his hand. He had above average looks, which he exploited, and an attitude that needed a reality check. He hated the students and the job for he considered his profession to be babysitting. However, he did have a strange affinity with one student, Jimmy Slattery, who was the most loathsome of individuals being a by-product of rich parents and poor genetics. I suspected Jimmy was taking steroids and God knows what else the little shit was cramming into his mouth for he was as volatile as a nuclear meltdown. Over time, his attitude had shifted from annoying to obnoxious and now precariously dangerous. I wondered why Phipps would tolerate a student like that.

Jimmy was six foot two, and weighed in at two hundred and twenty pounds. When he wanted to, he was as scheming as any

Sardinian syndicate boss and as disruptive as any mid range psychopath. He was into bodybuilding, wrestling, and his favorite – football, which was an excuse to maim the opposition.

Dee Washington was a classmate and what happened to her concerned me the most. Dee had been in my class since elementary and it was obvious she had little or no ambition other than to fit in. She wasn't stunning but then again she wasn't ugly. Her figure, well, that was a couple of notches above average, so in the overall scheme of things, Dee rated a seven out of ten. In class, she was positioned two rows over and constantly twirled at her long brown hair, this resulted in bouncing curly locks that framed her face and enhanced her vivid expression. Occasionally she would smile in my direction as classroom boredom set in.

Dee had a locker next to mine, and as I approached, she dialed her combination. I noticed 38 clockwise and then 24 in the opposite direction. Knowing what I know now, I shouldn't have opened my big mouth, for a simple question, completely innocent, was overheard and led to hell, "Dee, I was wondering if you…?"

"Yes," she interrupted half smiling, half concentrating. "What… what's up?" She lowered her shoulder pack to the ground, and turned to face me. I still considered that smile her best feature.

"I was wondering, could you store these books in your locker, just till tomorrow? I have training after school and my locker and pack are full." Her hesitation was obvious, I added, "Only if you want to."

"Sure… I'm sorry, of course, it's just… never mind." She sniffled, finished dialing and the door swung open. "Give me the books." She placed them onto the second shelf and quickly closed the door, spinning the combination to secure its contents. She scribbled the combination onto a scrap of paper and she pressed it hard into my hand, "Don't lose that. It's our secret."

She smiled again but that innocence was abruptly interrupted.

I noticed Jimmy, rather I sensed him. His breath was on the back of my neck. I crunched up the note hoping he hadn't seen it. My hairs bristled, "Hi Jimmy," I said without turning.

"What are you doing Constable, trying to score with my girl?"

Shocked that Dee would have Jimmy as a boyfriend, I turned and blurted out, "Of course not, I was just mentioning my training after school."

"Is that right?" and without diverting his eyes he kneed me in the thigh. I couldn't hold my weight. I reached for the locker to keep myself upright but the pain was excruciating. He plucked the note from my hand.

"Why the fuck are you lying Constable, leave my girlfriend alone – comprehend?"

"Why did you cork me?"

"Look Constable, it's quite simple, I don't like you. I don't want you around, so fuck off!"

I detected a hurt look in Dee's eyes as Jimmy grabbed her arm and moved her along the corridor. She looked back, but he viciously forced her head forward screaming a barrage of obscenities. Jimmy's control over Dee seemed excessive and their relationship was something I never expected.

Next day in class, Dee glanced at me quickly but appeared too embarrassed to say anything. Her face looked drawn from lack of sleep and her eyes were red as if she had been crying. By the end of class, Jimmy was at her side, there was no opportunity to ask if she was all right.

That night, around eleven, mom woke me and handed me the phone.

I sleepily asked, "Who is it?"

She shrugged, "A girl, she wouldn't give her name."

"A girl?"

I hit the hold button, "Hello…"

There was no answer, though I could hear her breathing in short shallow bursts.

"Hello… hello… Scott speaking."

"I'm… so sorry Scott… I didn't want to get you involved… I'm sorry, I'm so sorry," she kept repeating, "He made me do things…"

SHE REFUSES TO LEAVE

"Dee, is that you, are you alright, what's happening?"

"Scott, I don't want to worry you but you need to watch yourself, he wouldn't stop until I told him lies about us. He's insane and determined to cause trouble for you, please be careful. Remember 38-24-38..."

She paused and just when I thought she was about to say something, a muffled voice ordered her to put the phone down. The call was terminated.

Dee wasn't at school the next day but there was a lot of gossip about her photo appearing on the Internet. Word had it that Dee was 'way-out there' and once home, I switched on my computer and began a Google search.

Twenty minutes later, my stomach began to churn. In disbelief, I watched the screen load; in front of me was Dee, naked! Her legs... well, she was doing things no sixteen year-old should be doing. Gone was that sweet smile I was used to, instead she had a glazed expression that didn't appear sexually driven. Her arm had bruised puncture marks where she had been shooting up. How could she expose herself like this? How could she return to school? I felt embarrassed for her, talk about mixed feelings. I called Dee's house and within half a ring her mother answered, "Dee is that you?" There was urgency in her voice.

"No, this is Scott Constable, Dee isn't there?"

"No, no. She's not here, I have to go, I've got to keep the phone free." She hung up.

I was determined to establish what was happening and ran to her house. Outside I found three patrol cars abandoned one in the drive the others parked somewhat skewed to the curb. I hesitantly knocked on the front door. It took ten seconds for the door to open and it was the Chief of Police who questioned, "What do you want?"

"I'm trying to find out if Dee is alright?"

"Go away, we're working on something, scoot."

The door was slammed in my face. After a pause, I knocked again.

It was another ten seconds before the door re-opened, "Are you deaf or something? I thought I told you to get out of here."

"I had a call from Dee." To my surprise, he didn't allow me entry but rather shut the door behind himself. We walked down the stairs. His hand gripped my neck, so tight the nails almost pierced the skin. He directed me to the side of the house.

Once we were out of sight he began questioning me, "So you think you've spoken to Dee do you?"

"Is she in trouble?"

"I'll ask the questions. Now what's your name?"

"Scott Constable."

"Well Constable, when did this call happen?"

"Late last night."

"Mmm, how do you know the call was from Dee?"

"I recognized her voice."

"Did you now?" he said in a disbelieving tone.

I nodded.

"And tell me what she said?"

"She wanted to warn me."

"Stop right there. Tell me Constable, why would Dee want to warn you?"

"We are in the same class at school and she thought…"

He interrupted, "School mates, hey! You do homework together, cram for exams together, get chummy together, like really, really chummy?"

"Hey, I just want to help her, is she in trouble?"

"Why would you ask if she was in trouble?"

"I'm concerned, she seemed different, that's all, and then there was the Internet."

It was at that moment he turned aggressive and shoved me against the house, "So you've been browsing, hey?"

I was shaken by his outburst which resembled a four-year old temper tantrum, "What's wrong with you, I'm trying to help."

"Did you see her? Did you? You got excited… right, and then you decided to come around here and get involved. Making out you're trying to help when we both know that it's just a way for you to get your kicks… right?"

"What?"

The only thing that subdued him was the arrival of a television crew and their blinding floodlight.

"Is there anyone else I can speak to?"

"Like?" He glanced sideways to see if the crew was watching.

"Someone in charge, someone heading up this investigation, like the FBI."

"No… I'm pretty much it. I'm heading up this missing persons investigation and I don't want some dumb-ass kid coming around upsetting the parents. What I said originally, I suggest you do… piss off!"

He started to move to the back of the house. I said, "I think I know who she might be with. Jimmy…"

"Oh no," he abruptly answered and pivoted to make sure he had the protection of a large bush, "No… no, no, no you don't. Read my lips," he spoke nervously, his saliva ricocheting off my face. "Let me make myself clear, no you don't," his finger poked my chest, "Do we understand each other? You don't know nothing. Understand?"

I understood his command of English was wanting and felt desperately frustrated; even the television crew ignored me as I walked away. I tried to put the puzzle together – why had Dee started a relationship with Jimmy? Why Jimmy? On the surface, she appeared different, certainly more balanced and controlled but after looking on the Internet, I wasn't so sure. Of course, someone had to have taken those disgusting photos, maybe to teach her a lesson. I could never imagine her being a willing party to that, she just didn't seem that debauched or for that matter into drugs. Then there was the cop with attitude – he had purposely hindered my attempts to help. Somehow, everything pointed to Jimmy Slattery.

My parents sensed something wrong but I felt embarrassed to discuss my Internet search, only mentioning that a girl from my class was missing.

"What is her name?" mom queried. Before I could respond, a T.V. news update saved me the explanation and added to a perfect bastard of a day...

"After an extensive search, the body of missing teenager Dee Washington has been found. The sixteen year old was found face down in the Wasuma Country Club dam..."